Praise for

ROBIN D. OWENS

"Owens takes...elements that made
Marion Zimmer Bradley's *Darkover* stories popular...
and turns out a romance that draws you in...."
—*Locus* magazine

"Owens has crafted a...successful science
fantasy yarn with terrific world building."
—*Booklist* on *Heart Thief*

"Readers of Owens' earlier Celta titles, *Heart Mate*
and *Heart Thief,* will enjoy revisiting this fantasy-like
world filled with paranormal talents."
—*Bo*...

"A new voice in romantic fantasy fiction has arrived
and makes an outstanding debut. The alien world that
talented newcomer Robin D. Owens has created is
intricate...ould
welcome fu...Celta."

GUARDIAN OF HONOR

ROBIN D. OWENS

LUNA™

www.LUNA-Books.com

LUNA™

First edition February 2005

GUARDIAN OF HONOR

ISBN 0-373-80215-3

www.LUNA-Books.com

Printed in U.S.A.

To Deidre, Diane and Mary-Theresa
For encouraging me to breathe life into old dreams

In Memoriam
Sonya Roberts

Acknowledgments:

The Usual Suspects: Kay Bergstrom (Cassie Miles),
Janet Lane, Sharon Mignerey (www.sharonmignerey.com),
Steven Moores, Judy Stringer, Anne Tupler,
Leslee Breene (www.lesleebreene.com),
Sue Hornick, Alice Kober, Teresa Luthye,
Peggy Waide (www.peggywaide.com), Giselle McKenzie.

My Webmistress: Lisa Craig (www.lisacraig.com)

Excerpts of all my work available at
www.robindowens.com or www.robinowens.com.

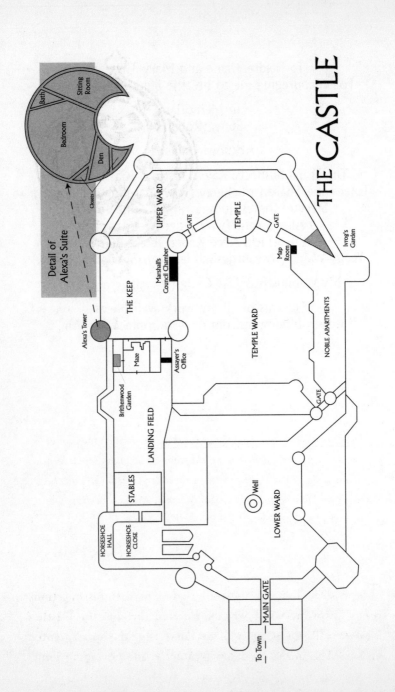

THE CASTLE

Detail of Alexa's Suite

Bath
Sitting Room
Bedroom
Den
Closet

Alexa's Tower
THE KEEP
UPPER WARD
GATE
TEMPLE
GATE
Ivrog's Garden

Marshall's Council Chamber
Map Room
TEMPLE WARD
GATE
NOBLE APARTMENTS

Maze
Brithenwood Garden
Assayer's Office

LANDING FIELD
STABLES

HORSESHOE HALL
HORSESHOE CLOSE

Well
LOWER WARD

MAIN GATE
To Town

I

Lladrana, early spring

When the Star Etalla glows bright and moves through the constel-lation Caen; when mists envelop the stone circle high atop Archer's Mound; when the face of the Moon is hidden—then the walls be-tween worlds are thin, and you may Summon saviors—or demons—from the Exotique Land. Send the Call. Choose well.

—Spring Prophecy

The rush of rain hit the stone pavement with hissing, tinny pings. Swordmarshall Thealia hurried through the Castle's cloister walk, ignoring the silver fall outside the open, pointed arches. The incessant damp weather made her aging joints ache even under three layers of robes. She'd once loved to watch the rain. Once. Now she avoided looking at it, listening to it, and wished she could avoid smelling the miasma that rose from it.

She'd been called the tough realist, harping on the harsh facts of Lladrana's desperate situation, demanding action—but she couldn't face the rain anymore.

Dread gripped her. She'd just stopped at the map room. She knew it was obsessive, checking the status of the land every morning and evening, but she couldn't help herself. She always hoped against hope that the tide of inhuman evil wasn't creeping into her country. That morning especially she'd prayed something had changed, so the Marshalls wouldn't have to risk the Summoning tonight.

A futile hope. She'd scanned the animated map of Lladrana, noting the breaks in the magical boundary set by her ancestors against the Dark. She'd counted each glowing white fence-pillar. Even as she had watched, two pillars had blackened and vanished. The loss was escalating and the new gap in the northern defenses stretched miles.

Fingers of the first taint of evil, the small nasty poisonous creatures signified by gray sludge, slogged to the border—and across. Stirrings of the more terrible horrors—slayers, renders, soul-suckers massed, ready to advance to the new breach. Chill fear had penetrated her bones.

Now with fumbling fingers Thealia drew the heavy key through the slits of her robes and stuck it into the iron keyhole of the thick wooden door made of grown tree trunks—sacred oaks ritually harvested in bygone times. The door opened smoothly, though she hadn't said the spell or pushed her shoulder against it. The Knight Lord of the Marshalls must be inside. She wondered if he had brought his brother—his Shield—too.

Her lips thinned in irritation. She'd wanted a moment or two in the chamber to soak in the sense of serenity that lived nowhere else in Lladrana. *He* couldn't appreciate the balm, even if he felt it.

Straightening her spine and shoulders, she set her steps carefully to glide with grace into the round stone Temple. The scent of rosemary and sage welcomed her.

Swordmarshall Reynardus paced the sanctuary, tall, broad-shouldered, the silver streak of hair at his right temple turned golden with age. Not even a small paunch softened the man. Lines bracketed his mouth. They had deepened over the past year as the Marshalls realized the ancient fence was failing and that they had no idea how to recharge the shielding posts, make new ones or lace the magical energy between them. Inhuman evil encroached upon Lladrana with sharp, monstrous teeth.

But didn't evil always encroach? It was Thealia's job to make sure the Marshalls guarded and defended Lladrana—even when the steps might be drastic and deadly to herself and others.

Reynardus frowned and stopped near the eastern point of the pentacle, his robe settled above the ankles of his metal boots.

"Tonight is the time." His voice echoed through the stone room, sounding as sharp as his footsteps.

"All is ready." Her gesture encompassed the freshly incised pentacle, the altar with the rainbow of glowing gemstone crystal chimes, the tools, the fruit and wine, the enormous silver gong. She hoped her quilted overdress concealed the shiver of apprehension that flowed along her spine like the touch of cold steel.

Reynardus scowled, thick black brows casting his dark eyes farther into shadow. "We will be using a great deal of energy for such a chancy enterprise, perhaps too much energy. Some of us may die."

Thealia inclined her head and folded her hands at her waist. The peak of her coif made her nearly as tall as he, and she was more than equal in Power. She had the golden streaks of age and Power at both temples. "The Spring Song foretold that only a Summoning has acceptable odds of success in beating back the horrors and saving Lladrana. We must try despite personal danger," she pointed out once again in their interminable discussion, wishing her more patient husband were here for this final preritual check of the spelldesign and equipment.

"I don't like the idea of draining ourselves completely or setting our lives in the hands of a stranger," Reynardus said.

Of course he didn't. A Summoning would be conducted by all the Marshalls, and guided by her husband and herself—out of Reynardus's control. The results too would be out of his control.

Reynardus tromped over to the white marble, blessing-carved fireplace that heated the room. He held his hands to the warmth and shot her a glance. "We are gifted with six opportunities to Summon Exotiques in the next two years. Why not wait?" he grumbled.

Thealia stiffened. Because they were desperate. Because it was their only hope. Because something needed to be done *now!* She'd argued so time and again. Thealia unclenched her teeth and managed a casual lift of her shoulders. "If you insist we wait, the rest of us will expect you to pay the price of such a gamble. We will want your Chevaliers dispersed to our lands to fight any slayers and renders that infiltrate our estates while we wait for your approval. Will you hazard your own domain until the next time for Summoning?"

He strode around the pentacle, his piercing gaze tracing the shining line of quicksilver. *Clank. Clank. Clank. Clank.*

No, he didn't like anything out of his control. Or anyone. His treatment of his grown sons had demonstrated that to all of Lladrana. He'd tried to control them with money and with Power, to form their lives as he pleased—and had driven them both away.

He might not be able to bend the Summoned Exotique to his will either. Exotiques were notoriously strange and as unpredictable as they were powerful. Thealia cheered a little.

"We Summon an Exotique female, correct?" He rubbed his hands.

"So the Spring Song advised." Thealia suppressed an urge to roll her eyes. He obviously thought women were more easily intimidated than men. She pursed her lips. He never should have married a spineless girl of the Chiladee family. Thealia had said so at the time. "Yes, a *woman,*" she said.

"*Hrrumph*. Hopefully someone who won't want to return to their own world, like the last one did a century ago. Wasted effort."

Thealia tapped her foot under her gown, counting beats until she could reply calmly. "Our chants and chimes and the gong will echo through her past to compel her. The pattern has been approved by we who rule, the Marshalls of the Castle."

She paused for emphasis. "All the other communities in our society have agreed with this course—the Sorcerers and Sorceresses of the Tower, the City- and Townmasters, the Knights and Chevaliers of the Field, the Seamasters. Even the Cloister—the Friends of the Singer and the Song who guide us spiritually—advise this action.

"A fighting woman of the greatest magical power will answer our Call and be Summoned to Lladrana to take her place as a Marshall. She will stay and help us triumph against the Dark."

"And not a female demon. There will be Testing?"

Thealia smiled coldly. "You made that a prerequisite of your cooperation, didn't you?" And won that point. Her loss still stung. She would have much preferred to have communicated their needs and the rewards honestly to the Exotique. "Yes, Reynardus, she will be Tested thrice as soon as she appears. The pool is ready." Thealia gestured to a large, square ritual bathing pool on the other side of the round chamber, beneath the lower points of the pentacle. "The next day she will undergo the Choosing ritual. Once she is Paired with a Lladranan by a blood-bond, we are sure she will stay."

She watched as he spun on his heel and a spur scored the stone wall. He examined the chamber with one comprehensive glance. He'd seen and evaluated every detail of their preparations in that brief scan—part of his Power.

"Everything seems in order. I'll take my place in the ritual tonight." Without another word he exited the Temple.

She'd thought so all along, but she was glad to see him go.

The tinkling of time-chimes reminded her of the hour. She let her shoulders slump. The moment had come to prepare herself for the great ritual of Summoning, and the Testing afterward. She gazed wistfully at the blue velvet pads atop the low stone bench that half-circled the room, the pillows and rugs on the floor. She wanted to sit and close her eyes and steep her soul in the comforting, powerfully magical atmosphere. But the Marshalls would need every particle of that calm magic to Summon the one who would help them save Lladrana from the Dark.

Thealia closed, locked and bespelled the door behind her. She walked to a pointed arch of the cloister window that opened into the wet-slicked pavement and verdant grass courtyard, and forced herself to look at the pummeling rain.

As each drop clinked against the stone, a tiny scaled worm wriggled from it. Most of the worms sizzled to death in a puff of greasy stench when they reached lush grass. The few remaining burrowed into the earth, purpose and effect still unknown.

Thealia shuddered. She hated rain.

Colorado mountains, early spring

Alexa Fitzwalter slogged through the knee-deep snow, every step difficult. She'd thought she had survived the worst of her grief over the death of her best friend, a friend who was more like a sister, but here she was, doing something completely crazy. Following a dream, a song that compelled her to trek through the mountains at night. Dangerous and mad. She couldn't explain her actions rationally, so it must be another aspect of mourning.

Yet she trudged on, knowing that although she couldn't escape the hurt inside her, she could leave Denver and all her problems behind for the moment.

Such sad thoughts on such a cold, perfect night. The soft feathery snowflakes were as heartbreaking as the sharp, pristine air she drew into her lungs. A night that spoke of mystery and life and challenge, if you dared to take it, shape it, *live* it.

Just that easily the image of her friend Sophie was back in Alexa's thoughts—Sophie who had been the sister and only family Alexa had ever had. Sophie laughing and dancing through the snow-crystal laden air, whisking sparkles of ice around her in a shimmering aura.

Sophie had been bold and vibrant; Alexa deep and brooding. But they'd both been risk-takers. Who else would be crazy enough to start up a law firm right out of school, trusting themselves and each other to make it work; knowing that they were both alone in the world with no family and no family money to cushion the start of a business? They had only themselves and their friendship to depend upon. But it had been enough.

Then Sophie died in a car accident.

Alexa's face chilled as tears froze on her skin. No use wiping them away since others would follow.

She stopped and adjusted her fanny pack, panting through her mouth, sending puffs of white vapor into the air. The cold made the inside of her nose crackle. She squinted up the hill—no sign of a track, but she'd hiked this area often enough to know where she was going. Odd that she was drawn to this point, never a favorite.

It was just one more crazy thing, part and parcel of the dreams and the auditory hallucinations. Alexa had been hearing things that weren't there, that no one else heard. Not instructions from God—she was no Joan of Arc—but a stream of rising and falling vocal music. Ripples of a chime that brought rainbow colors to her mind. And the gong. The gong haunted her.

It had sounded first, then the chime, then the chants. They had alternated and mixed. First the gong had been muffled as if echoing from a great distance. Then the sound had sharpened, become insistent, reverberating in her dreams until she woke. Awake, the memory of it would ring through her, shattering her thoughts all day.

Finally the sound in her mind had forced her into her car and led her here.

Obviously she wasn't coping as well as she'd thought with Sophie's death.

Sophie would have expected Alexa to handle the situation better, to be more flexible. Vital, ebullient Sophie would want her to *live,* not simply exist in a world temporarily bleak. She would expect Alexa to adapt again as she had so often when her life ruptured. Instead, Alexa followed a song.

The sky was so black as to be eternal, with sparks of light pinpointing lost dreams. The gauzy veil of the Milky Way draped across the bowl of night was so beautiful as to make her soul ache with longing—to be a star, to be the sky, to be a night goddess.

By the time Alexa reached the summit the snowflakes had

stopped. Brilliant white peaks encircled her, as if all the starshine in the universe coated them. She lifted her gaze to the stars again and pinpricks of light dazzled her eyes through the tears.

When she blinked them away, she saw the silver net descending, coalescing into a solid silver arch before her. She couldn't move a muscle. Her in-caught breath was so quick and big that she doubled over, coughing.

The gong sounded, the chimes tinkled a scale. The arch settled.

Her heart thudded fast and she heard her own gasps. She wanted to run, but before she could lift her feet, the beauty of the arch and the stream of music coming from it soothed the ragged edges of her mourning. The sheer relief at having her hurt gone made Alexa stay.

Reality or illusion? If she waited would it fade like all dreams?

Hunched, Alexa saw the shiver of rippling silver in the arch. Silver flowing like mercury, then parted to send a stream of voices lifted in music to her, along with a sparkling rainbow.

Now there were words, heard more in her head and her heart than with her ears, affecting her, *feeling* real, especially since the chants weren't songs of exaltation but pleas. "Help us. Come to us. We need you *here* as no one there ever will."

Alexa straightened and her throat tightened at the truth. No one needed her here.

The music enveloped, the gong enchanted, the words invited. She could only stand and stare, bemused. It went on and on until she couldn't feel her feet, and her fingers hooked around the straps of her pack, numbed.

"Come to us." Warmth and light and sound tugged at her.

She brushed a hand down the silver arch. It was warm to her touch. Planting a hand against it, she pushed. It was solid.

"Come to us."

The delicate scent of spring blossoms and renewal drew her to the rainbow. Most appealing of all was the small bud of hope that unfurled within her, the hope that she *could* help. She could find a place of her own where she was valued, where she fit.

At her back was the cold, friendless night.

Alexa stepped through the arch. Rainbow crystals bathed her and sunk into her skin to shimmer like glitter all along her nerves. Her loose hat fell off. Her fine hair lifted straight out from her head. She'd look like a brown dandelion. She threw back her head and laughed at the joyful effervescence. Hope and excitement flowed through her. She flung out her arms and twirled into a dance.

The monster attacked.

Big, twice as big as she. Black hairy bristles all over its body. Long fangs. Claws sliced, shredding her down coat, releasing a flurry of feathers into whistling winds.

Fear jolted her. She screamed but heard no sound. A paw-hand sporting foot-long gleaming claws slashed at her head. She ducked, but its hair brushed her face raw.

Move! How? She had no weight.

She rammed her own arms up against the beast. They stung with shock, but the blow propelled her and the monster apart.

Another clawed swipe. Her pack loosened and vanished. Her gloves whipped off in the wind. Better her stuff than her.

Alexa saw an opening. *Escape!*

It was a bright hole with rainbow traces. Panting in terror, she kicked with all her might, connected with the monster, ducked, rolled, spun, struggled to the hole and plunged into it feet-first. The last thing she saw was a huge red mouth and teeth dripping yellow spit. She didn't know if the beast growled in fury or tried to bite her head off. Or both.

The hole sucked her through.

And into a maelstrom of sound. A full orchestra rose in triumphant crescendo.

A flash swept across her vision—a pentacle? She landed hard in the center, on a pavement of multicolored stones. The groan rattling from her teeth echoed.

Solid. Real. The music faded to a background murmur.

She looked up. People in rich robes stared at her. She was among humans. She closed her eyes in gratitude.

When she opened them she was circled by swords.

"*This* is our savior? The one we risked our lives for? It's puny. And ugly," Reynardus said.

Thealia stared in shock at the small being in the pentagram's center. It was partially feathered, something she'd never seen before. Never anticipated. A female avian.

The chanting, gong and Summoning had gone well up to a point. Thealia had been sure they'd lured their Exotique fighter, caught her—the spirit and Power of her had sung through the connection. They'd lost her in the doorway, but only for a few seconds.

Looking at the entity, so different from the woman she'd anticipated, Thealia felt her blood drain from her face until her lips felt cold and stiff. There must be *some* way to save the situation.

Reynardus sneered down his nose at her. "This is the 'fighting woman of the greatest magical Power' you promised, Swordmarshall Thealia. Those were your words, were they not?"

If he said so, they were. His Power included a perfect memory.

He didn't wait for an answer. "Just as I thought. Wasted effort. The Power we used to bring this *thing* here will keep us all drained for days. This is a disaster." He dropped his sword and turned.

"Stop!" ordered the Medica. She was a healer, not a Marshall, but they listened. "You've already broken the link between us, but don't break the circle. And do *you,* Knight Lord Swordmarshall Reynardus, think small is weak? What of this?" She opened her hand and blew away a protective sphere. The glowing starlike atomball floated free. She flicked it to Reynardus.

Reflexively his ivory baton appeared in his hand and tipped the ball away, sent it spinning across the circle.

Thealia's wasn't the only gasp. A loose atomball, and the whole circle of Marshalls depleted from the Summoning! She froze with horror as it sped to her husband, Partis. He didn't have the Power to hold it even at full strength. His round face showed only minor strain as he caught the ball on the tip of his staff.

"I believe this is the first Test for the Exotique," Partis said, "to measure her Power." He tossed the ball directly to the small female rising to her feet.

Alexa wanted to believe she dreamed, but the physical sensations were all too real for her to ignore. She wondered—

Shit! The little star the strangers played keep-away with came straight at her! She ducked, held out her right hand, and the ball smacked into her palm with stinging force. It burned and sent rivulets of heat pouring through her veins, up her arm. And here she'd followed a song to help. Look where it got her. Somewhere else.

She gritted her teeth and bore the pain from the searing star.

Pretty nice tricks these people had. She had no intention of being "monkey in the middle"—and she knew by the tone of his words that the big guy with broad shoulders considered her something like a monkey. He swaggered with arrogance even standing still.

Holding the light made her dizzy, but when it finally cooled she loosened her fingers and dropped it. A golden walnut clattered to the floor and rolled away with a clatter.

The circle of people stared at her, some with their mouths open. She tried to suppress her shuddering, wishing it was from the lingering cold of the Colorado night, but she knew it was from adrenaline pumping through her. She fought to gather her wits, sure the fantastic events would continue to move at the speed of light—or magic. She must be ready and think on her feet, as she had so often done during her childhood in foster homes.

Alexa had concluded that they'd brought her here—the big silver gong shining within the circle was sufficient evidence of that. With the pentacle she was in, their circle, and another on the floor that they stood within, magic seemed to be the method they'd used.

Inhaling deeply, Alexa studied them. They were all taller than she. She lifted a shoulder. Nothing new. Everyone was taller than she.

They looked suntanned—a light golden brown—and all had black hair, though the tints and highlights weren't the same, nor was the thickness. Even the man with the most lines on his face had a full head of hair. No male-pattern baldness here. In fact, they all had streaks in their hair—silver or gold, over their left or right temple, or both. That was the oddest thing about them and she sensed it was significant.

Every one of them emitted a low note, something that she seemed to hear with her mind, vibrating her eardrum from the inside. Together their notes wove into a strong melody. She shook her head, but the song remained, as did the background music.

They stared at her with dark eyes. They were almost Asian, but the structure of their features was subtly different—a very beautiful people.

Alexa gazed back at them, conscious as never before of her pale skin, light brown hair and green eyes. She shifted awkwardly—knowing one side of her face was red and raw made her feel even more scruffy.

The elegance of their velvet robes adorned with fancy gold or silver braidwork looked too impractical for any activity other than magic. Each wore heraldry embroidered above their hearts. Or on their left side, Alexa amended. She didn't know where their hearts were. She recognized a coat of arms when she saw one, even if she didn't know what it meant. She figured these beings must be of high status.

They seemed to be grouped in pairs, two wearing emerald green, two sapphire blue, and so on around the circle—usually a man-woman pairing.

Most held their swords pointed at her chest, as if she were a threat. The big man wearing rust red turned to the angular woman—Alexa had decided they were the most important two.

He made another snide comment. Probably about her.

She looked down at herself and winced. She appeared to be molting. One side of her coat spilled feathers, some more drifted across the rest of her clothing, and with every breath a few separated to float around her. Her long jacket was dead.

She shed her coat and dropped her fanny pack. A mutter ran around the circle. Alexa raised her eyebrows at the big guy who glared at her, staring at her right hand.

Alexa folded her coat. Feathers puffed out. She flexed her fingers. Her right hand was pinkened, but didn't hurt as much as her face. Her down vest ripped when she moved. It, too, had tears. She realized the beast's swipe with the tips of its claws had come close to killing her. More adrenaline kicked in. She'd been very, very lucky. Particularly since she sensed the monster had been waiting for her.

With unsteady hands Alexa took off her vest and laid it on her coat, then stood in sweater and jeans.

The people spoke amongst themselves. The small round man ran a stick along glowing gemstone crystals arranged in a rainbow—the chime—and the sound shivered through Alexa. She jerked, sensing she was trapped here.

A pattern of tinkling chimes followed, each one affecting Alexa. At one, her balance tipped and she strained to keep upright, another sent her heart pounding loud enough for her to hear its rush in her ears. On and on the glasses rang as if testing every one of her reflexes, plucking at her organs.

It ended just before Alexa fell to her knees. Her body was coated with a cold sweat. She gritted her teeth and stiffened her spine. Posturing and attitude was all she had, and everything that counted in this game of strategy, as in all power games. Whatever safety, status and position she had in this world—in this time?— depended on this first confrontation.

The circle opened and a woman a few inches taller than Alexa left it, crossing to the edge of the circular room, to the gray stone wall. The woman was dressed differently than the others. No chain mail gleamed beneath her robe. This lady wore no armor. She wore a robe of dark red, with a coat of arms over her left breast, but in the center of her chest was a big white cross. Not hard to deduce that she was a doctor.

Alexa was profoundly glad that the woman was moving away from her. She shook out her arms and legs, steadied her breathing. No one else in the circle moved. They all watched the doctor and Alexa. And waited.

The healer unfolded a fur on a wide padded stone bench near a fluted pillar and murmured something soft and lilting. She picked up a bundle and proceeded straight across the room. To an altar.

Alexa looked wildly around. Everyone had sharp weapons. A fist of dread squeezed her stomach. Surely they weren't going to sacrifice a living thing. She couldn't stand that. She'd have to stop it—somehow.

She hoped it wasn't a dog. She would totally freak if it was a dog.

Breath strangled in her throat. What if they were going to sacrifice *her?*

The doctor stepped into the light cast by the chandeliers' wheels and Alexa saw it was worse than a dog.

It was a baby.

Face impassive, eyes hooded, the healer showed the naked infant to Alexa. It was a little girl of about one year old. Short black-and-silver hair was ruffled into tufts. The little one grinned at Alexa.

She moved to block the way to the altar.

The doctor glided across the room in front of Alexa to a square of blue polished marble.

Alexa didn't see the pool until the baby splashed into it.

2

Alexa had thought the dark pool was a slab of polished blue marble. Horror ripped through her as she ran to save the child.

There were six steps down. She slipped on the first and toppled into the pool, dog-paddling to keep her head up.

It wasn't water, but thick, like syrup. The liquid sliced fire into a raw blister on her foot, burned the tender quick of a fingernail she'd broken that morning. The pain in the cuts was bad, but worse on her scraped face, and now she felt scratches on her torso from the beast. The fluid even affected her bruises. Every ache seemed to be an open wound eaten by acid. It crawled from the edge of a bruise to burn hotter as it reached the center of the hurt. Alexa's breath came in anguished gasps. Her mind reeled.

She saw the little girl near the bottom of the far side of the pool. Alexa plunged into the liquid to reach the child, in too much pain to even prepare herself with a deep breath.

The fluid closed over her head. Tensing, she opened her eyes. And saw perfectly. She dove for the baby and grabbed her, pulled her from the pool. Staggered out.

A scream rose from her throat at the sight of the limp little body. She didn't know what to do. She looked at the doctor. Though tears ran down the woman's face, she stood with folded hands.

Alexa shifted from foot to foot in endless agony for a few seconds before wiping the baby's eyes, then pushed her finger into the girl's mouth, checking for obstructions, feeling if the child's tongue blocked the air passage.

She turned the baby over, grabbed hard when the infant slipped. Alexa patted her back. Thumped a little harder. Nothing.

Alexa cradled the baby and whirled to the people who stood on the other side of the room. She thought she cried, *What kind of fiends are you to do this!* But what came from her mouth was, "Shit. SHIT!"

Her frantic gaze scanned the room. The hole to Colorado was gone, though that wouldn't have done much good.

She didn't know where the door to the room was, what was outside, or if there were other people. The baby's only hope was those who'd already harmed her. So Alexa tried once more.

"Help!" she screamed. "Help her!"

A second later the doctor tore the child from her grasp. Alexa slipped and hit the floor hard. Again.

The healer pressed the infant to her breast and crooned a spell. Pulsing green light bathed them. An instant later the baby coughed, then screeched.

Alexa had never heard anything so sweet in her life, but she wondered what was going on. What were their intentions?

Growling drowned out the baby's cries. A man with a raised knife flashing in the dim light hurled himself at Alexa. She cringed and rolled, muscles protesting in new agony. Mad fury slammed into her, from *him,* her attacker. Again she fought to get her breath. She rolled, couldn't make it to her feet, was stranded on her back. He snarled, angling the knife.

His face twisted. In his eyes she saw revulsion, bone-deep hatred because she was different. Never to be trusted. Only to be slain.

She flung up her arms. Her soaked clothes constricted. Liquid trickled onto her skin and stung. The room spun, and a sea of emotions from everyone inundated her. Something in her mind broke free.

Her cry matched his. A weapon flew into her open hand. Unnecessary. With fear and panic, *with her mind,* she slammed her assailant across the room. She heard him hit the wall with a thud, then slither to the floor.

Oh God! Oh God, she'd hurt a man using her will alone!

She lurched to her knees, planted a foot, then another, and rocked to her feet. A couple of women moved to the still man, one wailing. Everyone else watched her.

Alexa bared her teeth at them. She'd never done such a thing in her life, but she now acted totally on instinct. This night was beyond belief. Beyond anything she'd ever imagined.

That she might have killed a man with the sheer force of her mind shattered the last rational belief she'd ever held. Nothing was the same. Nothing was right. Nothing was reasonable. Only primal intuition could save her.

She hefted the weight in her hand, considered what she held. It was a stick about two feet long and three inches thick, made of something like ivory and capped at each end with gold. One end was pointed, the other straight. Carved figures of knights fighting monsters covered the staff. It looked far too big to be a wand, but she'd bet anything that it was a magical tool. She slid it through her hands, enjoying the texture, though she sensed a nasty tingle of energy. Finding a button, she pressed it. A little brass hook with a blunt end popped from the side, as if it was there to hang the stick from a belt loop.

A shout attracted her attention. When she looked up, everyone was staring at her, as always.

Alexa raised the short staff.

The smallest man opened his mouth and began a chant. His melodious voice was the richest she'd ever heard, set in a soothing cadence. The others joined in, and though the music didn't sound the same here in the round church of *wherever,* Alexa knew it was that which had drawn her to this dreadful place. She could almost see the small man's voice as the stream of yellow in the rainbow that had compelled her into the arch. The big, mean guy's voice was jerky with some emotion, and his intentions didn't quite match the others, but Alexa felt he was the bright red, fluctuating band. The angular lady was indigo.

As he sang, the small man gestured, and the others slid their swords into sheaths. The leader's staff burned with a yellow flame at the tip. He set it aside and it stood by itself.

Alexa blinked. She was too exhausted and wrung out to goggle. The indigo woman stepped forward, raising her hands to her shoulders, palms outward. Another gesture Alexa understood.

She turned her back on them to check on the baby. Instead of the doctor, a teenaged girl held the child. The girl watched Alexa with huge eyes.

The baby was bundled warmly in a thick fleece blanket. Alexa motioned to her. "Is she all right?"

The youngster seemed to understand what Alexa said. She nodded. Alexa wondered if that meant agreement.

She hooked the stick in a belt loop of her jeans and pointed from the baby to herself and held out her arms. "Give her to me."

Wariness crept into the girl's gaze.

"Give her to me!" Alexa demanded.

The girl's glance slid from Alexa to the circle of people behind her. Whatever she saw reassured her. Carefully, she held out the baby.

Alexa cradled the child, pliant but live, in her arms. She flipped the corner of the blanket from the baby's face. Sleepy brown eyes gazed up at her. A little smile emitted a bubble of drool. Alexa sighed. She put her finger to each small fist in turn and smiled back when the baby clasped it, then the tiny girl snuggled against her and shut her eyes.

"Marwey," the teenager said.

Alexa looked up.

The girl pointed to herself. "Marwey."

"Alexa," Alexa said.

"Al-yek-ah," Marwey pronounced.

Alexa shrugged.

Marwey pointed to the baby. "Nyja." The girl gestured to the indigo lady, "Marshall Sabre Thealia." Then Marwey indicated the big guy. "Dom Marshall Sabre Reynardus." Finally, Marwey inclined her head to the short, round man. "Marshall Boucilier Partis."

All right. Alexa deduced that Thealia and the short man, Partis—probably her husband—had one title and the big jerk had two. Figured.

The healer came up and held out her arms for the baby.

Alexa clutched her closer.

The doctor said something that sounded gentle.

Alexa patted the baby. "Is she going to be all right?" Alexa emphasized the rising inflection of a question and raised her eyebrows, hoping such signals would get her meaning across.

"Ayes." The healer nodded vigorously, smiling.

Slowly Alexa handed the infant over.

The doctor unwrapped the baby and freed her arms and legs so Alexa could see them whole and moving. The baby girl's face screwed up and she cried. The healer shushed her and turned.

"Wait!" Alexa said.

The healer looked over her shoulder.

Alexa pointed to the shadows where the man she'd sent flying had lain. "Is *he* going to be all right?" Her stomach clutched as she waited for an answer.

In broad pantomime the doctor lifted her shoulders high and dropped them, frowned. Then she bobbed her head at Alexa, said something to Marwey and took the baby away.

Alexa's chest constricted. She'd considered the baby her only friend in this place. And how absurd was that?

Hard bootsteps striding in her direction made her pivot. Reynardus, scowling and muttering under his breath, marched to her. Again she felt fury—this man's fury—batter at her. Alexa shuddered.

The little round man, Partis, hurried forward and stepped in front of her, forestalling Reynardus. Once again Partis held his staff with yellow fire flickering at the top. Facing the others, he said a few sentences.

Raising his voice, Reynardus argued. With a motion, wind whipped around him, the nobles' robes flapped, Alexa's clothes plastered cold and wet to her skin. To Alexa's surprise, Partis stood his ground. Thealia came and stood next to him, raised her hand and stilled the air. Alexa's vision sharpened—she *saw* the energy fields of the man and woman. His was yellow and hers as indigo as her stream in the rainbow. They flowed together as if becoming a single entity, and the whole aura pulsed stronger— and malachite green. Their Songs melded into a lovely pattern.

Finally, Reynardus stepped around the couple and flung out his hand in demand to Alexa. Alexa jutted a hip, put her hand on it, and raised her eyebrows. She'd dealt with plenty of arrogant attorneys. She smiled with all her teeth. She could be a predator too. The memory of the sound as the man she'd fought hit the wall tugged at her and nausea rose. She pushed it aside. Pushed *all* thought aside. She had to be strong, show no fear, if she was to win the respect she needed to be safe.

The big jerk, Reynardus, barked an order at her. Gestured.

Alexa didn't get it. She widened her stance and set her hands on her hips, just noticing that her clothes had dried. She angled her chin up. God, she'd crash when the adrenaline stopped, but she was jazzed now. The ends of her hair lifted. Heat and energy throbbed along her skin, silky with power.

He growled, his eyes narrowed in frustration. With wide movements he tapped the empty sheath along his right side. He pointed to the stick she'd hooked to her jeans. He snapped his fingers, opened a broad, calloused palm.

Alexa smiled. "No!" She put her hand on the short staff under the pointed tip and angled it forward, curved her fingers around it.

She heard the grinding of his teeth as he repeated his actions.

"*No!*" she shouted. Grinned. "What part of 'no' don't you understand?"

"Ttho!" Marwey said from a little beside and behind Alexa.

When Alexa slid her gaze to Marwey, the girl continued. "No—ttho!" She smiled sweetly as if she too enjoyed thwarting Reynardus. "No—ttho!"

Alexa turned back to the big guy. "Ttho! What part of 'ttho' don't you understand?"

Thealia bit off some words. Then she spouted what could only be instructions, gesturing. Alexa watched closely, but only understood that the lady wanted someone to go and get something.

A massive man, even bigger than Reynardus, clomped over. He scanned Alexa up and down. She returned his stare. He snorted, took some huge gloves—gauntlets?—from his belt, pulled them on and went in the same direction as the doctor. Squinting, Alexa finally saw the door in the shadows, huge and pointed.

After he left, the others talked among themselves. The words hummed in the room like the low-level buzz of bees on a summer afternoon.

Alexa unhooked the stick, pushed the hook into the short staff and took time to compose herself. Though the others watched her, no one was threatening. She loosened her muscles and kept upright. So many emotions and reactions to the night's adventures tumbled through her that she kept a hard clamp on them and tried to use pure observation and reason. She glanced around the room while keeping an eye out for any more danger, holding the stick ready.

The chamber, round and very large, was made of white stone. All the furnishings appeared to be the very best any world could provide. Around half the room ran a built-in stone bench with padded seats, jewel-toned large pillows and rugs around its base. Colorful tapestries of pastoral scenes alternated with bright banners showing coats of arms. Windows were set high in the wall, about two stories up, and were as pointed as the door.

The altar was in the same quadrant as the pentacle and draped in maroon velvet, with a white lace over-panel. It held the bright rainbow of crystals—could they be huge precious stones?—the chime stick, two knives, a large smoking incense burner and two goblets, one of silver and one of gold.

Alexa was just wondering if she dared explore when the door creaked open and the huge man walked in. The scent of a damp, cold night wafted in with him, along with the hint of a smokey fire. The humid mixture of odors wasn't one Alexa would smell in Colorado. Her emotions threatened to break through the barrier she had erected. She couldn't let go! She couldn't afford to be seen as weak or vulnerable. She bit her bottom lip to keep it from trembling.

The massive guy stopped in front of Thealia. He held a rolled bundle—Alexa studied it and exhaled in relief—nothing living or newly dead was in it.

They talked a moment, then Thealia directed the others. They all formed a half-circle facing Alexa. Reynardus, still glowering, was the end of the half-moon to her left.

The huge man entered the half-circle and laid his bundle on the floor before Alexa. Just bending from the waist put him eye level with her. He stared at her as he unrolled the cloth. It clinked a little, made sounds of wood and metal and glass. The cloth was made of quilted felt, and she could see seams between pockets. The man flipped back the top flap.

Alexa reflexively retreated a step. The others murmured.

Before her were four rows of ten pockets. Most showed the top of a stick like the one she held. All looked old and valuable and powerful. Imbued with magic.

Thealia glided up, and the huge man took her former place in the half-circle. She gestured expansively to the sticks. "Batons," she said. Or something close enough for Alexa to understand it. Batons. Were they the same as magic wands? What could they do? What did they signify? The healer hadn't worn one. Nor did Marwey. But everyone else did.

"Deshouse," Thealia said, making the same sweep with her hand. When Alexa didn't move, the lady frowned. She walked down the long row and indicated each pocket with one toe of an elegant slipper, as if demonstrating the word *choose*.

Alexa got distracted by the slipper, peeking out and showing a narrow foot, then retreating under Thealia's skirts. It was pointed and looked to have jewels set in a pattern like a flower—

"Alyeka, deshouse!"

Mind wandering. Not surprising after all she'd been through. Still, the evening of adventure and discovery wasn't over. Alexa stiffened her spine and narrowed her eyes to see the batons better. She pressed her lips together as she concentrated, believing she could see faint outlines of energy. But how did she choose? By the attractiveness? The color and the jewels that appealed to her? By the "aura"? By smell? A couple of them were polished wood. Should she touch them?

No. Definitely not touch each one. Who knew what sort of electrical, magical, whatever, charge she might receive?

Still she felt as if she was coming to the end of her strength. If she needed to choose, she would. A smooth wand of dark green jade caught her eye. It looked slightly thinner than the others. Her fingers would close easier around it. The top was finished in tarnished bronze in the shape of flames, round at the bottom, pointed at the tips. Just below the metal was a small tube of a transparent material, glass or crystal, circling the jade. Now, that was interesting. What could the tube hold? Blood? She was definitely letting her imagination run away with her. There was another clear tube at the bottom of the staff.

Each time her tired eyes traveled up and down the myriad sticks, they lingered on the jade baton.

Alexa took a step forward and everyone hushed. She thought if she squatted she wouldn't find the energy to stand again, so she bent forward to scrutinize the wand. She couldn't see anything in the tube. She nibbled at her lip. When she looked up, she met the glare of Reynardus. Awkwardly she tossed him his baton.

He grunted as he caught it. Ran his hands up and down it as if checking for new nicks. Then he *sniffed* it and scowled at her. His eyes seemed to sink into the deep shadows of his sockets until they were lost except for a gleam of distaste.

Well, she probably had sweated on the thing. Or transferred some of the liquid from the pool to it. Still, sniffing seemed incredibly rude. She sent him a pointed glance and *sniffed* at him as if he were the inadequate one.

He muttered something under his breath.

"Sanctuaire!" reproved Thealia.

He shut his mouth, but Alexa thought he still cursed.

Minute trembling began in her calves and Alexa took the warning that she was at the end of her endurance. She slipped the jade wand from its pocket.

It blazed like a green candle, parts of it becoming translucent and beautiful.

The others sighed. She heard whispers of approval. Alexa blinked as she looked at the flame atop her new possession—her only possession besides her small fanny pack and clothes— Push that thought aside. The little sculpture glowed with copper and bronze flames, as if new. They seemed to flicker *inside* the metal too. Small white sparks flew from the tip of the longest flame.

Wow.

Seeing movement inside the upper tube, she brought it closer to examine. Mercury, also known as quicksilver. Mysterious and fascinating.

Thealia clapped her hands sharply. Alexa looked at her. She touched her chest with elegant fingers. "Marshall Sabre Thealia." She repeated Marwey's introductions. Thealia curved her hand over Partis's shoulder. "Marshall Boucilier Partis." Thealia inclined her head toward Reynardus. "Dom Marshall Sabre Reynardus."

Thealia nodded and waved at Alexa. "Marshall Alyeka."

Oh boy. Alexa hung on tighter to her stick—baton. She couldn't assimilate much more.

Thealia launched into a little speech with lots of gestures. She indicated the circle of Marshalls, the pentacle, goblets and gong. She hummed a snatch of the music, pantomimed Alexa whooshing down onto the floor. Then she clasped her hands and bowed to Alexa.

"Marwey?" Thealia gestured to Marwey and mimed talking, then indicated her head, Marwey's, and Alexa's. Alexa didn't like the idea forming in her mind.

The young girl, shorter and slighter than Alexa, slowly lifted thin arms. Marwey curled her palms around Thealia's face. They seemed to commune. Marwey stepped back.

Sure enough, Thealia indicated Marwey should do the same with Alexa.

There was a long pause as Alexa considered. She studied the girl, who looked young and innocent and good. When Alexa half-shut her eyelids she could see a bright aqua aura around Marwey. For some reason it reassured her. Like evil would show big black smears? Maybe. Maybe. Her instincts seemed to be guiding her well enough tonight.

Alexa jerked a nod.

Marwey eyed Alexa's baton.

Alexa sighed and dropped her hands to her sides.

Marwey came close enough that Alexa could smell her scent—girlish and floral, perhaps a prettily fragranced soap. Marwey put her warm hands against Alexa's face and the image came of soap in the shape of a seashell and the color of moss.

Alexa flinched as butterfly wings brushed her mind. Marwey's eyes grew big. She shuddered and jumped back.

She swayed and others crowded around her, leaving Alexa standing alone.

Marwey licked her lips. *"Leyu exotique,"* she said.

Alexa tried to translate. This time "exotique" sounded almost familiar. "Exotique." French? French for "exotic"? A French-based language? She didn't do well with languages. She was doomed.

The girl curtseyed to Alexa. "Bar," she said clearly. "You... haff...passed...the bar."

Bar? Alexa and Sophie had passed the Colorado bar a couple of months ago.

Marwey made a frustrated noise. "No. You...haff...*crossed*... le bar."

That sounded even stranger, but again a little familiar. Alexa shook her head, hoping to straighten out her jumbled thoughts. Crossed—passed...

This had been a *test*? All this stuff—the monster, the star-ball, the baby, the killer with the knife...had been *a test*?

Fury built in her, radiating from her belly to the soles of her feet and the top of her head. Again her hair stood straight out from her scalp. She shifted from foot to foot. She'd never been so angry. The baton in her hand began to hum cheerfully. Tiny figures incised in the jade that she hadn't noticed before glowed and almost moved. Looking at the staff meant she looked at her arm—and the golden aura streaked with red crackling from it.

Alexa angled the baton but didn't point it. Slowly she turned and, step by step, she looked at each person in the half-circle before her.

Too much. It was too damn much. Alexa whirled to the top nobles—Reynardus with the ivory baton and Thealia.

"This was a *test?*" she bellowed. The tapestries on the walls shivered. Alexa grinned. She turned back to the pool and pointed her baton, wondering what would happen if she sent a bolt of energy to it. She couldn't find the urge to care.

"Ttho!" Thealia jumped in front of Alexa. Locked gazes with her. "Ttho."

Alexa's nostrils flared.

Partis pulled Thealia aside and took her place. He was protecting his wife. He spoke to Alexa, his voice rising and falling in beautiful lilting notes. She ignored the words—as she thought he meant her to—and listened to the tone, the rhythms, the cadences. Warm yellow light pulsed from him.

The craziness of it all hit Alexa. She was a Marshall. But they all wore swords. And armor.

She wasn't a savior.

Hell, they *had* wanted Joan of Arc.

"I think everyone except Partis and I should leave," Thealia said.

Reynardus snorted and swept her a mocking bow. "As you will, Swordmarshall Thealia."

Thealia lifted her chin a bit. "Our mission was a success. We now have a powerful new Marshall. With her aid, the plague of evil invading Lladrana will be stopped."

"You think so?"

"You doubt the Spring Song?" His constant arguing wore on her nerves. She looked him straight in the eyes. "One of the requisites for a Marshall is appropriate visits to the Caves of Melody and a trance with the Singer and the Song. Reynardus, how long has it been since you have undertaken an individual Song Quest to tell of your path?" She knew, but wanted to hear him say it aloud.

A vein throbbed in his temple. "Are you challenging me for the leadership of the Marshalls?"

"I'm saying that I've received several Song Quests in the past decade, and most recently when the third fencepost vanished."

She waited a beat. He didn't speak. "When was the last time you consulted the Singer and the Song?" she repeated.

He paced with sharp-sounding steps to where his cloak lay. Whirling it around him, he replied. "I've been."

"When you were first confirmed as a Marshall. Before you even knew whether you were a Sword or a Shield," she pointed out. "Have you been other times?" she ended quietly. He had this coming, but it wasn't an easy thing to do—to force a Marshall to carry out his duty by shaming him.

"I'll go to the Singer and endure the Song Quest." He forced the words through clenched teeth as he clasped the brooch at the throat of his cloak shut. "Tomorrow." He stared at each one of the Marshalls, lip curling. "I trust you will temper our new little Exotique and make sure she is amenable and Paired by the time I return." Reynardus spun on his heel, then swept to the threshold and out into the portico in a dramatic exit.

Thealia caught the slamming door with her power and let it gently swing shut.

She turned to face the Exotique—Alyeka, Thealia corrected herself—and found the young woman still shooting out angry energy. Thealia glanced at the huge crystal points at the end of each rafter. Thank the Song such energy could be stored and harvested later.

Partis looked at the girl with his usual compassion. "She's not happy with us," he murmured.

"Who would be, enduring such Tests?" Marwey spoke up—out of her place.

Thealia frowned at her and the teenager faded back from the Marshalls. Then Thealia scanned the rest of her companions.

"What went wrong with Defau? He wasn't supposed to try to kill her. He was only to test her courage."

"Why ask, when we all know?" Shieldmarshall Faith said, rubbing her hands up and down her arms as if she were cold and didn't have the strength for a warming spell. Her skin showed an underlying pallor. "He hates Exotiques beyond reason. A flaw we didn't know and he didn't reveal. Perhaps he didn't know himself." Faith glanced at Alexa. "She is odder than I anticipated. Her coloring—the ebb and flow of her Power, the rhythm of it." Faith shook her head. "I don't know whether to be repulsed or fascinated."

"Obviously Defau was repulsed," Thealia said dryly.

Faith's eyes clouded and she tilted her head as if straining to use her Power. "His lifepulse is thready. I doubt he will live."

"We all knew there could be casualties among us," Thealia said. She felt the weight of their gazes.

"And you sent Reynardus away," Armsmaster Swordmarshall Mace said. His wife and Shield set her hand on his arm and squeezed. He shut his mouth.

Thealia passed a hand across her eyes, caught small beads of perspiration. "You only say what everyone thinks." She looked at them all. "We can't afford to have a negative influence in our Circle. We lost her for a moment. We could have lost her for good. Reynardus has challenged every step we took. I listened to the Spring Song and underwent a personal Song Quest." She nodded to a couple of friends. "So did some others of us. Reynardus won't listen to the Spring Song or believe our personal Song Quests." She shrugged. "He's always been a man who will only trust what he himself *knows* to be true—what he sees, or touches or perceives. Let him undergo trance with the Singer and hear his own Song. I only wish his results would be different and more hopeful than the rest of ours have been." Others nodded.

"Marshall Alyeka is about to fall into the pool again," Mace said. "Who knows what immersion in jerir twice in one night would do to her?"

Thealia hadn't seen any movement in her peripheral vision, but when she faced the woman, Alexa was swaying.

Straightening her shoulders, Thealia said, "Let's finish this business. Those who want to stay, can. Partis, call in all the unmated noblemen and women."

Marwey tensed as Partis went to the gong and hit three notes around the rim.

"Marwey?"

The teenager pressed her lips together. "You're including Chevalier Raston?"

Empathy for the girl's attraction to the knight touched Thealia. "I must," she said gently. "Alyeka must be able to choose from everyone eligible. Including Raston. Including you. The Song knows there isn't a *good* choice of quality available bedmates, just those courtiers usually here at the Castle and the Chevaliers assigned to us." She clicked her tongue. "I don't think our widespread call for a mate for an Exotique was taken seriously."

Marwey's mouth set; she looked strained about the eyes.

"And," Thealia said gently, "if Alyeka chooses a bedmate tonight she won't have to go through the formal Choosing and Blood-Bond Pairing ritual tomorrow. You've been the closest to her of us all. Surely you'd like to spare her that wrenching experience."

Marwey grimaced and dropped her gaze. "Yes."

"You've been linked to her to experience her world and help us communicate. Do you think she will want you or Raston?"

The teenager narrowed her eyes, recollecting and exploring her brief bond with the Exotique. Marwey shivered again. A dimple peeped from her cheek. "She likes men only. And older ones than Raston." Then Marwey sobered and glanced around the group of Marshalls. "Her world is completely different! They don't even believe Power exists!" She blinked rapidly. "I can't tolerate the glimpses of her world. I hope she can fit in here. 'Cause she *can* help us, a lot. She *will* make new fenceposts for us. I *felt* it." She pressed both hands to her chest.

They looked skeptically at her. She drew herself up to her full height—almost as tall as the Exotique. "I have not come into my full range or aspects of my Power, but I know what I know," she said with dignity, and walked to the bench beside the door and sat.

"Teenagers," Mace sighed.

"They can be dramatic," Faith agreed. "But Marwey is the only one who's linked with our new Marshall, and the Exotique chose the Jade Baton of Honor."

There was silence as they all thought of the ancient legends of blazing energy woven around the Jade Baton of Honor.

The gong sounded as the door opened and people trooped in.

3

Alexa jumped at the deep tone of the gong. She gathered her wits from the daze she'd fallen into.

More people. Now what? Was she going to have to weather more "tests"? Anger spurted through her and gave her energy enough to stand straight and glare at the newcomers. They brought a riff of music with them, individual notes, most of which weren't interesting to Alexa. Weird.

At Thealia's wave they stood in a line before Alexa.

Again they were all taller than she, a couple of the men far more than six feet tall. They were an attractive people.

Only a few had streaks in their hair, silver or gold. Several— men and women—were dressed in soldiers' uniforms, some with heraldry on their chests. The women wore long gowns of cotton or linen with wool surcoats in layered, bright colors that wouldn't have been matched together back home. None of the newcomers dressed like the Marshalls.

Definitely a class system here. Alexa wondered where an orphan who grew up in foster homes like herself would fit in. Lowest of the low, no doubt. A serving woman.

Ha! She'd climbed from poor beginnings in her own world, she could do it here too. After a little rest. God, she was tired! It was all she could do to keep her chin up. A warmth pulsed in her hand and she looked down to see her baton. Right, she thought fuzzily. She was already a Marshall, whatever that was.

A woman in the line squeaked as the jade staff glowed, then crumpled to the floor. Someone else snorted.

"Deshouse, Alyeka," Thealia said.

Alexa stared blankly at her.

Thealia tapped her foot and her eyebrows drew together as if she was figuring out how to communicate.

"Alyeka," said Marwey.

Alexa turned her head to the girl. Marwey ran to one of the young soldiers and threw herself into his arms. He flushed and stiffened until she pulled his head down and whispered into his ear. After a second, he kissed her with enthusiasm.

"Deshouse, Alyeka," Thealia repeated.

Alexa got the idea. They wanted her to choose a lover. So, they'd "tested" her to check if she would let a baby drown. Was this another test, to see if she'd have sex with someone she just met? Or was it more complex than that? Would her choice of lover reflect on her?

She didn't know what it meant that she had chosen the jade wand. Who had it belonged to, what traditions or history might it have?

What would it mean if she chose a person? Surely they didn't expect her to have sex tonight! She didn't even know if she could put one foot in front of the other to walk to the wall and collapse on a padded bench and sleep.

"Alyeka!" Thealia was stern.

After licking her lips and clearing her throat, Alexa called. "Marwey."

The girl said something to her boyfriend and patted his cheek, then ran over to Alexa, who could only admire her energy.

"Marwey," Alexa croaked. "Bar? Test?"

Marwey's brow furrowed, then her face cleared. "Ttho, Alyeka. Ttho bar."

"Huh," Alexa said.

Both Thealia and Marwey said it together now. "Deshouse."

With great precision, Alexa turned her back on the line of people. More than one sigh of relief came from behind her. She faced Thealia, met the gaze of every other Marshall. "Ttho. No." She felt like a two-year-old who only knew one word—no. Not exactly true—she knew *baton* and *Marwey* and *Thealia* and *Reynardus*.... Her mind numbed into a daze of weariness again. She wondered if she dared sleep. Maybe when she awoke she'd be in her apartment and this would all be a vivid dream.

The jade in her fingers hummed and drew a faint chime from the jewel-toned rainbow crystals.

While Alexa's mind floated, Thealia dismissed the others and only the Marshalls and Marwey were left to stare at her. Then Thealia was holding a purple cloak. It looked brand new. Embroidered on the left side was an impossible-looking fuchsia flower. Alexa touched a finger to the silken threads and stroked it, letting the texture of something beautiful soak into her—easing the rough edges of the night.

"Exotique," Marwey said.

Alexa understood. The flower was exotique. *She* was called "exotique." She didn't have enough energy to shrug.

The huge man appeared before Alexa's narrow range of vision. He held a belt with a tube-sheath that was green with silver traced around in an intricate, leafy pattern.

He bobbed his head, and with extremely deliberate motions, set the belt around Alexa's waist, buckled it, then faded back beyond Alexa's sight.

Thealia settled the cape on Alexa's shoulders and fastened the clasp. The cloak dragged on the ground. Sighing, Alexa tucked the baton in its sheath and gathered the excess material in her hands.

Marwey put the strap of Alexa's fanny pack over her arm, then grasped Alexa's elbow. "Ven, Alyeka." Marwey tugged.

They went slowly from the room. Someone opened the door and the chill of a humid night hit Alexa. Mist curled over her skin and brought with it an unpleasant odor of sulphur.

The walk seemed endless, up a curving ramp or two, down long corridors, then finally Alexa found herself dragging up an interminable set of narrow, twisting stairs.

She paid no attention to the rooms or furnishings around her, except to get the impression of great age and great wealth. At the top of the stairs was a half-circle room with a door straight ahead that had a little table next to it, and a door to the right. Evidently they were in a large tower.

The anteroom was done in purple. A thick rug of deep plum welcomed her feet. The pointed wooden door gleamed with a maroon-purple grain. On the purple-tiled tabletop was a purple fur muff to match her cloak. Alexa thought that purple would soon be her least favorite color.

Marwey urged her to the door. A golden plaque caught Alexa's attention enough for her to stare and blink. Diamond shaped, it had an inlay of purple enamel, then an exquisite representation of her jade baton—down to a tiny tube holding mercury at the top and bottom of the staff. Magic could certainly work beautiful—and quick—wonders.

There was also a set of wires on the door, looking like half an egg slicer. Alexa tilted her head, but the fog of exhaustion in her brain didn't let her even begin to figure this one out. Marwey ran a thumbnail over the strings, producing a melodious run of notes. She waited a bit, then opened the latch. Ah, a doorbell—doorsounder—doorstrings— Alexa gave up.

She took the muff and they went through the door and faced another curving wall. This room was a narrow hall, rounding to the right and left out of sight. Marwey tugged Alexa left and through another door to the bedroom. The chamber was large and wedge-shaped, with a curving outer wall. Alexa calculated that it was slightly more than the left half of the remaining tower. Long, dark windows in the round wall reflected an elegant, richly provisioned room. All Alexa cared about was that it held a nice, big bed. Marwey helped her off with her clothes and into the bed. As she sank against soft pillows Alexa watched the girl play with the zipper of her little fanny pack a few times, then the teenager whistled away the light. The door closed softly behind her.

Alexa shivered as cold sheets and a fluffy mattress embraced her—nothing like her own warm waterbed. "Warm," she muttered. Since she was alone, she allowed herself to whimper. "Warm." To her surprise a cocoon of luscious heat enveloped her. The orchestral music that played in the background of her mind surged and whirled her into darkness.

As soon as the new Exotique was taken up to her bed and the Marshalls were alone in the Temple, they relaxed…to an extent. The Summoning had been more surprising than any had expected.

Thealia ran her gaze over the rest of the Marshalls. They'd all seen each other bloody, covered in dirt, guts and inhuman matter, and other disgusting substances. Only the most innately elegant or the most prideful sat with spine straight.

She relaxed enough to lean against the tapestry-covered wall and let out a soft sigh. Partis sat beside her and took her hand, playing with her fingers. "It's been a very long night. It went well," Thealia said. The room amplified her words so all could hear.

"Very well. All things considering," Partis said.

Everyone murmured agreement.

"I believe the Song was right," Faith, the Loremarshall, said. "The Exotique will discover the key to raising new fenceposts to protect our land."

Faith was the most prescient of them all. They stared at her, and the mood lifted.

Thealia said, "I will remind you that it isn't often we can afford a pool of protection. The fight will start in earnest soon. I urge all of you to make use of it." Her gaze was drawn to the dark pool reflecting slices of light from the crystals embedded in the rafters and the wheel chandeliers.

It was mesmerizing.

Some grimaced. Mace rose. "My Shield and I will consider it." He led his lady from the room. Others stood and slowly gathered their belongings. It had been a long night of great effort, and though they'd succeeded in their task, it was evident to all that a new and strange era had begun.

Thealia started to rise too, but Partis pressed his hand to her knee and she subsided. "We will stay and take the plunge," he said.

The others nodded to Thealia and her Shield as they filed out.

Thealia eyed the pool. She didn't want to feel every hurt burned away, though her body would become stronger and more protected where her aches had been. But it was the right thing to do.

Partis was already out of his surcoat and chain mail before she unbuttoned her own robe at the shoulders.

"I wonder if the babe will heal now," Partis murmured in his musical voice, helping her discard her armor.

"We'll find out as she grows. All we knew was that she wasn't quite right in the head—nor were her Power paths clear and functional."

Partis touched the gold streaks in Thealia's hair. "Our granddaughter is a black-and-white, either graced with great wild Power or fragmented beyond repair. Still, it wasn't pleasant seeing the Medica drop her in the pool."

"The babe was the best candidate for the Test."

"It was very clever of you to find a Test of the Exotique's compassion that might also heal our granddaughter." He rubbed her shoulders, and Thealia let out a whimper of pleasure.

"If baby Nyja— If the Exotique hadn't saved her, her fate would have been better than living a life with flawed brain and Power," she said.

"Yes, dear. You don't have to convince me. It will be interesting to see the results."

They were naked now and standing at the pool. Partis eyed it with distaste, thinking about the pain to come. Thealia scrutinized her husband for bruises and scratches. He did the same to her. Neither of them wanted the other to bear the imminent agony.

"This isn't going to be easy," he said.

"No."

His lips curved into the charming smile that had won her heart so many years ago. He linked his fingers with hers. "So we do it together."

The minute Alexa woke the next morning, music filled her head. This time it was quiet, susurrant, again like a movie score, barely noticed.

So she knew she wasn't in Colorado. Probably not even on

Earth. More than the resurgence of mind-music, the basic scents were different. Even the atmosphere, the energy that pulsed around her, wasn't the same as that of her old home. It was as if this world possessed both magic and a different soul.

She stretched luxuriously. The sheets caressed her body in a soft silkiness she'd never experienced from cloth. The bed cradled her in a pool of comfort.

The coverlet tickled her nose and she inhaled deeply. Some sharp yet soothing herbal fragrance flowed into her lungs. She opened one eye, then the other. The room's walls showed the rosy reflection of dawn. It was light enough to discern a bright purple canopy with fuchsia flowers above her. She narrowed her eyes. This didn't look new, like her cloak. Somewhere in the back of her mind she knew that they'd had people like her—from Earth— here before. The whole setup indicated that.

Before she could face the situation, she had to find a bathroom. Alexa pushed the covers aside and dangled her legs from the bed. She scowled. It was too high. She slid to the floor. Her toes curled in the long plush loops of the purple rug. Alexa grabbed the top of her long underwear and put it on. The shirt came to her knees, which was decent enough.

She peeked under the bed skirt into shadows. No chamber pot. Perhaps a good omen. Spying a door in the left wall, she went and opened it. Clothes. A closet.

The far circular wall of the room comprised long-paned windows arcing out, brightening more each moment with the rising sun. She wondered if it was east, but didn't feel courageous enough to step to the windows and look out onto a strange landscape.

The right wall held another little door. She hurried and opened it. A triangular room held a toilet with the tank above it and a hand-pull to the left. A tiny basin hung on the wall and a shower stall was to the right. Another open door showed a large sitting room.

Alexa frowned—no bathtub. But people from Earth had definitely been here before—and had had some influence. Unless it had been the other way around—people from here had been to Earth. In any case, these folks had indoor plumbing. A very big plus.

Soon her relief that she was simply and gloriously alive would fade and the reality would crash upon her. She sensed it coming like a huge tidal wave—one the cobalt color of that dreadful pool.

It was only when she was back in bed, three pillows of the four propped behind her so she could think, that she recalled the pink fairy.

The Marshalls sat in their Council Chamber in the morning. Bright sunlight danced through the narrow windows, lighting dust motes until they glowed golden, bringing out the streaks of burnished oak in the table—and illuminating its scars.

Thealia could tell which of the Marshalls had availed themselves of the pool. The strain of the Summoning was there in them all, but those who'd used the pool of protection had an extra glow to their skin, a hint that their energy would return redoubled. It made her blink in surprise. Could the jerir in the pool be that powerful? Perhaps.

Bathing in jerir wasn't common, so she hadn't realized the effects were obvious. She noted everyone studying one another and saw a dawning awareness on the faces of those who hadn't taken the plunge.

Clearing her throat, she said, "The Marshalls' meeting is now in session." She inclined her head to Faith to make sure the Lorebook recorded the meeting. "Mistress Loremarshall, can you tell us how long the jerir is effective?"

Faith jerked in surprise. Stacked in front of her were three large tomes, all covered in the metallic hide of lizworm, one with an illustrated page of the jade baton. She frowned. "One moment." With a *whoosh,* a new book she'd summoned arrived on the table near her. She set her hand on it and lilted a spelltune. The book opened and Faith bent her head over it. "The amount of jerir in the Temple's sacred basin should last through an entire moonspan and a half."

"Ah," Thealia said. "In that case we will not drain the basin today as previously arranged. I propose that we let word spread that any who wish to use the pool may present themselves at the gates properly prepared. They will be escorted to the Temple and watched while they immerse themselves. Discussion?"

"Thealia, is this wise? *Anyone?*" asked Faith.

"We are at the prelude of a new age. Enough of us have heard the Song to know that the struggle before us will be long and hard. We will need *all* our resources."

Mace's—the Armsmaster's—grin was ironic. "Anyone who's bold enough to come to the Castle and request the use of the pool, and courageous enough to dunk himself, will be someone I can respect—and train, if needs be."

There was a moment of silence.

"Any more discussion?"

No one answered.

"Then we are agreed?"

"Agreed," everyone responded.

Thealia smiled in satisfaction. Meetings went so much more smoothly when their leader, Lord Knight Swordmarshall Reynardus, didn't attend.

"Let's talk about our new Marshall, Alyeka," Thealia said.

"She can't be allowed to keep that absurd name," someone grumbled.

"Oh, who's going to tell her that?" Faith smiled.

"Swordmarshall Johnsa, an image if you please," Thealia requested.

With the care and competence that she brought to all her duties, Johnsa built a foot-high, three-dimensional model of their new Exotique, startling in its likeness.

Thealia caught her breath. She'd forgotten how odd Alexa looked. Or perhaps it was that sunlight accentuated her pale coloring, light hair and green eyes so much more than the shadowy Temple.

Partis grasped her hand under the table and squeezed.

The harp on the door strummed.

"Enter," Thealia called. Of the Marshalls, only Reynardus's place was empty. She hadn't anticipated that he'd make the meeting, and he wouldn't courteously use the doorharp either.

The door opened and Luthan, one of Reynardus's sons—one of Thealia's dear godsons—entered.

Concern fluttered in the pit of Thealia's stomach. That he was here meant he didn't agree with the Marshalls on some point. "Do you come as the Representative of the Chevaliers?" Thealia asked. It was his right, but she didn't want an altercation with a man she respected, or a breach between the Marshalls of the Castle and Chevaliers of the Field. But she wouldn't let him turn her from the path she knew was right. "I trust you are not the only Chevalier who arrived for 'The Pairing.' I'd like to give our new Marshall a good choice."

His glance swept the table. He froze when he noted the model of Alexa. His expression of revulsion was brief but obvious.

Thealia's chest tightened. A pity he could not like her. They both could do so much worse. Maybe in time...

Luthan smiled, showing teeth. "No, I don't represent the Chevaliers to the Castle. I am here as the Representative of the Cloister of the Singer."

"The Cloister!" They hadn't sent a delegate to the Castle for as long as anyone could remember.

He slid into the proper seat, the one carved with a full moon sending rays down to a woman who Sang. "That's right. The Cloister wanted a Representative at the Castle if the Summoning was a success. They approached me as a man of good moral fiber and one with experience of the Marshalls."

No one could ever deny that. He'd battled his father all his life.

"The Cloister requested I turn over my representation of the Chevaliers to another whom I trusted, and attend for them."

This complete change shook Thealia. "Who did you choose to replace you for the Chevaliers?"

He hesitated. "The post is open for the moment."

Mace snorted. "The Chevaliers didn't believe we'd succeed in the Summoning. Caught them *and you* unprepared. Not a good thing for knights."

A flush crept to Luthan's cheekbones. He sat straight. "There is dissension amongst the Chevaliers as to the arrogance and the secrecy of you Marshalls. Further, some of us Chevaliers consulted the Song a week ago. It foretold only a sixty-percent chance of success."

Thealia flinched. "The last time the Marshalls consulted the Song, it was an eighty-percent chance of achievement."

Luthan lifted a shoulder. "Circumstances change."

"We were luckier than we thought," Faith said, smoothing the page of one of her books.

This change, and the new information, disturbed Thealia. But she couldn't afford to let it show. "And your replacement?"

"I thought to offer it to my brother."

"Bastien?" Mace laughed so hard he nearly fell off his chair.

"That rogue...in a responsible position? Impossible," Thealia said.

"What's impossible is the thought of the three of them—Reynardus, Luthan and Bastien—here on the Council." Johnsa shaded her eyes as if trying to banish the vision. "We'd never get anything done."

"Bastien is a good man," said his brother. "Undervalued and underestimated. Further, as delegates, we would follow the instructions of our patrons."

That started Mace laughing again. "As if Bastien ever followed any instructions, ever!" he said between snorts. "I thank you for the laugh, my friend. But we should proceed with business."

Thealia scrutinized Luthan. What *were* his instructions? He'd just made her job harder. She sought to keep him off balance. "Does your father know you're the new Cloister Representative and that you're here?"

His jaw tensed.

So. His father *didn't* know. Not surprising since the last she'd heard, the whole family had fragmented, Reynardus's sons moving to their own holdings or camping in the field with the Chevaliers.

She didn't press the issue. Luthan would inherit from Reynardus one day, and there was that wide streak of silver at his left temple as well as a few strands at his right. His personal Power was strong, and he might become a Marshall in the future.

"Why are you here?" Thealia asked.

Luthan's gaze went to the image of Alexa. "The Chevaliers heard the Summoning was a success. This changes the whole battle plan."

"As we told you it would," Thealia said dryly. "Though you doubted us. Do you stay to be part of the Choosing and Pairing?"

His eyes widened in horror. His cheeks reddened a bit. "Ah, no. I didn't come for The Choosing and Pairing. Nor has any other Chevalier."

Thealia just raised her eyebrows and stared at him. He shifted in his seat.

She continued. "That is the next step, you know. To Pair our Exotique—Alyeka—with a person of Lladrana so she will stay. The Chevaliers should be here."

Luthan frowned and leaned forward. "Let's call your 'Choosing' exactly what it is. It's a forced, involuntary life and blood-bond—a bossechain. Her Choosing will not be a ritual to find and love a mate. Her bond will not be a coeurdechain." His smooth and quiet tones had disappeared and his voice took on a harshness that echoed his father's.

"Semantics," she said, but her lips tightened. She met his eyes. "It isn't quite ethical, but over the centuries we've found it necessary and effective."

He sat up straight. "It is wrong."

She raised her eyebrows again. "We gave our new Marshall a choice of bedmates last night, in the hopes we could avoid the formal ritual. She retired alone.

"The rest of us are agreed. Do you choose to challenge us, Chevalier Luthan, with combat? Or call a vote of all the Castle, Tower, Chevaliers, Cloister and Towns?"

Luthan shoved his chair back and stepped away from the Council table, distancing himself from the decision. He leaned back against the stone wall, ignoring the chill that would bite even past the argenthide of his riding clothes, and folded his arms.

"I choose to personally disagree for the Lorebook."

Thealia sighed. "Always so contrary. Of two options you always choose a third."

A touch of a smile graced his lips. He glanced at the little model of Alexa and a hint of pity passed over his face. "And this Choosing will take place this afternoon."

"So, you did read the Castle information board?" Thealia stared coolly down her nose. "The funds and lands that come with Al-yeka as her dowry could greatly benefit you."

"Not at that cost. I won't be offering a token for the Choosing Table." He headed for the door.

"Luthan, before you go, cleanse yourself as if for a great ritual and use the protection pool," Thealia called.

He paused. His brows lowered as he studied the Marshalls. "It really does make a difference?"

"Now, and probably in the future," Thealia agreed.

"Is it true that it's painful?"

"Agony," Partis said cheerfully. "But you're a tough, young knight, you'll handle it."

Luthan grimaced, outlined the badge on his tunic in an absent gesture. He glanced at Thealia. "Is it a suggestion, or an order?"

Thealia felt her face soften, wondered if it was evident to the others. She had such a love and delight in Reynardus's sons, this one in particular. "Only a strong suggestion."

Luthan ran a hand through his hair. "I can be cleansed, in and out of the pool before the Choosing. I'll inform Bastien of this conversation this evening. I'm sure he will take advantage of the pool also—if for no other reason than his pride."

Mace cleared his throat and Luthan turned to him. "Yes?"

"If you flew in on a feisty volaran stallion, after the pool you might want to leave on a gentle mare."

Nodding shortly, Luthan bowed to them and turned.

"Luthan," Thealia said.

He looked over his shoulder.

"I don't believe your father thought of using the pool. You might remind him."

Luthan's gray eyes clouded, chilled. He inclined his head. "My squire will send him a note," he said stiffly, then left.

"The boy had a point about the Choosing and Pairing," said the oldest Marshall, Albertus.

"Do we have to discuss this again?" Thealia asked.

There was silence around the table. Several Marshalls wouldn't meet her eyes. She didn't like a forced blood-bond any more than the rest.

It could be chancy: if the drug mixture or amount wasn't right, or if the drugs affected the Exotique's judgment so she made a bad choice. To be tied her entire life, mind, body and heart to the wrong man— Thealia cut off her thoughts. She couldn't afford them. There were many others who had and would sacrifice themselves for Lladrana—Alexa was just one more cost.

It was unfortunate that she would be forced, but how they needed her Power! The Spring Song had prophesied that the Exotique was the solution to their failing boundaries—the melody rippling out in a hopeful trill.

Thealia hardened her heart and her expression. When she met each of the Marshall's eyes again, she infused them with her own determination. This had to be done.

4

"Call me Sinafin," the fairy had said in Alexa's dream, twirling and tinkling like wind chimes. The little being was no more than three inches high and completely pink—lacy wings, pointed ears, hair, tiny gown—everything.

Sinafin had stared at Alexa as much as Alexa had stared at her, and for as long.

"I must be dreaming," Alexa had said.

Sinafin had perched on the headboard and swung her feet. "You are. I'm not really a fairy. I just took this image from your mind." She shrugged and considered her wings. "It's not a bad form, but I don't think I'll wear it outside of your dreams."

"Then what are you?"

"That doesn't matter," Sinafin had replied with music in her voice. "What does matter is that you understand what is happening."

"What?"

Sinafin had sighed, studied her toes and flexed her feet. "You have been Summoned to Lladrana."

Alexa's heart had thumped. She'd licked her lips. "Heavy mojo. Chimes. Rainbows. Chant. Gong. Large silver pentacle. It doesn't look like I can get home easily." She didn't even want to think about disappearing holes and big hairy monsters. With fangs.

The fairy avoided Alexa's eyes.

She sat up straight. "What aren't you telling me about getting back?"

"It would be a massive undertaking for a Ritual to return you to the Exotique Land."

"But?" Alexa had spotted a hesitation in the little woman's words.

A minute pink tongue dampened pink lips. "There's a moment, a *Snap,* when your Land calls to you." She took off from the headboard and zoomed a circuit around the underside of the canopy. "Like when sometimes before you fall asleep, your body jerks."

This time Sinafin perched on Alexa's upraised knee. The serious look on the little pointed face didn't suit Sinafin. "You have a moment to go or stay. Wish to go, and you're gone. Hang on to something here, and you stay."

"When does this happen?"

Sinafin shrugged. "Who knows? Days. Months. Years. Different times for different people. Sometimes the Snap is easy, sometimes hard. Different for different people." She frowned. "Or maybe sometimes it's easier for people to stay or go."

"Duh," Alexa said, throat tight.

"But we really need you here."

"Joan of Arc," Alexa croaked.

Sinafin's entire being flashed humor. "Yes. But you can do it. You are stronger than you think. Stronger than *they* think. They cannot coerce you in any way—remember that."

"You're not one of them?"

She gave a tiny fairy snort. "Do I look like one of them? No. I sensed you were here and came. I am here for you." She launched herself into the air, dipping and whirling, wind chimes rippling with her movements. Alexa got the idea she was too impatient to sit still. Sinafin hovered before Alexa's nose, just far enough away that Alexa didn't have to look at her cross-eyed.

"Deep in your heart you need Lladrana. It can be a home for you. You can find your place here."

"Argh," was all that came out of Alexa's mouth.

A teeny fairy finger wagged at her. "So don't get scared, or depressed. Take it as a challenge."

"That's what they always call awful problems nowadays, 'challenges,'" Alexa muttered.

The fairy beamed. "I'm here to help you."

Alexa wasn't sure how a little pink fairy in her dreams could be of use.

Sinafin flittered around the bed, grabbed the fringe on the hangings and swung from it. "Don't think of going back. Accept your fate here and you'll live a long life of great fulfillment."

"You sound like a fortune cookie."

A laugh rippled from Sinafin. "I *am* good fortune. Now, I know you aren't good with languages. So *listen!*" A delicate wand with a star on top appeared in her hand. She waved it, and the whole evening rolled like a movie before Alexa's eyes. Only this time, she could understand what the people were saying. At least the words, but some of the meanings and concepts were beyond her. When it ended, she had a million questions. She opened her mouth to ask Sinafin, but with fairy capriciousness, the little magical woman had disappeared. A feeling of dark destiny crept over Alexa.

Now she shivered from toes to head as she remembered the

dream and the night before. She clutched a pillow almost as big as her. Her arms sank into it and she knew it was made of the finest down. Everything around her was the finest.

"Hard to go back," she muttered to herself, and knew that there wasn't much of a life to go back to. She'd have to start all over on Earth as well as here in...Lladrana? "Find my place here." Tears welled in her eyes and she was helpless to stop them. All she'd ever wanted was to fit in, be normal, know she was the same as everyone else who had a family and friends and a good home.

In Sophie she'd found a good friend, as close as a sister. Sophie had been outgoing and charming, had expanded Alexa's circle of friends. She and Sophie had graduated law school, passed the bar, and started their own firm specializing in domestic law. They'd had three clients.

Then Sophie died and the plans were shot to hell. Before Alexa had had time to regain her balance, she'd heard chimes and music and had gone through the silver arch to Lladrana.

She had *chosen* to go through the gate of her own free will. She knew that. But she sure hadn't known the consequences. Alexa was certain that in Colorado "ensorcellment" wasn't a valid defense for stupid decisions. What about here in Lladrana?

She uncurled from a fetal position and looked around her. Everything in the room—her own room—was of the highest quality. She had passed "tests" and been granted the status of Marshall. Alexa shuddered at the thought of the tests. She'd thought a month of studying for the Colorado bar had been bad!

That was then. This was now. And now was an entirely different world.

Tests. She'd focus on that. The little star-ball—atomball—had been a test. Partis had said so before he sent it to her. Many had been surprised she could handle it. The test was a measure of what they called "Power."

The next test was obvious. Did she have the compassion to save the baby? Then, she'd asked for help in keeping the baby alive. Had that been a test too? Alexa thought so. She wasn't too proud to ask for help. She could work with others to achieve a goal. She made a disgusted noise. Oh, their tests had been clever, all right.

The memory of how she'd flung her assailant against a wall *with her sheer will* burned in her heart. She couldn't sit in bed and face that fact so got up to pace the room. What could she have done differently? She wasn't trained in martial arts. She hadn't hurt him on purpose, had only defended herself. Self-defense was acceptable in Colorado and apparently in Lladrana too, since she hadn't been punished. But that she'd hurt, maybe killed, shook her to the core.

A sour taste coated her tongue, so she went to the bathroom and rinsed out her mouth. On the way back, she stopped at the windows and finally looked out. She was about five stories up!

Glancing down, she saw her Tower was built on the edge of a cliff. She flinched back, then looked out onto an expansive landscape. Before her were fields showing a fuzz of spring green, then wooded, rising hills.

She followed the window to the far left curve—in the distance was a large, tidy walled town. She looked down and saw a hedge maze just within the castle walls, and just beyond it a small garden centered around a tall, lovely white-barked tree. A sweet murmuring, almost beneath her hearing, beckoned to her. She pressed close to the window. The low music must come from the growing things, maybe even the land. Rocks? Who knew?

From what she'd already experienced, anything was possible.

She frowned, trying to separate the attractive lilt from other notes, and finally figured out that it came from the tree. She smiled. The tree had caught her eye, so it was logical that she'd hear its tune more clearly.

Alexa moved to the center of the window to once again study the vista of multihued greens. Her heartbeat picked up. *This is home,* a bone-deep feeling whispered. *This is what you've been searching for all your life.*

She shook her head and backed away, bumped into a piece of furniture she hadn't noticed before—a mirror on a stand. At her reflection her mouth dropped open and she stared. Her hair had turned silver in the night. Her eyes appeared very green—as deep and green as her jade baton.

Alexa ran to the bed, leaped on it and burrowed into the covers. She'd decided. She wasn't getting out of the bed, or out of this room. She'd wait for the Snap.

Alexa slept most of the morning, until the strings attached to her door rippled and Marwey called out. Alexa buried her head in the pillows and ignored her. After a while the girl went away.

Alexa dozed again until Thealia came and made demanding noises. The woman was impatient, not even denting Alexa's will-power to hold out before stalking off— Alexa could feel her irritated energy and hear hard footsteps.

Just as Alexa was beginning to relax, Partis chanted at her door, comforting, soothing. Lulling, Alexa thought with a snort. She wasn't moving.

Partis sang for about half an hour, then left.

The doorharp sounded again and Marwey spoke. She knocked. Alexa heard noises out in the hallway and wondered if they'd starve her out. Then the baby cried just beyond the door.

It went on and on. Alexa couldn't bear it. She got up and stood by the door, calling softly to the child, murmuring endearments. That only worked once.

She opened the door and scooped up the baby, who broke into a smile. Alexa smiled back, and a couple of women nabbed her.

Marwey, eyes wide, advanced and touched the ends of Alexa's shoulder-length hair. "Argent," she whispered in awe.

Alexa grimaced. She'd forgotten the color had changed from brown to silver.

"Alyeka, Alyeka, Alyeka." The women called her name. With a swirl of jewel-toned robes, Marwey and Thealia and the rest, laughing and coaxing—and cuddling the baby—took Alexa down long, curving stairs.

It wasn't a dungeon, but a big bathing room tiled in white and turquoise with slim graceful pillars. There were three pools of light blue, and lush greenery. The whole room was like something out of a harem. To one side hung a rich robe of dull gold. It looked Alexa's size.

She allowed herself to be led to a pool. Narrowing her eyes she examined the liquid. It appeared to be water. Thinking it would be easier to test the stuff than to try to ask what it was, she bent down and cupped some in her hands. It felt like water. No stinging. Alexa let it trickle through her fingers.

Lifting her hands to her nose she inhaled the scent the liquid had left. Herbs. Nice and somehow sweet, not astringent. As she scooped up the "water" again and lowered her mouth to taste, she watched the others. They looked amused but didn't protest or stop her. She darted the tip of her tongue out to lap at the water— again, it tasted of herbs.

Alexa stood and straightened her shoulders. She gestured for others to bathe before her. Thealia lifted her eyebrows, but moving a little jerkily, she disrobed and sank into a steaming pool. She leaned her head back on what appeared to be a padded cushion that rimmed the pool, shut her eyes and hummed. Alexa eyed the older Marshall and decided to follow her example.

Walking to the hot pool, Alexa summoned the courage to drop her bathrobe, and, ignoring embarrassment, trod the shallow steps into the pool. The hot water caressed her arches and Alexa knew why Thealia had moaned. It felt so good! The water lapped silkily at her as she submerged; the heat banished the aches and stings the liquid the night before had burned. Thealia sat on a ledge at the deep end of the pool. Alexa judged that if she joined the woman the water would rise to Alexa's mouth. She found a spot and a ledge where it reached her shoulders—ignoring the twittering of the other women, probably about her height—and flopped her head back on the pad. Oh yeah! The only thing better would be jets.

"Alyeka," Marwey said.

Alexa opened one eye. The teen offered a tray of soaps. One was green and Alexa had seen it in Marwey's mind the night before, one was oatmeal colored and textured, one peach. Alexa sniffed them all and took the green one that reminded her of the ocean. A pang went through her. Oceans. She wondered if she'd ever see one again.

"Shh," Marwey said, joining her in the bath and patting her shoulder.

Battling the ache of tears, Alexa looked at the girl. Marwey stared into her eyes and frowned. Then, slowly, an image took shape in Alexa's mind—a rocky coast with a gray-green ocean frothing spume. She closed her eyes and turned her head away.

Alexa drifted and listened to the cadences of the voices around her. Just from pitch she seemed able to differentiate the classes. Thealia's and Marwey's tones were lower, more decisive than those of some of the other women, whom Alexa had pegged as servants.

She wasn't sure what she thought of servants, or dealing with them. She and Sophie hadn't even had a secretary to call their own, let alone a receptionist or legal assistant. Tears stuck in her throat again at the memory of her good friend. Or maybe it was just all the changes she'd been through in a few hours—less than a day. God! Self-pity and sentiment were overwhelming her and she wanted to bawl her eyes out. Here in the pool would be fine if she were alone. She sniffled.

"Alyeka." Thealia sounded soothing too, and near.

Alexa sighed and opened her eyelids. She was pretty sure the Lladranans would never get her name right.

Swordmarshall Thealia held two goblets in her hands. They looked like gold. Alexa bit her lip. Thealia smiled and sipped from one, then held the other out to Alexa. She took it and tried a tiny taste. Not too bad—very thick and heavy with spices.

Thealia ostentatiously held up her glass, and Alexa got the idea she wanted to toast something. What? Anything the Swordmarshall thought was great, like Alexa's advent here, wasn't necessarily fabulous to her. She shrugged and little wavelets spread from her bare shoulders.

The Swordmarshall scanned the room, and Alexa followed her gaze. Everyone held goblets, though only hers and Thealia's were gold. A movement came from the dimness under a fancy, colorfully tiled cabinet. Alexa narrowed her eyes.

"Viva Alyeka!" Thealia exclaimed. Her voice boomed off the tiles.

Alexa jolted and turned to the woman.

"Viva Alyeka!" the other women returned enthusiastically, and her name hit her ears several different ways.

Alexa slipped. Thealia steadied her with one hand and clinked her goblet against Alexa's with the other. Gazing at her over the edge, Thealia gulped down her drink.

Alexa did the same. The brew slid across her tongue and down her throat, coating them like honey.

Everyone else drank too. Thealia smiled benignly at Alexa, took her goblet and handed both to a nearby woman. Then she gripped Alexa firmly by the elbow, pulling her through the water to the steps.

Bathtime's over. Too bad. Alexa blinked and blinked again, a haze gathering over her eyes. Her mind dulled.

Alexa!

Alexa stopped at the top of the pool and peered around the room as she was patted dry with huge fluffy towels.

It's Sinafin, Alexa!

Sinafin, the little fairy. Alexa's lips curved in a goofy grin. She looked harder for the tiny pink being, swayed, and was held upright by several sets of hands.

Alexa, think!

Think? It was hard to think. How could she think with the gold-colored robe dropped over her head? She couldn't see, could hardly breathe.

Her head popped through the neckline and she craned to find the fairy.

I'm not a fairy now, only in your dreams.

Did that make any sense? No. Nothing in the past twenty-four hours made any sense. Alexa frowned, started forward and stumbled. What a klutz! She hadn't been this clumsy in years. A thought nibbled at the darkening cotton of her mind. Can't think. Clumsy. Odd stuff. The drink! She'd been drugged!

She gasped, but couldn't stop her feet from shuffling along as the women walked on each side of her, holding her arms. Thealia swept ahead of them with decisive steps. Alexa wished she could dredge up fury, but sharp emotions were just as hard to find as clear thoughts. She took one last glance back at the cabinet. Something that looked like a foot-long dust bunny stared at her. Maybe it was a dandelion. With eyes... She grunted as she stubbed her toes on the first of a long set of winding stairs.

Time and mind fogged. When the mist parted, Alexa stood in

an elaborate rectangular room. The bright colors and sunbeams made her blink. People packed the room. Lots of soldiers in different uniforms, mostly men. She saw Marwey linking arms with her guy.

Click. Click. Click. Alexa followed the sound to Thealia's forefinger tapping on the table in front of both of them. A large variety of odd objects lay on the table. They zoomed in and out of focus. A smooth stone. A spur? A cap. A tin cup.

That made her think of the goblet she'd drunk from, obviously doctored. Her mouth was dry and tasted like mud. Her stomach quivered. Bile rose up her throat. Through willpower she forced it back. Swallowed.

The table was covered in silver-shot blue damask; the things on it looked well-used and common, like they didn't belong. Many brilliant lines wiggled from them. Alexa tried to step back, but was held in place by a couple of people. Her vision had narrowed, so she couldn't see them.

The lines seemed to writhe like a mass of worms. They all led from the objects to…men. She traced a bright yellow thread from the cap to a man leaning against the wall. She thought she could smell him from here. She gagged. Forced herself to stand up straight and take a deep breath. Maybe it would keep the dizziness and nausea at bay.

"Deshouse, Alyeka," Thealia said.

Alexa scowled. Didn't the woman know any other word? Choose, choose, choose…first a baton, then a lover. Alexa's stomach rolled at the recollection of the night before.

A lime-green line slithered to a guy in the corner. Alexa glanced at him and he grinned, showing broken, stained teeth.

Ick. Every strand from the objects looked neon-nasty, and when she squinted to see the men they led to, her stomach roiled. How many were there? Twenty? Thirty? None of them appeared to be anyone she'd care to meet, but she had the vague idea that this was like last night—the Marshalls wanted her to choose a man.

Time stretched. She heard murmuring and turned her head. The flash of silver caught her attention. A small side table contained long thin knives that looked extremely sharp, and several lengths of colorful silk that looked like ties. She couldn't force her gaze away from the ominous, gleaming knives.

Someone brayed a laugh. The lime-green guy. Too much. Her stomach revolted. She vomited on the table and sank into welcome darkness.

Very good, Alexa, Sinafin said, fluttering gauzy wings.

Bastien leaned back in the corner booth of the Nom de Nom Tavern and casually flicked his new hat with the broad brim onto the table. From the corner of his eyes he watched for the reactions of the other Chevaliers to his hat, and suppressed a smug smile.

Unlike most of the Chevaliers in the Nom de Nom, he was not a Lord's or Lady's Knight, but an independent. And the hat proved just how successful he was. Stretching out his legs, he admired it again. The hat was of his own design, with a great rim around it— wide enough to keep the frinks that fell with the rain off a man's face or from slipping down his collar—if you had tough enough material. Soul-sucker hide did just fine.

It had been his first soul-sucker kill, and the bounty had been prime. He grinned as he recalled the scene at the Marshall's Castle where he'd dumped the remains late in the afternoon. Oh, it was great claiming the prize from those tight-assed Marshalls who thought they were the best at fighting and believed they knew everything.

The assayer who'd counted out Bastien's gold had covered his initial revolted horror at the soul-sucker's body by donning a self-important air and informing Bastien that the Summoning had been a success—Lladrana now had a new Exotique who would save them all. Trust the Marshalls to dig up and follow all the old traditions instead of trying something new to defeat the invading horrors.

That had dimmed Bastien's pleasure for a moment—or until he had requested the assayer provide him with the soul-sucker's skin in an hour for his hat. It was Bastien's right to have the hide, and the clerk's appalled expression had revived Bastien's spirits.

Now that he recalled the scene, he frowned. There had been something else—something that had made the hair on the back of his neck rise—the silver hair that denoted Power, not the black locks. Had he seen a pair of glinting eyes in the rafters of the storeroom? He shrugged it off and gestured for some ale.

After he'd gotten the skin he'd spent some Power fashioning the hat he'd designed on the long volaran flight from the North.

Unobtrusively he shifted in his seat. That last fight the day before had been rough. A slayer, a render and a soul-sucker. They'd been gleeful at their supposed ambush of a single prey—a volaran-mounted Chevalier. He moved his shoulders to avoid a throbbing bruise.

He'd rarely been in worse shape. Bloody tracks from the render's claws covered his torso; a puncture from the slayer bore through his left thigh, far too close to his balls to think of the wound without a shudder. Bruises covered his body. Even the soul-sucker had marked him. Round, raised bumps from its suckers dotted Bastien's right shoulder and scalp—thankfully hidden by his clothes and his black-and-silver hair.

The conversation rose as his new hat was noticed and became an object for discussion. Only Marrec, who swore loyalty to Lady Hallard, actually had the guts to turn from the bar to stare at the hat.

When the serving woman Dodu brought his ale, she gave him a long, slow look from under her eyelashes. "I can cancel my plans for tonight, Bastien," she whispered.

More than Bastien's aches throbbed at her invitation. He looked at her plump hips and sighed. For the first time in his life he was in no shape for bedsport. He had the feeling that if he took her up on her offer his reputation as a great lover would shatter.

"Ah, Dodu, my lovely, I only wish I could cancel my own, but for once I must place duty before pleasure." He pasted a yearning expression on his face.

She narrowed her eyes.

Bastien lifted her fingertips and kissed them.

Dodu sighed and withdrew her hand. "Some other time, then."

He grinned. "Definitely."

With a swish of the ass she knew he admired, she served another table. Bastien shifted, trying to find a less painful position.

The door opened, letting in gray twilight and the stench of frink-filled rain. Bastien's smile faded. His brother Luthan scanned the room, spotted Bastien and strode to him.

Bastien's brows knit. Luthan didn't move with his usual fluidity, and pallor showed under the golden tone of his skin. He looked as if he'd been through an ordeal—more than just confronting the Marshalls in their Council, which Bastien had heard Luthan was going to do—as the new Representative of the Cloister. His acceptance of the position had spurred a lot of talk, since it now left the Chevaliers without a spokesperson to the Marshalls.

Was Luthan's streak of silver over his right temple wider? Bastien scowled. They were very different in personality, but close nonetheless.

Luthan stopped and looked down at the lounging Bastien, dressed in render-hide. Luthan himself had a pure white surcoat over his flying leathers, decorated with the coat of arms of their mother's family—the estate Luthan claimed for himself. When Luthan's eyes fixed on Bastien's hands scored by the tentacles of the soul-sucker, Bastien sat up straight. Then Luthan's gaze lingered on the new hat.

"That is the ugliest hat I've ever seen."

"You wound me to the core!" Bastien placed fingers over his heart.

Luthan scowled. "Looks to me like your last fight did that."

Bastien cocked his head and raised his eyebrows. "And you look like merde too." He swept his hat to a corner of the table. "Sit. I know Council meetings are bad, but it shouldn't make you look like a herd of volarans ran over you."

Grunting, Luthan gingerly settled his long length on the opposite bench of the booth, angling his body so he could keep an eye on the room as well as his brother, an automatic strategy for a trained fighter. Bastien, of course, had taken the last booth with the wall at his back. Standing at the bar gave Chevaliers more freedom, but Bastien hadn't been sure he could stay upright for long. Eyeing his brother, Bastien didn't think Luthan could handle the usual jostling at a crowded bar either.

"You look like merde," Bastien repeated.

Luthan stared at him, and his gray eyes seemed to have become darker. Bastien frowned, but when that pulled at the wounds in his scalp, he stopped and suppressed a wince.

"Jerir," Luthan said, as if that explained everything. He caught Dodu's attention and lifted a hand for ale.

"Jerir," Bastien echoed, mind racing. He was supposed to be the quickest of wits of his family, and Luthan usually made him use every one of them. "An Exotique and jerir. Knowing the old tales, I'd say the Marshalls must have used it as a test."

When the ale was set in front of him, Luthan stared down at the liquid. Then he looked up with gleaming eyes and a slight curve of the lips, lifted the mug in a half salute to Bastien, and drank. He set the glass down, pulled a pristine handkerchief from an inside pocket and dabbed his lips. "Right you are. There were several tests, but I don't know the details. I *do* know that they—"he jerked his head toward the Castle "—have a whole pool of the stuff."

Bastien choked, swallowed, breathed through a couple of gasps. "A pool?" He shook his head. "Can't be. Jerir is scarce and valuable."

"A pool. The ritual bathing pool in the Temple, to be exact." He closed his eyes and a shudder rippled his long frame.

Bastien leaned forward and pressed his fingers on his brother's fisted hand. "What is it? How can I help?"

"Take the job as Chevalier Representative to the Marshalls' Council."

5

"Become the Chevalier's Representative?" That jolted a laugh from Bastien and he leaned back against the padded wall—just the contraction of his chest hurt, by the Song. "Very funny."

Luthan didn't open his eyes. "I'm not joking. *Listen* to your last words. You want to help, to matter, to make things better."

Letting his eyelids lower, Bastien fingered the edge of his hat. "I think you take life too seriously and want me to, also. I'm willing to help my brother."

"And Lladrana?"

"The Marshalls believe *they* are Lladrana."

Luthan opened his eyes. "They are doing the best they can."

Bastien snorted and lifted his mug to drink again, let the smooth buttery taste of goldenale slip down his gullet. He licked his lips. "The Marshalls follow old ways. What's worse—they keep those old ways and old spells from the rest of us, so we don't know what they are doing, why, or what to expect. Most damning of all, they hid the knowledge that our boundaries were failing from us until we were invaded by the greater horrors."

"Perhaps they thought they could find a remedy without involving us."

"That's *your* supposition. Meanwhile Chevalier lives were lost," Bastien said. Including his childhood friend....

"They say the Exotique will solve the puzzle of restoring the fenceposts and boundaries. As in olden days, they Summoned one, and Tested her."

"Did you actually see her?" Bastien lifted a brow.

"I saw a *forming* of her."

His brother's voice held an odd note. Ever fascinated with something new, Bastien scooted a little closer. "You did? Where? And what did she look like?"

"During the Marshalls' Council this morning. She looks—odd. *Exotique.*"

"Hmm." Bastien eyed his brother. "What of you? There's something different about you. You didn't Pair with her, did you?"

This time Luthan choked. "*Merde,* no!" His mouth twisted. "Mind you, I was invited. The Marshalls were displeased that no Chevaliers showed up." His eyebrow mimicked Bastien's.

They grinned at each other.

"It's the jerir. I took a plunge."

Bastien's mug halted midair. "All of you?"

"And not just a quick dip. You know the size of the Temple pool—a nice dive and glide across to the other side to stagger out." He shuddered again.

Drinking deeply, Bastien finished his ale. He'd never seen his brother so twitchy, not Luthan the Calm. "Better you than me."

"No, better both of us." Luthan's fingers curled around Bastien's wrist. "Bastien, the stories are true. The jerir makes a difference in a person, an *obvious* difference. I could tell at a glance those who'd bathed and those who hadn't. Everyone can see the change, and I'd wager every Marshall in the Castle will be in that pool before long. It's an advantage they can't pass up, and neither can you."

"Ha, as if they'd let my little toe into a sacred jerir protection pool." Bastien withdrew his arm from Luthan's grip. An odd vibrancy to Luthan's fingers had set every silver hair on his nape rising. He waved to order two more ales.

Luthan's eyes blazed. "That's just it, Bastien. Word's gone out." His teeth gleamed in a grin that seemed to mock. "They're breaking tradition. Anyone who wishes to can immerse themselves in the pool for the next month."

"Must be desperate." With a smile, Bastien handed a couple of pegtees to Dodu to pay for the drinks.

Shoving his empty glass aside, Luthan took a swig from the new one. "It's a grand gesture, and a smart one. They'll find out who's the toughest, they'll get better Chevaliers and soldiers from this move, and they'll challenge the Chevaliers—the dissenters who don't think much of them, like you—to match them."

The ale turned sour in Bastien's mouth. A feeling deep in his gut told him he'd be swimming in jerir. Rot.

Luthan tapped an elegant forefinger on the wooden table. "Not only the Chevaliers. I'd bet there will be some guild-folk who'll have to bathe or swallow their pride." He spread his hands. "We all win."

"Huh." Bastien took a rag from his breeches pocket and wiped his mouth. "Huh," he said again, not at his most brilliant. He examined his brother again. "You don't look like the stuff has helped you."

"Not yet. I had some bruises from sword practice yesterday." He sucked in a breath and shook his head. "Rough."

"Everybody knows the attributes of jerir. It cleanses wounds and sets them to healing clean and fast. Wherever you were hurt becomes stronger, more protected from injury." Bastien culled from memory.

"Everybody's *heard*," corrected Luthan. "You don't *know* until you take that dive. I thought it was eating my body at those sores." His eyes narrowed, softened. "Give yourself a week or two to heal before you bathe. I wouldn't want to go into that pool with a real wound, and you look like you have one or two."

More like five or six. Bastien curved his mouth in a jaunty smile.

Luthan leaned forward again. "But spread the word. *Anyone* who wants can go to the Castle Temple and ask to swim in the jerir for the next month. They must bathe before using it, and will get a free meal, after. A Marshall or Castle Chevalier will be on hand to verify the submersion." He wiped his mouth with his handkerchief again and looked at the clock. "I have a courtesy meeting with the city guild Representatives to tell them of my new position. I'll also report on the Summoning and the Marshalls' Council. I'll tell them of this offer." Again his even, white teeth flashed. "That will stir them up. You spread the word to this lot." He touched Bastien's hand. "Think about the job of Chevalier Representative. It would be good for the Chevaliers *and* for you."

Bastien forced out the question he'd wanted to ask. "Did our esteemed father bathe in the jerir?" Not that he needed the answer. Reynardus would always have to prove himself tougher, stronger, better than any other man.

"No." Luthan's eyes met Bastien's own and reflected the same emotion. They would never receive the approval of their father, and they would always strive for it, consciously or not. Then Luthan's expression lightened. "Thealia prodded him into a Song Quest and he left before dawn. He should be back soon." Luthan unfolded himself from behind the table gingerly. "Good journeys, brother."

"Good journeys," Bastien said.

Luthan stared at Bastien's hat. "You know a dip in jerir might improve it. Couldn't hurt it any." With an absent wave of the hand, he left the inn.

A smile on his face, Bastien considered his brother and the Marshalls' challenge while making damp intersecting circles on the table with the bottom of his mug. Finally he gulped the last of the brew. Luthan hadn't looked good, true, but the dive through the jerir might not be as bad as he said. Luthan tended to be conservative—one of the reasons Bastien was sure the Cloister had requested Luthan act for them. Conservative and of strong moral fibre. Hell, strong emotional and physical fibre too.

Bastien didn't look as tough as his brother, and considered himself a flexible and genial man, but if this jerir Test must be done—and damn if he'd let his father and brother top him in this endeavor—it best be done quickly. Tonight. Just stepping up to stand on the bench hurt, but he managed. With luck, he'd have a few good souls like Marrec to watch his ass if he'd miscalculated. He scanned the room until several faces turned to him.

"Attencion!"

Though about thirty patrons of the Nom de Nom started up the winding road to the Marshalls' Castle, there were only two by the time they reached the drawbridge gate—Bastien and a reedy teenaged stableboy named Urvey.

Bastien glanced at the slight youth from the corner of his eye. "You don't have to do this, Urvey," he said gently. "No one will think less of you."

The boy's jaws set. "No one will think more of me either." He met Bastien's gaze. "This is my chance. If I do this, I can rise in the world, be more than a stable hand. I could even maybe be a squire." His eyes sharpened. "Do you have a squire, Lord Bastien?"

"I'm a very minor lord, Urvey, with one small parcel of land."
He shrugged.

Urvey pulled hard on the gate chain. A gong sounded behind
the first curtain wall. "But you have three volarans. You could Test
to be a Marshall, couldn't you?"

Bastien's lips twisted. "The last thing I want to be is a hidebound, tight-assed, nose-in-the-air Marshall."

"Huh. Well, you have the chance. I don't." He straightened his
shoulders. "Not 'til now. If I became a squire, maybe in a few years
I could even get a horse, maybe a volaran, then become a Chevalier. You really do need a squire, Lord Bastien. I saw how hard it
was for you to groom your volaran. If you had a squire and were
in a fight, *he* would groom your volaran for you. Please, Lord
Bastien?"

Bastien had no intention of becoming responsible for another
person.

The peephole darkened, then the gate opened. The Castle
guards scrutinized Bastien and Urvey and then waved them into
the lower bailey.

Without further conversation, they crossed the lowest courtyard to the second gate to Temple Ward. When they reached the
door, Urvey used the iron ring to alert the Marshall guards that
they wanted entrance.

Holding a lantern, Swordmarshall Mace ushered them through
the thick gateway. "Welcome, Bastien. Thought I'd see you tonight."

"Good eventide, Mace." The man had been one of Bastien's in-
structors in years past. Squinting in the darkness, Bastien noted
Mace had more vigor than the last time Bastien had seen him. If
Bastien used his Power and tranced in, he could pinpoint the differences. "You've dunked in the jerir pool of protection." He made
it a statement.

Mace nodded. "Right you are. It's evident, isn't it. That will help our cause by bringing others to dip in the jerir. My wife Shieldmarshall and I took the plunge together last night."

"Ah, the time difference. Luthan didn't look as well as you."

After locking the door behind Bastien and Urvey, Mace turned to them and smiled. "Still a bit white around the mouth, was he? He dunked late this morning." Mace frowned. "Didn't stay for the Exotique's Choosing and Pairing."

Bastien laughed. "Who'd want to be bound for life with a woman you just laid eyes on? None of the Chevaliers I know are that stupid."

Mace's gaze fired. "The Choosing is an ancient tradition. *And it works.* The ritual will match a man and woman who can love and bond forever."

Unobtrusively Bastien shifted from foot to foot. Sitting at the Nom de Nom with all his injuries had been rough, but the two-mile walk up to the Castle had caused sweat to sting in his wounds. Just being upright was a strain. "If you say the Choosing magic works, I won't deny you," he placated.

"I don't think you ever knew that my lady and I found each other through a Choosing," Mace said quietly.

That surprised Bastien. "No, I didn't." He would have liked to have swept Mace a bow in apology, but only half inclined his torso.

"It was a long time ago." He sent Bastien a pointed look. "But my love for my Shield grows every day. You Chevaliers should have attended the Choosing."

Bastien lifted and dropped his good shoulder. "For myself, I was traveling here by volaran at the time. So who did the Exotique pick?" He sidestepped a pace or two to the gateway's thick door wall and leaned against it insouciantly, exhaling in relief as the old stones supported him.

"No one." Mace's face grimmed. "No one. There wasn't a good choice for the new Marshall of the Jade Baton. Now we have a 'situation' on our hands. Who knows if she will go or stay? And we need her, by the Song!"

Bastien almost slid down the wall. "The Jade Baton of Honor? She wields the Jade Baton?" The stuff of legends. He'd never even seen the stick.

"She was Tested. There are more Choosing ceremonies than the one for a mate. I myself laid all the batons before her and she Chose the Jade Baton. She carries it well. It flames in her hands."

"Urgh" was all Bastien managed to say.

Urvey gulped too, opened and shut his mouth, then squeaked. "Lladrana really has a new Marshall? An Exotique? Not just rumor?"

Mace jerked a nod. "That's right. You might want to stay, Bastien, and Test for Marshall after you dip."

A half smile formed on Bastien's lips, he swooped his hand. "A dive and glide is what Luthan said."

Mace gave a crack of laughter. "Yes. It's all very well for you unmated athletic Chevaliers. My lady and I just dunked together." His brows lowered. "You could test for Marshall tomorrow."

"No. I thought the full complement of Marshalls was filled."

Mace grunted. "We will be expanding the ranks of Marshalls to defend Lladrana." Brows still drawn, he glanced at the hulk of the towered Keep.

"We already have one Marshall Pair vacancy—we wish to prevent another."

This startled Bastien. "Who died? And how? I thought you were all here in the Castle, none of you on the Field."

Mace grunted. "The Summoning wasn't easy. Who knew how many of us would die in the attempt?"

Urvey's eyes rounded. He gulped.

"Someone died during the Summoning?" Bastien blinked.

"Not exactly." Mace stared at Bastien. "Defau Disparu let his passions get the best of him while he was in a fight."

Bastien knew the sentence was directed as a reminder to him. "Disparu attacked the Exotique."

Urvey gasped. "Attacked our savior!"

Mace ran an eye up and down the boy. "That's right. He died. She has much Power, that one."

An atonal chant drifted from a low Tower window. Mace shifted his feet, looked up. "Swordmarshall Albertus and his wife and Shield used the jerir. She was weak to begin with, but she insisted on accompanying her Sword. She barely lives. If she can survive the shock of the next few hours, her health will be much improved. She's a wily Shield, we'd hate to lose her."

"Two Pair," Bastien murmured. From only six Marshall Pairs, it was a cause for concern—for them. "You wouldn't be at such a pass if you'd opened your ranks much earlier, as the Chevaliers advised. Too many of you wanted to keep your status and Power to a small group." Bastien jutted his chin.

Mace eyed him, but said nothing in defense. He shrugged. "That's past. No reason to ask why you are here. It's my watch to verify any who wish to use the pool of protection. Not that anyone has taken us up on our offer."

"I'm here!" Urvey said.

"So you are, boy. You want to dunk?"

"Yes, My Lord Marshall."

"Luthan's meeting with town guild members tonight. Tomorrow you should have some Chevaliers and townies," Bastien said.

"Good," Mace said. He cast a glance at Bastien then one at the window streaming yellow light where the chant was coming from. "You vouch for this lad, Bastien?"

"I'm his squire!" Urvey announced.

Bastien grimaced but didn't deny it.

"Huh," Mace said. "It's about time you showed a little ambition and responsibility, Bastien." He nodded shortly. "Good thing you took on a squire. Looks like he'll need some training—that will be good for the both of you. Staunch lad, to brave the jerir."

Urvey's thin chest expanded with the compliment. Bastien knew there'd be no dissuading him from the pool now.

Lifting a lantern, Mace scrutinized Bastien. "Stupid-looking hat."

"Soul-sucker hide." Bastien tilted his head so Mace could get a better look.

Mace grunted. "Seems like the soul-sucker laid a couple of tentacles on you, too." He gazed at Bastien's scratched hands. "Huh," he said again, still studying Bastien. "You appear a bit peaked—might want to delay your dipping in the jerir."

Angling his chin, Bastien said, "No." He grinned. "A dive and glide, said Luthan."

"That boy always understates the matter. It's a hell of a lot more. It's bad, especially if you have any aches or pains, any wounds or injuries. What's with you, boy?" Mace narrowed his eyes at Urvey. "You fit?"

"I have a coupla scratches. A flea bite or two. Maybe a bruise from a horse that butted me day before last."

"You'll do," Mace said. He stared at Bastien. "If you have any injuries that aren't showing, you better not try the pool of protection. Wait a day or two. I'd hate to haul you up to that sickroom too." He waved to the Tower window.

Bastien winced inwardly, thinking of the puncture, the rips, the sucker rounds... Ignoring the pain, he shrugged and grinned, tilted his hat to an even more rakish angle. "I can do it."

"You always had more mettle than sense. Your squire will watch out for you. Boy!" Mace called Urvey's wandering attention back to them. "You got any questions?"

Urvey gulped. His eyes gleamed. "I heard we get a meal—a *feast* afterward."

"That's right."

The chant faltered. Mace frowned, then nodded in the direction of the Temple. "I trust you, Bastien. Go take your swim and watch the boy. I need to get back to the healing."

"Fine," Bastien said.

With one last nod, Mace hurried up the right path to the Tower. Urvey started after him, until Bastien halted him with a tug on his sleeve.

"To the left for the shortest route to the Temple."

Urvey grinned but it looked more like the rictus of fear and anticipation than cheer. "A coupla Marshalls were down at the Nom de Nom for a short noonday meal and I saw them. They looked wrung. Musta taken the dip, I guess."

"Probably." Bastien recalled the pallor under Luthan's skin. He set his shoulders. It couldn't be *that* bad, could it? A whisper of the healing chant touched the nape of his neck and slithered down his spine like fear. He was pretty battered, but he was in fine health, strong, and had more stamina than was apparent. And he was a black-and-white; he had wild magic too. Usually under control.

Their boot-steps echoed hollowly before and behind them as they strode along the cobblestone path close to the buildings, passing the nobles lodgings and walking around the bulge of the Temple.

Urvey shivered. "I've never been up here in Temple Ward."

Bastien grunted.

The boy craned his neck, trying to see everything. "It's wonderful."

"It's a Castle bailey," Bastien said, but the large, round Temple, white stone instead of gray, loomed before them. He looked at it with new eyes—the building did seem to pulse with magic.

Finally they reached the great, pointed oaken door and Bastien swung it open. "After you," he said.

In an alcove separated from the main Temple by a carved wooden screen, Bastien and Urvey bathed. The usual cleansing pool was the one now filled with jerir.

Urvey wrapped a towel around boney hips as Bastien donned a robe. He'd convinced Urvey to dip first. Bastien wanted to have all his current strength to pull the youth from the pool, if necessary.

Without his baggy garments, the teen was even skinnier. Bastien surveyed him, noting a few minor scratches and the bruise the boy had spoken of. Urvey flushed a little.

"Just seeing how badly you might be hurt," Bastien said.

A quick grin flashed from the boy. He straightened. "I'm well enough."

"Looks like you could use the feast they promised us, though," Bastien said.

Urvey's grin widened. "I can always eat."

Bastien believed that.

They walked from the seat-ledge that held their clothes, to the pool. Bastien kept to deep shadows so Urvey couldn't see the extent of his wounds.

The jerir looked thick and dark blue, nearly filling the pool three man-lengths long and one wide. Bastien's stomach tightened at the sight of the still, viscous liquid and the thought of the pain that would come.

"Looks nasty." Urvey's voice sounded high.

"No, it looks beautiful." Bastien's voice was a lower rasp than usual. He didn't clear his throat. "A very beautiful blue. As blue as a fine sapphire. It's only the thought of the pain it can cause that makes you think it's nasty."

Urvey shot him a nervous glance. His black brows shot upward.

"But where you hurt, it starts to heal faster, and better than before. You're stronger than before, right?" He gazed down at both knees, which were shadowed with bruises Bastien hadn't noticed.

"That's what they say. I don't trust some of the old legends like the Marshalls do—"

"But they Summoned an Exotique!" Urvey said with awe.

Bastien had to nod. "They did. And I've never known Sword-marshall Mace to lie."

"Why should he? He's so big he can say whatever he likes."

Chuckling, Bastien said, "Very true. Do you swim, boy?"

Urvey looked horrified. "Swim? No."

Bastien led the youth to a corner. "There are steps into the pool here."

"Oh. I thought I'd just, um, jump in and pop out. I can do that in the water hole at the edge of town."

"Fine." Bastien surveyed the pool and walked to the middle of one long edge. "If I recall right, this should be about your height. Make sure you go all the way under."

Urvey gulped, sucked in a big breath. Then he glanced at Bastien, and down at the pool. Urvey's muscles tensed. He jumped.

His cut-off scream bounced off the circular stone walls and echoed. He popped up, screaming again.

Bastien reached into the jerir pool and helped Urvey out. Just the immersion of his forearm in the liquid made him bite the inside of his cheek with pain. How was he going to manage this?

But he had to. His pride was on the line. Every Chevalier at the Nom de Nom knew he'd intended to immerse himself in the jerir. Urvey looked up at him with pained and admiring eyes as Bastien helped him dry off and dress.

Not to mention that if Luthan could do it, Bastien could, and *would,* do it too. His mouth thinned. There was a different aura about those who had bathed in the jerir than about those who hadn't. Even now Urvey was showing the underlying glow of the experience. There was no way Bastien could simply lie.

He eyed the pool. It was going to be bad. Worse perhaps than even his last fight. Only fancy footwork and fast reflexes had saved him. And he didn't have his volaran to help him this time. He'd have to trust his wild magic.

"Shall I stay?" asked Urvey, looking longingly at the door, probably thinking of the good meal they'd been promised. Trust a growing boy to think of his stomach, even after such an ordeal!

Bastien said, "No, of course not. Go get some food and drink for us." He waved a hand at the door.

Urvey's brows came down. "Are you sure?" He opened his mouth as if to offer help, then shut it. They both knew about manly pride.

"I'm sure." Bastien grinned. Nothing to do now but to laugh at the situation he'd gotten himself into. "Go. Get some meat and mead. Take your time—" Bastien winked "—I may want to soak a little."

That reassured the boy. He laughed. "Fine. I'll get us *a lot* of good food and mead." He rubbed his stomach. He looked around and dropped his voice. "Can we eat in here?"

"Of course." Bastien made a wide gesture with his arm. "This is the Temple. A Temple is for all the rituals of people. Including breaking bread." He winked again. "Including sex."

Urvey flushed, dropped his eyes. "I'm a womanlover."

Bastien clapped a hand on Urvey's shoulder. "I am, too. We can eat here—there's a dining table over there." He waved to a darkened quadrant. "And you recall that behind the fancy screen is another bathing pool and a toilet. The pool with jerir is usually filled with water to bathe in, you know."

Urvey just stared. "No, I don't, Lord. *You* know. I can only guess."

"And learn," Bastien said gently. "You can learn."

Urvey brightened. "I can do that. And I know how to assemble a feast for us!"

He took off for the door while Bastien stared at the pool near his blistered feet.

Urvey hesitated by the door. "You *are* sure——"

"Go!" He didn't want the boy to hear him scream.

The door closed and Bastien rubbed his face. "Great, just great. What did you get me into this time, brother?" He swore under his breath. "What did my own stupidity and pride get me into? I damn well should wait." He should. But it was quiet and soothing here in the Temple. Surely he could manage a quick dunk—a hop in and dive through and hop out. That should be sufficient. But by the Song, he didn't want to dip in the jerir! He actually dreaded the idea.

Nothing for it. He'd manage. He'd been in worse spots.

6

Come, Alexa! Sinafin cried. She jumped up and down on Alexa, waking her.

Alexa cracked open an eye to see a blue squirrel, then shut it again. "No." She snuggled deeper into the soft mattress. As soon as she'd escaped the clutches of the Marshalls, she'd showered and hopped into bed, though the sun still shone.

After her humiliating sickness, they'd whipped up another potion that settled her stomach and fed her. Then Alexa had been stuck in a room and measured and given "little" clothes by giggling women. Following that, she'd been shown into a map room to watch some oddity on an animated landscape. Finally, she'd been plunked down and taught some Lladranan by a person who tried to keep a straight face at her pronunciation. Alexa began to wonder if the days here were the same length as on Earth.

Alexa, Alexa, you must come. Sinafin scrabbled at the covers that Alexa pulled over her head.

"No, I'm tired. I've had a *very* full day and I'm not going anywhere. I'm staying in bed, and if I'm lucky, the Snap will come and take me away."

Blue squirrel paws pushed the covers away, and Alexa found herself looking into bright black eyes. Sinafin clasped her paws together. *PLEASE, Alexa.*

"Your colors are off. There aren't any blue squirrels." Alexa rolled over.

She thought she dozed.

The baby cried. She shoved away fluffy comforters and half slid, half fell to the floor. Her bare feet missed the rug and jarred against cold stone. She swore.

Come, come, come! Sinafin, a golden ball, dipped and swooped, then vanished through the closed door.

Hopping from foot to foot, Alexa dragged on knit slippers that were warm and cushioned her feet from the stone floor. She muttered curses. In English. She hadn't learned enough Lladranan to know any good local swears.

What was it *now?* A person couldn't even barricade herself into her room for a little shut-eye.

NOW, Alexa! Sinafin—a neon purple bat—screeched in her ear and zoomed through the door again. Over her nightgown, Alexa whipped on a quilted robe that trailed on the ground, and rushed across the threshold—

And was jerked short when her robe stuck in the door. No infant was near. She heard a wail—would they leave the baby on one of the narrow landings? Surely not.

Follow me! cried Sinafin.

Gritting her teeth and taking precious time to open the door and grab the robe, Alexa knew she *really* needed those swearwords. She ran through the Tower room, down and down and down endless stairs following a flashing neon purple bat into the Cloisters. It was dark and raining again. Not twenty-four hours after her arrival in Lladrana and she was charging to the rescue again. Didn't a savior ever get a little downtime?

Apparently not. Sinafin led her to the huge oak door of the circular Temple. Were they trying to teach the baby to swim again the hard way? Alexa hated being manipulated by the Marshalls. But was this their work? The door opened easily under her hand and she rushed into the dim room.

Sure enough, Sinafin hovered by the end of that nasty pool as a large golden glow, flickering and fluttering wildly, as if trying to keep something out of the liquid.

Alexa's heart pounded and she peeled off her robe. Sucking in a big breath and whimpering inwardly, she dove into the pool.

Pain dimmed her mind like a lowering curtain. She fought against it, gritting her teeth to keep from opening her mouth in a scream and swallowing the stuff. The liquid slid against her, like it was measuring every inch of her before seeking each tiny wound to torture— She came up against someone hard.

It wasn't a baby this time. It was a big guy. Well, normal for *them,* but big to her. Apparently he'd made it into the pool, but not out of it. Alexa could understand that; the liquid gnawed at her bruises and sent biting pain along scratches. She vowed to never, *ever* pick at her cuticles again.

Thrusting her head above the liquid she gasped and thrashed to hold the limp, heavy limbs of the man. She sensed Sinafin trying to help, taking part of the man's weight.

Her nightgown tangled her legs, she floundered, slipped and sank, found her feet and tried again. Grunting and swearing she managed to roll the man out of the pool, but sank again before crawling out.

He lives! Sinafin caroled in relief.

Just as Alexa surfaced and opened her mouth to ask something instead of heaving a breath, Sinafin turned into a purple bat with golden wings and streaked from the chamber—through a closed glass window this time. As she did so she made the sound of a wailing baby.

Alexa allowed herself to collapse on the floor. She'd been had! By her own...what? Mentor? Sidekick? Friend?

After a few minutes the marble floor, though warm, felt really hard. Alexa rocked to her hands and knees, then stood and wobbled. Until she saw him. Then she was struck still and dumb with pure admiration.

Wow! Only the dim crystals in the rafters and the glowing gemstone crystals in a rainbow on the altar lit the room, but it was enough. He lay on his back, the outline of his muscles flickering wet and golden-hued. Alexa swallowed hard.

She took a step forward. Broad shoulders tapered to narrow hips, muscular thighs—she bet he had a killer butt—nice calves, long elegant feet. Oh yeah.

Naturally she looked at his sex. She was a red-blooded American woman, wasn't she? And she had to make sure that the people of Lladrana were like people at home. She peered a little closer and gulped. Yes, his parts were like those of the men at home. No, it didn't look like he was hurt there at all—but otherwise...

Just seeing the scars on him appalled her—new red welts, some slices that looked like they had come from the same sort of monster who'd attacked her. His body was a map of colorful bruises, scratches and circular raised bumps that made her think of leeches. She shuddered. He had a big, nasty puncture close to his, um, jewels that made her wince and shift from foot to foot.

She was warm and safe here, as was he, but how was she going to get help?

She eyed the gong and bit her lip. It was near the altar with those jewel-crystals and other magical stuff. She really didn't want to touch it.

"Sinafin?" she whispered.

No answer.

Alexa studied the studly guy again, this time making it to his face. She frowned. He looked a little like someone she'd seen before, but she couldn't place the resemblance. Nice jaw, good straight nose. Eyes heavy-lidded and tilted up at the corners. Soft, mobile lips.

Soft, mobile lips? She was losing it. Time to get her act together and see if she could help the man, but at least his wide, lightly haired chest rose and fell steadily.

Then she noticed something else. Unlike every other adult in Lladrana, he didn't have black hair or black hair with silver or gold streaks at one or both temples. No, the flickering light gleamed on his striped black-and-white hair. She stared. The baby had black-and-white hair like that too. Did they ritually drown those? She knew in her bones it must mean something.

His lids opened and she stared into deep brown eyes that slowly focused. He opened his mouth and started coughing. He stirred, moaned, then subsided again into unconsciousness. But his breath turned steady and deep.

The door pushed open and cold air swept around her, plastering her nightgown to her body. She whirled. A skinny teenager holding a tray and a pitcher stared openmouthed at her. She narrowed her eyes. He had that electric-blue outline that several of the Marshalls had had that morning. She glanced back at the man lying by the pool—yes, there was a slight electric-blue tint coating him.

She looked at her own hands. They radiated blue. Then she saw her own body, fully revealed by the thin, wet nightgown. She looked very white. She made a sound like "Eek"—a girly sound, she thought in disgust—hurried and snatched her robe.

"Voulvous? Vu?" The boy's voice rose in a question.

Alexa forced her lips into a grin, flopped a hand in what she'd intended to be a wave, and wobbled past the boy to the door. She'd done what Sinafin had wanted. Alexa didn't plan to hang around for questions she couldn't answer.

The man groaned behind her. She quickened her pace. The teenager frowned, then set the tray down and ran to the man.

Alexa slipped out the door and into the cloister walk. Silver rain fell tinkling around her, then sputtered into droplets and subsided into a soft patter.

Once back in her room, after showering—another pain, since some of the jerir penetrated her scratches instead of sliding from her body—Alexa was restless. She went to the windows to look out, and saw blackness over the fields. Her tower was one of the four large round Towers of the Castle Keep, but no one lived there except herself.

She dressed in leggings, a shirt and a long tunic, then she paced.

Though the weather had cleared and brilliant stars shone in the night sky, there was only the faintest luminescence where she knew the Town should be. No use going to the Town, since she wasn't even familiar with the Castle. The thought of walking alone down the hill to the Town daunted her. She shivered as the memory of the night hike she'd taken in Colorado flickered in her mind's eye. She'd been crazy, spellbound, grief-stricken—maybe all three.

She noticed the swaying white branches of the beautiful large tree in the garden below. Concentrating hard, she heard the soft murmuring of the tree's Song, which spoke of contentment and spring and growing and destiny. The strains came too quietly to grasp and the melody was such that she wanted to listen to the whole of it. Or maybe she just had cabin fever and wanted out. She drew her heavy, warm purple cloak around her, then slipped from her room and down the stairs.

Everything was quiet.

Hesitating, she cocked her head to get the tree's direction. With slow steps she followed the tune and found herself before a small door that would let her out of the Keep and near the garden. She opened it, and air laden with humidity and the rich secrets of night-growing plants wafted to her. As she inhaled, more notes joined the rich orchestral symphony. She exited, and a few strides later faced the tall hedge maze. Perfectly groomed, it stood a good fifteen feet high, dense and dark and green-black.

Still the tree Sang, and it Sang *to her.* She could almost hear it Sing her name. She pulled her cloak close and the cowl low and threaded her way through the maze by sound instead of sight. Low bird chirps accompanied the soft tread of her own footsteps.

A few minutes later she exited the maze at a right angle from where she had entered. There was a small lawn, then an old, low wall of stone with a little door that looked to be just her size. She smiled and walked to it, put her hand on the cold handle, pressed the latch and pulled, expecting an awful creak. The door swung silently and easily open.

The moon had risen while she'd been in the maze and now painted the garden in silver light. A profusion of bushes with stark branches of various shades of gray and black were all tangled together as though the garden wasn't well tended. Most of the Lladranans would have to stoop through the door.

But the white tree lifting graceful branches into the sky was the only life taller than the wall.

A bench circled the tree, and she picked her way through dead leaves along an overgrown path toward it. For a moment she hesitated, then slid her hands up and down the trunk, feeling the bark, smooth in some spots, rough in others. Tree-song enveloped her and she sat on the bench, leaning against the trunk.

She didn't know how long she rested there, her busy mind quiet, experiencing the tree's melody, imbued with serenity. It lilted of sap rising through it slowly, slowly, of the anticipation of each bud pushing through bark and unfurling tiny leaves, of the reaching of its branches and how it danced with the wind and the sky and the Song.

There you are! Sinafin said, the hint of a scold in her voice.

She was still the purple bat. In the recesses of her mind, Alexa knew she should be upset with the shape-changer, and there were questions she wanted answers to, but being in the tree's presence had made all her questions seem less urgent, as if she were measuring time more slowly now. So she just stared at the purple bat and admired its wings.

Sinafin hung upside down from a near branch and gazed at Alexa. Even this wasn't too disconcerting. She was operating on tree-time, with tree-serenity-philosophy still pulsing around her.

The shapeshifter whiffled, eyes bright. *You like the brithenwood tree, very good.*

Why? Another question that should be more important than it seemed. Only one concern rose to her mind.

"I'm here to make new fenceposts to defend Lladrana?" She'd culled that from Sinafin's mind-movie of the night before and the talk amongst the Marshalls in the Temple after she'd been taken to bed like a kid. But within the peace of the garden the spark of irritation failed to flame.

Yes.

"Tell me of the fenceposts."

They are the primary defense of Lladrana, made by Guardian Marshalls during the last true invasion of horrors, about eight hundred years ago.

Before my time. Since then we've had only little groups sneaking over. And the frinks. They are new in the past two years.

"I'm supposed to discover how the fenceposts are made and re-make them?" Alexa wanted to be clear on this point.

The bat stretched its wings, so transparent that some stars shone through the tissue-skin. *Yes.*

"How?"

The Song will guide you.

Alexa hadn't heard voices yet. "How?"

Sinafin was silent, her sprightly tune having faded. The background music hardly murmured. The tree was silent. Nothing answered Alexa.

The next morning the Marshalls had no sooner taken their seats around the Council table than the door flew open with a jar of harpstrings and Reynardus, Lord Knight of the Marshalls, strode in.

They all stood, Thealia slightly slower than the others. Though Reynardus marched to his chair at the head of the table and took it with a haughty look, pallor showed under his skin. He'd dipped in the jerir. Had probably swum back and forth the length of the pool, Thealia thought sourly. She narrowed her eyes. His expression hinted at controlled emotion.

"Events have not progressed well in the hours I have been gone. Hopefully now that I am back and can direct them, they will proceed better. I want to know what has occurred. I see we are all here except the dead Defau and Albertus's ailing wife," he said, still standing, knowing they all must sit after he did.

Thealia inclined her head. "I am sure you have been updated on all events."

"We lost Defau and nearly lost Veya. The Choosing Ceremony failed. If we spend hours on training the Exotique, give her jew-

els and land as is required, she might still disappear like this—"
he snapped gloved fingers, but the sound was still loud.

Thealia's temper simmered.

Reynardus continued. "Furthermore, I hear you opened the
jerir pool not only to the Marshalls and select landowners and
Chevaliers, but to *all* Chevaliers—no, let me amend—" He
peeled the gloves from his hands and flung them on the table. "You
invited *anyone* to immerse themselves in our precious jerir. The
jerir that cost us great effort to move from a natural pool to the
Temple pool. With the right care it could have been saved and
used for a year—"

"I thought we had agreed to drain the jerir," Thealia said. "But
you were the one in charge of that. Did you have plans that the
rest of us didn't know of?"

A touch of red lined his cheekbones. "That is moot now. I
cannot believe you will let any scum off the city street use the jerir.
I heard a stable boy dipped last night, a *stable boy!*"

Thealia looked at Mace.

His face hardened. "Your son's new squire," he said.

Reynardus's brows rose. "Luthan has a new squire?"

"Bastien," said Mace.

Someone turned a laugh into a cough.

Reynardus's nostrils flared. "I should have known he'd have
such poor judgment as to take a nobody stable boy for a squire,
but for the rest of you to issue a proclamation to all the Towns
for use of *our* jerir—"

"We are the guardians of the land," Thealia said. "Lladrana
needs all the staunch men and women available to fight the evil
confronting us. One of the ways to recruit the people we need is
to offer them use of the jerir."

"As I said yesterday, I will be honored to train anyone who dips
in the jerir," Mace said. "Both your sons availed themselves of the

jerir, as did some of the most important guild-people of the Town. Every hour more Chevaliers arrive to take advantage of our offer. We are building an army."

"An army of shopkeepers!" Reynardus sneered.

Protests ran the length of the table.

"With our magical boundary fields failing, more land than ever is being invaded by the greater monsters. And even the Townspeople are affected by the frinks falling in the rain, burrowing into the soil and turning the weak-brained into inhuman mockers," Thealia said, pursuing the point when the others didn't. "We need strong defenders. Lord Knight Swordmarshall Reynardus, do you have any report of your Song Quest you wish recorded in the Marshalls' Lorebook of Song Quests?"

Reynardus paled. He sat abruptly. "No." The moments it took for everyone to sit were enough for him to regain composure. He swept a piercing gaze around the table and verbally attacked. "I want a moment-by-moment recitation of what happened here at the Castle in my absence. I want a list of the names and ranks of those who have bathed in the jerir. I want an update on our borders. Most of all, I want to know what you have done to train our new Exotique 'savior' to control her Powers and to fight."

At that moment the doorharp sounded.

Reynardus scowled. Everyone looked at the door. Rapping came.

Thealia glanced at Reynardus. "It must be important."

He shrugged. "Come," he called.

The door opened only enough to let a Castle serving woman, Umilla, slide in. She was a bowed, thin woman dressed in bright green that emphasized her drab coloring. Her hair was streaked white and black—a sign of the greatest of Power or the most fragmented.

Several Marshalls gasped at her presumption.

Umilla twisted her hands in the dress that hung from her frame. When she spoke her voice was dry and whispery. "There's a fey-coocu in the Castle," she said.

Everyone stared at her. When the silence stretched, she turned and shuffled away.

"Stop, girl," Reynardus shouted. "Say that again, and speak up. I didn't hear you."

Umilla only turned her head. "There's a feycoocu in the Cas-tle." Her words were only a little louder, but the spells in the Chamber amplified them and repeated them: *There's a feycoocu in the castle. There's a feycoocu in the castle.*

Reynard stood. He leaned forward, both hands on the table, his Power focused on Umilla. "A magical shapeshifter? Are you sure, girl?"

"Blessings. It's been more than a century since we've been so graced. A good sign that our Summoning was right. A feycoocu can only help our cause," Partis said.

Snorting, Reynardus said, "You always take the optimistic road, Partis." He turned back to Umilla. "Serving girl, come here."

Steps halting, Umilla did. When she lifted her head, her eyes blazed. She ran a hand through her hair, emphasizing the streaks. "I know every heart pulse in the Castle. Every soulprint. There is a new one. Fun and new and happy and strange. It came after the new Exotique. It's *for* her."

"Who can tell what a feycoocu will do?" Partis murmured.

"As incalculable as Exotiques," Thealia said. "I agree it's a good sign. Others will be impressed, especially the Singer's Cloister, perhaps the Sorcerers in their Towers also." Thealia lifted her eyebrows at Reynardus. "Don't you agree?"

He chewed at the corner of his mouth, then jerked his head in a nod. With a flick of his fingers, he dismissed Umilla. She scut-tled from the room.

* * *

Hello, Alexa, Sinafin said.

She was a little mermaid swimming in a spherical aquarium hovering under the canopy of Alexa's bed. "I'm dreaming," Alexa mumbled.

Yes.

"The Lladranans call me 'Alyeka.'"

Your name is hard for our tongues.

Two names. She'd get confused for sure. She had no ear for foreign languages. During her childhood of foster homes, she'd changed schools several times and had ended up lagging behind in Spanish, French and Latin, and jumbling them all.

Sinafin flipped her emerald-green tail and waggled a fin. *Listen and watch closely as I show you what happened yesterday.*

The dream-movie as translated by Sinafin only rolled as far as the Choosing and Pairing ceremony before Alexa was wide awake, struggling into her new clothes of tights and tunic and tabard. This was far too much for her to take lying down. Time to do something about the Marshalls who were arranging her life in the pattern they wanted.

Stamping into some boots that had been made for a young Lladranan girl, she ground her teeth. She had to wear "little girl's" clothes. Anger already sizzled through her, and was fueled by her frustration over dressing in strange garments.

Wait, Alexa, you haven't seen all! Sinafin said.

Alexa looked for Sinafin, but couldn't find her. "Are you coming with me to confront the Marshalls?"

A beautiful tiny greyhound leaped to the top of the bed. Alexa narrowed her eyes. "I don't think greyhounds come this small." The feycoocu was only about a foot in length.

Sinafin sat and scratched her ear with a hind paw. *This is my nat-*

ural size. *I can be much larger or smaller if I use magic. You see, you don't know much about Lladrana.*

"No, but I don't think all Lladranans are like the Marshalls. I think I could take my chances in the Town. I work hard."

Sinafin cocked her head at Alexa. *You don't even know where the Marshalls are,* Sinafin pointed out smugly.

Frowning, Alexa tested a heaviness in her mind, like a dark cloud. The Marshalls. "I know they're here in the Castle and they're all together, as usual."

Sinafin tipped her head to the other side and twitched an ear. *Reynardus is back.*

Alexa snorted. "You think I care?"

You should. He is very powerful and important to your future.

"Huh. I've seen lawyers like him before."

And what did you do?

"Minded my manners. Walked softly. But now I have a big stick!" With a thought she called her Jade Baton, and it slapped into her open hand. Her fingers curled around it and the bar warmed and glowed, the bronze sculpted flames at the top blazing into real red and yellow fire. She was impressed. She grinned, showing teeth. Oh, she'd tell those Marshalls. Trying to "bind" her emotionally to a lover without her consent was the last straw.

She licked her lips and studied the wand, wondering about its powers. Maybe she could experiment. "Take me to the Marshalls," she said to her Jade Baton.

It tugged on her hand, pointing to the door.

Alexa threw a smile at Sinafin. "Coming?"

The little dog hopped from the tall bed, her tongue lolled briefly. *This may be fun.*

Alexa set her shoulders and marched out the door, following the inclination of her baton. She wound her way down the stairs, still angry and hurt. She knew she was far from emotionally accepting the changes in her life.

Even with Marwey to link with her mind, and Sinafin's dream-movies, all she understood was that Lladrana's magic Marshalls had Summoned her because they thought she could stop a great evil by making fenceposts to keep it out.

And that she had powers that had killed a man. She choked. She'd never thought that she could kill someone, not even in self-defense. If she stayed here, she'd have to learn how to control these strange mind powers.

She started down a long, gray stone hall. With her free hand, she wiped aside her tears and wondered if these people cried. Anger at the Marshalls' manipulations was an emotion she could recognize, one she could justify and act on. Grief at thoughts of her lost world, confusion and frustration at her new circumstances, creeping blind fear at the unknown could be squashed and hidden away and ignored. Anger was better.

Finally she reached a large pointed-arch door set in a stone wall to her right. The door had a big golden harp on it; strange letters decorated the harp. She bit her lip. She couldn't read them. She, who had been the journal editor for her law school, couldn't read. It was infuriating. It was humiliating. It was terrifying. With a cry of anger, she flung open the door.

7

Reynardus sat at the head of a long wooden table. He glanced up at Alexa. "Another interruption?" Then he turned to Thealia. "Things have certainly deteriorated in the short time I was gone."

"Marshall Alekya has a seat on this Council and is welcome here." Thealia stretched out her hand to Alexa.

Alexa stared. She could understand them! Sinafin pressed against her leg and Alexa realized that the fairy—whatever—was translating for her, the words' meanings coming to her mind a beat after they were spoken. She looked down at Sinafin, who gave her a doggy grin. Alexa was torn. She could pick up the miniature greyhound or hold her baton, but not both. She'd have to stand still and rant. Too bad. It was much easier for her to keep her thoughts in order if she paced.

Sinafin brushed Alexa's legs as she crossed to the table and set the baton down. It faded to a dull dark green. Parting with the stick was hard, but Alexa wanted nothing to do with the Marshalls or their Tests or their hidden agendas for her. She picked up Sinafin, who swirled a sweet-breathed tongue around her face, erasing tear tracks. Alexa was grateful.

But then the small hound pointed her nose at the wand and shook her head. *You do not want to do this.*

"I *must* do this," Alexa said. The words came out in English, then twisted into something else. She stroked Sinafin's ears. "Can you translate for me?"

Yes.

"Is that the feycoocu?" asked Partis.

Say yes, Sinafin said.

"Yes. She is translating for me. Listen up, guys."

A couple of the Marshalls winced. Probably not enough noble-speak for them. Tough.

"You brought me here without my express consent—"

"Wrong. You came through—" Thealia said.

Alexa waved her hand. "Very well, I agree on that point, but I didn't know what was happening or where I was coming. You didn't have the courtesy to ask me to help you. No, you all initiated a preemptive strike, forcing me to respond to Tests that could have killed me." She strode around the room, and several Marshalls craned to keep track of her. She remembered the baby, the man who'd been so repulsed by her that he tried to stab her, and whom she had killed with her mind. She fought new tears. "You could have killed a baby—"

"She's a black-and-white, flawed—" Reynardus said.

"Everyone's flawed in some way!" Alexa was old enough to have learned that lesson. "You set me up to be attacked and I took a life in self-defense. That's the worst of it. But that wasn't the last of your manipulations, was it? You wanted to keep me here by force, make me stay by somehow binding me to another—"

"Pairing—"

"Stop interrupting! Only *now* you try to explain. Only *now*, when your plans have failed."

Partis stood. "We need you."

"You didn't ask, and you didn't explain. You haven't been honest in any of your dealings with me. I've had nothing but manipulation and lies from you all. I'm leaving."

"You can't leave!" Thealia said.

Alexa glared at her. "Of course I can, unless you give me some good reasons to stay."

Reynardus leaned negligently back in his chair. "Let her go." He waved an elegant hand. "She won't get far. She can't live on her own. She'll come back."

Fury suffused Alexa. She'd heard comments like that before.

You won't make it through law school.

You won't pass the bar.

You won't make a living in a small partnership.

But she had.

"I'm sure I can find work in the Town."

Another Marshall stood and inclined her head to Alexa. "I am the Loremarshall, Faith. When an Exotique such as yourself is Summoned, you are given gold and the choice of an estate to support you. We will compensate you well."

A home, Sinafin said, just to her. *A home of your own. Your land. Your home.*

The offer made her hesitate, until she saw Reynardus's smirk. She'd have to work for these people. People she couldn't trust.

"I can't trust you," she said.

Partis dropped his eyes. Faith looked ashamed.

"You Summoned me, but you didn't trust that magic, and you didn't trust me."

"It's gone wrong before," Reynardus said coolly.

Alexa inadvertently squeezed Sinafin 'til she yipped. She loosened her hold. "I didn't know that, which only emphasizes my point. I know nothing of you, and none of you has been willing to explain or to trust me. I've heard no reason to make me stay—only a bribe. I'm leaving. I'll wait in town for the Snap."

Thealia gasped. "How do you know of the Snap?"

Lifting the miniature greyhound, Alexa said, "Sin—"

Don't give them my name!

"Since I came, this, um, feycoocu has helped me. She told me."

"It's a she?" asked Partis.

Alexa ignored him. "Anything else?"

The Marshalls glanced at each other, then at Reynardus.

Reynardus studied his clean fingernails. "She will be back."

Alexa's mouth turned down. She'd hoped for explanations, *something* that would tell her they respected her, accepted her. But there was nothing here for her. She turned and walked to the door.

"We can teach you to use your great Powers! Please, take up the baton again!" someone urged.

Another bribe. Like being a great magician was something Alexa should want. Power to kill with her mind. She didn't think so.

Alexa placed Sinafin on her feet and stepped away to open the door. Babble assaulted her ears. Since she couldn't understand any of it, it was easy to ignore. She looked down at the shapeshifter and said, "Are you coming with me?"

Her untranslated words silenced a few, as if they tried to decipher how her language was different from theirs. Sinafin sat and used a hind leg to scratch behind her ear, then yawned. *It might be fun.*

"You sound pretty cheerful all of a sudden."

The dog wiggled her nose. *You will change your mind. I tell you now and I will tell you again and again that you have a home here.*

Ah, there was a being who knew what buttons to push! Alexa shrugged. At least Sinafin had been honest.

Alexa opened the door and let Sinafin out first. "Lead the way." The dog trotted ahead and Alexa followed. Loud voices carried after her.

Sinafin turned left and zoomed down the hallway, sending a gleeful bark back to Alexa. *This strange dog-body likes to run. Very nice.*

"Yes," Alexa said softly, wondering if Sinafin could hear her—at what distance the mind-to-mind speaking worked.

She found herself smiling and blew out a big breath. Whew! Her steps picked up and became jaunty. Releasing all that anger had been cathartic. She refused to worry about what might await her ahead. She'd been uprooted and thrown into strange situations enough as a kid to believe she'd somehow manage. And she had a feycoocu. Things weren't all bad.

A distant *yip* had her stretching her stride. She came to the end of the hallway, where there was a door to the staircase to the front tower of the Castle Keep. This tower was on the opposite end of the corridor to the back tower that Alexa had been given. She turned right into the corridor that led to her tower staircase. She wasn't going back. Sinafin must have taken one of the other little passages, branching left off the Keep's hallway. The Castle was built for the Lladranans—slightly too large a scale for Alexa.

She paused, irritated. *Sinafin!* It was the first time she had tried calling with her mind. Nothing happened. Alexa frowned. Maybe words weren't the best way to communicate. What about pictures? She fashioned the best image she could of Sinafin—as the pink fairy—and tried again. *Sinafin!*

Faint, running claw-clicks came from a hall up a bit and to her left.

Sinafin shot from it, turned away from Alexa and ran down the corridor and back, panting and grinning. *Run, run, run!* Sinafin said.

"You run," Alexa grumbled. Her body still ached from the two dips in the jerir. At least now she knew what it was called, and that it was supposed to heal her and then be protective. She shook her head. Magic. Something to be as cautious about as a loaded gun.

Her thoughts went to the guy she had saved, and she winced. If she thought *she* hurt today, he'd be even worse off. His wounds had been awesome, but since he'd lived through the ordeal, he'd be one tough cookie, she guessed. And the baby—if she was flawed, would the jerir have cured her? Probably what everyone had hoped for. Alexa would miss the little girl, and Marwey.

Sinafin bounded up to her, lolling a tongue, then turned around and jogged left back down the passage she'd appeared from. *The closest way out is through the Assayer's Office, just beyond the Keep walls.*

Down a short passage the feycoocu waited before a big square wooden door. It was more roughly finished than most of the Castle doors. Alexa set her hand on the iron handle and an overwhelming dread flooded from her fingers up her arm to her mind, making her heart pound hard. She pulled back. *Death.* She could smell it now. The tang of blood and fleshy refuse. She swallowed hard.

Sinafin cocked her ears, looking too innocent. Alexa hesitated. She didn't want to go into that room.

Shuffling steps behind her made her whirl. A bowed woman in serving costume came slowly to them, her gaze fixed on Sinafin. Even hunched, she was taller than Alexa. The woman stopped, ducked her head a little and glanced at Alexa with shy eyes.

"I am Umilla. Is that the feycoocu?"

I am Sinafin. The words echoed twice, and Alexa realized the greyhound spoke to them both.

"Why did you tell Umilla your name and not the Marshalls?" Alexa asked.

A name is powerful magic. You can Summon me by my name, Sinafin said. *The Marshalls might use me if they could.*

Umilla snorted.

Alexa reckoned since the Marshalls couldn't pronounce her name, she was safe.

"I'm Alexa." She put out her hand.

The woman just stared at it. Her mouth fell open.

Sinafin trotted to Alexa. *Alexa.* Then danced to the serving woman. *Umilla.*

Alexa tried a reassuring smile and nodded. "Umilla."

"A-*lex*-a." The woman bobbed her head.

Alexa's eyes widened. Finally someone who pronounced her name correctly! She grinned.

Umilla ducked and leaned down to pet the dog. Her long hair swung to hide her face, and Alexa realized it was streaked black-and-white. Like the baby's. Like the guy's last night.

Reynardus had called them black-and-whites—and flawed.

Flawed? As she studied the woman, Alexa sensed wild fluctuations of energy—magic?—inside Umilla. Something the woman had never been able to control.

Umilla straightened, holding Sinafin.

Alexa watched the serving woman and Sinafin for a moment, then turned her attention back to the door and frowned. An itching at the back of her brain told her the Marshalls' meeting had ended and they were breaking up. Soon they'd disperse, and she didn't want to meet any of them. She didn't know of any door out except this one.

Finally a sigh escaped Umilla and she closed the short distance between them, holding Sinafin out to Alexa. Alexa took the fey-coocu.

"Merci." Umilla bobbed a curtsy. With vague eyes but a digni-fied bearing, she shuffled back the way she had come.

You should put me down now, Sinafin said, a note in her voice that made apprehension ripple through Alexa.

She set the dog on its feet. Facing the door again, Alexa clicked open the latch, pushed and entered in one motion. The smell was a mixture of antiseptic and dead things. The room was a nightmarish vision. Something that would haunt her dreams for years to come.

"What is this place?" Her voice rose.

The Assayer's Office, Sinafin replied calmly.

It was nothing like an assayer's office in Colorado. Not for min-erals—silver or gold. It was for monsters.

Alexa's stomach gave a sickening roll. Heads were mounted on the walls. Grotesque heads of creatures she'd never imagined in her most dreadful dreams. Above the heads the ceiling disap-peared into dimness around the rafters. One of the heads was like the thing that had attacked her when she'd come from Colorado to Lladrana. Its fangs glistened in such a realistic snarl that she shuddered.

Render, Sinafin informed her.

It was as huge as she remembered, the eyes small and red, the black bristly fur looking as rough as a steel brush. The muzzle was short, but open, showing black tongue, sharp teeth and the fangs. Beneath the head, a paw-hand was mounted, the foot-long curved claws extended.

Alexa put her hand to her mouth to stifle an involuntary scream.

Next to the render was a torso consisting of a bald, gray head with holes for eyes and lizardlike skin. It had two arms with suckers all the way down to its three-digited hands. Two tentacles draped before and behind each arm. The horror loomed directly above Alexa. All the hair on her body rose.

Soul-sucker, Sinafin said.

"Get me *out* of here!"

The room was taller than it was wide or long, with a wooden counter running the full length on her left. A heap on the counter caught her eye and she couldn't help staring. Yellow fur, as bristly as the render's, showed against glistening red muscles. The head and the back of the monster sported curved, wicked spines. The fur was nearly flayed from the thing.

Alexa bolted across the room, praying to find a door.

Slayer, Sinafin said.

A man with a neat gray goatee and thick black hair on his head skipped around the counter, blocking her way. Eyebrows raised, he stared at her with fascination. "The Exotique," he breathed.

He made her feel as unusual as the horrors surrounding them, and Alexa had an awful vision of herself stuffed and mounted. She couldn't bear it. She ran around him and hit the round-arched wooden door at top speed, falling into a stone-paved courtyard open to the sky.

At least it wasn't raining. The sky was a deep blue that reminded Alexa of home. She breathed air that was fresher than any the mountains provided, without the slight sulphur tinge she'd noticed when it rained.

She leaned against the stone wall next to the door, face in hands, trying to compose herself. "Was that really necessary?" she asked Sinafin.

Yes. Those are what threaten our lives. Those are what invade our land daily. Those...and worse.

Alexa couldn't contemplate what could be worse.

We need you. Wait and watch.

Again the note of warning.

With deep gasps, Alexa settled herself. She shoved fingers through her hair and wasn't surprised to find it damp at the roots from terror-sweat.

She looked around the courtyard. The Assayer's Office seemed to be on the right side of the main yard. The Temple dominated the far end, sitting in the center of the wall. Diagonally to her left and across the courtyard, tucked into a corner, was a gatehouse—in the direction of the Town.

Her breathing had just returned to normal and she was ready to leave again when she heard bells jingling from above her. She looked up to see a winged horse flying over the outer wall. Her mouth dropped open. The light brown horse spiraled down, blood welling from three claw marks on its neck. Claws like that had scratched her. Marks like that had crisscrossed the body of the man the night before—new wounds and silvered scars.

Render. The name fit.

The horse landed with a clatter of hooves, then tossed up its head in a lost, mournful cry that penetrated Alexa's very bones. She whimpered.

It fixed its gaze on her, then stared at Sinafin, its head lowered and feathered wings folded trembling against its heaving flanks.

The courtyard erupted with people. Doors Alexa hadn't noted were flung open around the square; some soldiers wearing the Castle livery jumped the low walls of the Cloister opposite her, into the yard. With a *yip,* Sinafin leaped into Alexa's arms.

The big Marshall—Mace—got to the horse before the others. His jaw tightened. "We've lost Perder." He stroked a soothing hand down the horse's neck. Two soldiers stopped and stood waiting for his orders. He nodded. "See to the volaran."

Volaran. Flying horse. Right.

More bells jangled. Like everyone else, Alexa looked up. Two struggling winged horses—*volarans*—with slumped riders whinnied and jostled. Even she could tell all four were in trouble.

Mace flung out his hand to the Marshalls near him. "Link!" A lady wearing the same dark burgundy surcoat as he, and Thealia and Partis in malachite green, joined hands. They frowned upward, and Alexa saw an opalescent white sphere coalesce around the volarans and riders. The horses stopped struggling.

Mace's woman gasped and fell to her knees. The sphere failed on one side, drooped like a deflating balloon. Volarans and riders screamed.

Alexa flung out a hand and jade-green energy poured from her fingers, hitting the sphere, making it round again.

"Bring them down fast!" Mace shouted. Sweat rolled down his face.

The sphere descended in a controlled fall and hit the ground— and the magic disappeared.

Suddenly weak, Alexa stumbled to a bench next to the Assayer's Office.

A metallic clatter came as one of the riders flung off a helm and let it hit the stones. Her long tangled black hair blew in the wind. She leaned over to hold the other flyer, tears streaking her face. "Help! Farentha, my mate, she's dying. The jerir! Healing spells, anything. My lifeblood for you. Anything!" She sobbed.

"Keep linked. Send energy to Farentha," Thealia ordered. Her gaze caught Alexa's. Thealia said, "We must take Farentha to the Temple for the jerir and healing. Will you help, Alyeka? We need your strength."

Alexa had planned on leaving these people, but she couldn't. Not right now when someone needed her, when she could save a life. Heart thudding in her chest, Alexa walked to the knot of people around the winged horses. She'd never been able to refuse a request for help.

Farentha's arm hung loosely, showing muscle and sinew and the round bone of the shoulder-ball. Alexa swallowed, glad she'd had no breakfast. Sinafin jumped from her arms, leaving them empty of warm, living comfort.

Other Marshalls came, linking hands in a circle and stretching their arms into the center to form a living pallet for the injured rider. Thealia broke her link with Mace and slapped Alexa's left hand into Mace's, then grabbed Alexa's right hand, hard. Alexa shuddered with the force of the current that shot through her. The energy spiked, then evened out as Thealia directed it.

Partis began to sing a powerful healing spell—that knowledge dribbled to her from the others. The rest of the Marshalls supporting Farentha joined in the Song. A wave of warm, bubbling energy swept from Thealia into Alexa's torso, tingling her nerves. She felt as if she stood in the strong flow of a river. Her head grew light with champagne fizz and giddiness. Then the force moved from her, taking the effervescence, letting her think again.

To her left, Mace jerked and whispered an oath. He glanced down at her with wide, brilliant black eyes. He was huge, his life-force incredibly strong. A big, trained knight. He could probably kill her with a blow. Yet awe at *her* shone from his eyes.

She shivered, and as the current of energy passed through her again, trembled more. Partis's Song segued into a chant that pushed her feet. The Marshalls moved in unison to the opposite end of the courtyard and the huge round Temple dominating the yard.

Alexa found herself humming with the others. She winced. She wasn't much better at singing than at languages. Her verbal skills were less than her written ones. The thought made her miss a step—sent the energy into a ragged beat. Thealia glared at her and smoothed it out. Then a golden glow of honey-sweetness from Partis soothed Thealia and trickled in to affect Alexa. She smiled.

They were healing the wounded one and she was helping! Through sheer willpower and magic. Wonder touched her. This was the bright side of the magic that could kill—the Power to save.

"Huh!" Reynardus snorted as he stood under the Temple's portico, at the entrance. "What do we have here?"

If Alexa let her mind rest, didn't try to force the sounds into words, she could understand him through her connection with the others.

Partis was spinning the healing songspell, Thealia handling the combined energy. And Mace was the strongest personality after Thealia.

"We have Farentha, close to death," Mace said, "and Dema, her mate, injured also. The Temple holds the jerir and is the best place to heal them. Let us pass."

Reynardus's face hardened. "They are independent knights, paid in coin. Why do we waste precious spell-energy and strength on such a couple? Neither of them has more than one volaran—and no land."

Anger surged in Alexa and she was surprised to feel it matched in Thealia. Thealia gripped Alexa's hand and clamped control over both of their emotions. To Alexa's amazement, Thealia siphoned some of the fury-heat into the healing spell.

Reynardus looked at the wounded woman they carried—pallid skin, face plain and round. His eyes lingered on her injured side, the arm aligned but wound gaping. He scowled. "She should be dead with such an injury." His gaze fixed on the other rider who was part of the Marshalls' circle. "And you, Dema, with that leg you shouldn't be able to walk. What is going on here?"

"The Exotique Alyeka," Thealia said softly. "She has the vitality and magic to keep them both alive."

Everyone looked at Alexa.

As all gazes turned to her, Alexa smiled weakly. For once she was glad she didn't know much of the language. She had no clue what to say. Sincerity radiated from the older woman. Everyone felt it. Even Alexa. Even Reynardus.

The harsh lines on Reynardus's face deepened as he frowned.

Alexa broadened her smile. She liked seeing the man nonplussed. In the light of day and without the haze of anger clouding her vision, he reminded her of a particularly pompous attorney she'd had to work with during her internship at a large law firm in Denver. Reynardus was tougher on the outside, solid fighting muscle, but Alexa would bet his mind was just as crafty, his will just as forceful as that of the lawyer she'd known. Oh yeah. She'd trust this guy just as far as she could throw him.

Partis's voice broke on a note and Thealia sent a mental command to concentrate on the injured Farentha. They inhaled as one, and the circle squeezed into a lozenge as they prepared to enter the door to the Temple. Rhythm picked up as they marched through the door from the bright light of the courtyard into the Temple's dim, incense-laden coolness.

Oddly enough, Alexa sensed the person watching her most intently was Dema, lover of the deeply wounded Farentha. Alexa met Dema's eyes, and though the other woman lowered her gaze, curiosity hummed from her.

The Medica joined them. In an exquisite blend of physical and mental management, Thealia and Partis rearranged the circle until only they, the Medica and Dema supported the fallen rider.

Legs shaking, Alexa backed up to the stone bench lining the circular wall and collapsed onto a plush pillow to rest and watch the drama. She'd wait until she felt stronger, and see what happened before she abandoned the Castle for the Town. She wanted to know whether the woman she'd helped would live or die.

"Jerir...Chevalier Farentha," Reynardus said.

Since Alexa wasn't connected with the Marshalls, those were the only words she understood. But she read his tone, gestures and stance well enough. He didn't think the woman would survive. She looked bad off, but the guy last night had been just as bad, and *he'd* made it. Hadn't he?

Of course he had. Sinafin would have told her if he hadn't. For reasons of her own, Sinafin took an interest in the man.

Alexa looked around for the feycoocu and saw a large purple furred muff a foot away from her on the curving bench. The same muff that had rested on the table outside her suite door the first night she'd come. "Sinafin?" she whispered.

I have to be invited through the door of a person's living space, Sinafin answered. *You brought me in as a muff that night.*

Just like a vampire, Alexa thought. She couldn't help herself: The image of a tiny, fairy-size vampire with white skin, long black hair and teeny pointed teeth, wearing a red-satin-lined black cape over a full-length black dress formed in her mind— A fairy vampire? A vampire fairy? A—

"Exotique Alyeka," Reynardus sneered.

Hearing her name jolted Alexa. She glanced over to the tableau. Reynardus stood, legs apart. With a broad gesture he pointed to her, then to the wounded women, then to the pool of jerir.

8

Standing by the pool, Reynardus again pointed to Alexa, then the liquid.

He'd done that twice. How rude.

As far as she was concerned, she'd done enough dunking in the jerir. The others could take care of the injured flyer. They were the locals, and they had the experience and knowledge. She'd be an observer, not a participant.

Alexa rose and mimicked Reynardus's stance. She jutted her chin, pointed to herself, then to the pool of jerir and held up two fingers, then raised her eyebrows and pointed to Reynardus.

Vrai...true, said Sinafin, and Alexa could tell by the others' expressions that they'd heard the feycoocu.

A rumble came from Mace, and an unenthusiastic agreement from the Medica. Alexa stared at Reynardus until his cheeks darkened a bit and he peeled off his gauntlets. She smiled sweetly. She'd won that round with him.

She kept the smile pasted on her lips as he continued to strip until he was naked. Obviously he didn't want to subject his clothes to the jerir. Alexa wasn't too comfortable with nudity, but she sure wasn't going to show embarrassment.

Alexa eyed Reynardus. His honed, muscular body was impressive, and she'd have said he had an impressive amount of scars too, if she hadn't seen the man last night.

Then Reynardus turned and his body was limned by a shaft of torchlight. Alexa jolted. He looked like the guy last night. She blinked and stared, but the fleeting likeness was gone. She knew she wasn't mistaken. The man last night must be a close relative. Probably his son. Now that she studied his face, the resemblance was obvious. She wondered what it said about her that she only figured out the connection after she'd seen them both naked.

Except the son had black-and-white streaked hair. Reynardus's words from earlier echoed in her head: *"A black-and-white is flawed."* So he had a flawed son. That couldn't have been easy on either of them.

Thealia and Partis moved to support the wounded rider while Mace and the Medica stripped. Alexa turned her gaze away from the large man. It was evident that this society—or this class of it—had fewer taboos about nudity than her own. Her mores regarding nakedness were deeply ingrained—especially since she'd fought all her childhood for privacy in foster homes.

The muff rolled until Sinafin was next to her leg, warming it, as if sensing Alexa's bad memories.

Keep your good customs, but take good from us, too, Sinafin said. *The mix has happened before and the blend has helped us survive.*

Alexa picked up the muff and set it on her lap. It had no discernable sensory organs or limbs. "Isn't being a muff uncomfortable?"

A chuckle came to her mind from Sinafin. *It is restful.*

Alexa turned her attention back to the drama. Now Mace cradled the fallen rider in his arms and walked slowly to the shallow end of the pool. Thealia was helping the other rider disrobe with tender briskness.

Partis's Song rose and filled the Temple. The dome and crystals reverberated certain notes back that reached inside Alexa and touched her very core.

Yes, she was seeing the other side of the coin—how magic could heal and save rather than destroy.

Sinafin settled more snugly into Alexa's lap. *You are meant to be here. Meant to help the Castle. Your home is with us.*

The light became diffused, adding softness to the scene. They all moved as if in an elaborate dance, truly a team, concentrating on the injured women. If she wanted, she could join with them, work with them, be accepted. One part of her yearned to do that, another rejected the idea.

The Medica held the unconscious rider's torn arm close to her body—ready for healing in the jerir pool, Alexa supposed. Alexa swallowed hard. The pain would be horrible.

Splashes, then screams. From the Medica and the less-injured flyer. The men's faces looked strained but determined.

They dunked the terribly wounded one.

Alexa couldn't stand it. The jerir ordeal was so rough, so demanding. They needed more hands. She could help. She ran to the pool in time to see Dema, the lightly wounded rider, go under. Oh hell! Alexa jumped in.

It wasn't as bad as the night before. More like being stung by a horde of hungry mosquitoes, then lashed with tiny whips in each scratch. Her hand slicked against a rounded limb. She grabbed it and found a female arm. Good enough.

Out! her frantic mind demanded.

She shot from the pool like a superhero, hung a couple of feet in the air, then collapsed onto the stone floor—with her rescuee. Damn! How humiliating. It was obvious that whatever magic she had was uncontrolled. She hoped she wasn't turning red.

Rolling to her feet, she tried to look as if she'd meant to be so dramatic in the rescue.

All the others were out of the pool too. Reynardus wasn't buying Alexa's pretense. He stood, thick jerir slowly rolling down his body, giving her a scornful glance. He made a comment and a gesture that Alexa could only interpret as "teach the fool some magic and manners," then stalked away to a screen near the edge of the room. Another splash came from that direction.

Dema scrambled to her knees, gasping, and crawled over to her lover. The other woman's chest rose and fell slowly. Tears joined droplets of jerir on Dema's face.

"*Vivant!*" She stroked the wet hair of her mate.

The others stared at Alexa.

"*Trey,*" said Thealia.

Three? wondered Alexa, or maybe she meant "very." Wasn't there a French "trey" that meant "very"?

Very stupid to go into the jerir three times.

Yeah. Her mouth set. That was it. Final. *Fini.* Latin for really done. Her soft heart had gotten the better of her and she'd helped. Now she'd get out of the Castle. She didn't owe anyone anything. No one was rushing to thank her; her effort hadn't garnered any respect. She was outta here.

She stalked over to where she'd left her muff, Sinafin. The little greyhound waited with perked ears.

"Come on, feycoocu. Let's go. Lead the way to the Town."

Ignoring curious glances, Alexa left the Temple. The doors were too heavy to slam satisfactorily, so she just huffed a breath. She stepped from the portico out into the yard.

It was full of people. Alexa recognized servants in their rainbow garb, the nattily dressed man from the Assayer's Office, soldiers in the livery of the Castle, and more flyers dressed like the pair in the Temple. Chevaliers.

And five different flying horses. She eyed them as she followed Sinafin, fascinated, tempted to linger just to look at them. The small dog danced across the large paving stones, attracting attention.

"*Feycoocu.*" The murmur ran around the square.

The sun was warm on Alexa's clothes and they gave off a faint, astringent steam. She tried to look as if she walked around in steaming clothes all the time.

The Temple was at one end of the wide courtyard. About a block from it, a gatehouse sat between small towers, showing a shadowed opening through the deep walls. A door?

Along the opposite side of the courtyard ran cloisters—covered walkways with openings of triple-pointed windows. Next to that wall was a long two-storied building. On her own side of the Castle was the large Keep with several towers. She could even see the top of the back one that held her former rooms. The walk here was open, just part of the pavement. She started down it and soon reached the gatehouse.

Marwey's young, handsome soldier was there, along with a thirty-something, stern-looking man, equally attractive. One glance at his expression and Alexa knew he was related to Reynardus. Another son? But who cared? She wanted *out*. Out of the politics, out of the Castle.

As she came near, distaste lit his eyes and he drew back. His mouth turned down and she sensed it was more because of his own reaction to her than to herself.

She nodded to the men and went through the archway between the low gateway towers and up to the doors, whispering from the side of her mouth to Sinafin. "How do these damn doors work?" Hell, she'd never been a history buff.

Sinafin barked and an unobtrusive smaller door set in the huge ones swung in.

"Good job!" Alexa grinned. She was on her way out of the courtyard! She could *feel* people's mouths drop open as they watched her and the feycoocu. At least they weren't interfering, trying to stop her.

The Lladranan-size door didn't reach the ground. She had to step over a thick partition. A security measure, Alexa supposed. The next yard was larger than the one behind her. How big *was* this Castle, anyway?

Frowning, she glanced back into the other court and found the Assayer's Office just off the Keep.

Sinafin followed her gaze. *The Assayer's Office also opens onto the landing field.* She jumped back over the edge of the door and trotted to the men. Marwey's soldier faded back; the other stood stolidly, a wary look on his face. She circled around him, sniffed his knee, barked in acknowledgment and let her tongue loll. The Chevalier grinned.

Sinafin ran and hurdled the door again, skidding to a stop in the dust before Alexa. *Luthan,* she said. *Brother to Bastien we saved last night. Sons of Reynardus.*

Why it was important, Alexa didn't know, but she tucked away the information. She held out her arms and the dog leaped into them. Luthan watched them, eyes narrowed. Feeling a little foolish, Alexa bobbed her torso in an abbreviated bow. Luthan's eyebrows winged up. Aha! She'd surprised another person with simple courtesy. Good, she had the feeling it would be in her best interest to keep the Lladranans guessing.

Alexa turned and studied the new courtyard. She sighed. This one was about a block and a half long—various buildings jutted from the stone walls, in various sorts of architecture, interesting little alleys running between them. Some of the buildings were of the standard gray stone; a few older, smaller ones were made of a creamy yellow stone.

She glanced back and saw the top of the round Temple in the previous courtyard. It alone was a striking white. She started forward, out of the Castle.

This yard had stone sidewalks around thick grass, brown-tinged with blades of renewing green. A small round stone cupola stood in the center, looking new.

They had to cover the well, Sinafin said.

Alexa didn't want to know why. She had enough on her mind. So she strode down the right-hand outside path toward the huge gate in the middle of the opposite end. Since this gate was between two substantial towers, it must be the main entrance. She wondered if there'd be a moat and drawbridge. Cool.

But the coolest thing was that she felt in control of her life again. She was escaping the Castle.

Bastien had gnawed a turkey leg as he watched the incredible events in the Temple courtyard—Temple Ward. He tossed the bone in a trash box and listened to an excited Urvey report all the gossip. The Exotique had plunged in the jerir again and saved Dema, she'd flown around the inside of the Temple, then she'd argued with the Marshalls, stunned them all with her Power, and left for the Town with the feycoocu, vowing never to return.

When Urvey stared yearningly after the strange Exotique as she left the Temple with an equally strange-looking small dog, Bastien had given him leave to follow the new Marshall. Bastien had always been of a curious nature himself. His new squire could be a boon.

It sounded like the Marshalls, and specifically his father, had made a mistake. If the woman left the Castle, Bastien guessed, the Chevaliers might also make a mistake and invite her to join them as *their* Exotique. He pondered whether he should intervene in the matter.

At that moment, Marrec, a Chevalier with Lady Hallard, hurried down the cloister walk, then slowed as he saw Bastien. "Good, I'm glad you're here to accompany me. Lady Hallard wants a report on the health of Farentha and Dema from the Marshalls."

"Yes, I voted for her to be the new representative of the Chevaliers. Good woman. She sent you to question the Marshalls and you don't want to face them alone? I don't blame you." He clapped the man on the shoulder. "Just think of it as being in a den of clever thieves ready to skin you."

"Thanks a lot," Marrec muttered as they entered the shadowed Temple.

The Marshalls didn't look stunned into immobility by Exotique Power. They looked angry and even divided—until they noticed Bastien and Marrec. Then their auras melded into solidarity.

Still smiling, Bastien addressed Reynardus. "My congratulations, Father. With your usual charm you alienated the powerful Exotique, Savior of Lladrana." Bastien put as much swagger into his steps as he could and still tread carefully so as not to jar any of his aches and pains. He felt as if any major effort would break something loose inside him.

The Marshalls turned in a body to stare at him, some squinting. Even with light from the windows near the ceiling, the Temple was dim. Bastien grinned. One of *his* natural gifts was excellent night vision.

"Don't you think you should be more diplomatic?" muttered Marrec.

Bastien ignored the comment, continuing to approach the people around the jerir pool. He ignored the pool too, not wanting to remember the pain and how close he'd come to dying from sheer stupidity.

His father's mouth thinned into a stern line and his gaze flattened—his usual expression around Bastien.

"*Alien* is right," Reynardus said. "A small woman of no account. No doubt her Powers are much exaggerated."

"Oh?" Concentrating, Bastien mentally located his quarterstaff in the stables of the Castle with the rest of his gear and volaran. His legs had started to tremble, but he had no intention of appearing weak before his father. A person was foolish to show any weakness to Reynardus.

With a thought he summoned his quarterstaff, liking the sound as it smacked into his outstretched hand. He leaned insouciantly on it. "I've heard that even untrained she had enough Power to kill Disparu. That she claimed the famous Jade Baton. That she's survived three plunges in the jerir, and brought Dema and Farentha back from the gates of death. That a feycoocu has come to companion her."

Not to mention that she'd hauled his own sorry ass out of the jerir pool. He was glad he only remembered a flash of startled female eyes. "Quite a list for someone who has been in Lladrana barely two days. And now you have let this paragon walk away from the Marshalls."

"Quit baiting your father," Marshall Thealia said, coming up to him and brushing a perfunctory kiss on his cheek.

Bastien ducked his head in courtesy. Doubt and concern clouded her eyes.

"I don't need you to defend me, Thealia, especially not from Bastien," Reynardus said.

She spun on her heel and faced him, face tight. "There is such a thing as common courtesy. It is obvious where your younger son gets his rudeness."

"Too true, Godmama," Bastien said. "Unlike my good brother Luthan. But witnessing my father making a major mistake was something I had to see."

"I made no mistake," Reynardus snapped. "The woman is useless to us."

Bastien lifted his shoulders and let them fall in an elaborate shrug. "If you say so. But Luthan is in the courtyard, the Representative of the Singer. I wonder if he will agree—or Marrec's liege, Lady Hallard, the new Representative of the Chevaliers. If the Exotique reaches the Town, there might be guildmembers who think otherwise." Bastien rubbed his chin. "Not to mention the Sorcerers in their Towers. I'd imagine one or several would be very interested in an untrained, powerful Exotique. No telling what potential *use* they could put her to."

Reynardus stiffened to statue immobility, inflexibility. His head tilted slightly. The unheard but *felt* buzz of quick, mental communication among the Marshalls hummed around Bastien and Marrec. Marrec widened his stance, ready for anything. Bastien's smile came and went at his companion's action. Completely solid. Completely reliable. That was Marrec Gardpont.

A flush rose under Reynardus's cheeks, anger lit his eyes. He was wrong and he knew it. But he would never admit that his pride caused mistakes. Not in dealing with the Exotique. Certainly not in dealing with his sons. He wouldn't admit his arrogance was anything but a sterling quality.

There was a flash of Power among the Marshalls, as if they'd come to a major decision, and the humming energy among them quieted to the usual intricate melody that bound them.

Partis, Thealia and the other Marshalls whirled as one and started past Bastien and Marrec for the Temple door.

"Swordmarshall Thealia, I would like confirmation that Farentha lives," Marrec said.

Thealia paused. "She lives and will heal. Well enough to fight, we think. She and Dema are in apartments above the volaran stables in Horseshoe Close."

Marrec bowed. "Lady Hallard on behalf of the Chevaliers thanks you for their healing and lodging. We will pay the proper fees."

"Difficult," Thealia said, obviously wanting to leave and find her precious lost Marshall, "as it was the Exotique who enabled us to heal them and she isn't a member of the Marshalls."

Bastien chuckled. "Then she will have coin enough to live in Town for a while, won't she?"

With a nasty glance, Thealia hurried after her fellows.

Swordmarshall Mace stopped before Bastien too, and shook his head in exasperation. "You like to cause trouble, don't you."

"You should all thank me for making this a very short and easily corrected error," Bastien said.

Mace snorted. "You don't know a damn thing about how much this will cost."

A wide, beatific smile stretched Bastien's lips. "Oh, I know it will cost my father some of his pride, if I figure right. And you so very *noble* Marshalls."

Mace grunted, said, "Good day to you, Marrec," and loped off.

The Temple emptied of the Marshalls, all on their new quest for their Exotique.

Marrec sighed. "Don't you think we could have used her?"

Bastien flashed him a look. "Don't you understand? The Marshalls Summoned her. With *their* ideas of what Lladrana needed, *their* requirements. They brought a woman who would fit in with *them*. She is predisposed to work with *them*. So let them have her, especially if she will stir them up a little. Then we can figure out how to Summon someone for *us,* the Chevaliers."

Marrec's eyes widened. He met Bastien's gaze, then looked at the black-and-white streaks in Bastien's hair. Marrec shook his head. "You are a scary man." He turned and walked away.

Bastien laughed.

They all marched out of the Temple and into the courtyard. Thealia raised a hand to halt. "We can't *all* go after the girl. It might overwhelm her."

Reynardus snorted.

Thealia's jaw flexed, but she said evenly, "Partis can keep a low mental connecting Song with you all, while we convince her to come back to the Castle."

"Let her go," Reynardus said.

She whirled to face him. "You say that when you've seen what she can do? Such energy she has for our songspells, such Power that she flies from the pool. The battles are only going to get worse. What if it is you who needs great healing?"

Reynardus paled, his eyes narrowed. "It won't be me."

"How can you say that? Any of us could fall. I, for one, would want Alyeka near if that happened."

The others exchanged glances. Mace spoke for them. "Thealia, you and Partis go, as a Pair."

"I'll go too. I am, after all, the Lord Knight of this gaggle," Reynardus said.

There was internal muttering through their link, but no one voiced an objection.

Partis grinned. "Very well, the three of us. Should be interesting."

"I think that's what the shapeshifter keeps saying. I'd rather a predictable path," Mace murmured.

"We're losing her—let's go." Thealia pivoted and started down the courtyard.

* * *

Alexa had just reached the end of the straight part of the court-yard and started angling inward to the main gate when she heard the voice.

"Exotique! Exotique, halt!"

She'd been half expecting someone to try to stop her, despite Reynardus's encouraging her to go. But she bit her lip and kept walking, telling herself that leaving was the right thing to do. Sin-afin ran beside Alexa, but she suspected the little magical being knew Alexa was thinking hard.

It was true she'd been wronged. But it was also true that she'd listened to the Marshalls' Song and her own heart's yearning and stepped through the gate to this place. She had always wanted to find a home of her own, and had wanted to make a great and vis-ible difference to the world. She just hadn't realized it wouldn't be *her* world.

Huge goals, and huge goals came with huge price tags.

Could she walk away? Even as her steps took her closer and closer to the main entrance of the Castle, Alexa didn't think so. Setting aside the tempting idea of land and a home of her own that one of the Marshalls had offered her that morning, Alexa doubted she would ever be able to forget the wounded woman this morning, the scars on the man last night, or the mounted mon-sters in the Assayer's Office.

They were the stuff of nightmares even if she managed to get back to Earth. And who could she talk to on Earth about such hor-rors?

But she could have second, even third thoughts about her fu-ture in the Town. Time to act, not to react. The Town was even more unknown than the Castle, but she'd landed on her feet often enough before.

"Exotique, halt!"

Someone darted around her. Oddly enough, it wasn't any Marshall, any soldier, any Chevalier that stopped her. It was the young, skinny teen from the night before.

He stood in front of her and stared.

She stared back, realized that he was taller than she, and frowned. He squared thin shoulders, then lifted his hands in a gesture that matched the plea in his eyes.

"Exotique, je audio—"

Alexa, pick me up! Sinafin pawed at Alexa's boots.

Scowling, Alexa did so. Sinafin slurped a tongue around Alexa's face, then turned her pointy muzzle to the youngster.

Speak again! Sinafin ordered.

The boy's eyes rounded and a nervous smile twitched on and off his face as he stepped back a pace.

"Exotique—" the boy said.

Exotic, Alexa heard in her mind as Sinafin translated.

Quick words tumbled from the teenager. "I heard you turned in your baton and are leaving the Castle. Don't go! We need you so badly."

Alexa flinched. The word *need* always touched her heart, short-circuiting logic. She raised a hand to stop the boy.

He shut his lips but watched her intently with large brown eyes full of desperate hope that tugged at her.

The heavy thump of metal boots came to her ears and she looked up the courtyard to see Thealia, Partis and Reynardus marching toward her, a phalanx of fighters. Unlike her, they didn't keep to the path, but stepped off it to cross the grassy yard.

She glanced around but didn't see anyone else they might be after. They'd catch up with her shortly. She wondered if she was insane enough to try another superhero flight.

"I can't stay here in the Castle," she said, and waited a beat for Sinafin to send the mental words to the teenager. "The Marshalls have manipulated and lied to me since I arrived. I can't trust them."

Colorful tunics flapping around their armor, they proceeded down the yard. Ahead of her were the two big Towers with the large arch between them. She eyed the points of an iron grille near the top—a gate that could descend to block any entrance...or exit.

The skinny kid stuck out his chin. "The Chevaliers didn't lie to you. You could trust them."

"I can't be a Chevalier. I don't ride," Alexa said. And though the flying horses were beautiful beyond belief, she had no *intention* of riding them either.

"You don't ride?" he squeaked, goggling.

"No. And I'm not going to learn."

The Marshalls looped left around the well.

"Time to go." Alexa turned.

"I'll take you to the Mayor! He'll help you, make you welcome in Town," the boy blurted.

Alexa glanced back at him. "The Mayr?" She tried to pronounce it like he did.

He gave a quick nod, whipped around her and jogged to the gate. Alexa put down Sinafin, then hurried to catch up.

Posted on one of the towers was a board with notices. Alexa compressed her lips. She couldn't read the papers. No matter; she had brains and hands and a willingness to work hard. And magic. She could survive outside the Castle.

People streamed in both directions through the arched entry of the Castle, and the boy knew how to weave through them, Alexa noticed approvingly. But the youngster didn't look prepossessing. His pants were of rough brown material and sagged over his skinny behind, where a large patch had been crookedly sewn. They were held up by a hank of rope at his waist. His shirt was a faded red and spotted with unidentifiable stains, with a rip under the right arm. His black hair stuck out in all directions.

And he was going to introduce her to the Mayor?

Their footsteps echoed hollowly as they crossed the drawbridge. Looking down, Alexa saw a beautiful, flowing blue stream in the moat. She sniffed. It smelled clean—no refuse or sewage. No monsters or human body parts.

The road on the other side of the drawbridge was muddy. Tiny blades of grass poked through the earth.

It was all downhill to the walled Town—no more than a couple of miles. The Town looked as neat and tidy as it had when she'd glimpsed it from her window the day before.

The Castle towered behind them, and they would have to travel some distance before she'd be able to view the whole thing.

It was a fortress, and the Lladranans were fighting monsters. Like the one who had nearly skewered her on her way here. Would it be waiting for her when she went back?

A heavy hand clamped on to her shoulder and spun her around. She faced an irritated Reynardus.

9

Alexa glared up at Reynardus, flung a hand toward the Town and said "mari" for *mayor*.

The boy giggled high behind her. Reynardus's mouth fell open in shock, and his grip loosened enough for Alexa to slide away and start jogging down the path to the Town, to her new life outside of the Castle, away from the Marshalls. As she waved the boy ahead to show her the way, she got the distinct impression that she'd mangled the word somehow. Unsurprising.

Thealia whispered urgently behind her and then the woman's husband, Partis, joined Alexa, walking fast. Alexa grumbled inwardly. Even a short man of this race had no trouble keeping up with her at a quick walk. She'd never be able to outrun them.

"Feycoocu?" Partis asked, and held out his arms to a gleefully bounding Sinafin.

The little greyhound cocked her head at him as if measuring

the man, looked past him to Thealia and Reynardus, then ahead, ignoring Partis.

"Feycoocu...fey-coooooo-cooooooo." The lilt in Partis's voice plucked a chord inside Alexa.

She watched him from the corner of her eye as she hurried. A bead of sweat ran down his temple, but his round face glowed with good humor. He clanked beside her, and her own lips widened into a smile as she picked up her pace. The Marshalls following her ran in metallic armor under their tunics. She'd give them a workout.

Partis continued to croon to Sinafin, modulating his tones until the range made Alexa shiver. The man had a magic voice, for sure.

Sinafin twitched an ear, then stopped and let Partis scoop her up as they ran. Sinafin barked, and Partis laughed with the same note of pleasure.

"Mari..." Partis panted.

Husband, Sinafin said to Alexa.

Alexa stumbled, windmilled, but caught herself before she hit the muddy ground. "What?"

"You are going to Town to meet your husband?" Partis's eyes twinkled at her.

It was impossible to be irritated with this man. Reynardus could annoy her by just edging into her vision—but Partis? No. A premonition that between Sinafin and the boy and Partis and Thealia, they'd talk her around, descended on Alexa. They had a lot going for them. She was a stranger in a strange land, didn't know the language or the customs, had no money. What she *did* have was magic she couldn't really control.

Still, she was outside the Castle now, not completely in their territory, and had an ally in Sinafin. She should be able to negotiate good terms. She was alone and ready to fight with words. That had happened often in her life. Just one more time. Frame it in a situation that she understood so the unknown couldn't freak her out…and she could win.

They were coming up on the Town wall and gate, the wall much lower and the gate much less impressive than the Castle's, but made of the same gray stone blocks.

Alexa slowed to a walk on the path that was packed hard enough that even the recent rain hadn't stirred up much mud. A slurping sound caught her attention. Sinafin was licking Partis's perspiring face.

Four guards in blue and green, the colors of the shield over the arch of the Town gate, drew aside as she and Partis came near. They seemed torn between staring at her, the Exotique, Sinafin or Partis. They didn't even seem to notice the boy.

Then they looked up the wide path. As one, the four seemed to melt into the shadows of the gate. Obviously they would be no help against even three Marshalls.

Squaring her shoulders, Alexa pinned the boy with a look. "Mayr," she enunciated, hoping it was right this time.

The boy chewed at his lower lip. Alexa sucked in a breath, ready to demand, when Sinafin barked and sent a mental command that rang in Alexa's ears. *Nom de Nom!*

The teenager nodded hastily and turned to lead again.

Sinafin broadcasted, *The Exotique has left the Castle. Those wishing to meet her, including the Mayr, may join us in the back room of the Nom de Nom for consultation.*

From the reverberation in Alexa's head, she thought everyone in the whole Town had heard Sinafin. The shapeshifter hopped down from Partis's arms, and Alexa skipped to keep up with the youth and the dog. As she passed through the gate the road widened into a small, cobblestone square. She heard the *clomp* of many boots following her and saw two of the guards separate from the shadows to join the little parade.

Heat crept up Alexa's face. All she needed was a baton to lead this— Suddenly her Jade Baton hovered before her.

She heard gasps. Sinafin made a sound like a gleeful doggy gurgle. Alexa set her teeth and gestured to the young man to continue on.

All the streets opened into squares. The way she followed was a street large enough for two carts, though sometimes narrow passages branched off. The buildings against the city walls were usually three stories high and made of stone. As they went deeper into the Town, the buildings became two or three stories, and were sometimes of plaster. The plaster ones were multihued, showing the Lladranan love for color. The more elegant, newer buildings flaunted bow windows.

There was no shade of purple in sight. Must be reserved for Exotiques. Too bad.

Finally they came to a three-story stone building that leaned a little. Alexa blinked. Something creaked overhead, and she looked up to see a square sign with a black-and-white circle. As she watched, the circle spun and changed colors. First it was white lettering on black, then black lettering on white. *Nom de Nom. Nom de Nom.* She blinked, but felt a little dizzy. She couldn't figure out how the sign worked. Must be magic.

Reynardus's snicker broke into her thoughts. No doubt she looked like a perfect fool, staring at something they all knew was simple and standard in their world. She wished she could turn the man into a toad.

Finally the press of the stares prodded her to enter the inn. Not only had the three Marshalls come down from the Castle, but others had too. Reynardus's son Luthan, Marwey's soldier, even some fliers. They all watched her and waited.

Straightening her shoulders and lifting her chin, Alexa strode in as if it were the diner where all the law students hung out and she was about to announce she'd been named valedictorian.

It was smokey, but from open fireplaces, not cigarettes. The light was as dim as the Temple, but the inn exuded a totally different ambience. Pretty different from the diner hangout too, except... Except the conversations held the same note of exhaustion after trials, of conviviality, of desperate living before more Testing. The similarity stopped her for a second before she moved on in.

The inn reminded her of her undergraduate years—scarred wooden booths with worn cushions, a long bar— Then she saw the heads on the walls. Her mouth turned down. She supposed now she should be grateful that there had been no heads gracing her suite of rooms in the Castle.

There have never been heads in that room. This is where the Chevaliers gather, Sinafin said. *Of course there will be trophies.*

Alexa grimaced. She *greatly* preferred diplomas. Sinafin snickered, jumped from her arms and trotted through the room, taking a right at the end of the bar and scratching a demand that the closed door be opened.

The boy that had led them there looked at the bar man, lifted his shoulders as high as his chin in a shrug, and hurried to do the greyhound's bidding.

Keeping her steps and expression steady, Alexa walked into the room. Serving women and the barkeep followed, opening indoor shutters to the fading afternoon light, whisking dustcovers off deep chairs, and wiping down the large round table that dominated the room.

As they bustled, lights came on from faceted crystals that looked like huge hunks of quartz set in the walls.

Send energy to one, Sinafin said.

Narrowing her eyes, Alexa concentrated on the nearest quartz.

A brighter spark appeared within it, then it glowed white, while the others in the room showed yellow.

Silence.

Alexa looked around to find everyone staring at her again. She smiled. The inn people rushed from the chamber. The Marshalls and the man Sinafin had named Luthan marched in, along with an older woman in gear that looked like the fighting clothes that the riders of the flying horses wore.

Sinafin whined and Alexa picked her up.

Go to the biggest chair, she advised.

Alexa frowned. It was wise strategy, but the chair would dwarf her. She sighed and went to the chair, drew it close to the table. Then she laid her baton down on the table, discreetly climbed on the chair, scooted until her butt hit the back and crossed her legs. Who from Lladrana would know that she didn't usually sit in a chair like this? It sure beat sitting on the very edge and letting her feet dangle.

Sinafin curled on Alexa's lap. *No heads here. See the banners? They are those of the Chevaliers fallen to the Invaders in the past two years.*

The banners crowded the rafters; most were tattered. Some showed stains that were probably mud. Some had huge swaths of a dark red-brown—dried blood? Some had holes that looked like they'd been made from claws—or worse, acid. The scariest ones had lots of blotches: red-brown blood, greenish old-slime stuff, thick black ichor blobs. There were even a few puckered tentacle marks like those that had shown on the body of the man she'd saved from the pool. Pretty evident that would be from a soul-sucker.

See how many there are? You can't see the ceiling. We need you!

"I get it already," Alexa grumbled as the Marshalls scraped back chairs to sit around the table.

Reynardus sat opposite her at the round table, his usual sneer on his face. Thealia sat to his right at ten o'clock in relation to Alexa. Partis was between Thealia and Alexa, on her left.

That sneer really got on Alexa's nerves, setting her temper simmering again. She leaned back in her chair, back straight, composed her expression and petted the shape-changing dog. Tension and anticipation coiled in her. This discussion would be all about her future. She wasn't going to be manipulated or steamrollered. She was going to play it cautious, and canny—and *win*. What concessions she could get, she didn't know. But Sinafin would be able to keep score and tell her.

She did know that the first one who dickered would lose, and she was ready to sit silent until the inn closed and the bartender threw her out.

The inn does not close, Sinafin said. *It is open all day and night, every day.*

"Twenty-four, seven," Alexa murmured.

What does that mean? The little dog pushed a warm, curious nose into Alexa's palm.

"Twenty-four hours a day, seven days a week." Alexa wondered if the days were the same.

Yes, answered Sinafin. *But we go by moon-months.*

Before she could say more, the older woman clomped forward and bowed to Alexa.

Lady Hallard, a major landowner, now the Representative of the Chevaliers to the Castle. And Luthan— Sinafin pointed her nose at the man sitting at three o'clock in relation to Alexa *—was the Chevalier Representative before you came and now represents the Singer. He offered the Chevalier position to his brother, Bastien, the man you saved from drowning in the jerir. He refused.*

Alexa had heard this before in her dreams, but Sinafin's recitation helped ground her, get her mind around the players again and put names to faces. Reynardus and his sons, one of whom was a flawed black-and-white. The Marshalls...

"On behalf of the Chevaliers, we thank you for healing our

members, Farentha and Dema. Here is our offering for your fee," Lady Hallard said, placing a worn leather drawstring pouch on the table before Alexa.

Money! Alexa exulted. Oh, she was better off now. She didn't have to depend on the Marshalls for everything.

Enough money, "zhiv," to house you in Town for two years. Little enough for two lives, but the two you helped heal are independents, and all the Chevaliers took up a pool for them.

Alexa had contributed to enough pools, and been the recipient of one or two when she'd been down on her luck, to understand how they worked. She frowned. She couldn't possibly take it all.

"Tell me, what is enough for one year of middle-class living?" she asked Sinafin.

Inside there is a large diamond. It is enough.

Opening the bag, Alexa gently sent a stream of jewels, silver and gold coins pouring onto the table. She caught her breath. Jewels. She was sunk. She had a weakness for even the cheapest costume jewelry. It would make her greedy, for sure.

Gemstones glittered. Alexa's fingers itched. Oh, the large sapphire and the little square emerald were lovely. She could *not* stop herself from scooping up the bloodred spinel. It looked a lot like one in England's crown jewels.

She took the diamond, which was the largest and dirty white, to pay her way in Town, and the spinel, just for herself. The rest she slid back into the pouch and shoved into Lady Hallard's hands before her avaricious streak got the better of her.

Setting her hands firmly on Sinafin for translation, Alexa met the weathered woman's eyes. "This is enough. Divide the rest amongst the Chevaliers who contributed."

First Hallard looked surprised and pleased, then she stiffened, and ruffled pride showed in her expression.

Alexa lifted a hand to forestall Hallard's protest. "My needs are few. *This is enough.*"

Again they matched gazes, then Hallard nodded and went back to her chair next to Luthan.

Alexa let out her breath unobtrusively and faced the Marshalls. Thealia looked dismayed. Reynardus still sneered, as if the entire incident was of no import to him at all. The glow from doing a good deed evaporated.

Leaning back in her chair, Alexa wished she knew more about yoga so she could curl her fingers right and chant "om" and look seraphic as events played out.

Silence unfurled from a seed to a blossom as they all waited.

"Enough of this silliness!" Partis said. "We Summoned you, Alyeka, and we need you. The events of this afternoon amply prove that." He slapped a hand down on the table, cocked his head as if listening to distant voices. "I speak for all of us."

Then there was more quiet.

"I'm tired of this," Partis continued. "Lord Knight Swordmarshall Reynardus has disapproved of what we've done for months, and in disapproving, has made everything more difficult. I call for a vote of confidence to remove Reynardus as Lord Knight of the Marshalls."

Gasps ran around the table.

Alexa thought one of them was her own. But this was interesting, seeing real law and Power altered before her very eyes.

"Not all of us are meeting. This is not private," Reynardus protested.

"I am linked to all of us, and time flees with every second, letting horrors invade our land. We must ensure our future."

Reynardus flung his chair back to clatter to the floor as he stood, towering over the smaller man. "The position of Lord Knight is determined by combat. Who is going to challenge me, *little man?* You? You aren't even a Sword who fights monsters, but a Shield who provides *defense.* Or do you plan on letting your wife, your Sword, combat me?" he sneered.

Thealia rose too, her face set in pale, angry lines. "If you wish to battle Sword to Sword, I agree. If you wish to fight Sword and Shield to Sword and Shield, both Partis and I agree. I do not see your Shield here to support *you.*"

This was good. Better than watching a mock trial. Better than watching some real jury trials Alexa had studied.

She wouldn't have thought that Partis's face could harden, his eyes go cold, but they did. He gestured to Thealia to sit. She hesitated, but did as he requested.

Partis smiled widely, not a nice smile. "Combat isn't the only way to determine the Lord Knight of the Marshalls. There is also Testing, or have you forgotten?"

Reynardus's expression froze.

"We all have to Test to become a Marshall. Difficult Tests that few pass. But we can also designate Tests to name a Lord Knight. And who has been Tested the most the past couple of days? Who has passed Tests to prove herself a Marshall, who has saved a life and taken one, who has healed, has braved the jerir *three* times? Who has shown honor, and independence, and leadership?"

Everyone looked at Alexa.

Uh-oh! This wasn't a play anymore. It had turned personal, and nasty.

No. No way. Not Joan of Arc. Not right now—maybe never.

"Marshalls choosing a new leader, in a time of war, *which this is,* can measure the actions of candidates in a three-day period—"

Three days. Alexa jumped on the thought. She was used to winnowing out important information from an oral argument. She hadn't been here three days. Maybe she was saved.

Now Reynardus really did snarl, with sound and all. "I will not be mocked! How can you think to put a *thing* like her in my place!" His ivory baton was in his hand, pointing at her, a stream of dark red shooting straight at Alexa.

Sinafin jumped to the table. Barked. The red energy bounced off her and shot to the crystal lights. She'd shielded Alexa.

Alexa's baton flew to her hand. Without thought she pointed. The bronze end turned into real flames and sparks of green hit Reynardus square in the chest. He made a strangled sound. Alexa's arm, palm and fingers tingled.

The silence seethed with emotions—shock, anger, fear.

What would have happened to her if Sinafin hadn't taken the hit? Alexa's insides chilled. Cold sweat dampened her spine. She had the nasty idea that she'd have been fried for good.

A minute passed. Reynardus stood as still as stone, mouth half open, eyes bulging with effort—to speak? To free himself?

What had she done? He appeared trapped. How long could the spell last? She'd used all her will, but she didn't know the specifics of a magic spell—such as how long Reynardus would be statue-like.

When it didn't look as if he was going to move, Alexa regained control of her temper. But she had some points to prove. "Don't anybody move," she said, knowing she sounded like a character in a bad movie.

She set her baton in her lap, hoping it didn't show that all the strength had left her fingers. She leaned against the chair. Every muscle in her body had strained in her self-defense. Even her toes hurt.

Sinafin jumped back onto her lap and Alexa grunted. The little dog sat at regal attention.

Put your hands on me and I will bring energy from the storage crystals to you.

Alexa petted Sinafin with both hands.

Hold still.

Alexa did. In a few seconds, she felt a spritzing energy on her skin that sank into her, revitalizing her. She grinned and said, "Listen up." She met Reynardus's furious eyes. "I am not a 'thing.' I am a mature woman. I will not be treated as a thing—manipulated and lied to and sneered at. This is how it's going to be."

She stared around the table and wished she had pen and paper to draft a list of demands so she wouldn't forget something. She did so much better with notes.

"First, Partis says everyone's linked together. How many of you are there?"

Thealia said, "Presently, not including you, we are ten. When we Summoned you, we were twelve."

So Alexa had made thirteen. Bad or good luck? A witches coven was thirteen, wasn't it?

The older woman studied Alexa consideringly. "We have decided to expand the ranks of Marshall to the greatest number historically, thirty-eight members—nineteen Pairs of Sword and Shield. When you Pair—uh—*find* your Sword or Shield, that will make forty members of twenty Pairs."

Alexa's mind reeled. Only forty People of this status! This was a real high-stakes game. She'd thought to work up to the big leagues....

"Only three of you are here," Alexa said.

"The others in the Castle are all linked with me," Partis said.

She tried to remember all the faces, and recalled the Pairs had been color coded. Reynardus wore fox red. Alexa didn't recollect seeing his partner. What woman would put up with him? Thealia and Partis were in malachite green. At least she didn't have *too* many new people to learn to work with. About the size of the law journal staff. Her mouth turned down. That was all gone. Before.

"We are all linked," Thealia agreed.

"Right. Good. Well, then. I don't want a leadership position. In fact, I doubt that I can stay a Marshall. There would always be bad blood between Reynardus and me. Working in a small group with such friction is impossible. The group could never come together in a cohesive whole." Feeling major disappointment, she took her baton from her lap and shoved it into the center of the table. The wand had become so important to her in such a short time. That smacked of unnatural magic, too.

Everyone frowned.

Thealia looked between Reynardus and Alexa. The Swordmarshall's jaw tightened. "You are right. We *must* be unified in our actions and goals. But you miss a point. Reynardus has been a source of discord all along the way. It does not appear that he will change his attitude. One reason that your spell was so strong was that it used his own negative energy focused on you, another Marshall, against him. This is against our rules. If we choose, we can dismiss him from our ranks."

Very interesting.

A chair scraped the floor as Luthan stood and gazed at his father. "I have consulted with the Cloister of the Singer regarding Reynardus and his recent Song Quest. I would remind us all that most Song Quests show differing life courses and melodies for a person, based on crucial choices. This seems to me to be a time of decision for him."

The crystal lights dimmed. A wind whisked around the room, as if gathering an element of the atmosphere—magic—and drawing it to Reynardus. He was trying to free himself from the effects of her trapping spell!

She hadn't liked Reynardus standing like an evil statue and glaring at her, but hadn't had a clue how to break her own spell. She would have lost a lot of face before the Marshalls if she'd tried to release him.

Reynardus glowed yellow, his face contorted in a rictus, every muscle of his body strained.

The wind whipped again. Alexa ducked her head and closed her eyes, gathering all her strength and will, and every scrap of memory of fantasy movies to help her. *Release!* she chanted in her mind to the wind. It pulled at her, plucking the command from her, and thundered toward Reynardus. She opened her eyes to see that he glowed white, blue-hot. Then the heaviness of the storm inside the room broke and he was free.

From his teeth-snapping grin, Alexa knew he thought he'd broken free on his own. Had he?

Sinafin turned big brown eyes on Alexa. *You were the one who forged the spell to bind him. You freed him. He merely showed you how.*

"Don't tell him that," Alexa murmured in a pointy ear.

Thealia stood and addressed Reynardus. "Do you wish to remain a Marshall or not?"

"Of course."

"Alyeka has Tested to become Marshall and has shown her valor. We need her in our ranks. I will remind you of our Oaths as Marshalls to respect and support one another."

His nostrils flared. He turned and strode to the door.

"Running away?" asked Partis softly.

Reynardus's spine stiffened. He spun, baton in hand.

"As the Representative of the Singer, I need to report whether the Marshalls continue to be a viable body of leadership for the rest of Lladrana. Do you cooperate with each other or not?" Luthan asked.

The question hung in the air, fully as ominous as the wind that had zoomed around the room a moment before.

Thealia murmured, "The evil wins if we are not united."

Reynardus took his seat, placed his baton on the table so gently it didn't make a sound. He steepled his fingers and looked over the tips at Alexa. A series of emotions flickered in his eyes— anger, pride, triumph...and finally, acknowledgment and resignation.

Alexa sensed his feelings. He wanted to continue to resist the will of the rest of the Marshalls because she was an element out of his control. But he'd have to bend his pride if he wanted to keep his leadership position.

"Welcome to Lladrana, Alyeka," he said in a melodious voice that she'd never heard from him, a tone that rivaled Partis's. Reynardus smiled wolfishly and separated his hands to tick off points. "We will need to explain our Oath and Rules to you. You must learn to control your magic, master our language, and fight with us as a team. We will start your training immediately."

She just leveled her gaze at him. "No."

10

Shock ran around the inn's table. Reynardus sat up straight. She thought she could see how his mind was working. He scanned the others and his mouth soured. He must have realized that he would have to truly modify his behavior toward her or leave the Marshalls.

"I will not have you dictate to me." She looked at Thealia. "I will not allow you to manipulate me further. If you wish me to do something, you will request it of me, and you will explain until I understand your reasoning. I will then follow your request or not. I agree that there are many things to learn. Magic——" with a snap of her fingers her baton leaped to her hand "——your language——" she stroked Sinafin's head "——fighting." She kept the frown from her face. "But I will work out a schedule for that with you. I will have final approval of my teachers."

She stood and lifted her chin. "You Summoned *me*. You must trust yourselves and this Song of yours that you chose the right person. If you don't, we can part company. I passed your Tests. I killed with magic." She hurt just saying the words, still had trouble acknowledging it to herself. "I saved a life." Now that was an achievement. "So I think I have proven myself to you. You, however, have not proven yourselves to me."

They gazed at her. Partis broke the silence with a chuckle. He lifted his left hand and clasped Thealia's, then offered his right hand to Alexa.

"Sit and *feel* us, then. Learn us through your senses." He winked. "A good first real lesson in the Power."

Good advice, Sinafin said.

Thealia held out her left hand to Reynardus and kept her nose in the air until the Lord Knight took it. A strong current sizzled from the others to Alexa. Reynardus was still plenty hot with anger.

She smiled sweetly at him before sinking back into the chair, and then closed her eyes and tried to *sense* the Marshalls. Maybe she could get a handle on them that way.

At first she felt them in Pairs, and the auras of the individuals mingled together in the couples. Something else she envied. The Pairs *were* bonded, linked in some inextricable way, by love or by blood. Each had complete faith in his or her partner, had trusted one another with their lives, their hearts. More, there was a synergy that flowed among the Marshalls—all had been in battle together. Whatever their arguments and conflict with Reynardus off the battlefield, they trusted his leadership implicitly in a fight.

The Marshalls vibrated with intensity. They believed in their vision to save Lladrana. They were dedicated. As devoted to service as any public defender Alexa had known. She respected such commitment; it resonated with her core beliefs.

Alexa liked what she sensed in these people—honor, dedication, willingness to sacrifice and put the greater good of future generations above their own lives.

She couldn't deny that their purpose was the best she'd ever known. She couldn't deny that it was a great and worthy cause that appealed to her. Saving lives, defending a country from truly inhuman monsters that only wanted to destroy—this was an ideal she could wholeheartedly embrace. Most of all, she couldn't deny that she felt a kinship with them and knew that they would come to respect her and call her friend. She could finally fit in and make a place for herself that would earn her the respect she needed, the companionship she craved.

Taking a deep breath, she opened her eyes.

"Well?" asked Partis. "I felt your touch." He cocked his head. "Everyone says they did." His eyes crinkled. "A very unique, Exotique, but refreshing touch." He let loose of her hand and the rest unlinked too.

"You are good people," she said simply. For the first time she noticed the beverage an inconspicuous server had set in front of her. Frowning, she lifted it to her nose and sniffed. As expected in an inn, it smelled alcoholic. "What's this made from?"

"Hops," someone said.

"I don't drink alcohol," she said primly, not since that close escape from date rape at a party in college. She waited for their reactions. They didn't disappoint.

Everyone stared at her, horrified. Sinafin gave an undoglike squeak.

Then Partis laughed. "This will be interesting."

Fun! Sinafin lolled a tongue.

"Do you have anything made from…" She didn't know whether to say tea or leaves or what. Since *hops* had translated well, maybe tea would also. "Tea?"

More stares. Reynardus sighed. "An expensive woman. I should have known we would Summon an expensive woman."

Alexa guessed that tea was as exotic as she was. She tried to remember if she'd had any in her fanny pack and if so, how much. If she did, it would be good quality. She'd been indulging in top-grade Assam since Sophie's death. She sniffed again at the lager, ale, beer, whatever. Sophie had loved beer.

The whole *alien-ness* of the scene crashed down on her...again. Golden-skinned people with subtly different beautiful features. Light from large crystals. An inn that smelled of beer and sweat but not cigarettes. And a Jade Baton with a bronze flame that glowed before her, signifying Power and magic that she didn't understand.

How her expression changed, she didn't know, but Sinafin dug sharp dog-claws into her thighs and Partis hummed low.

Thealia cleared her throat. "I have the *pleasure*—" she glanced at Reynardus and lifted her chin "—to inform you that according to custom you may choose an estate—land and manor house—tomorrow."

Your home! Sinafin exclaimed.

Alexa thought the feycoocu had only spoken to her. *Yes, there are some rich vacant properties. Be guided by me.*

Oh boy. All her emotions were being tugged to make the decision they wanted. Her heart was with them. With what they offered. Her head reminded her that if she returned to Colorado she would have to start a new life there too.

The Marshalls would be her colleagues, and perhaps her friends. She thought of friends and acquaintances back home. None pulled her enough to know that she should return.

Lady Hallard tapped a fingernail on the table and all eyes turned to her. "It is well and good that the new Marshall will be integrated. But as I understand it, she has been wronged by the Knight Lord Marshall Reynardus Vauxveau. I, myself, saw how he tried to use his Power against an untrained novice."

Reynardus flushed at Lady Hallard's condemnation.

Alexa stared. She wouldn't have thought anything could get to him. Women—maybe *strong* women. From the dream-movies Sinafin had shown her, Thealia had manipulated him too, until he went away to do the Song Quest.

"I believe the new Marshall must be assured that we are not only a good people, we are a just people. If the Lord Knight Marshall broke any vows and oaths, he must pay," Hallard said.

Nothing in her voice or demeanor showed anything but seriousness, but Alexa thought there was something of glee underneath.

Partis said, "We guarantee you and the Representative of the Singer—" he nodded to Luthan "—that we will handle this matter. In private."

Yeah, this was good.

Lady Hallard drew riding gloves from where they were folded over her belt and drew them on. Her jaw was firm. "Before I accepted the position as Representative, I spoke to many Chevaliers—nobles and their household knights as well as independents. There are many who don't respect you Marshalls, who call you secretive and obsolete."

From the stony faces of the Marshalls, Alexa figured this wasn't news.

The Lady continued. "We of the Chevaliers do not hold as much Power, but we are many, and we are fighting as hard as you are. Further, we have more contact with the general populace. As it stands, I am willing to wait a couple more months to see how the new Marshall works out. Be warned, shifts of influence have happened before in our history, and in this dire time *results* are more important than posturing." She snorted when she caught Reynardus's stare.

"I think that is a very good introduction for us," said a voice from the doorway.

Two men stood there, both tall, one middle-aged and fat, the other Alexa's own age and handsome, but stern-looking, with a small streak of silver at his left temple. Both were dressed in robes, dark brown and dark blue respectively. And they both had the faint blue aura of a jerir bath around them.

The younger man strode in, and Alexa realized he was the one who had spoken. His stare was fixed on her. "I am Sevair Masif, Stonemaster of Castleton and one of the Citymasters. The Mayr sent me. Greetings, Marshall Alyeka." He bowed.

"Greetings." Alexa bowed back.

The older man's face had turned pale, then ruddy. Masif gestured him forward. "This is Trademaster Dragee."

"And your business?" Reynardus stood too.

The trader shrank back, but Masif's lip curled. "Obviously you do not recall, Lord Knight Marshall, that I have been requested by my fellow Citymasters and Townmasters to interact with the Marshalls. I would agree with Lady Hallard. The city and town folk are not pleased with the Marshalls at this time."

"Is that so?" Reynardus said.

"Perhaps if you truth-vow that the Marshalls did *not* linger in telling us that Lladrana's fenceposts were falling, it would mend the suspicion."

Alexa sorted that out. The Marshalls hadn't told the rest of the players that the land was in danger? Jeez. Where was the media when you needed it?

There was silence. Color crept into Reynardus's cheeks.

"Further," Masif continued smoothly, "you Marshalls have been secretive in giving us the cure for the frinks."

"There is no cure," Reynardus said, grinding out the words.

Masif lifted his brows. "It seems to me that we have asked that very question for the past three months, and this is the first time we have received an answer."

Partis shifted beside Alexa.

The trader puffed out a breath, straightened his shoulders, and swept around Reynardus and the table to stand before Alexa. He pulled a large satchel from beneath his cloak, reached in to take out a smaller linen bag and put it before her. Then he opened the bag to reveal a casket. "A welcoming gift from the cities and towns to Marshall Alyeka," he said in a high voice, bowing.

Thankfully, the box didn't appear very strange. It looked like tin, and had two little hinged latches in the front. Alexa flipped them up and opened the box. The fragrance of good tea wafted to her nose.

"Aah," she sighed, then grinned at the man.

He blinked in surprise, then smiled back.

"Thank you very much," she said in Lladranan, then continued in English. "Your thoughtfulness is very much appreciated."

His eyes widened at her words, being translated and broadcast mentally by Sinafin, and he bowed again. "Our pleasure." He shot a narrow look at the Marshalls. "We of Castleton, and the other cities and towns of Lladrana, wish to assure you of our delight in having your help." He gestured to the box with a be-ringed hand. "A token." With a speaking glance at Masif, he bowed again to Alexa and hurried from the room.

"Dragee reminds me that should you wish to leave the Castle, we of Castleton will find a place for you here or in another town, and work that pleases you."

Some of the tension left Alexa. Options, how nice.

"Ha!" uttered Lady Hallard. "Masif took the words from my mind. You, girl——" she nodded at Alexa "——are welcome in the ranks of the Chevaliers, with or without that Jade Baton. If you don't want the land or annuity the Marshalls will give you, you're welcome to join the Chevaliers."

Alexa didn't deceive herself—they'd all want her magic, her

help, and had ideas about how they'd want her to help, but at least they were up front about it. "My thanks, Lady Hallard."

When the woman winced at her name, Alexa knew she'd muffed it.

Reynardus turned a cold gaze on Luthan, his son. "Isn't the Representative of the Singer going to try to seduce the Jade Baton into the Cloister?"

The phrasing and tone would have put Alexa in fighting mode, but Luthan looked as cool as his father.

"The Song has visited the Singer twice since the new Marshall came to Lladrana," said Luthan. "I have instructions to act only if certain events transpire."

Well, *that* seemed to have everyone thinking hard. Good one.

A clanging alarm pounded in alternating short and long bursts. Alexa was surprised to see the auras of Hallard, Luthan and the Marshalls flow together in a pattern of sheer determination as they shoved back their chairs and ran from the room. Shouts came from outside the tavern, and she heard running as the building emptied.

Fear flooding her, she reached for her baton.

No, Alexa. Not today. No battle for you yet, Sinafin said.

When Alexa curled her fingers around the baton and felt the warmth, it reassured her as much as had Sinafin's words. Wherever she ended up in Lladrana, she was sure she'd be fighting. She hooked the baton in her belt.

"Marshall Alyeka," Sevair Masif, the Citymaster, said softly at her elbow.

She looked up at the man and wondered what he might have seen in her expression.

"Let me walk you back to the Castle. It has been an eventful two days for you."

Alexa found her voice. "Yes." She closed the linen bag over the box of tea and put the drawstrings over her left wrist.

He offered his elbow in a gesture Alexa had seen in old movies and she curved her fingers around his arm and found it as muscular and hard as iron, then recalled he'd said he was a Stonemaster. Stonemason? It wasn't a profession you heard about much on Earth, especially in Colorado. No doubt it'd give a man some solid muscles, though.

"I heard you received a diamond as payment for saving two Chevaliers. Should you want it converted to coin, let me know," Masif said as they left the private room for the taproom of the tavern.

"Thank you," Alexa said.

The innkeeper and his staff were clearing the detritus the Chevaliers had left, and cleaning the tables. Masif dropped some coins on the bar and the barman looked up.

"For the use of the back room and the Marshall's refreshment," Masif said.

On their way back to the Castle, Alexa heard a commotion and detoured down a narrow alley that opened onto a small cobblestone square. In one corner cowered a couple, surrounded by an angry crowd tightening a circle around them. Alexa tugged away from Masif and started forward.

Sinafin jumped in front of her and barked. *They are no longer human. Look at them closely!*

Alexa did. The man and the woman had pasty faces, unusual amongst the golden-skinned Lladranans. Their bodies looked puffy and their bellies hung over their belts. The man's hair and beard were scruffy and the woman had long, lank hair. Hair had started to grow between her eyebrows. Their mouths hung open in complete idiocy. They were revolting.

Alexa took an instinctive step back.

Mockers, Sinafin said, and Alexa knew she was looking at more monsters.

Tainted humans with small brains and big mouths. Too stupid to come out of the rain. Frinks got them. They can cause great damage if not identified and killed. Sinafin jumped into Alexa's arms. *Watch.*

More people had gathered behind Alexa, and she was caught in a crowd and unable to leave without calling attention to herself. She'd had enough excitement in her life that day and was sure she wasn't going to like what was coming.

"What are frinks?" she asked Sinafin.

The dog didn't answer.

"Does anyone have clean rainwater?" Stonemaster Masif asked.

"There hasn't been a *clean* rain for months," said a guy near Alexa.

She didn't like that news either. Bad piling on bad, and Sinafin and the Marshalls expecting her to fix it.

"Here!" A woman standing in the doorway of a shop said, holding a bucket. With her other hand she tossed in a clot of white stuff.

Salt, said Sinafin.

"I knew there were Mockers around, just didn't know who." The shopkeeper fixed her eyes on the repulsive couple. "Should have guessed it was those two. Always were mean and selfish."

Masif took the bucket from the woman with a nod and thanks.

"Make way for Citymaster Masif!" someone called. The man beside Alexa made an approving noise. "Good to see one of the Citymasters here. Not afraid to do a dirty job."

Oh yeah. Alexa was *sure* she wouldn't like what happened next.

The crowd opened for Masif. He stood in front of the cowering man and woman. Incoherent whines came from their open mouths.

Impassively he threw the salt rainwater on them and stepped back. The water hit them and they shrieked as if being burned. Their bodies swelled, then burst open. A multitude of white slugs wriggled from the carcasses, along the cobblestones. People stamped and spit—both actions shriveling the slugs.

Alexa's mouth had dried in horror, so she had no spit and could only watch the white worms slither by her. Sinafin jumped down and howled. Hundreds of the slugs died instantly.

Everyone turned to stare at the dog. Then at Alexa.

"Exotique." The word rippled through the crowd. People withdrew from her.

"Um…" Alexa said. Warmth bathed her thigh—the baton! She pulled it from the belt loop.

People "aahhed." The baton flashed an eerie green that flowed onto the cobblestones. When it was done, no slugs moved, and the bodies had turned into unrecognizable husks. Murmurs of satisfaction rose from the crowd.

She slipped the Jade Baton into her sheath with trembling fingers. Sinafin leaned against Alexa's legs.

Bootheels rang on the stone as Masif joined her. A soldier from the Castle—the teenage girl's, Marwey's, lover—pushed forward. He bowed smoothly to her, then to Masif, then to Sinafin. "I would be honored to escort the Marshall of the Jade Baton of Honor to the Castle." His tone was stiff, resolution flashing in his eyes. Alexa was sure he wanted something.

Masif cocked an eyebrow at her. He'd evidently seen the same thing in the young man, a need. Alexa suppressed a sigh. Masif was already an ally, and the soldier could be one more. She needed all the friends she could get. So she held out her hand to the Castle guard. Gingerly he linked her arm with his. His muscles were solid but shivered with nerves.

"My thanks for seeing the lady to the Castle," Masif said. Smiling briefly and showing white, even teeth, he bowed to them, then spun away and strode off at a pace that would have been too fast for Alexa. Off on Town business, no doubt.

Sinafin barked and the young man started, dropping Alexa's hand. The little dog jumped into his arms. She must have said something to the man, because he tucked her under his left arm and held out his right elbow to Alexa again. She took hold of his biceps. The soldier started walking slowly, then quickened his pace until he and Alexa matched steps. She realized that he'd walked the same way with Marwey, who was about her height. That relaxed her a little.

He cleared his throat. "I am Pascal, a Castle guard of the second rank. I have ambitions."

Well, who didn't?

Pascal looked down at her. "I want to Pair with Marwey, but I have little to offer. I am the third son of a farmer. I am a good guard and want to be a good Chevalier."

"How can I help?"

His face set into determined lines. "You will soon have lands of your own, but no Chevaliers. Marwey said——" He stopped and flushed. His posture stiffened. "I have trained with the Chevaliers and am close to winning my volaran reins."

What had olden guys won when they became knights? Spurs? Better reins around a halter than cruel spurs digging into horse-flesh.

Pascal bit his lip, looking as if he were drowning in interview-mode. She'd been there. She patted his arm. He jumped.

"I want to be your Chevalier," he blurted.

She missed a step, and he steadied her without even noticing. Nice. No way was she going to be able to answer in Lladranan. She was glad he was holding Sinafin. "You would be my..." What on earth was the right word to use? She cleared her throat. "Employee?"

He flushed again. "Yes," he said. "I would vow my loyalty to fight for you."

Alexa didn't like that idea. She couldn't see herself sending this young man out to face monsters and die. Maybe she could keep him on her land, when and if she got it. He and Marwey, safe. She glanced at him and didn't know whether safety would appeal to him. At least she could give him options.

"You would vow loyalty to me, and I would pay you...how?" She squashed irritation at her own ignorance.

But he'd brightened. "With payment for my further training as a Chevalier, with advancement in your ranks—"

What ranks?

"Perhaps even with a little land—or a volaran," he said in the same tone of reverence with which she'd once said "diploma in law."

She liked his energy, his directness, his politeness. "Very well, if I receive an estate and funds, you're hired."

His bearing took on a little swagger of male pride, but his voice sounded choked. "My thanks."

He took her back to the safety—and restrictions—of the Castle.

In Castleton, the square once swarming with frinks was silent and shadowed. It started to rain. Hours passed.

As the husks of the Mockers crumbled, a black fog rose from them and mixed with frinks. A shadow coalesced, made of mist and frink and Mocker and powered by the ancient, deadly will that lusted after Lladrana and what it held. The shadow formed into a cobweb of almost-substance.

No one in the land would recognize this new threat, know it existed. The tool had not been used for centuries. But it had been successful before and had been called into being once more. It could be web or more solid, manlike, but nothing else. Still, that would do. That would do very well.

It raised a shadow like a protrusion the size of a head, featureless except for the glowing red orbs where there should be eyes. It looked up the hill to the Castle. Its prey was there—rich, exotic dreams to succor it.

Its awful, gnawing hunger must be fed with simpler fare first. A rip opened, mouthlike, and the cobweb billowed in and out though there was no wind. It would feed on energy and magic and dreams and souls. Beads of gray-dew dripped from the mouth.

Pure malicious glee ran through it at the thought of a kill and the luscious draining of the prey as it fed. It drifted, then tumbled faster into the narrowest pathway between the first two buildings it could find. Stretching, it attached to each of the walls, a dark net lost in even darker shadows. It was weak now.

When it was strong and gorged and powerful, it would feast on otherworld flesh.

11

Alexa slept that night in luxurious comfort with no nightmares of the render that had attacked her between worlds or Sinafin dream-movies. Slowly she woke, and as her senses filtered information—the deep softness of the feather mattress, the hue of light from the sun illuminating stone walls, the scent of magic—she knew she was still in Lladrana.

She stretched and rolled onto her back, then looked at the canopy over her bed, past the bed curtains and around the room. She liked the bedroom, and her Tower suite with the large sitting room and a small office.

Sinafin, as a pink butterfly about a foot wide, fluttered to settle on Alexa's stomach. *You slept late. It is midmorning.*

"It felt good to catch up on my sleep. That jerir of yours takes a lot out of a person."

It is good you dipped three times.

Alexa grunted.

The Marshalls are having their morning meeting.

With a groan, Alexa rolled to the edge of the bed and slithered until her feet hit the rug. "Better get at it, then." She needed to make sure they accepted her as one of them, if she was going to fight for them.

Thealia will tell you true what happens at the meeting.

Alexa considered that. It would mean she'd only have to deal with one person she knew instead of face the ten of them, most of whom she hadn't sorted out, and the jerk Reynardus, to boot. "I think Thealia might leave out things I need to know." It would be like reading notes of a lecture, or a trial, and not being there herself. She'd miss nuances.

From the wardrobe she took underwear that resembled the long underwear she wore for hiking in the Colorado cold, except the pants were footed. They fit. She pulled on the long, thin under-robe of purple. It fell to midcalf. Then she donned a lavender tabard—more like a serape—a long rectangle of cloth with a hole in the middle that draped over her front and back. She fingered the white fur trim along the surcoat and sent a glance to Sinafin, who'd landed on one of the top corners of the bed.

"You explain to whoever made these, that I never want fur on my clothes again." Alexa shuddered, remembering the Assayer's Office.

We eat them. You wear and sleep on things you eat.

"You eat ermine?" Weren't they little minklike creatures? Ferrets or weasels or something?

Not me, but some nobles think they are a delicacy.

"Huh. Well, I'd bet some monsters would think *me* a delicacy." Gruesome thought. She cinched her leather baton-belt around her waist. The stick lay heavy against her hip.

An exotic-looking flower was embroidered over her left breast in purple on the tabard. Glancing into the closet, she saw her wardrobe was lavender and purple, with one gold gown. She grimaced, shut the door, and hurried from the bedroom into the narrow semicircular hallway.

New shoes are outside the door, Sinafin teased.

Alexa had forgotten about shoes, but none of the Castle corridors was carpeted. She opened the door with a yank that set the harpstrings singing. In front of her were several pairs of exquisitely made shoes. One pair of black, one brown, one jade green, one purple. No one was in the half-circle anteroom of her tower, so she sat down and pulled on the shoes. The leather was soft and molded to her feet when she laced them up.

When she stood and shifted back and forth, she nearly moaned in delight. They were the most comfortable shoes she'd ever worn. Finding size fours outside of the children's section had always been difficult, though sometimes the Velcro fastenings made up for it.

It was a fact of life: she was small. Small there and even smaller here. And she was supposed to be a warrior?

Sinafin fluttered to her shoulder, folded her wings. *The Song would not have called you if you were not the right person to save Lladrana.*

Alexa supposed she'd hear a lot of that stuff in the future, but she straightened her shoulders, lifted her chin and took the stairs down at a quick pace. She was pretty sure of the way to the Marshalls' chamber.

When she reached the door with the fancy writing she couldn't read, she felt a twinge of anxiety again. Well, she'd learn to read, and to speak, and to fight, and she'd do her best...until the Snap. She grinned. Her best had always been good enough to scrape through, and the Marshalls hadn't seen her in action!

She flung open the door and marched in.

They were all standing. Reynardus touched his baton and the ivory flared white. "This meeting is adjourned. We all have much to do."

If she'd been paranoid, she'd have thought they had deliberately finished before she could participate. Maybe it was just that they'd always done things one way, that they weren't used to her being there.

Maybe.

The room was long and narrow, with tall multipaned windows inset with stained glass in the center showing coats of arms. The large wooden table had fifty chairs, with the Marshalls clustered at the near end. One of the wooden chairs had a carving on top of a knight riding a volaran; another, a woman reaching upward, mouth open; a third, a Tower with lightning around it; a fourth, a town; a fifth, a ship. Representatives' chairs, Alexa figured. All the other chairs alternated—a sword or a shield carved on them. The last one had a carved shield—and a stack of cushions. Yep, the Marshalls had expected her and had noticed she was small.

All except Thealia and Reynardus filed out. Since she was irritated, Alexa hitched herself to sit on the huge table. With a final flutter of wings, Sinafin sat on Alexa's shoulder.

Alexa swung her legs. "Mind telling me what was discussed?" she asked the two.

"Since we had no Representatives today, we decided what information we would give them," Reynardus said.

The pompous jerk. She knew "spin" when she heard it. She kept her voice mild. "I hope you decided that the best policy is full disclosure." Dammit, now *she* sounded like a politician. "Tell them everything."

Reynardus's heavy eyelids lowered.

Before he could make a snide remark, Alexa pushed ahead. "From what I could tell from the map, and what the feycoocu has

shown me, you are fighting a losing battle. Your defenses are falling and you don't have the army to stop the, uh, creeping evil."
How different the evil here in Lladrana from that spouted by
politicians in the States. *This* was evil. *These* were true monsters,
not humans with differing beliefs. "You need all the help you can
get. Arm the Chevaliers with magical weapons, give them the
right spells to use in battle." Were these words really coming from
her mouth? They should have sounded silly; she should have *felt*
silly. She didn't. She felt determined, fierce. And it was good to
have a passion again.

She heard Reynardus's teeth click together.

"There are several problems," Thealia said. "We don't have the
time to train them in battlespells. It takes more Power to prime
the magical weapons than we can spare."

"If everyone had knowledge of our battle spells, there would
be worse fighting amongst the Chevaliers and in the towns,"
Reynardus said.

It sounded to Alexa as if they'd done too little, too late, and
time was running out. Alexa stared at the Marshalls. "Am I allowed
any opinion, any input to the Marshalls at all?"

"Of course," Thealia said.

Reynardus curled his lips.

Alexa had magic enough to gain their ranks, but not enough,
yet, to have them listen to her. It would take time, but she'd be
like a faucet drip and wear them away. Deep inside, she knew that
was one of her functions here, and she would follow her instincts.

"I ask that you tell the other Marshalls my concerns."

"It will be done," Thealia said.

Alexa fixed her stare on Reynardus. "You don't have a very high
opinion of the Chevaliers and townspeople. And they don't have
a good opinion of you Marshalls either. Don't you think someone needs to mend fences here? To be honest, I think the Mar-

shalls, who are in the ultimate position of power, should be able to bend. That's my recommendation."

"We'll discuss it—" Thealia choked.

"We *have* discussed it, and nothing will change," Reynardus said.

Acid pitched in Alexa's stomach. She wished she could pound some sense into their heads, but she was the youngest and most inexperienced. Too new. Too Exotique.

"What else was talked about?"

Thealia's expression softened. "We decided to open Marshall Testing and increase our team to forty. We already have a few applicants."

Reynardus grunted.

This was news to Alexa. She perked up. With an increase of Marshalls, especially younger Marshalls, she bet she'd have a better chance at change. The balance of power within the Marshalls could shift. She could only go along now, make sure she was accepted and fit in. Later, she could help the Marshalls steer a new path.

"That sounds good."

"And we are inventorying the magical weapons in our armory in case we wish to disperse them in the future. The batons are the fiercest weapons, but we have several swords—broadswords and short swords. A mace or two, and some quarterstaffs like Partis uses," Thealia said.

Again, too little, too late. And too late for Alexa to do much about it.

Thealia looked at Alexa. Like this was supposed to placate her?

"Speaking of estates," Thealia said, "we also dealt with Reynardus's fine for oath-breaking and gifting you with your estate. Reynardus and I were on our way to the map room."

A thrill ran through her at the idea of land of her own. She could hardly believe it—it seemed to be coming to her too soon and almost too easily. Discreetly she wiped her suddenly damp palms on her tunic. Then Alexa looked at Reynardus, maybe not so easily. She figured she'd have to battle him every inch of the way.

He looked as if he had tasted something bitter.

"According to the Lorebook, Reynardus must be fined lands or volarans for his oath-breaking."

Now Reynardus didn't look happy with following ancient tradition.

"Two square miles or seven prime, war-trained volarans," Thealia said.

"I told you I only have six," Reynardus said.

"So we agreed on the land. I believe that my ancestor sold a bit of land to yours in nearly that amount."

"One-point-eight," Reynardus said.

"That will do," said Thealia.

Reynardus huffed a breath and strode from the room. Thealia followed.

Sinafin-butterfly rose to flutter in the air and Alexa slid from the table to her feet. "We're going to the magic map room that shows Lladrana and those falling magic fenceposts, right?" she asked.

Yes. You will be guided by me, Alexa. It's important.

Sinafin flew ahead of her, pink and silver wings flickering in the gray corridor. They exited the Keep and crossed the courtyard to an opening in the Cloister walk that led to the small map room.

Reynardus stood stiffly, hands clasped behind his back. A big chunk of land in the middle of Lladrana glowed fox red on the map. It was far from the long northern border where the horrors came from.

Since she often accompanied Thealia to the map room, Alexa

knew the placement of the fenceposts. None had fallen during the night. She sighed with relief.

Thealia tapped a small portion of red land that intruded on her green-tinted estate. "I accept. I'll have Faith draw up the papers for you to sign, Reynardus." Thealia smiled broadly. "You *do* have a time limit, according to past Lorebooks."

"You studied up," Reynardus snapped.

"I had Faith brief me. I can invoke a penalty if you don't make the transfer within twenty-four hours." Thealia smiled sweetly. "The usual penalty is a hundred acres an hour. The oath-breaking was serious."

Boy, were they gouging him. Alexa made sure her glee didn't show and tried not to think what would have happened to her if the guy had fried her with magic. At least the Marshalls were taking this seriously. It nearly satisfied her.

A tic jumped near Reynardus's right eye. "I'll sign the land over as soon as the ink is dry on the contract."

"Now for a more joyful land transfer." Thealia beamed at Alexa. She walked to the animated map. As large as a king-size sheet, the map's backing was stiff, but the colors were vibrant, the northern border glowing and with minute peglike fenceposts. The outlines of Thealia's and Reynardus's estates faded.

Thealia picked up a huge book from a shelf on the wall. "Currently the Marshalls oversee several vacant estates." She waved a hand and different portions of Lladrana lit up.

Alexa had a bad feeling about how they had become "vacant," but the deep yearning for her own home kicked in. She wanted this so much she could taste it like her lost tea. And if the price was forsaking everything else she'd ever known, it was higher than she'd ever expected. But it was a price she would pay.

She looked at the mountain range to the north. She'd like living in view of the mountains again, but didn't want to be on the front line of invasion. Since most of the North was "vacant," she figured others felt that way too, or had died trying to preserve their land.

There was a little curve of mountains to the east. Hard to think of mountains in the east, but still...

Sinafin flapped in front of the map, indicated with an antenna a decent-size chunk of land. *Here, Alexa, pick here.*

It was in the west, several miles in from the coastline. Since the map had reverted to the green-brown of a geographic-altitude map, the land Sinafin pointed to showed green with rolling hills. Alexa thought that meant it would be good for farming. And pretty to walk on.

"A very good choice," said Thealia.

It wasn't anywhere near Reynardus's estate. That was a point in its favor.

Thealia found a page in the Lorebook. "It was an Exotique's land many years ago, and has a four-story brick manor house, three villages and a good annual income."

Would people who once lived with an Exotique be more friendly than those who hadn't?

Here, Alexa!

She shrugged. Sinafin hadn't steered her wrong yet. She nodded. "Ayes."

Sinafin pulsed pink and silver like a flickering neon light. "Si— Feycoocu, you're hurting my eyes." Alexa remembered Sinafin didn't want the Marshalls to know her name almost too late. Sinafin stopped the light and zoomed around the room. Alexa had never seen a butterfly zoom, but Sinafin managed it, and as she did so, she inserted images into Alexa's mind. Green grass and large deciduous trees, a pretty red house with bay windows on several floors.

Alexa swallowed hard. This looked like a place she'd only dreamed of. "Yes," she whispered.

Hers. A place of her own and a high place in this society if she fulfilled her potential, and she was used to fulfilling potential that only *she* believed in. Others had expected that she'd spiral downward from the foster homes; instead she'd climbed upward. Steady and determined. She could do that here too. Win a home and land and even the *hearts* of some people. She could make friends. She could finally fit in. "Yes!"

Six mornings later Alexa cracked open an eye to see the bright landscape out of her turret windows. She wanted to roll over and sleep, but her new waterfall chiming clock wouldn't let her. She dragged her weary and aching body from the soft comfort of the bed and donned her new clothes.

She wished she was back in law school. It had been easier. The classes for the bar, the shared anxiety, the camaraderie and Sophie—all had gotten her through. Her lessons hadn't been as hard and her memory hadn't been as taxed as it was here in Lladrana.

Her brain felt as if it would leak out of her ears any minute. And nothing compared to the bruises and aches of her body as she learned how to ride and fight with the other Marshalls.

She had no real friends except Sinafin, who absented herself from the boring daily grind-Alexa-into-the-mud to play and take care of unknown feycoocu business. The little shapeshifter still experimented with forms for Alexa. Sinafin seemed to enjoy plucking images from Alexa's brain and trying them out. Alexa had shared her rooms with everything from a Gila monster to a penguin. Mercifully the foot-long cockroach had only lasted an hour.

Since Sinafin wanted Alexa to learn the language, she didn't visit Alexa in her dreams to explain things. Even riding wasn't as bad as struggling to speak, read and write Lladranan. Alexa knew gloomily that she'd always have an accent. And if it never got any better, it would be an accent that people laughed at. Apparently she sounded drunk.

Since her voice was a tool of her trade, she was painfully aware when she slurred her words. But if she wanted to speak in any sort of natural manner, she had to accept that her tongue would mangle words. She could only hope that with use and time, her verbal skills would improve.

Alexa turned off her alarm and looked at the view while she dressed. The brithenwood tree was the same spring green as the fields. Bushes and trees were budding. The rains had been heavy this year. Even so, Alexa had never seen a frink. It didn't rain frinks in the Castle grounds anymore. The Marshalls believed Alexa's presence had something to do with that, which made her feel even more odd.

She couldn't see past the heavily forested hills to the piece of land that was now hers, and which she hadn't visited yet. A *large* estate with a lovely four-story brick manor house, Thealia had said. The thought of it, the support of Sinafin, and her daily healing of Chevaliers were the only things that kept her going.

The Marshalls were helpful, but distant. Reynardus had stopped outwardly sneering and now treated her with exquisite courtesy and a smirk that drove her crazy.

Most of the Chevaliers accepted her, glad of another strong arm in the war against the invading horrors. She'd experienced a couple of instances of instinctive revulsion like that Luthan had shown at their first meeting, but no further attacks.

With effort and care and conscious sensitivity, she could make friends. Sinafin liked her.

And Pascal and Marwey. The former soldier now wore her purple livery and was in a more advanced Chevalier training than she was. He used one of the five volarans that had come with the estate.

Baby Nyja liked her too. Alexa spent at least an hour every couple of days with the baby, making sure she wasn't abused, that she received all the care she should have.

Alexa pushed herself hard, harder than the Marshalls expected, but she needed to prove to herself as well as them that she was as good as any one of them, and equal to Reynardus.

She'd actually moved from one-on-one training to being with a class of squires to working with young Chevaliers. Six hours a day of fighting and sheer determination to learn made her the equal of anyone in her class. Except with volarans.

Her five prime flying volarans made her a wealthy woman. All but the one Pascal used lazed their days away in the pastures of her estate. She didn't think she'd ever master the skill of flying on a horse, and after the third time she broke her arm and it was healed magically, the Marshalls agreed with her assessment.

The fighting force would be split, some on the ground and most in the air. The Marshalls worked with the Chevaliers in this way too, though they mostly flew. Alexa had chosen to stay on the ground. Learning to ride a horse was daunting enough.

Now, still grumbling, she left her suite and descended her Tower stairs. The other Tower rooms were empty and Alexa didn't know whether to be pleased or wary. She often liked being alone, but it was a long way from the other Marshalls' apartments, though with one instantaneous mind-cry they'd come running, if she cared to have them here.

The day was cooler than it had looked as Alexa hurried to the map room. She'd developed the habit of meeting Thealia there in the morning before they started their work. Alexa had shaded her estate on the map in deep green, with the emblem of her baton on it. The land of other Marshalls was also shown on the map, as was the estates of the Chevaliers. Alexa knew where the land of Lady Hallard, the new Representative of the Chevaliers, was, as well as that of Reynardus's son Luthan. The most important location was Singer's Abbey, where the oracle of Lladrana lived. It shone gold on the map, and Alexa had vowed to defend it with her life.

She'd sworn to defend Lladrana itself with her life.

Most of the time all she had to do was call up the image of the baby Nyja, or Pascal and Marwey, or the Chevaliers she helped, or the map with her estate on it, and the vow would connect bone deep.

Not this morning. She hadn't slept well; a chill of foreboding had plagued her with black dreams. She'd discovered that a night like that usually meant something bad had happened—Chevaliers died, or more of the magical yellow fenceposts were down, or horrors had been seen in the newly turned fields for planting.

She'd reached the map room and hesitated. It was rough walking in and seeing the changes, worse knowing that the gray and black that breached Lladrana's borders and inched inward showed lesser and greater evils. Really bad was when dots of red, or a large blotch, showed where people had fallen—usually Chevaliers, some local people, some mercenary foot soldiers.

Dragging in a deep breath and straightening her shoulders, she entered the chamber. It was a medium-size room with good light from high windows and the ever-present crystals. Thealia was already there. Alexa frowned. The Swordmarshall was obsessed by the map, and her own estate and relatives weren't even near the failing borders.

"Another fencepost failed and three Chevaliers were lost in a skirmish at dawn. They stopped the larger monsters—four renders, a slayer and a soul-sucker—but such a cost!"

Alexa drew near and saw a red smudge in the northwest. She

scanned the map with the blue force-lines that showed the magical border between the magical fenceposts, the missing fenceposts and the boundary. In the few days she'd been in Lladrana, two fenceposts had gone dark and the defensive border that depended on the energy had failed between them.

When Thealia turned, her face was haggard. She gestured at the map. "It's only a matter of time before the occasional greater beast becomes an onslaught we will have difficulty in stopping. Look here!" She pointed due north of Lladrana's center. "These were the first fenceposts to fall and it's the hardest boundary to defend. Every day the light of the fenceposts on either side of the hole dims. Soon they'll go out." She clenched her hands. "We don't have enough people. We became complacent, didn't realize the knowledge we'd lost. Then the fenceposts started dying and *everyone* in Llandrana knew we were weak and vulnerable. Morale fell and fear increased."

Thealia spoke a little too quickly for Alexa to understand her every word, but most of the terms were unfortunately part of her daily vocabulary—"fenceposts," "boundary," "borders," "defense," "beast," and all the monster names too.

"That's why you Summoned me, right? To heal the boundary?" Alexa asked.

"Yes, you will show us how to make new fenceposts. That is your fate." Thealia went to the bookshelves, pulled out a large volume and thrust it at Alexa. "This is the history of the fenceposts. But it doesn't tell us how they are made! Not even the Sorcerers or Sorceresses of the islands know."

Alexa took the heavy volume and opened it on a nearby table. She still couldn't read well, so she flipped to pictures. The fenceposts were shown, about twenty feet tall.

"Take the book," Thealia said. "Perhaps when you read it, you will understand something we don't." There was a mixture of bitterness and hope in her tone.

Alexa shivered, reminded herself she wasn't alone. Forming her words slowly, Alexa said, "A new class of Chevaliers will be fully trained soon." She knew because she'd trained with them. "More young men and women are contacting the Chevaliers to fight." For service to their country, for glory, for wealth. They'd find mud and horror and death. So would she.

A little strain disappeared from around Thealia's eyes. "Yes. It is a good class. You were right to choose Pascal for your first Chevalier." Now she watched her words and spoke more slowly. "You are all good in that class. Some excellent volaran riders."

"Let me know if there is someone very talented in other classes that would need a volaran," Alexa said.

Thealia frowned. "We should not just give away volarans."

"A person of extraordinary ability should always be given a chance. We need all the strong fighters we can get." Alexa gestured with her Jade Baton.

A corner of Thealia's mouth turned down. "None of those who have Tested for Marshall have passed."

Alexa frowned. "Fledele did."

"Her husband failed. She did not want to bond emotionally with someone else, or by blood. She has no close relatives who wished to Test for Marshall. She declined the position." Incredulity tinted Thealia's voice.

The door swung open with a loud *creak,* spilling bright light into the room.

"Ah, Swordmarshall Thealia and the Marshall Alyeka, studying the map, as usual," said Reynardus with a false smile.

"Salutations, Reynardus," Thealia said.

"Shalutashhuns," said Alexa, and felt herself flush. She knew her accent sounded "drunk" again.

Reynardus looked down his nose at her. Alexa gritted her teeth.

She really hated that—he was too tall and had too straight a nose, and he had that insulting look down pat. She longed to see the nose broken, his white tabard smeared, but that wouldn't happen. He was an excellent fighter, and if his nose ever was broken, it would only lose the arrogant straightness temporarily.

He smiled, sending a twinge of alarm up Alexa's spine. He was up to something. Striding between them, he went up to the edge of the map. His smile widened and he tapped an elegant finger to where the skirmish had taken place the night before, on the northwest coastline, near a fallen fencepost.

"I think it is time we showed our new Marshall the reality of the Field," Reynardus said.

He didn't do "benevolent" well. He still came off as pompous and patronizing. Alexa's stomach lurched. She had the sensation of being on a bicycle and having the training wheels yanked away. Inhaling unobtrusively, she said, "Of course." She gripped her baton a little too tightly, but it was better than letting her fingers tremble.

There might be fighting. There would probably be magic to perform. And she'd have to ride there or be taken by someone else on volaran. Three things she didn't do well. Yet.

"Good, good." Reynardus dropped a heavy hand to her shoulder in false bonhomie.

He didn't even sway her. One thing she *had* mastered was achieving her balance—physically, mentally and magically. She could stand straight and steady in a gale.

She smiled too. "I mush change into m' paddin', an' pick up m' new sh-chain mail 'n town." Tailored to her, she'd already spent a bunch of Power on making it magically light and tough. "I'll ride down." She trusted a gentle mare to take her there.

Thealia cocked her head in the way that meant she was mentally communicating with someone. "Luthan has agreed to fly you. He'll meet you at the Nom de Nom."

Dead monster heads again. Oh fun.

"Ayes." That she could say well. She nodded to the Marshalls and left.

12

Sitting in the Nom de Nom, Luthan stared at the Exotique woman before him. Ever since he'd met her, he'd tried to mask his aversion to her—based mainly on her appearance, for which he was deeply ashamed.

With reluctance, Luthan had agreed to fly the new Marshall to the Field of the last skirmish, where three Chevaliers had lost their lives.

She looked at him with clear, green eyes and he sensed that she was well aware of his discomfort with her and hurt by it. He winced inwardly. Lladrana needed this woman, and if the Song was right, this Exotique would be only the first to come to Lladrana in the next two years, when the harmonics of the two worlds resonated in syncopation. So he should try to accept her as soon as possible.

It was not only her alien looks that put him off—she was such an unknown quantity, capable of strange actions that disrupted life. For the Marshalls, that might be good. For Luthan personally, he disliked illogical starts and turns in a person—he'd lived with enough disruption in his childhood, with a brother he loved but didn't understand.

The worst was that he believed his godmother Thealia was trying to matchmake, Pair him to this strange Exotique woman. He imagined the Marshalls were desperate to keep her in Lladrana, and Pairing would do that. But such an emotional tie between him and this one would never happen.

She drank her tea, her eyes as watchful and examining as his own, making no effort to break the silence engulfing them. He wondered what she thought of him. More, he wondered what sort of man *would* be attracted to this odd little creature.

Ping! The sound inside his head froze him. He strove to keep his breathing even, his pulse steady, his mind at rest so the vision would come clear, and last.

The woman's aura trembled, then was replaced, and Luthan saw true. Now she sat in front of him with skin a darker hue and a long scar running down her left cheek. Her hair was longer. Behind her, his hands on her shoulders, was Luthan's brother Bastien.

He looked more contented and relaxed than ever in his life. His dark eyes gleamed with self-knowledge and purpose. As he caressed the woman's shoulders, love shone in a golden aura around them.

Bastien! Bastien in love with a Marshall! The rebel and rogue and troublemaker. A black-and-white, Bastien had always gone off like a rocket in any direction his brilliant mind took him, followed his emotions as if they were oracles from the Song.

Bastien! Oh, how he deserved this lady. She would shake *him* up, perhaps help make him into the man all sensed he could be— a great man. In the vision, she reached up and placed her hand on his in a touch that spoke of equal love. Luthan softened. Yes, Bastien deserved love. He'd had little enough of that from their parents.

The Exotique met Luthan's gaze with an amused one of her own and said something. Bastien shifted behind her and winced, obviously the butt of teasing.

"Arr you alll righ'?" The Exotique's accented words in the here and now, the hesitant touch of her fingers on the back of Luthan's hand, broke the vision.

A small line of concern showed between her brows. Luthan laughed. She sat back quickly.

Now when he looked at her and saw a lady who would sort out his brother, all his uncomfortable feelings about her vanished like mist. His *sight,* as always, left him a little giddy.

Luthan reached out and patted one of her hands. "I am very well, Lady."

She eyed him with suspicion, then shrugged. "I am called Alexa."

"Alyeka," he said, and frowned when he knew he hadn't pronounced it correctly.

He leaned back in his chair and drank deeply of his beer. It grounded him, but he couldn't keep from smiling around the rim of his glass. The complications between Bastien and Alyeka would be entertaining to observe.

"I'm called Luthan."

"I know. I have heard of you. You are a Chevalier, the Representative of the Song and the son of Reynardus." Her words were very slow but distinct.

Luthan thought it a good sign that she put his title first. She saw him as an individual, then, not merely as the son of a man her voice told him she disliked. Many people disliked his father. Including his sons.

Reynardus would loathe this one. Small and female and too strange to be understood and manipulated.

But Bastien—her Power and her uniqueness would snag Bastien's lively curiosity, just as her status as a Marshall would repel him.

Now that he knew she'd be Bastien's, Luthan studied her. Her short, fine hair was pure silver. Her face was attractive enough, coming to a pointed chin and holding those big eyes.

"Yes," he said. "Reynardus is my father." He shrugged. "You can't choose your forebears."

A fleeting grief shadowed her eyes. She sat up straighter. "No."

"I have a brother, Bastien." He watched closely, but saw no flicker of recognition. Had the two met yet? Bastien was in the Field, due north.

"Ah've heard of Bastien." She pronounced their names correctly, even if she misspoke words.

Luthan smiled, trying to calculate what gossip she might have heard, who might have spoken to her of his brother. "Don't believe everything you hear of Bastien. He's a good man." *Even if he is misguided.* But Luthan cheered to think that this woman would put Bastien on the right path.

Luthan stood and bowed to her, offered her his arm. As her eyebrows rose, he noticed they were a light brown. Odd. But no instinctive twinge of revulsion occurred, and he grinned. He was over that affliction.

A few minutes later Luthan introduced her to his volaran. The volaran was huge, as large as some of the great horses in Earth's past. It was a beautiful black, and when it had studied her in the Landing Field with big brown eyes, she saw intelligence in its gaze. Perhaps not intelligence that the Lladranans recognized, or intelligence that was humanlike, but a cleverness all the same. She got the idea that the Lladranans underestimated these creatures, but it wasn't something she felt qualified to comment on.

Luthan set her on a long saddle and mounted behind her. Alexa figured that Thealia was trying to matchmake, but knew it was futile. Alexa would always be an Exotique first to Luthan. A pity, because he was a strikingly attractive man, better looking than both his father Reynardus and his brother Bastien, whom she'd rescued from the pool. She'd hesitated to mention Bastien because she didn't want to get into family dynamics. Still, she sensed Luthan was the most honorable man she'd met in Lladrana. Yep, really too bad.

They took off in a steep ascent that clutched at Alexa's lungs and gut.

When they steadied, Luthan yelled in her ear, "Sing with me."

He sang a spellsong through, then Alexa joined in and they repeated it twice. At the end, they were encased in a magical bubble she'd formed. She admired the sheen of the outward curve of the spell. *She'd* helped in the magic! Formed the bubble that kept them warm and the air quiet around them.

"Are you going to Test to become a Marshall?" she asked.

Luthan hesitated. "Not now. I have responsibilities to the Singer and her Friends. They convinced me that the best use of my talents would be to represent them. I probably will Test for Marshall sometime in the future."

When his father retired from the Marshalls? *Did* they retire? Alexa wondered if he worked well with his father. He certainly was more diplomatic than Bastien. She'd heard how he'd baited Reynardus, pushing him into following the rest of the Marshalls into Town after her.

Luthan said, "Has anyone told you of the distance-magic of the strongest volarans?"

She didn't think so, but could extrapolate. "Um, they can shorten it?"

"Ayes. Instead of flying one volaran-length with their wings, they can fly a furlong, a mile——" he patted his mount "——more. It depends on their physical strength, the strength and wildness of their Power. Or my Power. My brother Bastien, raised my volaran. All of our relatives have volarans he trained. All of the Marshalls and the best Chevaliers have horses with great distance-magic. We'll be using a little distance-magic this flight."

"Intereshtin'," Alexa said.

Since the little attempt at conversation had included several explanations and definitions of words from Luthan, and neither of them seemed to care whether they spoke or not, Alexa leaned back to enjoy the flight.

They flew northwest to the coast. Under them, slightly distorted by the bubble, were fields, rolling hills, forests—all a patchwork of different greens that tugged at her heart. A beautiful land, a verdant land, a land too lovely to be desecrated with nasty monsters, blood, war and rotting bodies.

Was that why they invaded? Because Lladrana was so pretty? Alexa didn't know. Nobody had told her why the horrors invaded. Maybe no one knew.

She caught her breath as she saw the ocean. From the map she'd known of the ocean, but hadn't emotionally understood the landscape of Lladrana. The sea was a changeable panorama of blue and green and gray, stretching to an endless horizon, dotted with islands. To someone used to the jagged peaks of the Rockies defining the western horizon and man-made buildings blocking the east, the ocean was mysterious and too vast for comfort. But it too, was awesomely beautiful, and she had wanted to see it.

The coastline was rugged, like pictures she'd seen of Oregon. Alexa looked inland, trying to see the magical fenceposts.

This was the northwest border of Lladrana, and though the fence was failing here, the monsters didn't often creep over. They seemed to prefer invading where no water existed.

Straining her eyes, Alexa discerned a faint blue-white line a few miles inland. She followed it to a glowing yellow beacon, tall and straight. A fencepost!

The line between the good beacon on a rough outcropping, the end post, and the next fencepost inland, one lying on the ground, was a dull white. She narrowed her eyes. The downed fencepost barely glowed, as if its energy leached into the ground. Squinting, she peered into the distance. The third post inland was down and black on the landscape, looking like a huge fallen tree trunk. She wondered what it was made of. Everyone wondered. No one knew.

Luthan murmured a command and the volaran angled to a gentle descent. Details of the land jumped out at Alexa as she tried to wrap her mind around another aspect of her new reality.

Two fenceposts were down, cut off from the energy of their neighbors and the whole line. At least it wasn't like a string of cheap Christmas lights in which, when one went out, all of them failed. With a hint of nausea rising in her throat, Alexa realized that if all the posts went out, there would be no Lladrana.

A group of Marshalls and Chevaliers were already surveying the site. The ground where the volaran settled showed trampled, short spring grass and mud. Dark patches of blood stained the ground, and the dark outlines of the fallen Chevaliers. According to Lladranan custom, a spell was cast on the dead and they sank into the ground to fertilize it. Memorial tablets were erected in their home chapel. Everyone accepted that the death would lead to new life on the land.

Since the battle had happened just after dawn that morning, three shields of independent Chevaliers stood point-down where they'd fallen. The banner of a lesser noble waved over her grave.

Alexa felt Reynardus's gaze on her. Everyone would be watching her, seeing if she could fix the boundaries, if she was a true, powerful Exotique. She hadn't ever thought of herself that way. Hadn't ever wanted to be a warrior except in the courtroom. But she would fight and defend, and, if necessary, die to make this land safe again. She thought of the gurgling baby Nyja she had played with the night before.

Yes, this was a bad time for Lladrana, and if she could save it for the future, what a triumph that would be! What a difference that would make in so many lives. To save a whole culture. She'd have made her mark.

She hadn't wanted fame, but she did want to make a difference. Even if the memory of her deeds was never recorded and lost in the mists of time, *she'd* know that she'd made a difference. Her life, her struggle to be the woman she was, would be validated. The result was more important than any acknowledgment or fame.

Sliding off the volaran, her knees gave way, and she would have fallen if the flying horse hadn't shifted to support her. Oh boy. This *was* reality. And did she have any incredible deeds within her? What happened if she didn't? Would they throw her out of the Marshalls, just as she'd begun to think of them as her peer group?

The other Marshalls approached. Reynardus smiled that nasty smile of his. "Now, let's see what you are made of." He jerked his chin at the boundary line, then waved an expansive hand at both the downed fenceposts.

Alexa wanted to frown, but sucked in her breath and nodded. She was circled by sober-faced Chevaliers and people planting fields who'd stopped to watch. The two fallen posts were relatively close together, no more than a few hundred feet apart. This too was something that had no explanation—how far apart the magical posts were. Thealia was of the opinion that it was determined by their creation, and that circled back into the complete lack of knowledge of how to make the fenceposts, how to revive them, how to regenerate the boundaries.

Deciding to start at a logical place, Alexa walked to the first dead inland post. Wind whipped her tabard over her surprisingly comfortable chain mail. She clinked as she walked.

With one last glance at the gathered onlookers, she pulled her Jade Baton from the loop at her hip and curled her hands around it. As always it warmed to her touch and began to glow. A sigh escaped her. She could only do her best, and hope that it would prove her to be a true Marshall.

Placing one foot on the boundary, she walked it like a tightrope. Her cares fell away and she was conscious as never before of the world around her. Whatever expectations others had of her, she was free to enjoy this moment of lambent sun behind pearly clouds and a brisk sea wind that left the taste of salt on her mouth. Her nose twitched and the light scent of brithenwood came with its tune. She glanced around and found a copse of trees nearby. Clouds blew away and left a dazzling sky. Sunlight caressed her face and warmed her tunic. The earth beneath her feet felt soft and welcoming. Lladrana accepted her.

A simple melody rose from her heart, a melody she'd never heard before, and didn't really hear now. She *experienced* it. Notes comprised the sun and blue sky and the greenly budding brithenwood and the whiff of rich earth and salty ocean and the susurration of waves and wind. It bubbled through her, giving her peace and joy. She began to dance.

You have found your Song! The pink-and-silver butterfly danced with her.

"Salutations, Sinafin," Alexa said.

Sinafin's eyes gleamed and she curled her antennae.

Alexa flung out her arms and twirled. The bronze flames at the end of her wand fired into reality, burning strongly in the wind. Her tabard whirled out with her, like petals on a blooming flower, and she almost liked purple again. She laughed, caught her breath and gathered her dizzied senses and continued along the border, weaving dance-steps along the boundary.

Soon enough she found herself at the next fallen post and stared down at the dimming beacon. It looked a little like a telephone pole. With shock she realized that the deep carvings in the post were depictions of monsters. Various slayers, renders, soul-suckers and other monsters she didn't recognize, including some flying ones, were shown in various death throes.

She stared. Walked down to the base of the pole that was thicker than the top end, then back to the rounded top. Every inch of the thing was carved, even the ends. Each image was about three inches tall or wide and incised about an inch into the pole. She couldn't tell what the beacon was made of—in some spots it looked like wood, in others like stone. Its color varied from black to deep red to pink, in no design she could deduce. Occasionally a monster image even looked as if it were fashioned from a jewel—ruby, sapphire, topaz.

Her baton tugged at her hand and she followed it. Acting like a dowsing rod, it angled to the post. About a foot and a half up the thing, pale jade gleamed. Jade, like her wand. Alexa swallowed. Two friezes of dying jade monsters circled the pole.

She slid her own piece of jade into its sheath and touched her finger to the jade. It flared bright green.

Sinafin perched on Alexa's shoulder.

"Watch out!" Screams bit the air.

Alexa pivoted. Monsters headed straight to her in a jangle of dissonant notes. Time slowed and her mind numbed as she saw the horrors up close and alive, with their sole aim to kill her.

They carried no weapons, they needed none.

The slayer was huge. Taller, wider than the render, with long, bilious yellow fur. Two horns curved among the nasty spines covering its head, larger spines marched down its back. Its arms had spines too. Both legs had a spine-spur on the hock. Tiny red eyes full of kill-lust stared at her.

Two soul-suckers glided on each side of the slayer, tall and thin, reptilian skin glistening with natural ichor. The long tentacles near their arms writhed as if waiting to hold her and suck the life from her. The huge black eyes of one of them caught hers, and she felt trapped, unable to move. Chill infused her.

One of the renders slid in front of the soul-sucker and broke the spell. Tall, nasty, steel-bristle hair, fangs dripping. Its eyes too, were red. Its claws were already extended from the paw-hands to kill. It should have lumbered, but when it ran, the motion was smooth and deadly.

A warhawk's scream broke the moment. Alexa stumbled back, then watched Sinafin, in bird form, dive-bomb the soul-sucker. A tentacle whipped up but missed the hawk. A render jumped at the bird and claws clanged together on empty air. The slayer swiped, and several spines shot from the back of its arm, peppering the air where Sinafin had been an instant before.

The monsters were a stride away. The Marshalls and Chevaliers were too far away and too scattered to save her.

Alexa acted as trained, raising her wand, using it as a weapon—a sword with a green blade. Words tumbled from her mouth, and they were the right words, a fighting chant. Blood thundered in her ears. She ducked, slid under the razor-claws of a render, swiping at its middle as she jackrabbited by. Guts and gray ichor spilled.

Panting, she turned, slipped on gore, fell and rolled. A good thing, because the soul-sucker's tentacle-arm whipped to where she'd been. She kept rolling, cut the feet off another render, scrambled away from more pouring blood.

She was smaller than what they usually fought, reacted differently, took chances she shouldn't have, jumped through holes that should have been too small.

She lit on her back, head thunking against the ground. As another render bounded to her, something blocked the sun behind him. He swung.

"*Helleva!* Fry, you hulking beast!" Alexa called.

A burst of jade energy hit his chest. He staggered back, then pawed at himself. Jade fire burned him.

Shouts. Ground vibrations. Volarans ran like horses into the fray. Marshalls and Chevaliers joined the battle. Thealia, face grim, leaned down, grabbed Alexa and jammed her on the rump of the volaran.

Alexa's bones jarred. Her jaw snapped shut. A golden bubble coalesced around all three of them as the volaran took flight.

Alexa wrapped her arms around Thealia and goggled at the iridescence curving around them.

Partis is my Shield. Now you know what that means. I fight. He protects. We work as a team.

They rose higher and the bubble thinned. As they circled back and landed, Alexa saw Partis leaning on a staff, watching them, baton ready.

But the small influx of monsters was dead. A slayer, two soulsuckers and four renders. Their bodies littered the ground. This time Alexa hummed an antinausea spell under her breath. Better to look white and shaking with fear than to stand and puke her guts out.

Wrong image. Guts already strewed the ground. She breathed through her nose. The spell blocked some of the stench.

Partis approached them, round face serious but otherwise pristine. Reynardus had hung back—but his brother and Shield hadn't come along, and it was against the code for a Sword to fight without a Shield.

Alexa had had no choice. And no one had thought she'd be fighting anyhow. Like most women, she'd probably be a Shield.

Thealia was an exception in that. Looking at Partis, still fresh, and thinking of her own clothes covered with mud, spattered with nasty stuff, Alexa figured defense work would suit her fine.

That's what she'd been trained for at home. The only clients she'd had at the start of her career had been those in need of defense.

Partis lifted her off the volaran. Though he was the smallest Lladranan man she'd seen, he had plenty of strength to toss her around—as he'd proven in their fighting exercises.

Everyone stared at her, apparently checking her out for wounds.

"I analyzed her energies. She is fine," Thealia announced.

Partis lifted her purple tabard and held it up. Huge blotches of mud and ichor caked the tattered garment. Alexa swallowed. She hadn't even been aware that the thing had ripped, had been shredded in the back by render claws. A strange singe darkened the left side near her shoulder. Alexa patted her left shoulder and under her arm. Everything seemed fine. Excellent armor, maybe a little warm to the touch.

"Well done, Marshall Alyeka," Partis said.

The Chevaliers nodded.

Reaction hit. The adrenaline supporting her faded. She needed to sit down...now! Forget about saving face or pride or anything else. She'd almost been killed. By monsters more horrible than any nightmares. She didn't know how she'd survived. Her blood drained from her head at the same time her sweat turned cold.

"What—" Thealia sounded startled. Suddenly her volaran was steady against Alexa's back, and the horse's big blue eyes studied her.

Alexa managed a weak smile. Ducking death and fighting overwhelming horrors might be all in a day's work for the Chevaliers and Marshalls, but it was damn new to her, and she didn't care for it.

Concentrating on keeping her feet, evening her breathing and heart rate, she almost missed the concerned glances and mutterings of the group. She heard her name mangled, and her attention sharpened.

"Yes?" she said loudly as if a question had been addressed to her.

Shieldmarshall Faith's mouth thinned. "We promised not to lie to you ever again. Or manipulate you."

Uh-oh. Alexa was sure she wasn't going to like what was coming next.

"It is extraordinary that monsters attacked in the same place they'd been defeated hours before." Faith's brow wrinkled. "I can't recall the last time this happened."

"They came for the Exotique Marshall," Reynardus said coolly.

He probably wished they'd gotten her too.

"Yes." Thealia's jaws worked. "We were distracted and not protecting Alyeka as we should have. This whole matter is very odd." She looked straight at Sinafin, who had settled atop the volaran's head.

"Si—the feycoocu?" Alexa's voice cracked. Horror rose through her. Surely Sinafin wouldn't betray her.

The butterfly curled antennae in Alexa's direction. *You needed to be blooded.*

13

Sick with betrayal, Alexa stared at Sinafin.

You needed to be blooded, Sinafin repeated.

Blooded. Spilling blood of monsters? Alexa shuddered. Her lips went cold. "We'll speak of this later." When she'd sorted mixed emotions, predominantly hurt, and could think rationally instead of feel...

Someone cleared his throat. It was a Chevalier Alexa vaguely recognized, a tall, loose-limbed man with a tough face. He wore Lady Hallard's colors. His name was...Marrec.

"There was a dreeth," Marrec said.

All sound ended, even the slight *swish* of Sinafin's wings.

"It was more shadow than substance, not fully materialized, but it loomed over the last render to attack Alyeka."

"Impossible," Reynardus said. "Did anyone else see this?"

"Improbable, perhaps," Faith corrected. "But not impossible.

The war with the Dark is escalating, the reason we Summoned *Marshall* Alyeka. That means additional monsters will invade. A dreeth sounds like the next logical step up."

Worse and worse. The volaran's warm, curved side behind her comforted Alexa. "What's a dreeth?" she asked.

People stared at her. "A large bat-winged creature with sharp curved beak, poisonous teeth and bloated belly," Luthan said.

A dragon? She'd always had a soft spot for dragons. Didn't seem like that would survive reality.

Luthan frowned as if in concentration and an image formed before Alexa. Not a dragon. A flying reptile like one of those during the dinosaur age, only bigger, fatter. A pterodactyl, pteradon. Ick.

She thought through Marrec's words. It had not completely materialized. Apparently it could come out of thin air, just as the other monsters could rise out of the ground at their last, farthest penetration of Lladrana if there was no magical boundary behind them. The rules of magic in this place were as convoluted as the rules of law at home.

Alexa recalled the shadow blocking the sun right before she'd killed the last render. She didn't want to think of killing the render, of fighting for her life, of being betrayed by Sinafin. She didn't want to think at all.

It was all too much. How did she pretend to be normal?

She paid little attention to the discussion around her as she fought another battle. Terror.

A small bark came at her feet. Sinafin again. This time as a cute black cocker-spaniel puppy with big brown eyes. That didn't help her fear.

As a scrawny kid, Alexa had seen such a puppy and yearned for it with all her heart. But it played happily in a pet store window with littermates and the price wasn't even within the realm of Alexa's dreams. No one would buy a puppy for a foster child who'd been in their home for a couple of weeks and would probably move on in another couple.

Sinafin lolled her tongue and tilted her head with long ears. *This was the shape you loved the most in all your dreams. I can keep this shape forever, if you want.*

Alexa sniffed, picked up the puppy, and walked with the shape-shifter away from the group and to the fallen post, then back out to the cliff. Alexa whispered into silky ears. "Why did you do it?"

You needed to know what it is to fight and fear and kill and survive and know that this could happen tomorrow too. Your training is not a game.

Maybe Alexa had wanted it to be.

More, you needed to know that you are a natural fighter. Your body and mind and spirit and magic will meld together and protect you when you fight, and you will win!

"I don't think so."

The puppy wriggled in her arms as if impatient, and licked her under her chin. *I would never ask anything of you that you could not do.*

"Huh." But Alexa rubbed her face against the puppy-soft fur, wiping the tears that had leaked unwillingly from her eyes.

Do you want me to keep this shape? Sinafin twisted until her tongue lapped up any trace of Alexa's tears.

"No. It isn't natural for a dog to remain a puppy forever." Alexa's own words rang to her soul. She had wanted to remain a novice Marshall forever, playing at fighting instead of the real thing. Well, who wouldn't? So she was human. So sue her.

Sinafin yipped. *I thank you, then, for your courtesy.* She sounded sincere. *I will continue to experiment with shapes until I find the proper one for us.*

Us. That sounded good too. A unit. Alexa looked across the field. The Marshalls were walking or riding volarans in pairs, as usual. "Do Shieldmarshalls fight too?"

Of course, when necessary, but their primary function is to defend their Swords. Sinafin jumped to the ground.

Alexa shrugged. Well, now she knew what it was to fight and kill and nearly die, just as she'd known what it was to be part of healing and helping others survive. Someday she'd have a partner of her own, be one of a Pair. Then she'd be integral to the Marshall team.

Not wanting to stand alone anymore, she crossed to join the rest.

"There should be a blooding ceremony," Albertus, the oldest Marshall, said.

A gleam appeared in Reynardus's eye. "Oh, by all means," he purred. With a negligent wave of his ivory baton, he transported a mangled render—probably the most revolting one—that lit with a sickening *thud* between them.

Alexa shortened her breath and stared beyond it, not focusing on her kill. The thought made her shiver. Killing would be a part of her life now. Maybe even daily. She'd have to accept it.

Though killing monsters, especially those who tried to kill her, was a whole lot easier to justify than any other killing she'd done in her life, renders and soul-suckers were not flies or mosquitoes.

"Allow me to do the blooding," Luthan said, emerging from the group.

His leathers looked unstained, and Alexa wondered if he'd been in the short massacre. He wouldn't avoid battle.

Luthan continued. "As a blood relative to a Marshall—" he nodded his head at Reynardus "—a Chevalier in good standing, and Representative to the Singer, I am a symbol of three of the six communities of Lladranan society."

Reynardus's lips thinned, but he inclined his head.

With fascinated repulsion, Alexa watched as Luthan bent to the still body on the ground and dipped his right index finger in a dark messy wound. She gulped. She was not going to like this. She stood soldier straight, eyes ahead. Suck it up, tough it out. If this was the price for being recognized by the Chevaliers, she'd pay it.

Luthan's finger was warm. And sticky. And it smelled awful. She froze as he dabbed once on her cheek.

Cheers rose.

A gentle smile curved his lips. "Very well done, Marshall Alyeka. I salute you."

Beneath disgust, pride bubbled, triumph even. It was just as fantastic a feeling as being sworn in as a new attorney to the Colorado bar. She was part of a community, had the knowledge and skills that that community valued, spoke a common language. Her mouth turned down at that—not quite, not yet, but she would! She'd redouble her efforts.

"You call that a proper blooding streak?" Reynardus sneered, swiping his own fingers knuckle-deep in gore.

Luthan straightened and looked down the aquiline nose he had inherited from his father. He raised one brow. "Yes. It's a proper blooding, especially since we don't know how render-ichor will affect Alyeka's skin. I know you would not wish to harm our newest Marshall."

Alexa hadn't thought whether the green monster blood could hurt her, but her cheek didn't tingle or burn. Just smelled nasty. She wondered how long she'd have to wear the mark.

Reynardus stood, emanating waves of frustration. He said a string of words and not only was his hand clean again but the various heaps of dead monster flesh disappeared. His voice rose. "I trust none of you wanted to claim the bounty for these kills."

"None of us are independents that need zhiv," Luthan said.

Alexa guessed that meant this little foray had been open only to top-ranking people or their trusted Chevaliers. In any event, they'd made quick work of the horrors. "And none of us would claim the new Marshall's kills."

"I will ensure Alyeka receives her bounty," Thealia said.

Huh. She'd made money in defending her life. Alexa shifted and felt the pull of sore muscles and bruises that would stiffen later. Not the best way to make money, and not the easiest, but it would be good to have, all the same. She wasn't sure how much she had.

A butterfly again, Sinafin fluttered into sight and lit on Alexa's head. *It is time to go,* she said, booming to all minds. *Alyeka will ride with Luthan. There is another stop we must make.*

Alexa couldn't catch the faceted eyes of the shapeshifter to protest, so she just sighed and accepted Luthan's offered arm.

Ever since he'd gone zombielike in the tavern, he'd changed toward her, and she didn't think she liked it. The whole thing screamed of some sort of magic at work.

Though she was learning quickly, and controlling her own magic didn't spook her as much as it did originally, the thought of someone else having a magical vision about her creeped her out.

"Look!" Marrec called, and pointed.

Everyone followed his finger to Alexa. Again. As usual.

A loud gasp came from the crowd as people pointed at her, and behind her. She turned to look back. The boundary line that had been dull, glowed, and jade flames about a yard high flickered.

She was a hero! She grinned. She could like being a hero.

Luthan lifted her up onto his volaran. She liked the stallion and sensed it approved of her too. That it was even proud to carry her. She wondered if its attitude had worn off on Luthan.

Sinafin flew up and perched on the volaran's head. The flying horse rolled his eyes and flicked his ears.

I think it's time you see something, Sinafin broadcast. Her eyes twinkled.

"What?" asked Alexa.

A surprise. The feycoocu proceeded to flap her wings, pointing with one, then the other. After Luthan and Thealia nodded, Sinafin took off in a spiraling rise.

Luthan mounted and gathered her to him. The pulsations of his aura made Alexa think he now thought of her as the way he would a close relative, a cousin or even a sister. She cleared her throat. The last and only other person who'd considered her that was Sophie. And Alexa would have died for Sophie, *had* done all she could to help her lost friend, in law school and after.

Then the volaran ran to the edge of the cliff and took off. Alexa was too petrified to scream. Instead she clutched at Luthan's steely arms. He hummed at her as they fell.

The flying horse spread his wings, and they caught an offshore breeze and circled upward into the blue sky.

Alexa trembled and mentally checked her underwear. Still dry. She hadn't actually wet her pants, it only felt like she might. As they flew near the cliffs, over the rocky beach below, she huddled next to Luthan. He continued to croon, but there was a note of amusement in the lilt of his voice. Alexa didn't care. She preferred flying in airplanes.

About fifteen minutes later they angled inland and beneath them lush green fields turned into a rising plain and then rolling hills. The landscape was so appealing that Alexa was able to breathe normally and watched the clumps of sheep and cows and villages below. Finally, they started an easy descent. They landed on a big green lawn attached to a mellowed red brick manor house of four stories.

Luthan dismounted, set gauntleted hands on hips and surveyed the countryside. He muttered, sounding a little irritated, "Who chose this estate?"

"What?" asked Alexa, yawning to pop her ears.

"Who chose this estate?" he repeated, slowly and distinctly.

"Ah heard yoush the firs' time," Alexa replied.

Sinafin drifted down to land on Luthan's shoulder. He flinched and she nearly fell. Rolling her antennae, she flew over to perch on Alexa's shoulder.

Alexa smirked at Luthan's narrowed eyes. He took his gauntlets off and slapped them against his leg, looked at the lawn, the house, across the land into the distance. "Why did you choose this particular land as your Exotique estate?"

"What?" Now Alexa looked around, trying to absorb everything. This place was beautiful. Absolutely, positively beautiful, obviously well-kept and equally obviously wealthy.

Your home, said Sinafin.

"Mine?" Alexa had never dreamed of having something as beautiful as this.

Do you like the house?

"It's a dream house," Alexa breathed.

Sinafin preened. *I told you to trust in me.*

"You did good," Alexa said. Since Luthan was still staring into the distance, it didn't seem like he was going to help her down. She slipped onto her stomach, then slid off the volaran, her tabard rucking up. It was a couple of feet before her soles hit the ground. The volaran whuffled.

Luthan came forward as her knees sagged, and braced her with a muscular arm. "The feycoocu advised you to choose this land as your Exotique estate?" He was looking at Sinafin, who pulsed silver and pink. The Lladranans sure liked color.

"Yes, she told me to pick this land." Alexa reminded herself to speak as slowly and precisely as Luthan. "But it was on the map. I didn't know it would look like this." Now steady on her feet, she detached herself from Luthan to walk around. The lawn rose gently to frame the house. There weren't any bushes in front of the place, but she could plant some.

Frinks got the bushes.

Alexa's mouth turned down. The only frinks she'd seen were a couple of nasty little dead shells Sinafin had dragged in as a cat.

Luthan stared at her with solemn brown eyes. "There haven't been frinks in the rain at the Castle or Castleton since you were Summoned."

"Oh." She couldn't think of anything else to say.

Joining her, Luthan offered his arm. "Do you know the history of this place?"

"Not all of it."

He started walking up to the manor house. "Many generations ago, it was a Marshall's house. An *Exotique* Marshall's home. Then it passed to his son, who didn't care to Test to become a Marshall and accepted a lesser noble title. After a while, a daughter married a wealthier man, moved to his estate and sold this one."

"Who owned it last?" They'd come to the covered portico in front of the house.

Luthan shrugged. "Again, minor nobles of the Janin family. The last one was a young Chevalier who died two years ago, leaving no family. A soul-sucker got him."

"Oh."

This was the physical evidence of her place in this world—land and a home of her own that she would have had to work decades to achieve in Denver.

She took a step to it, and her muscles ached. Oh yeah. The price for this place would be steep. Alexa glanced around at the fields, the woods, the landing place for volarans, the stables housing volarans of her own. Partial payment for this place of hers had already been taken from her in the form of the Testing of the Marshalls. She had killed for it.

She could *be* killed for it. She could pay more in blood and flesh and stress and other ways she didn't even know.

But she could belong. All the Marshalls were considered powerful and odd—being an alien Exotique would just be a little harder for regular folks to accept, wouldn't it? And among the Marshalls, as they came to know her and she to know them, would come respect and friendship. With most of them, she sensed that.

Alexa took the wide steps to the door, and there, slightly above her head, was a knocker in the form of the Exotic flower. A knocker, not a doorharp.

"What is it about this estate that interests you?" she asked Luthan.

"Pardon?" He raised his eyebrows.

Alexa shook her head. "Don't act innocent now. You were fascinated that this estate was mine. Why?"

His lips curved upward in the merest hint of a smile. "I don't want to frighten you off."

She straightened to her full height and waggled a thumb at her chest, an action he watched with fascination. "I am the big, bad Exotique Marshall. Able to wield the Jade Baton. Able to slice renders to bits—"

"Able to dance along the magical border and revive the boundary lines. The Singer's Friends will be interested in that," he murmured.

Her mood deflated. "Probably won't last."

"Perhaps not, but that you could resurrect them at all is incredible."

Alexa shrugged, feeling a bit uncomfortable under his scrutiny. "We've wandered from the subject. This manor in relation to myself interests you."

Luthan inclined his head. "True."

"Why?"

He turned her and pointed. "My brother Bastien's holding adjoins yours. It is small, but fruitful."

Bastien, the guy she'd rescued from the jerir. The black-and-white that taunted his father, Reynardus. If Luthan was the honorable firstborn, good son, Bastien was the rebel and rogue of a bad son. Too bad they weren't twins—they could have been the basis for a good-twin, bad-twin story....

"Not impressed with Bastien," Luthan said. Now he was actually smiling.

"Will he be a good neighbor?" she asked. She glanced again in the direction Luthan had pointed, but wasn't too interested. She wanted to get inside the house. *Her* house.

"He will probably not be much of a neighbor at all. Bastien is usually in the Field."

That meant he was a Chevalier who fought a lot. Well, he'd had the scars and muscles to prove it. Sounded very macho. Huh.

"So he has an estate and a couple of volarans?" She traced the door knocker with her fingers, trying to get a sense of the place before she entered. It exuded cheer. Her heart started to thump hard.

"Twelve volarans."

That got her attention. "Twelve? I only have five." She pouted. It didn't matter that she had no intention of riding any of them.

"He likes volarans." Luthan lifted and let the knocker fall. It echoed inside.

A moment later the door swung open and Alexa faced a man as tall as she was, and much rounder. His eyes widened at the sight of her, his face puckered into a grin, and he squealed with delight.

"The mistress is here. The Marshall Exotique!" he called over his shoulder, as if addressing the entire household.

How many people were *in* her entire household?

Luthan took her hand and led her in. The entryway was tiled in brown-and-white marble squares. A sweeping staircase to the right curved upward to the second floor, and beyond.

The proportions of the place appeared to be slightly less than Lladranan standard, more Earth-like.

"The Exotique built this house," she said.

Luthan raised an eyebrow. "Right."

Alexa swallowed again as she saw the staff arrayed before her. Then she smiled. In typical Lladranan flamboyance, they formed a rainbow. The butler and housekeeper wore purple. Down at the end, a boy in his young teens wore deep reddish brown. Servants she didn't know the names for, let alone the names *of,* were clad brightly in blue and red and green and yellow.

The butler bustled forward. "Welcome, welcome." He bowed, and bowed again.

She did the greeting thing, knowing it would take months to learn the names of all the staff. She only hoped she *had* months in the future to do so. Then she took the butler up on his offer to show her the house.

At the door of her suite, Alexa dismissed him. Luthan had gone to inspect the stables for her. She had a feeling he was also calculating how far her place was from his brother's and trying to recall who else were her neighbors so he could tell her more stories. Be informative and helpful. She didn't know what had happened between them in the tavern, but he could be a staunch ally. Especially with his father, Reynardus. She got the impression that neither of his sons was afraid to stand up to the man. They must be a pain in his ass.

She smiled and stepped into the first room. It was the sitting room, with a desk near the window, a lovely fireplace, and some chairs, settees, tables and other furnishings that looked old and well-cared for. Somebody had taste and money. She sighed, glad she didn't have to furnish a house herself. She hadn't spent any time in houses like this to know what would fit or what would look tacky.

Her smile broadened as she noticed there was no purple any-where. She walked to the bedroom and looked at the bed. Little stairs again. Too bad. Yet, the windows were large and curved at the top and had nice dull-gold-colored curtains. Everything in here pleased her too.

Alexa climbed the small stairs and sank down into the rich feather topper of the bed and knew she'd made a mistake. It felt too good against her sore body. Before she could settle, she scram-bled off the thing, but looked at it with longing. She'd like to spend the night here, but her rounds of lessons and meetings at the Cas-tle tomorrow would prevent that. The Marshalls would probably have a meeting to discuss what took place today, ad nauseam.

Meetings in Lladrana were only slightly better than the meet-ings at the big law firm where she'd interned. The best meetings she'd ever had were partnership meetings with Sophie over pizza and beer. Those days were gone and never to return.

And the Lladranans didn't have pizza.

Alexa stood and closed her eyes and tried to *feel* the house around her. It was a good place, no terrible tragedies, no hideous monster invasions. Day-to-day life. And she wanted the home with every iota of her being.

The tiny chimes at the threshold of her sitting room-bedroom door tinkled and Luthan looked in. He smiled if he sensed her magical probing, and approved.

"We should leave now if we wish to reach the Castle by dark."

Alexa realized she was holding on to a bed-curtain rope of vel-vet she'd used to steady herself. Reluctantly, she dropped it and nodded. "Yes, let's go."

"We can fly over Bastien's land so you can get an idea of your neighbor," Luthan said, a little too casually for Alexa to believe that he didn't care about her decision.

"Sure," she said.

He offered his arm, and she took it, feeling a little silly. Odd. She hadn't felt silly in the house or with the folks that worked here, but now was awkward. It was Luthan. He no longer acted as if she were totally repulsive, but she wouldn't ever forget that his instincts had been against her.

With great courtesy and easy strength, he helped her into the saddle and settled behind her. The volaran nickered, and Alexa sensed again that he was pleased she rode with them. It lifted her spirits a little at leaving a place where she'd prefer to stay. To explore every room while knowing that everything in it was hers. To learn the quirks of the people who kept it comfortable and safe for her. To claim her home.

She sighed.

The volaran ran and lifted off with a *whoosh* of great feathered wings, rising in a large circle into the sky. Luthan moved with the beast and Alexa tried to follow his lead in how to sit, where to place her hands, how to balance her weight. It was easier this time.

Luthan gestured below. "That's Bastien's estate, Freehold."

Alexa glanced down to see well-tended fields and a lot of corrals that indicated volarans. Friendly neighs and greetings came from a cluster of animals, and there was some lifting of wings. She sensed Luthan expected some comment.

"Everything looks cared for." Even from this height she could see the flying horses were healthy and just plain beautiful.

Luthan relaxed incrementally behind her and she realized another thing that bothered her was that he was so stiff all the time. His bearing would do a rigid Marine proud.

"Bastien is a good landholder and an excellent Chevalier," Luthan replied. It was the last he spoke during the entire trip.

The guy was odd.

14

Alexa hated being a hero. Word of her reviving the border—even for the short time of a day before it died again—had spread through Lladrana and the Marshalls had sent her on a goodwill tour. Alexa deduced they wanted to prove that their decision to Summon an Exotique was a good idea. To show the rest of Lladrana that the Marshalls were still viable, strong leaders.

She felt like everyone was now looking to her to save them. A load of responsibility burdened her, like invisible weights on her shoulders.

Though she was learning a lot about Lladrana and the status and popularity of the Marshalls, Alexa didn't like the travel. It rained continually, so the countryside looked more mud brown than spring green from Alexa's carriage window.

She supposed the inns she stayed at were the best each town had to offer, and some rivaled the Castle's luxury, but she was tired of sleeping in alien beds. She traveled with a retinue, only two of them of her choosing—Sinafin, who was having a great time, and Alexa's new maid, Umilla.

The Marshalls hadn't been pleased with Alexa's choice of servants, but Alexa had ignored all their protests. She liked the black-and-white; the woman treated her with respect, didn't laugh at her accent, and Umilla pronounced her name correctly. Umilla now wore Alexa's purple livery. Alexa had had qualms about that, until she noticed Umilla took pride in the clothing and no longer walked with a stoop. There was no denying that Alexa needed help in dressing herself in the chain mail.

Three others traveled with Alexa—her language teacher, the Castle Medica, and an older woman who taught Alexa magic and was the strictest prof she had ever experienced. Alexa was doing well in her magic lessons, but not as well in her language lessons. Just when she thought she understood some concept of grammar, the rules seemed to change.

The worst was that everywhere she visited she was a curiosity, the *Exotique*. She'd never been a wildly outgoing person, and now she struggled to keep a smile on her face and be civil—she had pat responses in fair Lladranan to common questions, but anything unusual meant halting speech. She felt stupid, and she felt like a freak.

After ten days of touring, they reached an inn called The Singer's Hand, and Alexa desperately needed time alone. Time pretending to be a normal person. The past two nights she'd awakened in the middle of the night and nearly wept for home and faces she knew.

That day Sinafin had been prodding her at every instant, impossible to bear. Alexa had managed to talk to the folks who approached her in the private room behind the taproom until everyone's questions were satisfied—all during the day and until the gray, rainy evening. With a little strategy, she eluded every-one, even Sinafin, dressed in some ordinary clothes and pulled on a royal-blue cloth cloak that the innkeepers kept for guests.

She opened the back door and peered out at a small cobbled courtyard between the inn and the stables. The light was bad in the sputtering rain, and the sun had just set.

To her right was a passage between outbuildings to a field of long grass and an old orchard. The air smelled fresh and the heavy drops were now just intermittent splats. She closed her eyes, lifted her face and took in the scent of Lladrana. Sweet rain fresh with hints of blossoming trees, a scent near to one she remembered from her childhood.

A little walk would be just the thing to refresh her spirits. She wouldn't go far, just to the orchard. The inn stood on the edge of a midsize town, and Alexa had no intention of getting into any more complicated situations. She'd been in enough over the past weeks to fulfill anyone's craving for adventure…and it was just the beginning.

So she drew the cowl of the cloak over her head until it nearly reached her eyes, and stepped from the building. She'd learned by experience that wet cobblestones could be very slippery. Picking her way, she headed down the path between the stable and the inn.

She must have misjudged the path, because she ran into a thick cobweb. It clung to her, blinding her, covering her nose and mouth. It smelled of rotted bodies…death. The more she fought against it, the tighter it became.

Panic struck.

She broke the binding on her left hand and pulled it into the cloak, fumbled with the baton fastened on her left hip. Her feet slipped and she landed hard, the jolt of pain clearing her mind just enough. She freed the baton. Comfortable in her hand, it stead-ied her enough to mentally order *Fire!*

Heat pulsed from her, constriction vanished. The smell dissipated. She lay in the wet courtyard for a minute, panting, trying to gather her thoughts. What had happened? She'd run into a spiderweb. They were stronger and stickier in Lladrana, she guessed.

"Hel-lo there, darlin'. Did you slip?" A man swathed in a rain cloak and with a broad-brimmed hat shadowing his face grasped her arm and lifted her easily to her feet. When she swayed, he steadied her against his body.

She gulped air, her mind still dizzy. "Shal-shalutashuns," she gasped.

He hugged her closer, chuckled. "I can see why you slipped. Tricky walking out here. Did you see some sort of green light?"

She shook her head, trying to dispel the muzziness. It had just been a spider web.

"Ah, well. Must have been an illusion."

He settled her better against him. Her head rested on his chest.

He was warm and strong and smelled really good. Like a spicy pastry. She could do with a good piece of pie.

Or with a man.

He wouldn't have to be good. Just good in bed.

This was the first time since she'd stepped through the silver arch that she'd thought about having sex. It seemed a damn good idea.

More, she realized that she hadn't been intimate—physically or emotionally—with anyone while in Lladrana. Well, maybe Sinafin picked up on Alexa's emotions now and again and had been a good friend. But it was difficult to identify with someone who was about three inches high in her dreams and a foot max in real life. She'd held Sinafin, but Sinafin had never held her.

No one had held her with tenderness and affection since she'd been Summoned, and the press of events had kept her from that realization. She had put her physical needs in storage, just as she had as a child.

But this man reminded her of all the wonderful activities men and women could do together—and being held ranked very high on that list, maybe even higher than sex. Kissing should definitely be a priority too.

As she let him take more of her weight, he seemed to get the same idea.

"Well now, do I have a willing woman?"

The lilt and rich texture of his voice more than pleased her.

For a moment caution lit her brain. She rubbed her eyes. The cobweb seemed to have affected her mind and her senses. It was taking a while to recover. So she stared at him without seeing much, noted the worn flying leathers of a Chevalier, and a couple of patches of rank. That was good enough testimony for her.

He stood her in front of him, and tipped up her face, his still shadowed by the hat. "You look a little peaked, darlin'. You sure you know what you're doing?" He adjusted the cloak around her, smoothing it down, making no attempt to hide that he lingered on the curve of her breast and hip.

She liked that simple honesty. Little sparks of interest signaling real attraction flickered inside her. With proper blowing, those sparks could ignite into hot flame.

Absently, she dropped her baton into the cloak's deep inner pocket.

"Ah know what ah'm doin'." She decided to be honest too. No thinking about every word before it passed her lips, trying to regulate her speech into proper Lladranan. She didn't care that she sounded drunk. He wasn't laughing at her.

She looked up and his face was shadowed by the broad brim of a hideous hat made of something she didn't want to think about. In the twilight, she couldn't see his features, but his jaw was strong and his mouth soft. He didn't smile. No, he wasn't laughing at her.

"Do you work here at the inn? I haven't seen you here before. 'Course, I haven't been here for a couple of months."

"No, Ah'm travlin'," Alexa said.

"Ah." Now he smiled. He sifted his fingers through her hair. "Very fine. Very silky. Almost unusually so. You arouse my...curiosity."

That wasn't the only thing, and she knew it. She felt his erection. It built a low fire in her, feeling a man's passion for her. No man in Lladrana had touched her with desire, had expressed any interest in her sexually.

She put her arms around his waist and leaned against him. A very *big* erection. For her, a very big turn on. "Mmm," she said, almost humming. The Lladranans and their preoccupation with sound had rubbed off on her. She wanted him to rub against her for a good long time. All night. And she was willing to rub against him too.

"A willing woman," she purred.

He enveloped her. He was larger than she and he brought his cloak around them both and bent his head over hers, moving his cheek against her hair. He sniffed as if inhaling her scent and enjoying it.

His body was hard and strong and masculine, something she hadn't experienced for too long. *His* scent was slightly wild, musky, foresty, spinning her into a little erotic fantasy equally wild.

"It's been a rough spring. A night of comfort and passion and grace would be very welcome for me," he said softly.

His hands stroked down her back to her hips. When they came up to her shoulders, he massaged her tense muscles there.

Comfort and passion and grace. What an odd combination of words to describe lovemaking, but the words and the way he said them melted something inside her. The simple sentence gave her images of rolling and laughing and being completely unselfconscious as they slaked their desire. There was a gentleness about this man too.

"Works for me," she said.

"I'm bunking in the stable loft. It's warm and dark and, most especially, private."

"Oh yeah," she said in English. "Ayes, ayes," she said in Lladranan.

This time his hands went beyond the small of her back to slide over her bottom. He let his hands roam over her, then squeezed, lifted and angled her into his body, where his hard arousal met her sensitive flesh. She moved her own palms to his shoulders and found they were as tense as her own. His apparent nonchalance wasn't completely true. She dug in and he grunted. When she returned his massage, he let out a little groan.

He could give. So could she.

She could receive. She was sure he could accept that with grace too.

His breath came more quickly near her ear. "You are so small." He set his fingers on her waist, felt her butt again, squeezed. "This will be a delightful madness." His voice had roughened, grown husky.

"Ayes," Alexa said, for once very sure of her accent.

He smiled, a flash of white, even teeth. His face shifted, and she snatched for a memory. Then his soft mouth came down on hers and her mind spun away and she let the sensation rule.

His kiss was soft, testing, first pressing against her lips, then withdrawing. He swept his tongue across her mouth and she surrendered to him, to his tenderness, to his desire, to her own needs so suddenly unlocked.

She opened her mouth wide and accepted his probing tongue, caught it and sucked it and drew the taste of him into her to savor.

He groaned softly. "Let's take this inside. I want to feel you. More."

She wanted to feel him too, over her, under her, *in* her. Covering her with his body, blocking all thought and all responsibilities and all considerations of tomorrow. Her hands shaped his shoulders, slid to the back of his nape to play with his hair. Then she speared her fingers into his thick mane. Textures. His hair was full of textures, some strands thinner and silkier than others.

He stilled. "Do you still want me?"

"What—?" What was he talking about? Of course she wanted him. She stroked his face. His mouth had set into a flat line.

"Is your need so great that any man will do, even a black-and-white?"

"Huh?" She framed his face with her hands; smooth skin with the slight roughness around the jaw of incipient beard. "Yu arhhh bee-yu-tee-ful."

"I'm a black-and-white," he said.

She sniffed in disdain, "Shtupid." She tugged his hair. "Feels great. More kisses... Ah haven't had kisses that sing to me for a long time."

Now his mouth quirked. He set a muscular arm behind her body and lifted to bend her back, curving her lower body hard and intimately against him. She whimpered at the contact, the fierce anticipation that sizzled in her blood. Her back was bowed and he took her mouth, rougher now, parting her lips, thrusting with his tongue, letting her feel the edge of his teeth.

Heat filled her. She grabbed his hair with both hands.

He laughed into her mouth. Laughed! She was ablaze with desire and he was playing games.

Her feet didn't touch the ground as he whirled her into his arms. Great move. He had a lot of great moves, with hands and tongue and body. She supposed she should be concerned, but nothing mattered except slaking this great need for sex, for intimacy.

"I *will* assure you that all those old legends about black-and-whites are true." He chuckled and hurried sure-footedly across the cobblestones. "We are phenomenal lovers. Women just have to get past the fear of taking a lover with wild magic."

She didn't doubt it.

The stables were too dark to see a thing, and smelled of the sweet musk of volarans. Another different scent for her. He flung her into the air and she shrieked until she sensed the strong lift of magic that whisked her down onto a soft cushion. He was there in an instant. More magic. She spared a brief thought for how magic could change sex, then forgot everything as he came down on her.

The sheer pleasure of his weight, of someone close, of a *man* close, made her gasp. She felt too good to protest.

His legs spread hers until his arousal settled where she needed it most. Just the pressure of him drove her higher. She reached up, found his head and brought his mouth back down to hers.

She *needed*. She needed him more in that moment than she needed anything else Lladrana had given her. His warmth. His simple desire for her as a woman. His honesty.

Sliding her fingers through his hair as she sucked on his full lower lip, she reveled in the textures. Using the tips of her fingers, she traced his bone structure. Elegant. Yes, he was beautiful. She wished she could see the golden tone of his skin, the brown-black of his eyes.

Then he rocked his hips and nothing mattered except the climb to bliss.

His hands released the clasp of her cloak, undid the tie at the top of her dress, then slid under the breast-strip and covered her breasts.

She shuddered in delight as he palmed her. Flesh touching flesh, finally. But it wasn't enough.

Her fingers were fast and agile as she rid him of his cloak. She pushed at him and he rolled and she was on top of him and yanking his shirt from him and throwing it aside and sliding her hands all over his firm chest and—

Feeling a lot of scars.

A small cry of distress escaped her. His larger hands covered hers, brought them back to his chest, to his nipples. She rubbed. He bucked and groaned.

But she touched his face again, the smoothness of it, even as her other hand traced old wounds.

"I've been lucky," he said, his voice raspy. "But I believe we are both thinking too much. Time for action. Time only for feeling. I need to be in you or I'll die."

He set her aside and, with an oath, stripped off his pants. She scrambled to find him. Touched the hard muscle of his arm.

His fingers hooked in the neckline of her dress and ripped it from her. Then he lifted her and brought her down on him.

They both whimpered in passion.

Only mindless heat. Only the rough climb. Only hard thrusts.

Just as she was at the edge, she saw two huge, beautiful crystals. The crystals resonated, drew close, touched.

Exploded.

Alexa climaxed. Behind her eyelids, little shards like rainbows drifted and sparkled.

She went limp and fell on him. Above the pounding blood in her ears, the fast thud of his heart, she heard him give a long, low moan.

They lay together in a damp tangle.

"Merde," he said, more prayer than curse.

For a moment her heart clutched. This was now *the after*. How would he treat the after? How would she? With grace? She hoped with all her heart that it would be so, and wanted to curse herself at the return of reason.

He rolled a little and she lay loosely beside him. He tucked her close to his body, her head pillowed on a strong shoulder.

"I'm Bastien Vauxveau."

Shock zipped through her to her toes. He wasn't a nameless, uncomplicated lover. This could mean trouble.

He laughed harshly. "You go stiff. I suppose you've heard of my esteemed father, the Lord Knight Marshall of Castle." He snorted.

Obviously she had to say something, but she didn't know if her tongue still worked after such incredible sex. She sure wasn't thinking in Lladranan. Her mouth worked a couple of times before she could form the words. "Yes, and of your brother Luthan, and of you."

Bastien shifted a little. "I hope I lived up to my reputation," he purred.

Alexa cleared her throat. "I think you've lived *down* to it."

With that, he sent a questing hand down her body, touching her nipples, sliding over her stomach to the delta between her legs.

"I *can* go down."

"Not neshesh—necessary," she croaked, completely aware by the tingling of every nerve in her body where his hand was, how easy it would be for him to sweep her up the road of passion again.

"And who do I have the pleasure of pleasuring?" He continued to put a purr in his tones. What was *with* the men of this country, anyway, that they could wring emotions from her with just their voices?

His left arm jiggled her a little, as if prompting.

"Alexa," she mumbled against his arm, and tensed, wondering if he would withdraw now.

"Very nice." No purr. He sounded distracted. His fingers went lower on her body, between her thighs, and began to work ancient, natural magic.

She reached out and found him, ready to go again. Bastien

Vauxveau. Incredible sex. And that crystal thing. Wow. Fantastic. Over the top. How could it be more than one night? So she'd better make the most of it.

This time it was faster, more intense, as if they'd both memorized exactly what the other liked best.

And this time she was ready for the vision of the crystals, shining, meeting, joining, shattering. But this time melody was added. Naturally. It was her last thought before she cuddled closer to her fabulous lover and they subsided into sleep.

She woke to his hands on her and a raging need. She pulled him upon her, needing to feel him. She might be alone and untouched by anyone the rest of the day, the week, but in her memory she could steep herself in the whole of him...and remember.

The weak gray light of morning insinuated itself into the room through a small window. Narrowing her eyes, she could finally *see* him, his intense expression, his heavy-lidded eyes and sensual lips. No, she hadn't forgotten how he looked, and she suspected she'd measure every Lladranan man by Bastien Vauxveau.

She grabbed his strong shoulders, ignoring scar ridges, and arched with precision, sheathing him. He closed his eyes and flung his head back, a droplet of sweat trickled down his throat. She wanted to taste all of him. She was too short. He was too strong. The need was swamped by others.

God, how he'd learned to move within her to build her desire to the limit. She panted, clung to him, focused on the dance of their bodies together. Every time it was better—too much better. Too spectacular. It couldn't continue.

But it did. He was relentless, focused on his body and hers, how they meshed, how he could move to increase their passion increment by increment. She hadn't ever been *pleasured* like this. Single-mindedly. Totally. Every sensual spot on her body singing with need. Surely she'd go mad. Die, maybe. Go mad, then die.

His skin under her hands slicked. His breath came in ragged moans, yet he gave himself as little quarter in this struggle for the ultimate climax as he did her. Control was all. Sensation was all.

She knew the shattering neared when the crystals appeared, drawing together to make a bright star.

Music started again. Her song? Was the other his? They twined together in a melody, strengthening as the crystals flowed to each other.

They touched.

Fireworks burst inside her, *were* her.

Her cry mingled with Bastien's.

He collapsed on her and she welcomed his weight, a sign of earthly reality in a fiery universe.

This time the star that was two crystals lingered.

There was a dark streak along one of the star points. It offended her. Didn't belong amidst all the lovely wonder.

She sent a lightning bolt of her jade magic to the point, splintering it. In the next instant, she grabbed crystal shards and reassembled them into new, bright angles.

Bastien jerked and howled, clutched his chest.

Alexa sat up, watching, horrified, but it was too late. She hadn't thought that she'd hurt him. She'd just seen a flaw and fixed it.

A flaw. The flaw he was born with as a black-and-white? Surely not. It wasn't that difficult to correct, so someone should have done it a long time ago.

She shouldn't have repaired it. She had no right to mess with a person's magic. She just hadn't realized.... She leaned over Bastien and stroked his bare chest, glistening with sweat that highlighted his scars.

"Are you all right?"

He grimaced, then smiled, stretched his arms and legs. "A pang is all, darlin.' I have them now and then." Picking up her fingers that played with his chest hair, he kissed her hand. "Don't usually have such *frissons* with a lady, though. Please accept my deepest apologies." Even in the dim dawn light, the red of embarrassment touched his cheeks.

Frissons. A Lladranan word she didn't know.

His smile froze, he glanced away. "I am a black-and-white, after all," he mocked himself gently.

Alexa didn't like that he put himself down. The frisson-thing must be something that manifested in "flawed" people. She bent down and brushed his lips with hers, softly, softly, tasted his mouth with her tongue and hummed approval. Then she leaned back to observe him again. This time she combed his wonderful hair with her fingers. The black strands had a different texture than the silver, and the contrast was as pleasing to the touch as it was to the eye. "You are verr-y beau-ti-ful, black-and-white," she murmured. His chest hair was vari-colored too.

His body relaxed under the covers—at least most of it did. She saw one muscle that was raring to go. Since she didn't want to discuss anything, or admit her tampering, she let him draw her mouth to his for another kiss.

"And I suspect you're still drunk, darlin'," he whispered just before their lips met and rubbed and explored.

This was much better than any explanations. She'd deal with any complications of sleeping with Bastien later. Way later.

She woke again and knew not much time had passed. Bastien still slept, so she studied him. So sweet and sexy. The sex had been fabulous, and the intimacy had filled her lonely heart. Most of all, they'd given and received equally. He'd been honest and hadn't wanted anything but a little loving. She sighed.

Time to face reality. Holding and kissing and sex and intimacy was for the one night. No matter what sort of connection she'd felt, it wouldn't last. The simplicity of being with him would be fleeting. Real life would intrude.

She should just take the gift of the night and leave. But she lingered. She liked how he looked, roughly handsome, not as elegant and classy as his brother Luthan. His cool hair, silver and black and tantalizing to the fingers. Incredible body, though scarred, strong, muscular, damn good on top and inside hers.

Wincing at the thought of the scars and how much pain he'd endured, she flopped onto her back and stared at the beams of the stable. This guy was a real hero. He'd fought and probably felt the bowel-watering fear and still fought some more. She didn't know how he did it. Frankly, she didn't want to learn.

She'd like him in her life, but quashed the thought. She'd always considered a relationship a partnership and had tried a couple on, but they hadn't lasted. Her best relationship—business partnership and deep friendship—had been with Sophie.

At the thought of Sophie, she sat up and put her head on her knees. It was easier to recall Sophie, and all the fun they'd had together, here in Lladrana, than if she were back in Colorado where everything would remind her.

Heaven knows what people thought had happened to her. Though she'd left the business in as good shape as she could have, that wasn't saying much, since half the partnership was gone. She shoved those issues aside. Nothing she could do about them.

Nicer to stare at Bastien and remember the night. They'd been great together. Maybe, just maybe, it could carry over to the light of day. A partnership would be good, and perhaps easier in Lladrana. Partis and Thealia had a great intimate partnership, as did the other Marshalls who were married. Some Chevaliers were the same.

She found she was needy, more needy than was wise. But she'd been alone so long, with everything and everyone very strange in this new world. Having as her closest companion a tiny pink fairy or a shape-shifting muff was more than a little odd. Was it too much to hope that maybe, just maybe, the intimacy with this man could last?

He snuffled beside her, drawing her attention. Even sleeping he looked like Trouble—rough and dangerously attractive. It would be better if she locked away her odd yearnings. The upset he could cause in her life, just when she thought she was coping well and had found a place she finally fit in, could be more than the great sex and whatever "bond" they had between them was worth.

But she *wanted* him. She set her teeth. This indecision wasn't like her. This emotional dependency. It may have been all too human to want a lover by your side, and she could understand her need, but it wasn't wise.

And there was the sweet Song rippling between them, meaning a bond had been formed, no matter how small.

What *was* that bond? Could it happen between a lot of people, or just a few? She knew it didn't have to be sexual, though she could understand why that would be a strong bond. Reynardus's Shield was his brother—this man's uncle—she realized. She hadn't asked the Marshalls or Sinafin or her teachers about the bond or bonds between Sword and Shield or lovers, so she only had herself to blame for being ignorant.

"You're looking too thoughtful after a night of extraordinary sex," Bastien said, smiling.

She glanced down to see him studying her.

He stretched, his left arm extending from the blankets and wrapping around her. He pulled her back down to settle next to him. She had to admit the rumor was right. He had a great way with women.

Alexa stroked his face. "Shalutationsh, Bastien."

His face went completely still. His eyes widened, narrowed. "You're the new Exotique Marshall."

It was her turn to freeze.

15

"You are the Exotique the Marshalls Summoned, aren't you." Bastien jumped from the hay and started dressing. "You must have a Jade Baton about you somewhere."

"How do you know?"

"I can see you now."

She flinched. "Of course." She kept all intonation from her voice. Racial prejudice again.

His gaze sharpened. "I didn't mean it that way."

Alexa shrugged and stood shakily. She picked up her ripped dress, hunted for her underwear.

The man cursed. "Everyone knows of the new Exotique, and my brother kept me apprised of events."

"The very honorable Luthan," she said. "Bastien who is Trouble."

His lopsided smile was completely charming.

Finished dressing, he swept her a graceful bow. "That's me."

"The rebel." She eyed his hair again. "You use the stories about black-and-whites to your own advantage."

He raised an eyebrow. "Of course."

Alexa blinked. She understood every word he said, every inflection of his voice, every nuance. Further, her tongue now mastered the language better. It was still difficult and imperfect, but she could now speak and be understood. It must be from the link during their lovemaking. No wonder the Marshalls had wanted her in bed with someone that first night. When minds and powers connected during sex, some qualities were transferred. She wondered what Bastien had got.

"I speak better now."

It was the wrong thing to say. He stared down at her. "Merde, the Marshalls set this up, didn't they. And you were oh-so-willing. I should have guessed, but my magic is wild, it fluctuates. Sorry, the plan won't work."

Her spine stiffened. She enunciated each word. "I did not seduce you. I did not even know you were here."

His eyes narrowed. "Didn't you?" His lip curled. "You were a very convenient damsel in distress last night."

She recalled the spider web—how natural was it? Shook her head, it wasn't important in this discussion. She lifted her chin. "I did *not* plan this."

He raised his eyebrows. "Then the Marshalls did. They used us both. And they'd continue to use me if I hung around. I won't do that. Nothing will make me stay. When you Pairbond with someone, he will be your Sword or Shield. Fight with you and the Marshalls. You come with too many complications, Lady."

Just what she'd felt about him, but she'd been willing to take a chance. Now he was rejecting her.

So much for any intimacy, for any pitiful bond *she'd* felt. All illusion. Story of her life. Anger, hot then cold, swept her. "I would not dream of keeping you."

"Good." His scan of her was long and penetrating. "I can't believe I didn't know it was you. Maybe I didn't want to. Maybe there was a befuddling spell?"

"I don't know such a spell," Alexa said through gritted teeth.

He shrugged. "Doesn't matter, this stupidity won't go any further."

Humiliation and anger bubbled through her. She'd never had a one-night stand. She'd never had someone leave her so fast. True rejection.

He slid down the ladder and led his volaran out of its stall. With a quick tuneful whistle it was saddled.

Alexa crawled to the edge of the loft and peered down at him. "Thanks for the fu—" She got the correct, derogatory word from his mind but just couldn't say it. She'd thought it had been more than sex. He'd been tender, charming. She had thought they'd shared real intimacy. She licked her lips and substituted another word. "Thanks for the sex. It helped me immensely." Her clenched fists were out of sight.

He turned back and looked nearly as angry as she did. The slant of sunlight coming through the half-opened door lit the silver in his hair, creating a blazing white aura.

Bastien bowed low with a sweep of his ugly hat. Though she didn't know all the nuances of bows, she was sure he scoffed.

"My pleasure, Lady Marshall."

Then he and his prime volaran disappeared from view.

She *hurt,* and wondered how in heaven she had gotten emotionally tangled up with him in just one night. Maybe it wasn't just last night. Maybe it had started even earlier…the night she saved him. A lot of people believed that saving another's life formed a bond. *She* remembered doing the deed, but it didn't seem that he did. He'd been out of it that night, so it wasn't surprising. Nothing in the land of Lladrana would drag the fact that she'd saved his hide out of her. She couldn't bear that he might feel a burden and look at her with forced gratitude.

But that wasn't the problem. The problem was that she *felt* something for him—some emotion that she didn't want to scrutinize. Felt a bond to him, more than to anyone else on Lladrana, even Sinafin—and just from sex. That was scary. What sort of hold on her could he have through sex if he pursued this affair? A *good* thing that he wanted to walk away—okay, face facts, he was running away as fast as he could, *flying* away. Could he have used magic on her? Since a black-and-white was supposed to have strange energies, maybe he had bewitched her without meaning to. Not good for her.

Good that he was flying away home— Shit! His home was next to hers. She muttered a few more Anglo-Saxon words at this turn of events, then remembered he spent little time at his estate and more in the battlefield. She didn't think he'd be knocking on her door to borrow anything, and she certainly wasn't going to traipse over to his place.

Time to shove the emotions aside and skate on a flippant surface, concentrate on shallow thoughts. She looked disgustedly at the dress he'd torn off her. She had her breast-strip, and the panties she'd insisted on having made, but she couldn't see slinking into the inn clothed only in underwear and a cloak. Besides, she had liked the dress a lot. It was very comfortable and a bright blue that flattered her very pale coloring.

She chewed her bottom lip and tried to recall a mending spell. It was really a healing spell to be used on rent flesh, but it should work on cloth too.

She started humming, remembered the three-note memory key to prompt the spell. Then the whole tune came. With a tip of her finger shooting jade energy, she ran it down the rip and watched in great satisfaction as the fabric rewove itself. It only took a minute, and such a small amount of energy, that she'd recharge it just by walking back to the inn, drawing on earth energy.

It still amazed her that she could tap into energy from the natural elements—earth, fire, water, even air sometimes, though that was the hardest for her. There were a lot of cool things about magic and Lladrana—including acceptable plumbing. Right now she really needed a shower.

She dressed quickly, descended the ladder. Volarans peeked over a couple of stalls and whickered. She greeted them, then left the stables to step into another gray day. Except for a couple of vacations, she'd always lived in Denver, where the sun shone an average of three hundred days a year. This gray weather wore on her nerves. But at least it wasn't raining.

When she reached her room, Sinafin sat in the middle of Alexa's bed, a big, fat, white Persian cat. Sinafin grinned, a grin all the more irritating because it was cat-smug.

Have a good night? Sinafin purred.

"It was a great night. This morning hasn't been so hot." Alexa stripped and ducked into the small corner bathroom, which held a shower cubicle. Turning the water on hot and hard, she decided to spare her vocal cords and communicate mentally with Sinafin. *I told you I don't like it when you become Mrs. Morris's cat.*

That cat had been the bane of her existence when she'd been fostered by Mrs. Morris. Arguments about the cat had led to Mrs. Morris passing Alexa on to someone else. Just as well. Mrs. Morris had treated the cat better than any child she'd ever fostered— at least she'd given it more affection.

I felt like a cat this morning, Sinafin said.

Great. Dumped by a one-night stand most gracelessly, and now stuck with a snotty cat. *Where are the others?*

*I told them you were sleeping in. They are shopping for supplies in
the city.*

Relief fluttered through Alexa. At least her humiliation
wouldn't be public. The water streaming over her refreshed her,
cleansing her of the sweat of man and sex. Good.

Where is Bastien? Sinafin asked, purring again.

Alexa snapped the faucets off, grabbed a towel to scrub her
body so only her own scent rose to her nostrils. She tromped into
the bedroom. Sinafin was lying on her back in the middle of the
bed, front paws curled over a fat stomach, back paws sticking
straight up, looking at Alexa upside down. Sinafin did cat very
well.

"How did you know about Bastien?" Stupid question—Sinafin
knew everything. Alexa recalled Bastien's words. "Did you use a
befuddling spell?"

The cat didn't reply. Jeez, she really hated when Sinafin was a cat.

Alexa asked, "Did you cast a spell on us to make love?"

Sinafin purred. *No. I would not flout your free will.*

"Huh. Bastien's gone, taken off into the blue."

That got action. Sinafin rolled to a crouch, whipped her tail
back and forth, growled. She stared at Alexa, then her whiskers
twitched and her big blue eyes narrowed. *You corrected his energy
stream. He will be very powerful now.*

"Good for him." Alexa dug out her brush, went to a mirror and
pulled it through the tangles of her hair.

He is good for you too.

"The operative word here is *was*. Past tense." God, she was glad
she could talk to Sinafin and use a large vocabulary, not halting,
short words in Lladranan. "We *had* great sex. He *was* a wonderful
lover. He *was* a...jerk this morning. He couldn't get away from me
fast enough." That sounded like a whine. She would not whine over
a man, especially a man she'd known so briefly.

Everything about him was past tense. She had to get a grip. One night of hot sex and adieus shouldn't wind her up like this, even if she'd never before had a one-nighter.

Sinafin leaped off the bed to cross over to a chest under the bay window, craning her head to look outside. *He is gone.*

"Told you so." Now that felt good. Telling off Mrs. Morris's cat and having the damn thing know what Alexa meant. Alexa pulled from her bag her "longies," the shirt and tights worn under chain mail, and put them on.

The cat turned back to her, stared at Alexa, then back out the window. *There is a melody spinning between you.*

Alexa shrugged. She didn't think so.

He will be back.

Alexa snorted. "See if I care." But she'd decided. "I'm tired of traveling. It's time we return to the Castle." She was ready to study hard, fight hard, win her place in this world, prove to everyone, including a sweet-loving, hardheaded man, that she was the best Exotique ever Summoned.

Joan of Arc step aside, Alexa had hit town.

She trained and studied determinedly. When the alarm that called the Castle to arms clanged, she took the Field on horse-back—four times the first week. She worked with a Sword and Shield team as an extra Shield, learning all the defensive tricks. Oddly enough, working with Mace and his lady was the easiest on everyone. Unsurprisingly, Reynardus refused to link with her.

Alexa also Paired with various Chevaliers. She and Luthan were a competent but uninspired team. She thought she'd have trouble connecting mentally with the man—son of Reynardus and brother to Bastien—but the bond was smooth and comfortable.

After the battles, Alexa walked the land and examined the fenceposts—those fallen and dead and those still pulsing with vitality. The inert ones were interesting to look at, but told her nothing. When she touched the live ones, there was something about them that she almost recognized, like an answer to a test question lurking in the back of her brain. And like such an answer, it couldn't be forced.

In her rooms at night she studied the Lorebook of Fenceposts, read each word for hidden meaning. She looked at the pictures— excellent drawings of individual fenceposts. The battlefields were familiar—near the gray-green ocean, or with mountains towering in the background, dotted with trees, oak, brithenwood and pine.

One morning during her second full week back, Alexa sat cross-legged on a thick pile of carpets in a small chamber with her magical professor, Madame Fourmi. Alexa was pretty sure she'd progressed from Magic 101 to Advanced Spelltuning. Of her various lessons, magic was her favorite, mostly because it was less "kill" oriented. Learning to ride a horse wasn't too bad either, except that it made her body hurt, and she'd much rather have a headache or energy drains from magic than an aching body.

To add a surface familiarity, she'd made up names for the other classes—Learning to Be a Marshall (Shield Defense), Teamwork with Marshalls and Chevaliers (Level Two), and The Language of Lladrana. She still disliked the language lessons the most, though she was progressing satisfactorily, up to a C+.

"Very well, Alyeka, breathe deeply and center yourself," Madame said now, giving her standard instructions.

Alexa could take three breaths and fall into a light trance where logic didn't whisper that magic was crap and where she could access her magical energies. This was the best state in which to learn the skills she needed.

She met Madame's eyes. "I'd like to ask a couple of questions and see if we can't solve a problem that's bothering me."

Madame looked intrigued. Alexa had gone along with the syllabus until now.

"Ayes?"

"Is there a process where I could lock away some memories or emotions so they don't affect me?" She'd had some miserable nights dreaming of Bastien. He had revived her interest in sex all too well, but she sure didn't need to relive again and again the humiliation of their last scene. Not to mention the nightmares where she fought monsters and awoke in a cold sweat.

"Are you speaking of fear? Being an intelligent woman, you must realize there are good reasons for fear."

Yeah, it triggered adrenaline to prepare her body for combat, and she didn't like it, but she'd sure use it. She chose her words carefully.

"I am most concerned with the rejection I feel when I meet certain Lladranans. Occasionally it is instant revulsion on their part. I can't change what they feel, but I can change my reaction. When this occurs it distracts me. If it happens on the battlefield it could be fatal." She'd thought up her logic beforehand.

Madame pursed her lips, but there was a softening in her eyes. She'd have heard how a Marshall had attacked Alexa and been killed the first night she was on Lladrana.

"Ayes, there is a way to do this—to separate the emotional content of memories, or use a keyword to set aside emotional reactions."

"Good!" What was the use of magic if it couldn't enhance her life?

Tapping a finger to her lips, Madame considered Alexa. "You know, there was once an Exotique who was Summoned who disliked looking alien so much that over the course of several years he was able to gradually change the color of his skin and his eyes. Even his bone structure. Would you want to do this?"

"Ttho!" She wasn't any beauty, but was happy with her appearance, even her prematurely silver hair. She just got tired of the stares, hated the revulsion, and would gladly tuck Bastien's rejection into a lockbox deep inside and throw away the key.

"Very good." Madame nodded approval.

"Very good" had been her highest praise so far, though if she hadn't been a good teacher and Alexa hadn't respected her, Alexa would have asked for someone else. She didn't think they'd ever be friends, but they got along well enough. Alexa would have added her to her holiday card list with some of her other profs.

With a tilt of her head, Madame said, "We might also consider a small spell rather like a 'glamour.' It would initially make you more 'likable' upon first impression, then gradually wear off as the individual came to know you."

Madame rubbed her hands. "A challenge. I knew you would be a challenge, Alyeka." She smiled widely. "Of course, if a person took a dislike to you, it would not sway them." She slipped back into her standard serious mode. "As for those who…have an extreme reaction to you, we can prepare your response, and I will teach you how to separate your emotions from the memory. But I believe it would be wise for you to know of their repugnance and be on guard."

"Yeah, shurr," Alexa replied, knowing her speech sounded slurred. Hearing and comprehending Lladranan was much better since sex with Bastien, but her speech still fluctuated.

"Very well. We will start on a meditation exercise, then segue into the spelltune you wish to learn."

A tune—that meant it would be of medium difficulty. Not a few notes of a simple spell, and not a long, laborious major Song.

"Very well," Alexa echoed, and an hour later she could look back on that last scene with Bastien and feel nothing at all.

* * *

Bastien lay in the hospital bed in the northernmost Chevalier Clinique of Lladrana. The building was a simple rectangle, the only floor a hospital ward with beds on each side of the wall and a tiny office in the back. The walls were a little too pink for his taste, so he usually looked at the white ceiling.

He'd tried to put the country between him and the woman he'd made love with and who had mended his flaw. Looking back, sampling the Song between them, he knew she'd spoken the truth when she'd said she hadn't planned to seduce him. He also believed it hadn't been set up by the Marshalls. They'd have followed up by now. Sheer coincidence. Or his wild magic at work. But he'd felt trapped and wanted to run, so he had.

He'd tested his Powers in battle, taking risks he shouldn't have, trying to learn his new limitations.

Now he was in trouble. His brother had found him.

He could tell Luthan was in a bad mood just by the quick ringing of his spurs on the stone floor. Bastien turned a groan into a sigh and refused to open his eyes, flinging an arm across his face in an effort to avoid his brother's gaze.

He yelped at the pulling pain on his triceps.

"I've heard you've been courting death. Are you crazy?" asked Luthan.

"I'm a black-and-white," Bastien said.

"You use that as an excuse. Just what are you doing? Are you trying to kill yourself? If so, I would like an updated copy of your will to file with the Chevalier Loremaster. You look worse than our father, and *he* has forty more years of fighting than you."

Bastien would have sighed but knew his ribs couldn't take it. His brother was so stern and upright. The silence stretched, and though it was comfortable between them, the quiet was unusual. Carefully, Bastien removed his arm from his eyes.

Luthan studied him with narrowed gaze. Then he smiled. "But you aren't a black-and-white anymore. The brilliance you were gifted with by being so shines true and strong, unimpeded by any block to your energy flow." He spotted a chair near the next bed, drew it over and sat. "This is very interesting."

Luthan took on a patient stillness, trance-deep in his own Power, and closed his eyes.

Bastien stared. It wasn't like Luthan to leave himself so vulnerable, even with Bastien and in a place guarded by Chevaliers and dogs.

If Luthan was seeking his *sight* the matter of Bastien being cured was more important to others than just the two of them.

Bastien shifted uncomfortably. He had known he'd changed, but hadn't wanted to acknowledge it. Most of all, he didn't want to admit that it was the woman who had changed him.

But his mind worked faster, clearer than before. It scared him that he was no longer the man he'd been. He'd taken chances that should have killed him...but hadn't.

His brother started to hum, slow and lilting, making the space between Bastien's shoulder blades tingle as if an arrow were pointed at his back. When Luthan used that Song it was bad news for Bastien.

It was *their* Song, the Song of the sons of Reynardus Vauxveau, the Song they'd made between them and shared. When big brother Luthan hummed that song and used his Power he was always right. He always won the argument and Bastien lost.

He wanted to pull the covers over his head. He had a bad feeling about this. He was sure Luthan would want him to do something he didn't want to do. Like see the woman again.

As he'd flown away from the Exotique who'd sizzled his blood, melted his bones, and straightened out his energy flows, he'd assured himself he wasn't a coward, and knew he lied. It didn't matter that she was an Exotique, or that she was powerful. It mattered very much that she was a Marshall.

He'd tried very hard not to think about how they'd come together, to forget the best sex of his life.

Luthan's eyes opened and he grinned. "Will you look at that."

Merde. Bastien could plainly see the sparkling magical line— shining white, coming from his balls and his heart and his head, merging and shooting out of sight. In the direction of the Castle. Luthan had shown him what he hadn't wanted to see.

"You have a connection. I can guess to whom."

Bastien kept his face stony.

Luthan leaned forward. "I know, Bastien."

It was a losing battle, but he fought anyway. "You can't know."

"I *saw.*"

One of Luthan's visions. Worse and worse. Bastien said, "I don't want to hear about that."

"You don't want anything. Especially nothing that's good for you. So you try to forget in battle. That won't work, brother."

Luthan had tried the same thing after he'd left their father's house. That time, Bastien had deliberately gotten into enough trouble to need Luthan's rescue. After that, Luthan had accepted his responsibilities and turned into the most honorable Chevalier.

"It's odd that our father hasn't noticed the connection, but he hasn't been looking for it." Luthan studied the thread. "It's very thin, but strong. Must have been at least two meetings and an exchange of blood or other bodily fluids."

Though Bastien hadn't admitted it to Alexa, he vaguely remembered that she had rescued him from the jerir. He wondered if he'd bled on her somehow, or if the jerir connected them somehow too. As for the other time— His cock twitched just thinking about it, which was why he tried to forget.

"I wonder when that happened and how." Luthan tilted his head. "No one knows. You were always a wonder, Bastien."

Quiet for ten heartbeats.

Luthan stood up, pulled his riding gloves from his belt and drew them on. "Go to the Castle and formally Pair with her. Make that connection stronger."

"There is no connection."

With one whistling note Luthan plucked at a cord deep within his body and had Bastien arching out of bed. "You can't deny that. Not to me. Not to yourself. Not anymore. I won't let you."

Bastien had been afraid of that.

Luthan got in his face. "We need Marshall Alyeka Paired sexually and with a fighter. Go to the Castle, accept your destiny. You will be an excellent Swordmarshall." He straightened.

Bastien could feel the look of stubbornness mold his features, his bottom lip stick out. Childish, but satisfying. What was it about relatives that always brought out the child?

"The North needs good fighters, needs me."

"I will not allow you to continue to try to throw your life away," Luthan said.

"Oh?"

"If you leave this place for anywhere except your own estate or the Castle, I will have the Singer's Chevaliers hunt you down and take you to her for a forced Song Quest."

"You can't do that."

"Yes, I can." Luthan's smile was smug. "I have the trust of the Singer. By the way, she is interested in you, as is a certain feycoocu. If I were you I would not irritate either one of them."

"A feycoocu? Marshall Alexa's feycoocu?" He hadn't seen her in the stable, had a wavery memory of a blue light near the jerir pool, of eyes looking down from the rafters of the Assayer's Office.

"And shapeshifters are as unpredictable as Exotiques and black-and-whites." Luthan flicked his fingers in goodbye and exited on a laugh.

Bastien fell back against a hard pillow. Luthan was obviously enjoying the hell out of this. *Merde.*

16

"Today we will study the movement of air," Madame Fourmi said as Alexa entered the chamber where she took her magic lessons.

The air in the room was stuffy and held a heaviness that oppressed. The air outside had been spring fresh with a light breeze carrying the scent of newly turned soil and blossoms.

Everything in Alexa rebelled. "I don't think so," she said, then smiled widely. "Not today. I think I'll explore the Castle instead."

Madame raised little pointed eyebrows. "That is perhaps not wise. You need to learn all you can as quickly as possible."

"A person can't be wise all the time," Alexa replied. She took a stride back into the hall and ran lightly along the passageway and down some stairs, and rocketed out of the building into the Temple Ward.

She had no doubt that *someone* would keep a mental eye on her—maybe Madame, maybe Thealia—but Alexa didn't think they'd interfere. She'd always been a perfect little student. They'd cut her some slack.

It was a great day to ditch class. She abandoned the cloister walk. She hadn't explored the Castle yet, and wanted to know her surroundings. She'd think of it as a walk around campus. She chuckled and lifted her face to the sun, closing her eyes.

For a moment she relaxed, breathing deeply, letting her senses rest, though she felt magic—Power, they called it—all around her. When she opened her eyelids she noted the gazes of the soldiers and Chevaliers. She didn't care. Being an Exotique had some privileges and one was acting as strange as she wanted to. She'd lost a lot of her self-consciousness. Maybe because she'd begun to fit in. There were no Marshalls around.

She sauntered to the north end of Temple Ward. By now she knew the Castle was made up of three courtyards—wards. There were also a couple of cul-de-sacs, like Horseshoe Close in Lower Ward where the Chevaliers stayed.

Temple Ward was the middle courtyard, and the places she usually went were in the yard—the Marshalls' living space, including her tower, the eating hall, the kitchen and the Council Room. The magical map room Thealia haunted was across the ward from the Keep. Of course there was the Temple itself, huge and round and dominating everything else. There was also the Assayer's Office, which she avoided.

She'd been in the Lower Ward several times, mostly passing through, and had seen Horseshoe Close and Hall, gone out to the Chevaliers training ground and the Landing Field.

But she didn't recall ever being in Upper Ward, so it drew her feet today. She passed the curve of the Temple and approached a gatehouse between two small towers. Smiling at the soldiers on duty, she greeted them and passed through the small building, then stopped to survey the courtyard.

It was a skewed rectangular shape, with the left set of buildings against the wall that probably defined the edge of the hill on which the Castle was built. She thought most of the servants lived here.

The right wall bulged with the huge curve of the back of the Temple. Little storage areas seemed to crowd in the straight sides of the available space.

She walked until she reached the very end of the ward and found a wall with a wooden door bound with iron. With a tug and an application of magic, the door opened outward. She peeked through to see a charming tangle of vines showing large buds of green draping courtyard walls that angled to a point.

When she sniffed, the scent of spring wafted to her. Smiling, she entered the garden. She was halfway across it before she realized it wasn't empty.

On a stone bench a man slumped against the wall, staring at her with a serious, lonely gaze. A Marshall—Shieldmarshall Ivrog Vauxveau, brother to Reynardus and uncle to Bastien and Luthan. This was the man who kept Reynardus from death, who defended him on the battlefield.

"I didn't mean to intrude," she said, pronouncing her words carefully. "Should I go?"

With a graceful gesture, Shieldmarshall Ivrog invited her to sit beside him on the bench in the garden. Feeling a little uncomfortable, but curious, Alexa did. For a while they sat in silence.

Since she'd joined the Marshalls, she'd come to value all of them except Reynardus, and since this man was bonded to Reynardus, she'd never learned to know him.

He gave her a slow, sweet smile that amazed her. Rumor painted him as an angry, bitter drunk. Unobtrusively she sniffed for the smell of liquor.

Not unobtrusively enough. He laughed, then sank back against the sun-warmed wall again and closed his eyes. "I'm not drunk and won't be in the future. You've changed my life, Lady." He found her hand and held it.

A huge orchestral melody swamped Alexa. She'd never mentally "heard" anything like it. Even when the Marshalls wove a Song between them, deep and rich, it was never more than six "instruments," one for each Pair. She swallowed, but the music was so fascinating that she didn't pull away.

She could almost, almost grasp the Song of the Vauxveau family—that's what the melody had to be, the whole, rich tunes of each family member that this man knew and carried. She sensed he was tied to them all at this very moment—a live performance. Reynardus, of course, was the strongest, a trumpet, but she was surprised to understand that neither Luthan nor Bastien were overwhelmed by Reynardus in any way. The smallest, threadiest noise was that of Reynardus's wife, a whining, plaintive note.

For a moment she just listened, and as she relaxed and let the music take her, she closed her eyes and could actually "see" it. It appeared like a living tapestry, woven of individual threads.

Reynardus was the rusty fox red of his tunic, the color of the Vauxveaus for ages.

Luthan was a deeper red, more like a maroon. He was the heir. Would his vibration turn red when he ascended?

Bastien was midnight blue approaching black, with glints of silver as his complex Song twisted and turned.

And the man beside her was pale blue, the blue of a hot Colorado summer sky.

Fumbling with her Power, Alexa tried to "see" into the past. There wasn't much there. The threads led into darkness in the past, yet she sensed that Bastien's Song had been kinked and uneven, and Ivrog's nearly flat and gray. Now they were both vibrant.

She opened her eyes and the pastel colors of new spring in the garden around her were pale and uninspiring in comparison.

Ivrog didn't stir beside her, but said, "Did you see your Song?"

Alexa sat up straight. "Mine?"

He chuckled. "You are a slow pattern of notes, very infrequent, but twining about Bastien's still. You and he have a bond. If I were to guess, I'd say it was a sex bond of very limited duration, but a strong connection forged between you all the same." He squeezed her fingers. "Do you want to 'see'?"

Alexa pulled away. The Power had taken her warmth as a price for seeing the melody. She was cold now, all the way to her lips. "No."

"It's not everyone who can see the melodies that bind us together. It's my special gift, one not valued much—not a very great gift. But I sense that you come from a people more visual."

With TV and films that was true. "Yeah," she said. "I guess so."

"Perhaps that's why I was given this gift. To help you. Now that you have 'seen' the melodies once, you will always be able to do so. Your mind has learned the skill. Will this benefit you?"

She was pretty sure she'd be able to figure out the patterns and connections around her more easily now. "Yes. My thanks, Shield-marshall Ivrog."

"So I've repaid you for helping me," he said.

She cleared her throat. "How?"

He opened eyes that were the lightest she'd seen in Lladrana, an amber brown.

"You came and changed Reynardus's song. Because of you he was forced to visit the Singer. And while he was in the Singer's Cloisters, he was away from me." A long sigh escaped him. "For the first time in decades, he was not so close, not there to carp or criticize. It gave me time to see myself for what I'd become and start changing. Then there's Bastien."

Alexa stood up. "I don't think——"

"We won't talk about your connection, if you don't want to, and I won't tell anyone of it. People could know if they looked or listened closely, but I doubt they will." He grinned. "Your melody is not of the world of Amee. Your Song does not flow the way we expect. It corkscrews."

"Figures," Alexa muttered. "I suppose it's purple."

Ivrog closed his eyes, frowned. "It changes color. You aren't of Lladrana yet."

"Okay."

"But back to Bastien. You mended his Song, smoothed his tangled thread. Something I don't think the rest of the family has realized either. He was in dire straits during a fight and reached for anyone who could help——unconsciously, I think. I gave him my energy. When all was done, his triumph blazed through me and it cured me. So simple. I have no more craving for drink."

He unfolded himself from the stone bench, and as he stood, she saw for the first time that he was the tallest member of his family, taller than Reynardus.

Ivrog placed a hand over his heart and bowed. "I will always be grateful."

She flushed and rose to her feet.

"Very beautiful," he said simply. "Your coloring."

They stood in the lovely silent garden, looking at each other, and Alexa felt peace emanate from him.

"I know everyone you meet tells you how much we need you, and the Marshalls expect you to find a way to revitalize our boundary. That was the Singer's prophecy, that you could keep the invading horrors out. But I would have you know that you have other gifts for touching and helping our people. You saved Farentha, the independent Chevalier. You mended Bastien, and by that, you helped me. Thank you."

Tears rose to the back of her throat at his quiet tone. "You're very welcome."

He nodded. "It is good we shared this time together. Now when you try to link with Reynardus, I know you better and can ease the bond."

"My thanks to you," Alexa said, feeling uncomfortable. No one had thanked her for anything since she'd gotten here and she hadn't realized how much she'd needed validation from these people.

Now that she had it from Ivrog, she wasn't quite sure how to handle the "you're welcome" gracefully. She gave him back a little bow. "Fare well," she said.

His lips curved and he settled back onto the stone bench in the sun. "And you."

The garden was noticeably cooler to her now, though Ivrog didn't seem affected. Probably since she'd spent energy "learning" her new skill visualizing the Song-bonds between people.

As she left the little courtyard for Upper Ward, she realized that she'd had a magic lesson after all. Madame would be pleased.

During the next few days, Alexa looked at the unattached male Chevaliers with new eyes, considering them as lovers.

Since she was now very wealthy and of high status, and looked to remain that way, she was a good catch. Further, she was still an unpaired Marshall. The man who bonded with her would be sure to become a Marshall in his own right and might find the Testing process easier than others.

There were several men who had asked her on a date—a couple of soldiers at the Castle, a couple of noblemen, and four or five Chevaliers. It was as if she were wearing a sign saying "I'm available." They seemed to sense she was looking around. For a fighting partner and a bed partner if nothing else. The one Alexa liked most was Faucon Creusse. So she accepted when he asked for a second date.

Alexa met Faucon at the Nom de Nom. He escorted her to one of the back tables with the elegance of a nobleman deferring to a princess. She liked it, a lot. She liked *him* a lot. And the nobleman bit wasn't too far off the mark. Like many Chevaliers, he had a rank and a title and an estate, but she hadn't quite figured out the system. He seated her in the back booth of the tavern and took his place opposite her, facing the room. Now she knew it for the protective gesture it was and felt touched.

When Faucon lifted a hand and a man with a superior air glided to them, she guessed Faucon was pretty high on the noble list. The servant carried a tea set. Alexa caught the fragrance of steeping tea and she nearly moaned. The tea she'd received from the Trademaster had been good, hearty stuff, but nothing special, and she'd used it all.

She hoarded her small stash of teabags as if they were gold. She only had one Assam bag left, and the lowly emergency store brand bags were now treasures.

The man set fine china cups and saucers before her and Faucon, and poured a stream of golden brown liquid into each. Alexa's nose twitched. Her mouth watered.

"My valet, Broullard." Faucon gestured.

Alexa hoped her mouth hadn't fallen open. *Valet?* Had he actually said the word? She repeated it. "Valet?"

"Yes, quite estimable, and an excellent fighter too."

An edge of Broullard's mouth lifted. He nodded to her, and she nodded back. Both Broullard and Faucon wore tailor-made flying leathers of the highest quality with shirt and trousers underneath of richly patterned silk.

"Broullard will be overseeing our meal." Faucon smiled and a dimple flashed. "I had some delicacies flown in from my estate. Some foods I don't think you've sampled yet."

Uh-oh. She sure hoped she didn't disgrace herself. So far the food had been fine, something she hadn't thought much about, good and filling and tasty. But now she wondered how her stomach would take "delicacies."

Broullard put a tile trivet on the table, acting as if it weren't scarred by generations of Chevaliers. He placed the teapot on the tile. "Hauteur." Broullard nodded. That was Faucon's title. "Marshall." Another nod. "I am needed in the kitchen." He glided away.

When she'd agreed to a date with Faucon at the Nom de Nom she'd had no idea that it would be such a production. Live and learn. They sat in a pool of relative quiet, and no one seemed to be watching them. Alexa could only guess that in this time of war, a quiet social date was respected. Or maybe it was just that the Chevaliers were as eager for her to Pair with someone as the Marshalls were.

She'd worked with several males and females, including Faucon, but no Pairing had really clicked as a fighting team. She hadn't wanted to Pair with anyone and have them become her Sword or Shield.

Everyone wondered about the Snap. If she Paired with someone, it was much more unlikely that when the Snap came, she'd let it take her away from Lladrana. Sinafin repeated to Alexa that the timing of the Snap was incalculable, individual to each Exotique, so Alexa had put it from her mind.

"Alyeka." Faucon put his hand over hers and drew her back into the moment. "You must know that I find you very attractive. Fascinating and unique." His fingers stroked the back of her hand. His gaze sizzled with male interest.

"Thank you." So being an Exotique could work the other way too. Some men would be turned on by her unusual looks and background. That was interesting.

With Faucon covering her left hand with his, she used her right to pick up her tea and sip. The taste was *so* wonderful that she had to keep from gulping it. How easily she'd gotten used to fine teas from around Earth.

The habit of drinking tea had been both a declaration that she was an adult and her own person, and a statement that she was someone more than an orphan shuffled around in foster homes.

She lifted her cup to him in a personal toast. "And thank you for the tea. It's exquisite."

He flushed, squeezed her hand, and she wondered if he could answer some questions. Delicately she placed her cup in the saucer and smiled a guileless smile that she'd practiced for hours and had hoped to use on pompous attorneys and hostile witnesses. She'd been operating too much on instinct to use it her first days in Lladrana, and now Reynardus wouldn't buy it.

"You must have heard that the Lord Marshall Reynardus and I occasionally are at odds." Big understatement. "Tell me what you know of the Vauxveaus."

Faucon's glance sharpened. "The Lord Marshall has a wife and two sons. He is a difficult man to work with." He took enough time to pick his words. "I trained under him a season. He is more impatient with those who aren't his equal."

When Faucon looked back at her, she saw a gleam of humor in his eyes. He shrugged. "And who of us is equal to a man of great Power who is one of the richest in Lladrana, of the highest rank, and has proved himself in battle for over forty years?"

"Thealia Germain," Alexa said without hesitation.

Faucon chuckled and lifted her fingers to his lips, brushed them with his mouth. "You fly in exalted company, my *shere*."

She wished that gesture had lit a fire low inside her, but it hadn't. Maybe she was thinking too much and should go with the flow.

At that moment Broullard herded a couple of flustered tavern maids to the table. One woman carried a towel-covered steaming dish. Broullard placed a large stone tile painted with orange and red flourishes on the table, set a thick, round wooden plate carved along the edge on the tile, then gestured to the maid to deposit her burden.

Visibly nervous, the woman lifted the towel to reveal a large puff pastry.

It smelled delicious, the golden brown crust looking ready to fall into flakes at a breath. So Alexa held hers and salivated.

Wielding a huge, thin paddle-spatula, Broullard transferred the delicacy from a kitchen serving dish to the wooden platter. Not a flake fell to the table.

The maid sighed in relief.

Broullard directed the second woman to set the table for Faucon and Alexa. Cream-colored china edged in gold with Faucon's orange-and-red coat of arms, and heavy silverware was whisked in front of them.

Alexa looked at the brash heraldry and glanced at Faucon, wondering how it felt to know you were always associated with certain colors and symbols. Well, she had a law degree, right? That meant she could put an Esq. after her name and her partnership had had a scale as a logo. Not so different. She caught a glimpse of the purple cloak embroidered with the big, strange flower. Yeah, way different.

The valet now sliced the round pastry with a pie server. As the scent of crust brushed with powdered sugar and cinnamon rose, Alexa leaned forward. He placed a nearly melted piece of cheese dotted with nuts and covered in pastry on Alexa's plate, then did the same for Faucon. Broullard stepped back.

Alexa couldn't wait. She nipped off the point with her fork and popped it into her mouth. An incredible mixture of tastes flowed over her tongue. Best of all was the cheese. She closed her eyes and savored.

When she opened her lids, Faucon was watching her and smiling. His expression was the softest she'd ever seen on a Chevalier. Maybe her heart was melting a little like the cheese. She hoped so. This was a man she could really like and respect.

He took a bigger bite and forked it into his mouth, let the taste linger on his tongue and then swallowed. He looked at Broullard and the maids. "Very well done, Broullard, Shemma and Dodu. Very well indeed. Thank you."

The way he said it made Alexa think there were bonuses in the wait staff's futures. Oh yeah, this was a nice man.

Too nice. She suppressed a sigh. He might be feeling the hots for her, but she found the dish more arousing than she found him. She'd work on it.

With a hand, Faucon dismissed the servants.

Alexa tried not to look like she was gorging. She took sips of her tea between bites and didn't hurry.

"You like the sweetcheese?"

He'd pronounced it "antremay." She rolled the word around in her head as she let the pastry slide down her throat. "Yes, I like it very much."

His eyelids lowered. "I hope to always provide you with savories you like."

She thought of them together on a bed and a trickle of desire stirred inside her, she was sure. "Perhaps," she said.

After a couple of minutes of blissful eating, she went back to pumping Faucon for information.

"Tell me..." She hesitated, picked up the teapot and poured herself another cup.

His tongue flicked a bit of pastry into his mouth. "Anything, my shere."

"Luthan Vauxveau..."

His brows lowered. "Surely you aren't interested in him." He looked at her, then relaxed back and took a bite of the sweet-cheese. "I can't see it." He said it with the confidence of an observant man. "You spend time together, but not a great deal. You treat each other with respect but no passion."

"There are some people...Luthan Vauxveau—" she drew in a relaxing breath "—and the late Marshall Defau Disparu." The man she had killed. "They react to me with an almost instinctive revulsion." She'd been plodding through histories about past Exotiques word by word. That phrase had appeared time and again, so she'd memorized it. "Most people stare and point. Gawk. Why?" Maybe she could get answers from a person instead of books.

Faucon put his fork down and looked at her steadily. "I think it is a matter of Power. Some of us sense the utter *difference* of your thoughts and your Power and the life you came from. Things we will never understand, even if you sit and tell us about them all life long." He frowned as if displeased with his choice of words. Then he made a wide gesture. "Power is like a Song. It flows from us like melodies. Our melodies seem like simple human folk tunes, and your Power, your melody, like the call of a hawk to his mate before he kills."

Appalled, Alexa stared at him, grappling with his words. "I don't feel *human* to you?"

He frowned. "Yes, of course human, but completely different."

Alexa thought of songs and singing. Thought of bird cries. And thought of whales and dolphins—they sang too, didn't they? It wasn't just noise, or calls, but communication and joyful pleasure. Hadn't she heard that somewhere? She knew she'd heard recordings of the sea mammals' songs. But they were a different species. Was she *that* strange to the Lladranans? Unknowable? *Never* knowable?

"Alyeka." He took her silverware from her fingers, set it aside and grasped her hands in his own. "Others' reactions to you is not something you can control. Especially on a basic level. And I've seen you with Luthan. He acts like a friend toward you. Whatever his initial reaction, he has overcome it, or changed his mind—"

"Perhaps." She withdrew her hands. "But never enough that we could be lovers."

Faucon's eyebrows raised. "Did you want that so much?"

"No. Ttho!" Alexa picked up her fork and ate some more sweetcheese. It was delicious and that helped her get over the moment. She met Faucon's scrutiny. "I don't want to be lovers with Luthan, but it...hurts...to think that someone would literally cringe away from you in bed just because of what you are. Something in them could never wholly accept something in you."

"And some of us are extremely attracted to the unique and wonderful, instinctively," Faucon said, with a smoldering look. "It is a matter of Power flow. Some people will never be compatible. Some people would never work with another once they have Paired."

Chemistry. Magnetism. Or just plain Lladranan magic. She decided the Lladranans were just more aware of each other because of it. Another sense. Sensor. Yes, an added sensor that Lladranans used to measure each other.

Luthan had been repulsed by her, but when he'd come to know the real her, had overcome his feelings to treat her like a friend. The man across from her was drawn to her just because she was an Exotique, not because he knew who she really was.

The idea didn't appeal. But they could learn of each other in time. Wasn't that what they were doing right now, learning about each other? Just like any other couple on a date.

Alexa smiled. "A matter of Power flow, you said. Perhaps you are right."

Robin D. Owens

"I'm not sure I like your habit of saying 'perhaps' around me."

"Tell me about Luthan Vauxveau's Power flow."

"Strong, powerful, focused. Like the man. He is a good man, perhaps the most honorable that I know." He grimaced a little. "Like his father, hard to live up to. Almost perfect, that one."

"There's another Vauxveau." She'd finally worked the subject around to the one that had prodded at her for weeks. She didn't know what to think of *that* Vauxveau, *that* lover. So many stories, such a brief night.

"Bastien Vauxveau." Faucon laughed. "We trained together for years. A good man in a crunch, but it has to be a crunch before he shows his true colors, sings the true Song. I don't presume to know him. Who knows what goes on in a black-and-white's head?" Faucon divvied up the last piece of sweetcheese and topped up their teacups. He shook his head. "Bastien, such a one! Often beyond brilliant and sometimes so stupid and gauche."

Alexa could attest to that. She leaned forward and ran her fingers down Faucon's long, elegant hand, hardly scarred. "Back home in Exotique Terre, if women were talking, we would say such a man was sometimes as brilliant as a diamond and sometimes as dumb as a sack of rocks." She gave him a slow smile. "Of course, if women were talking, that wouldn't refer to only one man, but *all* men."

Faucon's eyes went wide, then he threw back his head and roared with laughter.

Suddenly she felt more on an even keel. He was suave. Noble. Rich. Strong in every way. Excellent sense of humor which included being able to laugh at himself. What more could a girl want? She was sure if she gave him a chance he could make her toes tingle. Time to put heavy thoughts out of her head and enjoy herself. She settled back into the booth.

A second later, she was pulled away from her seat by Luthan Vauxveau, who carried a red bird with a long tail on his shoulder. Sinafin.

"Sorry to interrupt, Creusse, but Singer's business. You must come with me now, Marshall Alyeka," Luthan said.

17

Luthan lied. Alexa knew it in her bones. His damn Power flow told her so. And he was awful at lying too, but his grip on her arm was solid.

"Are you crazy?" she said. She'd just spotted Broullard and attendants coming through the kitchen door of the inn with a baked and stuffed bird that smelled like the best Thanksgiving Day meal she'd ever had. She dug in her heels.

"Singer's business," Luthan repeated, not meeting her eyes, ignoring the inn full of people watching the little drama.

Sinafin transferred herself from Luthan to Alexa. The bird's claws hurt. With her beak, Sinafin tugged at a lock of Alexa's hair.

Time to return to the Castle.

Alexa swept her hair away from the bird's hold.

Faucon stood, face expressionless in the usual Chevalier's way, but Alexa thought everyone around him could gauge the anger in *his* Power flow. What a useful concept. She hadn't transferred the knowledge from her lessons to real life.

"Vauxveau," Faucon said, holding himself arrogantly. He was not quite as tall or broad as Luthan, but Faucon's attitude made a statement.

Broullard hovered with the—whatever—too little to be a turkey, too large for a Cornish hen; sure didn't smell like chicken. Alexa's stomach grumbled. She noticed all the Chevaliers in the tavern were focused on the group. Only one of them was looking at the people; the rest were drooling and ready to pounce. On *her* dinner.

"You can't do this," she said in a near whimper.

"Singer's business!" Luthan announced.

Faucon gave way, Luthan dragged at Alexa. She glanced back. The stuffed bird looked glorious; only the tiniest of crumbs marked where the sweetcheese had been. The maid beside Broullard held another pot of tea.

"Noooooo."

Luthan didn't listen. One of his brawny arms encircled her waist and lifted her off her feet. Where was her baton? How could she use it to get out of this mess?

She couldn't. *Everyone* on Lladrana followed the oracle, the Singer. She smacked the flat of her hand on Luthan's shoulder. He didn't wince. Didn't let go. He was trying not to make a scene. Her stomach gurgled again.

"You jerk. You creep. You…" She continued to swear, and he took it stolidly.

She figured her cursing lacked a lot since she was swearing under her breath and in English. All the good Lladranan swearwords had gone clean out of her head. She wriggled around and almost slipped free before Luthan did something magic—and suddenly they were out the door into the cool night. Her last sight had been of Faucon, staring at them thoughtfully.

As soon as her bottom touched the volaran's back she went still. She didn't want to spook it; she knew it fought in tumultuous battles. She didn't want to spook herself either.

It was a moment's ride to the Castle. Sinafin chattered in bird talk that sounded cheerful.

Since she'd left her cloak at the Nom de Nom, Alexa hurried off the Landing Field and into the Castle. There she swung to confront Luthan.

"What Singer's business?"

Leaning against one of the Castle walls, Luthan looked at her blandly and stuck his hands in his pants pockets. "It doesn't look as if you've had dinner yet. How about joining me in the Castle kitchen?"

Stew with stringy beeflike stuff, mushy dumplings. That's what she'd get. She snarled, hauled out her baton.

Luthan's expression turned quizzical.

Alexa fumed. She studied the glowing green of her baton. Surely there was some way to get from the Castle to the Nom de Nom instantly. Before those wolves of Chevaliers devoured her dinner.

She stomped her feet. "Moron," she shouted.

He looked pained. Yeah, that was one of the words that was the same in both languages.

"Moron," she said again, then, "Jerk!"

He didn't react, so that word hadn't achieved the effect she wanted.

She slid her baton into its sheath at her hip, narrowed her eyes and pointed a finger at him.

Nothing changed. She must not look terrifying enough.

A thought came to her and she smiled.

Luthan pushed away from the wall, wariness flickering across his face.

She waggled her finger. "You can tell the Singer," Alexa said sweetly, "that she owes me one lovely baked and stuffed bird of the sort Faucon provided *and* three large pots of excellent tea, and whatever else the man had in mind for my dinner."

His eyes widened. She could almost see him tallying up the cost. He swallowed.

"A week from today. I want it served in my suite a week from today. And as punishment for that very poor lie you told, I want the sweetcheese too." She turned on her heel and marched away.

Sinafin squawked a laugh and flew next to Alexa.

Alexa thought again of the dinner she was missing. She sniffed, trying to remember the fragrance of the new pot of tea. It had been different from what they'd drunk with the sweetcheese, another variety. She still had the yen for more tea. Her stomach felt hollow and she nearly groaned. It would have to be the generic tea, after all.

When Bastien was discharged from the clinique he flew home. Luthan had given him the option of home or the Castle, and Bastien wasn't ready for the Castle, yet. Didn't know when he would be.

Within five minutes the caretaker of his estate had informed him of his new neighbor—the Marshall Alexa—that she'd visited her estate twice and her staff were pleased. Always curious, Bastien sauntered to her house himself.

He met with Pierre, the head of the stables, who was the best vet around and had helped Bastien with his horses and volarans.

Bastien sat with the tough old guy in the front room of a cottage that looked out on the main wing of stables. The walls were whitewashed plaster and held paintings of volarans. Wooden beams protruded from the low ceiling; the wooden floor was plain scrubbed pine planks. They drank ale.

Tipping his chair back on two legs, Bastien asked, "What do you think of the new Exotique Marshall?"

"Doesn't like horses, wary of volarans," Pierre said, and took a gulp of beer.

"Not like the Janins, the previous owners," Bastien said.

Pierre snorted. "Those folks were worthless. I misspoke. The new little Exotique doesn't know horses, and I heard they don't have volarans where she comes from." He shook his head in pure disbelief.

"I've heard that too. Bad if she's not interested in the stables."

Clunking his mug down, Pierre wiped his mouth with a purple napkin. "Didn't say that. When I heard that she toured the house but wasn't coming to the stables, I went up to get a good look at her—you can believe that."

Bastien nodded.

"She's a funny-looking one, but she had this expression in her eyes. Like she'd already come to love the place and would die before she'd let anyone take it from her. She's a fighter. She'll be good for the estate, and good for Lladrana. The Marshalls picked a good one, there."

That wasn't what Bastien wanted to hear.

"Furthermore, I'll make a horsewoman of her in three years, and in five she'll be dive-bombing her volarans. Or you'll train her."

Bastien choked.

"Guess I wasn't supposed to hear those little notes running from you to her? Wasn't supposed to know you came here for information or advice?" Pierre chuckled. "This is her home, she has ties to it already, and come Summer Solstice and the Land Bonding ritual, she'll do it, mark my words. It holds some of her energy and yours from when you've visited. Of course the energies Sing when they're linked."

Bastien was surprised. First Luthan knew of the bond between Alexa and Bastien and accepted it, now Pierre. It didn't sound as if fighting his destiny would work. He'd still try.

Pierre continued, "I approve of her. I approve of you. You're both fighters. Go to her. That's my advice."

"Marshall—" Bastien strangled on the word.

Pierre sent a sizzling flick of energy against Bastien's hands in reprimand, not as much painful as shocking.

"You were always slated for a Marshall's baton. Go do it. Now. It won't take more than an hour to fly to the Castle using one of the wild volarans and your own magic to shorten the distance." Pierre stood, stalked to the door and opened it.

After swallowing the last of his ale, and adjusting his hat, Bastien strode out the door.

"By the way, that hat could use a few horses trampling it to make it prettier!" Pierre shouted.

His laughter followed Bastien as he walked home.

Thoughts circled in his head. If Alexa was such a fighter, why wasn't she fighting for him? The curiosity that had gotten him in so much trouble throughout his life piqued; Bastien stopped and leaned against a tree. The cheerful burbling of a nearby brook helped him visualize the bond between them.

There it was. It wasn't white now, but midnight blue—his main color—and purple, braided together. He wondered what she'd do if he gave it a nudge, just a tiny quiver. Would she even notice? With the bond, could he put it in her mind to come to him instead of him having to go to the Castle and her?

He moved it a finger's breadth.

Nothing happened.

Bastien plucked it again.

He was yanked from his tree to land in the soft mud of the cold, shallow stream. He sputtered and laughed.

She didn't. He felt her mental presence now, but it was distant and shielded, nothing like when they'd coupled together above the stables at The Singer's Hand. In his mind's eye an image coalesced. A pair of very large scissors with a handle in a color of purple he'd never seen before—maybe a color from Exotique Terre. The scissors positioned themselves on each side of their thread.

"Wait!"

The scissors paused an instant. Bastien thought fast, sent this thought: *Do you know what will happen if you cut that thread?*

He did. It wouldn't be pleasant, but it wouldn't be debilitating either. He'd wager *she* didn't know. She didn't know a lot of things about Lladrana, especially that the Marshalls were a bunch of self-centered, obsolete snobs. And he had to admit he'd like to teach her some customs, especially some sexual ones.

Jaws yawning wide, the scissors hovered, then withdrew—as she did—leaving him to pick himself up, shake himself off and slosh back to his stables for a quick ride to the Castle.

Her emotions about him had been strangely flat.

He'd known enough women to believe that his quick departure after a night of sex—no, it had been more, a real closeness of body and emotion—should have engendered hurt and anger and perhaps even bitterness. But none of those emotions pulsed from her.

Oddly enough, that irritated him. Pierre had said she was a fighter, and Bastien had sensed the same basic characteristic when they'd been together. What, he wasn't worth fighting for?

That steamed him enough to rationalize going to the Castle.

He let the Chevalier coordinator know where he could be found and flew to the Castle on his best volaran—one he'd bred and raised himself, one his father deeply coveted.

He smiled. Perhaps his fate wasn't too bad after all. He'd be in a position to rile his father and the other stiff-necked Marshalls, at every opportunity. Shake them out of their ruts and hidebound ways. Helped along by the very Exotique they had Summoned and who was ruffling their feathers as well. Then the Chevaliers could get some answers, some help.

This could be fun.

And the thought of having sex with Alexa wasn't too hard to accept either. He hadn't gotten a good look at her and wanted to. Wanted to explore her differences, inside and out.

Bastien and his volaran glided to a halt on the Landing Field of the Castle. He was met by Urvey, who looked at Bastien reproachfully for having left him behind, even though Bastien had paid the boy to stay and take care of his room in Horseshoe Hall.

No need to ask how Urvey knew he was arriving, since the feycoocu in warhawk-form flew beside him and settled on Bastien's shoulder. It too, watched him with disapproving eyes set above a wicked bird's beak. He sensed that if anyone was behind the meeting between Alexa and him, it was this being. And he didn't want to think of that. *Very* wild magic at work.

"Where's the...Marshall Alexa?" He had almost said "the Exotique," but recalled how he hated being called "the black-and-white."

Urvey and the bird sniffed in unison.

Bastien smothered a smile.

"In the training yard," Urvey said stiffly.

"Look, Urvey, I'm sorry I left, but if I'd taken you with me, you'd be dead." Bastien dropped a hand on the youth's shoulder. It hunched under his fingers. "All right. I owe you an apology. I apologize."

With lips pressed together, the teen looked up. "Do you want me for your squire or not?"

He hadn't thought he'd face his new life so soon. Accept responsibility for another? The boy studied him anxiously. It was unlikely anyone else would keep him as a squire, dip in the jerir or not.

Time for Bastien to become an adult and a true Chevalier. *Merde.* "Yes, I want you as my squire. I'll be needing one here, especially if I Pair with Marshall Alexa."

The bird squawked and flapped its wings. *About time.*

Now Urvey's mouth curved slyly. "Chevalier Faucon's squire has been training me."

That must have taken guts and initiative on Urvey's part. Good boy. But Faucon...that smooth bastard. An unexpected bite of jealousy nipped at Bastien. He wondered how far Faucon had gotten with the Marshall.

The Exotique is innately attractive to some, the feycoocu said.

Like me, Bastien thought.

Like Faucon, it ended smugly. *He is sparring with her in the training yard.*

"Huh" was Bastien's brilliant reply. He set off at a trot that caused the bird to rise and caw.

Sure enough, he found the pair in the first training yard, a fenced circle. Half of the Marshalls and many Chevaliers watched, including his brother Luthan. Bastien could *see* the aura around them as they willed the newcomer to learn.

Alexa and Faucon fought with short sword and shields. She was doing well, augmenting her strength and her blows with powerful magic, good in her footwork. A glow of jade green surrounded her. The Jade Baton lay on her left hip and could be deployed in an instant.

Bastien frowned. Faucon was holding back.

"Time!" Bastien called.

The fighters dropped their weapons. Everyone turned and stared at him. He opened the low wooden gate, strolled through and latched it behind him. The feycoocu landed on the gate.

Bastien walked up to Alexa and gave her a kiss on the cheek.

"Hello, sweeting." The scent of her rose to him and went straight to his loins. *Merde!*

"I'm not your 'sweeting.' I am nothing to you. We are nothing to each other." She looked up at him with strange, cool green eyes, her face expressionless.

Bastien didn't like her words, but kept a smile on his face as he turned to Faucon, who looked at him with a resigned, knowing gaze. Bastien offered his hand, and Faucon met his grip. They were well matched in every way, except Power. Bastien had been a black-and-white, and his hair still proclaimed him that, but he was now fully in tune with his Power.

Faucon's eyes widened and he dipped his head, a wry smile curving at his mouth. "Now I understand why Luthan has been so protective. You have a good brother."

"The best."

A little yearning flickered in Faucon's eyes. He was an only child. Bastien suddenly realized his life had been better than he'd thought. He had a weak mother and Reynardus for a father, but sharing kinship with Luthan made up for all of that.

"You are doing her no favor in holding back," Bastien said quietly.

Faucon shrugged. "I can't help it. She's so small and delicate—"

"Are we going to practice or quit?" asked the lady sharply.

"May I cut in?" asked Bastien, loud enough for all to hear.

With a nod, Faucon sheathed his sword. He smiled and saluted Alexa and strode from the field.

Slowly Bastien turned to face Alexa.

She'd picked up a quarterstaff that was all wrong for her—too long and heavy, and leaned on it. He couldn't see her hair under her helm, but her face was so pale it seemed to glow, the color of cream with a touch of rose in her cheeks. Striking coloring.

Her figure was like many women's and she was dressed like a

Marshall, but the way she held herself, her attitude, was not of Lladrana. He couldn't pinpoint the differences, but they were there and would always remain so.

Her gaze met his and he probed. She should be angry with him, but he sensed the distance she'd put between them, the magical block on her emotions. Whistling, he prepared for the fight by stripping off his riding gauntlets and untying the lace anchoring his sword to his thigh. He took a shield from Luthan, who handed it to him with a serious face but a twinkle in his eyes.

Alexa set aside the quarterstaff and did some stretching that was nothing of Lladrana, but looked useful. When she was ready, her gaze met his with remoteness.

Bastien smiled wolfishly. All his life he'd learned to demolish mental blocks of others and to work around his own. Whatever was keeping her from feeling the natural emotions she should for him, would soon be gone.

"Go!" shouted Luthan in a tone that warned Bastien, but which he disregarded.

Most of the time it was interesting to play with fire.

He crossed swords with her, starting easy, testing, teasing. As they feinted, riposted, thrusted, he slipped a probe into her mind and sensed the emotional block she had regarding him. There were other blocks, but right now he was only interested in the one with his tune on it.

She beat back his blade, entered under his guard and sliced his good leather tunic. When he hopped back and looked at her, she was grinning. Sweetly.

Bastien increased the pace of the fight. They moved well against each other, and would move better together. He heard murmuring from the sidelines as the Marshalls and Chevaliers recognized that their fighting patterns complemented each other, showing that their energies would merge well too.

Alexa frowned, not understanding. Bastien winked.

Showing her teeth, she pressed him, making him fight faster, concentrate more on his sword and shield, on his footwork instead of his mental probing. With sheer strength, he deflected her blade with his shield and touched her shoulder with his sword.

She scowled. Their gazes locked, and through that look, he touched her mind and broke the block she had against him with a piercing whistle. All the emotions she'd suppressed flooded from behind the block—humiliation, rejection, anger.

Alexa's eyes widened. She stumbled back. He let her go. She shook her head. Her face, her stance, her fighting *changed*.

Fire lit her eyes. Energy crackled around her.

"You jerk!" she screamed.

He didn't know what the second word meant, or many of the following words, and had no time to think as she rushed to him in a fury, her sword moving faster than his eye could see.

He reacted on instinct and thanked the Song for his years of training. He'd thought that she might lose her concentration when angry, make mistakes he could take advantage of. The opposite was true.

Suddenly she was *there*, totally and completely enveloped in her Power, using it, channeling it, fighting as no one he'd ever seen in his life.

Wham! A slap of her blade on his shield and he was flat on his back gasping for air, her sword swooping to his heart.

"Halt!" Luthan cried.

Her sword point tickled Bastien's chest. He wondered if she was going to carve something on him. One of those words she'd shouted.

She glanced at Luthan and sneered, stared down at Bastien with the same expression. It sat oddly on her features.

"I won't lose control," she said.

Chevaliers and Marshalls poured into the yard, but they all kept a distance from her. She glowed jade.

As far as Bastien was concerned, she'd already lost control. And too damn bad it hadn't been in bed instead of in a fight.

A cackle of bird-laughter came from the feycoocu.

"I came to the Castle to apologize," Bastien said.

She laughed and threw her sword into the air. It spun high, twirled and sparkled in the light, plummeted down and slid into the sheath at her side with a tiny *snick.* Bastien had never seen the like. The shadows of the onlookers, which had been nearing, faded back.

Alexa put her hands on her hips and laughed some more. Then she shook her head, turned on her heel and swaggered away.

Luthan loomed over Bastien. "Well, brother, I would say that you brought the lady full into her Power."

Luthan stretched out a hand and Bastien took it, let his brother help him to his feet.

"You continue to push your luck, and by all the Songs that sound in the Universe, you *are* lucky."

Since Luthan was taller than Bastien, he could pull off the trick of their father's and stare down his nose. "You are in trouble," Luthan said cheerfully. "And it will be fun to see you get out of it. It's evident to all—" he swept a hand at the observers "—that you somehow, somewhen became intimate with our new Marshall. *And* despite your usual charm, you did not endear yourself to her. We will all be watching to see how and *if* you can fix this latest mess of yours."

"Go to hell," Bastien mumbled, and limped to the gate.

She felt *great.* As if she'd drunk some amazing elixir that had flowed through every vein, simmered down every nerve to energize it. When she took off her helm, despite damp sweat, her hair stood straight out with the static electricity and she liked it. She grinned and danced down the corridors to the stairs to her suite, and when anyone saw her, they got out of her way.

She almost wanted to meet Reynardus. She thought she could beat him now. She sure had beaten the pants off his no-good son. It had felt really great, and in doing so, it was as if everything she knew of Lladrana and all the qualities that she'd carried from home had clicked together and made her whole.

Flexing her fingers, she saw the outline of faint blue from her dips in the jerir, then the jade green of herself. Yep. She done good.

She raced up the stairs and into her rooms, and Umilla was there, bobbing and smiling and helping her with her clothes. The maid seemed to be as happy as she was—sensing her victory, maybe. Alexa didn't think the gossip of her great win would have reached Umilla by now, but who knew?

Before she went into the bathroom to shower, Alexa carefully penned a note to Luthan. "I want my good food. Now." She put it in an envelope and turned it over. Placing her finger on the front she thought of Luthan's coat of arms and it appeared etched into the envelope in color. She handed the missive to Umilla for delivery, then hit the bathroom.

Oh yeah, she felt good. She'd whomped both of Reynardus's sons in different ways today. Soon she'd take on the old tiger himself.

Back in his rooms in Horseshoe Hall, Bastien was grateful that Urvey kept his snickering to a minimum. The squire gasped when he saw the state of Bastien's body.

"I told you that you were lucky not to come along with me," Bastien said to the openmouthed boy.

Urvey glanced away but his chin jutted.

Bastien sighed. "I'm going to bathe. I know you're good with horses—do you have one?"

Gaze hopeful, Urvey met his eyes. "No."

"A friend of mine is bringing three." Two had been for himself, the third a gift for Alexa, since Pierre believed it a better mount for her than the one the Marshalls had provided. But it would be a good incentive for the teen to have his own horse. "The sorrel will be yours."

"Thanks!"

"Take care of them, and me, and I will send for an old volaran for you to learn to fly on."

The youth's eyes were filling with tears as Bastien hurried to the communal Chevalier bath in Horseshoe Hall.

18

As Bastien stripped and waded into the medium-hot pool in the basement of Horseshoe Hall, he suffered the joking comments on his scars and his latest loss.

On the whole, he'd spent a lot of time with the independent Chevaliers, or the minor nobles, like himself—knights who were the most dissatisfied with the progress of the Marshalls in repairing the fenceposts and defending the land.

He leaned back, closed his eyes and let the water lap over him. He'd decided to win Alexa. The idea had snuck up and clobbered him when she'd walked away from the training ground.

Everything within him told him that Lladrana needed this woman. He'd joined the majority in that. The best way she could be incorporated into Lladrana was to be Paired. So he'd had to decide whether to Pair with her and live with the machinations of the Marshalls, or cut the bond between them so she could Pair with another man.

The thought of her body shuddering in climax under any other man's ignited a storm of jealousy within Bastien. *He'd* been the first one to have mind- and body-shattering sex with her, and he wanted to keep it that way. He felt possessive. Jealousy and possessiveness weren't emotions he admired or wanted to feel, but they were undeniable all the same.

Soaking with other men and women, he sensed their underlying excitement that the rogue of the Chevaliers would soon be inside the Marshalls' inner circle. They were proud of him too, an emotion that threw him a little since he'd only ever felt it from his brother.

And as usual, as soon as he thought of his brother, the man appeared. He took in the common bath with its dingy brown walls and puddles on the concrete floor with a pained glance.

Since Luthan had a large estate and was the heir to Reynardus, as well as being the former Representative of the Chevaliers and now the Representative of the Singer, he had a suite in the Nobles' Apartments of the Castle. Still, Luthan stripped, folded and placed his clothes on one of the stone shelves along the side of the room, and sank into the heated water next to Bastien. The others who had been sharing the pool with Bastien discreetly withdrew.

Luthan moaned in contentment, leaned his head back on the round stone neck-rim and closed his eyes. Bastien smiled at the all-too-human sound.

"The things I do for you, brother," Luthan said.

"This bath isn't too troublesome. I know for a fact that the water is hotter and the minerals more efficacious than in the Castle buildings proper."

No answer.

"And I don't recall asking you to do anything for me."

Luthan's eyes opened and he pinned a sharp stare on Bastien. "You *always* press your luck. I don't know how you get away with it." Then he smiled. "But sometimes you don't. That fight in the training yard will be remembered for a *long* time. The stuff of tales around encampment fires."

Bastien grunted.

Luthan continued. "I trust you have an idea to win her back. You know, there's betting going on as to how long it will take."

Bastien shifted and leaned his head back too. "I hope you put your zhiv on me, and for tonight. I have a wonderful idea, one that will get me into her suite tonight. Once I am in her suite, I am hopeful the Pair bond will help me out."

To his amazement, Luthan scowled. "Tonight Alyeka is dining on sweetcheese and roast dinfais fowl and drinking tea from the island of Brasser."

"Is that so? What time?"

"In about an hour."

Bastien nodded. "That will do. I will join her."

Luthan groaned again, this time with disgust. "That was what Faucon was feeding her when I saved her from seduction. It cost a month's worth of my estate profits to replicate that meal. Now *you* will partake. I should have known."

"You really shouldn't do me so many favors, brother. But my thanks," Bastien said softly.

"I was sure she would fall to his charms that night," Luthan said. "Her concentration was all on him. Ever since she returned from her travels, she's been looking around. You met her then, right?"

"Yes. I handled it badly. The *afterward* I handled badly. I was my usual superb self in bed."

Luthan grinned. "You must have truly bungled, for her to be so angry that she wanted to skewer you."

"Huh."

"Be careful of Father. He won't take this news well."

"I know. He wrote me off as an acceptable son a long time ago."

"Don't underestimate him. Don't push your luck."

"I'll try not to."

An hour later, dressed in a new surcoat of his colors of midnight blue and silver, over equally new trousers and shirt, Bastien strummed the doorharp on Alexa's suite. He was a little surprised when Umilla opened the door a crack. He'd heard, of course, that Alexa had chosen the black-and-white as a personal maid, but had thought Umilla would never retain the post. The woman had fractured energy pulses that she hadn't been able to work around as Bastien had done. Black-and-whites often had mental problems.

But Umilla held herself with pride.

"May I see Alexa?"

Umilla gave him a sharp look. "You say her name right."

"So do you. We are more flexible."

She studied him. "You are whole, now, together."

"Alexa did that for me."

Umilla shuddered. "I am happy as I am."

"Each to his own." Bastien wasn't about to tell the woman he hadn't exactly agreed to the change in his circumstances. After examining the entire matter from every angle, he knew that Alexa had felt guilty in curing him without his consent. He could use that too. "Please, just ask her to come to the door to speak to me."

Umilla looked at his offering. "She will like those." She closed the door on him.

Bastien couldn't hear Alexa's dragging footsteps, but sensed them. Whatever exultation she'd known after trouncing him was gone.

The little square door at his eye level opened. She was too short to be seen. "What do you want?"

"Alexa." He lilted her name. "I have a bouquet of the first spring flowers gathered from my estate and yours. Don't you wish to see what grows on your land?"

There was silence. A great wistfulness emanated from her. He watched the peephole and saw her face bob up and down as if she stood on tiptoe, then relaxed, then pushed up again.

"They're beautiful" came from behind the thick door.

She sighed. People often sighed around Bastien—usually a sign that he'd worn them down and he'd get what he wanted. The door swung open.

She was lovely. Her hair fascinated him, light and silver and so fine it lifted from her head with her Power. He gave her the flowers. She cradled them like a baby and buried her nose in the scent of them, then stroked a petal or two.

"Can you forgive me?" he asked, voice low.

"What do you want?"

"To lie with you and live with you and Pair with you." His own words scared him, and he wished with all his heart they were having this conversation in bed, where it would have been so much easier.

"Don't want much, do you? The sex was great, but you screwed up after."

He winced. "I know. I was wary of all the circumstances. Can we talk about this over dinner?"

She snorted. "Everyone in the Castle knows that Luthan provided my meal tonight." She glanced back and to her left. "He wasn't stingy. There's enough for three." She turned and disappeared into the narrow curving hallway that led to the bedroom and sitting room. The small passage was a security measure.

Since she left the door open, Bastien took this for grudging invitation, stepped into the little hallway and closed the door behind him. Three? Umilla must be joining them. Odd, but endearing. Harder for him to woo Alexa, though.

"We could continue to have great sex—" Alexa's voice came from the right "—but I don't know about the living together. You don't like the Marshalls."

He turned and followed the rounded wall until he reached another open door. "I think the Marshalls are secretive and far too proud. I don't have to like them to work with them. There are several Chevaliers I don't care for that I often team with."

"I see," she said over her shoulder.

He'd been in other Tower suites that were arranged like this one. This room was large and wedge-shaped, comprising the right side of the Tower. Lush, layered rugs covered the stone floor and tapestries hung between the windows on the wall. A huge painting of Alexa's house graced the wall separating the room from the rest of the Tower. Behind that wall was the bathroom that connected to the bedroom.

Bastien crossed to the table situated near the outer wall. The tablecloth was cream-colored damask with purple napkins laying under heavy silverware. Three places were set, and a vase for the flowers sat in the middle of the table. He thought the teapot had been moved from the middle to the side.

Like everything of Alexa's, the room was slightly different from any he'd been in. The atmosphere was imbued with her Song, the furniture set in a cozy pattern, but one that differed from any Chevalier or noble arrangement.

Discreetly he glanced around. No wine, no ale—only tea. Well, the food would make up for the lack of drink.

"Too many flowers for that vase, Umilla. Maybe I can have another vase for my bedside table?" asked Alexa, halving the bouquet and putting one bunch on a side table.

Umilla stared at the vase and the flowers and frowned, as if she still tried to figure out whether they'd fit. Then she screwed up her face.

As Alexa arranged the rest of the flowers in the vase with surprising artistry, Umilla said, "I told Bastien's boy. He will bring another vase. One that will look good in the bedroom."

"Thank you, Umilla," Alexa said, then glanced at Bastien. "Your boy?"

"My squire, Urvey."

"Oh, Urvey. I know him. I didn't know he was your squire. I thought Faucon had taken him on."

"He's mine." Bastien smiled ruefully. "Time to live up to my responsibilities, I think."

That brought an approving look from her, but he wanted more, needed more if he was going to overcome his previous mistake and grace her bed tonight.

"Your stableman, Pierre, is doing me the favor of bringing in a horse for him. Urvey is good with horses. I have no qualms in giving him one of my steeds."

She sent him a sharp glance as if unsure of his motives.

He smiled.

"You going to seat me?" asked Umilla, standing in front of an ornately carved wooden chair with a plush velvet seat. The sweetcheese in pastry, now on the table, steamed with a tantalizing odor.

Bastien swallowed and crossed to seat Umilla.

She smiled up at him, her eyes wickedly sharp. She would never lose this position, and she would always claim whatever prerogatives the Exotique would grant, against all class and tradition. He bowed his head in acceptance. She was a Power in Alexa's life. Another black-and-white had found her true place—and with the Exotique.

When he turned to Alexa, she'd already seated herself. She

looked at him with considering eyes, though the Song between them had taken on a warmer tone, a richer note. She liked him, at least. That and the sex would be a good basis. If he didn't make a mistake. If he could bring some grace into the process of winning her again.

He sat, unfolded his purple linen napkin and laid it on his lap.

"Bastien will sing the thanks to the Song, tonight," Umilla said.

His eyes widened. He cleared his throat and stared at the cooling sweetcheese, trying to think of a short gratitude. A brief one thanking the Song for the bounty of the land and good friends came to mind and rustily he opened his mouth and sang.

When he looked at Alexa, she was blinking her eyes. The Song had had an effect on her—a softening effect! Well, of course only those who truly appreciated music would be Summoned.

He served her first, then Umilla, then himself. As the first bite of sweetcheese melted in his mouth, he thought to thank his brother as well.

They had nearly finished the sweetcheese when the doorharp sounded.

Umilla's brows dipped, then she smiled. "That is Urvey with another vase." She stood.

"One moment." Alexa whisked the last wedge of pastry encrusted cheese onto a plate.

Bastien had been eyeing it, wondering if it would be rude to snatch. She handed the plate to Umilla.

"Give this to Urvey for his effort."

Umilla nodded and left.

"Urvey probably has never tasted sweetcheese in his life," murmured Bastien, listening to a surprised and pleased exclamation from his squire.

"So?" Alexa stood and placed the top set of dishes into a basket.

"So you are generous to your servants."

"Lladrana has a class structure. I'm still figuring out the ramifications and the fluidity of it. You are a second son, but have an estate of your own?"

"One of my mother's minor properties. My father would not let loose a clod of dirt that belongs to him."

Her smile was sharp. "He has had to, lately."

Bastien's temper rose as he recalled the story of Reynardus shooting magic at her, and the fine.

Alexa tilted her head. "You are considered an independent Chevalier. Do you get most of your income from your estate, or what? I have a Chevalier of my own, Pascal. I'm paying for his training and gave him a volaran. But I know some Chevaliers fight for gold and are mercenaries." She frowned as she mangled the last word.

Umilla entered the room with a large, lustrous purple vase, and disappeared into the bathroom to fill it with water.

"Some Chevaliers are associated with a noble landowner, who sends them to fight, like your Pascal."

"He's very young and will only win his volaran reins in a couple of days. I plan on sending him to my estate to become familiar with it."

"A good idea."

"And other Chevaliers?" Alexa asked.

"Some are minor nobles, some major nobles who have Chevaliers under them. Some knights fight for pay." He leaned forward. "But we *all* believe in defending Lladrana."

Alexa frowned. "No corrupt Chevaliers at all?"

"Perhaps one or two. On the whole, no."

Her gaze shot to him and he felt her mind probe. He allowed it through his upper layers.

"If we stay together," she said with a heavy accent. "You must promise to be honest. Not to lie. I must be able to trust you."

She looked out the window at the twilight landscape. "After—at the inn, when we woke up that morning, you weren't nice, but you were honest."

Bastien winced. "I—"

Umilla traipsed in, beaming. "It's full of water and be-spelled so the flowers will stay pretty longer." She thrust the vase dripping with water into Alexa's hands.

"Very good." Alexa looked at the vase and sighed.

"What troubles you, sweeting?" Bastien asked.

Her expression didn't lighten as her gaze moved to him. "I'm tired of purple."

"If we Pair, we can choose our own color."

She snorted. "A stupid reason for Pairing." She wiped down the vase with her napkin, picked up the other bunch of flowers, arranged them with nimble fingers and walked into the bedroom.

Bastien watched the sway of her hips, unlike the walk of other women, then found Umilla staring at him, gnawing her lips in thought. He felt the brush of her Power.

"You could be good for her," Umilla said.

"Good for me? Ha!" said Alexa, entering the room.

Umilla looked back and forth from Alexa to him. "You have a sex bond," she said. "Not a blood-bond yet, but it can grow."

Alexa sat down and gestured to Umilla to serve the next course. "How do blood-bonds happen?"

"Through the sharing of blood," Bastien said matter-of-factly, accepting that this would be the strangest dinner conversation he'd ever had. That amused and intrigued him, much as did the woman herself.

"I guessed that. What does that mean, exactly?"

The scent of perfectly roasted dinfais made Bastien's mouth water.

"Light or dark meat?" asked Umilla.

"Dark," said Bastien.

"Light," said Alexa.

"And I like both because I am a black-and-white." Umilla giggled. A moment later all three plates had a serving of fowl and a medley of tender steamed vegetables. Umilla sat.

"Blood-bonds?" prompted Alexa.

"Blood-bonds are those of Paired people, or those who need to work closely together with a mental and emotional tie, like the Marshalls. I have a blood-bond with my family, since we share blood."

"Obviously." Alexa popped a bite of dinfais into her mouth and closed her eyes with pleasure.

Bastien's body stirred at the sight of her, so he distracted himself by taking his first bite. As the tasty, moist meat fell apart in his mouth he hummed in satisfaction.

"So good!" Alexa whispered. "The best meal I've eaten here."

"Me too," said Umilla.

Alexa smiled at her.

Umilla said, "The Marshalls tried to make you Pair with someone the morning after you arrived. They gave you the Choosing drug, then took you to the Great Hall and wanted you to bond with someone there."

Alexa put her fork down and stared at her food. Bastien guessed the memory was bad enough to affect her appetite.

"Drink." He poured tea into a delicate cup. "Savor your tea." She did.

He drank too. The tea's flavor was something he'd never had— must be a special variety. He still wished he had ale.

"A bunch of nasty men attended the Choosing," Umilla continued, naming them. "No one nice, so of course Alexa didn't Choose or Pair."

More anger roiled in his gut. Not one of those men would treat a woman well. Alexa had surmounted more obstacles than he'd realized, and he had only made her journey harder. Shame joined the anger. He reached for his own tea cup and took a swallow.

"But some good nobles have been taking her out lately." Umilla dished herself more dinfais.

Alexa's eyes met his, green and steady and wary. "A blood-bond is more important than just a sex bond, then? Will you want a blood-bond?"

His pulse roared in his ears. Such a *huge* step. "It might come naturally."

Her face lightened with curiosity. "How?"

"If we are fighting the same enemy and both bloody our hands at the same time and clasp hands—also a blood-bond."

She scrunched up her face and said a word he'd never heard. "Eeeeewwww."

He stared as she gulped more tea, then he ate a bite of vegetables and continued. "Or if we both get wounded and our blood mingles, another type of blood-bond."

"All those?" asked Umilla. "I didn't know that."

"The Binding, ritual blood-bond, where our veins are cut and our arms tied together for a day and a night for the blood to mingle and we say vows—that is the strongest."

"But you won't ask that of me." The words rushed from Alexa.

"No." He shouldn't have been disappointed at her sigh of relief since he didn't want such a bond, but he was.

For the rest of the meal, he kept the conversation light. Helped Umilla with the serving and clearing, judged the rhythm of the event, and finally spoke at the best time—after Alexa drained her first cup of tea.

"Walk and talk with me," he said.

"Where?"

"How about down to Castleton? I have a new chain-mail tunic

waiting for me at the blacksmith's that I told him I'd pick up to-night."

Alexa's brows rose. "Taking me away from the Castle?"

Bastien smiled easily. "That's right. We can talk about whatever you like."

She propped her elbow on the table and set her chin in her palm, studying him. "Interesting strategy," she said. "Talking. In-stead of trying to remain here in my rooms and seduce me."

With his Power he kept the heat that wanted to redden his cheeks from showing. He took her hand and lifted her fingers to his lips. "We'll get to the seduction. Later tonight," he whispered. Her increased pulse made him smile. She didn't withdraw her hand so he nibbled her fingertips.

A moment later he stood, pulled her to her feet and tucked her hand in his arm. "Let's walk."

"All right."

Umilla hurried to the wardrobe and returned with Alexa's cloak. Bastien took it from her. Standing before Alexa, he draped it around her, touching her nape, her arms, even above her breasts. All the while he held her eyes. Shadows of hurt and caution and yearning showed in her gaze.

He ran a thumb over her cheekbone. "I won't hurt you again."

She stepped away coolly and leveled a serious gaze at him. "Don't promise what you can't deliver. I don't want—" She gri-maced and shook her head, obviously frustrated with her lack of vocabulary.

"No bread crust promises, easily broken," Bastien said. Giving in to temptation, he closed his fingers over a handful of her hair. It was like holding silk, soft and tickling against his palm, not the heavier, coarser silver hair that most Lladranans had. "No bedroom promises, made at the height of sex and lasting no longer than the act."

Slowly, he tipped her head back and lowered his lips to hers, stopping just before they touched, enjoying her slight breath that brushed his lips. He closed his eyes and knew with Alexa he could weave each stroke of fingers, each touch, each kiss into the choreography of a formal dance, important and essential and perfect.

Umilla grunted and Bastien straightened.

"Let's go," Umilla said. She was dressed for the cool night too.

Narrowing his eyes, Bastien said, "You aren't invited." He hurried Alexa from her suite.

Umilla chanted a clean-up spell, then followed them. Bastien frowned as she joined them on the tower landing.

"I will visit my friend Crin. He's the farrier for the Castle," Umilla announced with pride.

"Go, Umilla." Alexa grinned.

The serving woman patted Alexa's shoulder. "Black-and-whites are excellent lovers. It's the energy fluctuations. You are in good hands with Bastien. The feycoocu trusts him too." She hurried down the stairs.

Alexa looked up at Bastien. "What's a 'farrier'?"

"Fa-ri-er," he pronounced. "A person who makes shoes for horses and volarans."

"Thank you. You don't make me feel stupid when I ask questions. That's good." Her expression turned serious. "You must promise to be honest. You didn't, before."

19

Bastien took both her hands in his own, enveloping them, warming them, liking the tune that hummed between them with layers of budding friendship, heating passion. He stared down into her eyes.

"I promise."

More harmony was added to the melody between them. They both shivered.

He kept her close as they descended the stairs from her tower. "I want you. All the time I've been apart, I've wanted you. More than just sex. More than the notes that tied us when you cleared my flaw." He led her into the yard and down the paved walk. "More than the bass rhythm that rolled between us since you saved my life."

She caught her breath, glanced at him.

"I remember," he said. "Your beautiful eyes. The strength of your will. Your unusual Power. It was like a dream for a while, but then I found the stream of notes between us and knew the experience had been real. Even then, I thought more about you than any other woman in my life."

They walked down Temple Ward and through the gate to the Lower Ward. Bastien gestured to the right where Horseshoe Close and Hall was reached through a short passage about three horses wide.

Alexa strode over to the alley and peered down it. "It's interesting." She sighed. "I've been here more than a month and still haven't explored all the Castle, let alone Castleton."

Bastien squeezed her hand. "Tell me."

"You won't laugh?"

"You're an Exotique, strange to all of Lladrana. I'm a black-and-white, never fully accepted either. We are both seen as…different." He meant what he said.

"Not worse. Not lower. Just different," she said.

"Yes."

"I doubt that I can do what the Marshalls and Chevaliers have Summoned me here to do."

"And that is?"

She laughed shortly. "Defend Lladrana. Find the way to make new fenceposts, mend and rePower the boundaries so Lladrana has secure borders again. Maybe even kill all the monsters. I don't know. I think they expect everything of me."

He drew her close to his body, until their clothes brushed and they shared their heat. Since she didn't meet his gaze, he spoke to the top of her head. "I don't expect anything of you."

Alexa stepped away, face remote again, and he hated it.

"Wrong," she said. "You expect me to be your lover, your Pair, to be of use in your angry one-upmanship with your father and the other Marshalls."

"No!" He framed her face in his hands, tilted it upward to

meet his gaze. "I won't deny that there will be times that I will goad my father. I'm human, and if I were to promise you I'd never spur him, I'd lie, because I know my emotions will carry me away now and again. And I'll tell you that I *will* prod the Marshalls to change, but I think you want that too. We can work together on that. We can be together, work together. That's what a Pair bond is."

Her gaze examined his face, her mind touched his, explored—she felt his emotions, his desire for her, to live with her. To *be* with her.

She smiled, stood on tiptoe to brush his lips. "We can try."

Huge, giddy relief washed through him. He kept her right hand and urged her through the lower gate and down the path to Castleton.

They didn't talk, but there wasn't silence between them. Their Song bloomed and grew, twined around them, connected them. The melody was rich and varied, with lilting measures as well as crashing chords. Already they'd shared life-altering experiences, already they were journeying on a path together. Bastien intended that journey to be long and sweet. And full of grace.

Since he wanted only her company, and wanted her in bed as soon as possible, Bastien took the shortcut to the armorer and kept the transaction brief. From the interested look in the man's eyes when he saw Alexa, Bastien judged the tale of their training combat had reached the town and he'd just given the man a new installment in a good story.

When they left, he carried his mail under his arm. Alexa took very little steps. He'd shortened his stride to match hers, but the rippling desire inside him mounted each moment and the path to the Castle had never felt so long.

They were just out of the town gates when they were hailed. "Marshall, Chevalier Vauxveau!"

Bastien cursed under his breath and Alexa smiled, sensing his impatience. She really didn't want this peaceful time between them to end either.

She turned to see a young man about the age of Urvey, but with an air of confidence and a healthier aspect, hurry toward them.

He bowed. "Will you come with me, please?"

Bastien's hand slipped up to her elbow, and he bent in a gesture both courteous and protective. Some sort of guy-body-language that had an intrigued gleam showing in the teen's eyes.

"He's the journeyman of Sevair Masif, a Guildmaster of the Town."

She recalled Masif, the man who had interrupted the Marshalls at the Nom de Nom. He'd taken a jerir bath, and he'd destroyed the Mockers.

Bastien had already begun following the youth. "Masif is a good man. Smart."

"I agree."

Bastien scowled. "You've met him?"

Alexa lifted her chin. "He brought me tea." Or arranged for the Trademaster to deliver it. "He's young and personable."

More muttering from Bastien, then he pasted on a smile and said, "A good friend to the Chevaliers."

"In what way?" Alexa asked.

A faint smile curved Bastien's lips. "He keeps us apprised of what's going on in the Town and whatever he learns is happening in the Castle—with a different perspective. Also, when there are disputes between townsfolk and the Chevaliers, he usually is one of the calm heads on the side of the townspeople that prevails. He's an arbitrator."

"You must know him well, then."

Bastien laughed. "Are you hinting that I might have been in a brawl or two?"

"Would you rather I say it straight out? And how many brawls have you been in? How many times hauled before an arbitrator?"

He shrugged. "I can't recall. Masif is a friend of my brother's too."

Alexa got the idea from Bastien's tone that the Guildmaster was not a friend of Reynardus's. "He doesn't see eye to eye with your father?"

"Let's say that he is a forward-thinking man, one willing to explore new ideas, like most Chevaliers and Citymasters, and unlike the Marshalls who are stuck in old mind-sets."

"Hmm," Alexa said. She was still figuring out what might be traditional and customary and what was considered breathtakingly innovative.

They turned a corner into a square that was rimmed with lampposts consisting of large glowing crystals atop metal poles. The neighborhood seemed to be prosperous, maybe even more than upper middle-class, maybe rich. The houses were all three stories, made of stone, and some had bay windows. Each door was painted a different color.

As she recalled, Masif seemed to be in his early thirties—young like Luthan and Bastien to have such responsibilities and status. A definite contrast in age to the Marshalls, who all seemed to be sixty or older. She supposed age and wealth and Power—magical and monetary—clustered together here in Lladrana as often as they did on Earth.

"He's a stonemason?" she asked as they walked along the square. A large, green park was in the center, with trees blossoming, including a copse of brithenwood. The scent was heady, yet comforting.

"More, he's a brilliant architect. If you have any Exotique ideas about building on to your home, he'd be a good one to see. Like I said, a man willing to think in new ways."

As always, the mention of her house made a warmth bloom inside her. She had a home. Land. She was making a place for her-self here.

The young man stopped at a small walkway up to stone stairs and a lovely stone house. He opened the door and ushered them in.

A beautiful chandelier with slim, pointed white crystals illuminated a small entryway. The walls were hung with bright tapestries of forest scenes. Alexa didn't have time to study them before they were shown into a library.

It was a comfortable room full of wooden bookcases and rich carpets. On the desk was a neat pile of papers that looked like a report, and nothing else.

As they entered, Masif himself stood in the center of a grouping of two large chairs and a small couch near the fire.

Alexa liked the room a lot, though it seemed as if everything was a shade too neat, too precisely placed. Still, she took mental notes so she could compare her own library to this one. She wanted one as homey.

"Please, sit. Refreshments?" Masif asked.

"No, thank you," Bastien said. He seated her and sat himself, then gave Masif some guy-look that made the man look amused.

"I'll get right to the point, then," Masif said, and sat once more. "We are concerned about some missing people…. The Citymasters have been divided regarding whether to bother the Marshalls with the discrepancies, but I believe we have a problem." He gestured to the papers on his desk. "It appears that the disappearances started with animals—pets or food animals—then escalated to children, the elderly, then adults in their prime."

Bastien tensed beside her. "How many people?"

Masif tapped steepled fingers together. "Twenty confirmed disappearances of people. About twice that of animals."

"Bad," said Bastien.

"Yes. It seems the horrors have touched us here—something more than the frinks or Mockers. We don't know what. Our Lorebooks don't record anything more threatening. It is interesting that the area first affected was near the place where the Marshall and I disposed of the Mockers."

Masif met her eyes for the first time. They shared that memory.

Bastien draped his arm around Alexa's shoulders. Masif smiled. Bastien traced circles on her shoulder.

"You think it might be something associated with the Mockers?"

"I don't know." He glanced again toward the report. "But it is interesting that no one was designated missing during a certain time period."

"Yes?" Bastien asked.

"When Marshall Alyeka was away from the Castle on her travels," Masif said softly. "The disappearances resumed when she returned. And they seem to be increasing exponentially."

When Bastien's face went tight, he looked remarkably like his brother, even a bit like his father, Alexa thought.

"Whatever it is will have to get through me to touch her," Bastien said.

"I can see that." Masif nodded. "Good. The one thing all the Masters in all the City and Town gatherings agree on is that Marshall Alyeka is a boon to Lladrana."

Joan of Arc again. Alexa suppressed a sigh.

Masif smiled and looked much younger, more approachable. "I don't recall if I said it before, Marshall, but welcome to Lladrana."

"Thank you." Alexa inclined her head.

Bastien drummed his fingers on her shoulder, tugged at her hair a bit, like he was thinking hard. "I don't know if you've heard..."

Masif's gaze sharpened.

"The Chevaliers of the Field have seen dreeths near battles."

Alexa had seen pictures of dreeths—huge, bloated ptero-dactyl-things—in a Lorebook. She shifted a little closer to Bastien.

The Citymaster paled under his golden skin. "Dreeths," he breathed. "No. We haven't heard this. Things are getting worse. These strange vanishings. Dreeths. The horrors are invading our land." Stern again, his eyes met hers, then Bastien's. "We must stop this. At any cost."

"I agree. I'll let Lady Hallard and my brother Luthan know of your concerns." Standing, Bastien pulled Alexa to her feet.

Masif frowned as he rose. "Do you think we should notify the Sorcerers and Sorceresses of the Tower?"

A crack of laughter escaped Bastien. "I'd wager they already know. Who speaks to them on behalf of the cities and towns?"

Grimacing, Masif said, "We've expected the Marshalls to do that for us. Either we will have to appoint a spokesperson or you will have to ensure the Marshalls earn our trust again."

"We're doing our best, but it's a slow process," Bastien said.

"One last thing," Masif said.

"Yes?" Bastien asked.

"There have also been accounts of an unusual gray dust—"

Something in his tone chilled her to the bone. Visions of Mockers and frinks and people being sucked dry until their bodies turned into dust particles sped through Alexa's mind. Since the two men were unnaturally quiet, muscles tensed, she got the idea they imagined the same thing.

"Bad," said Bastien.

Masif nodded. "Very bad."

"We'll take care of it," Alexa said, not knowing why she said it, where the words came from.

"Of course we will," said Masif.

"Of course," Bastien echoed.

Their walk back up to the Castle was different from their stroll down to the Town. The silence wore on her.

"Bastien," she said.

He looked down at her and squeezed her hand. "Yes?"

She licked her lips. "I think I know what sort of horror it might be. I think I ran into it."

"What!" All his attention focused on her.

She sensed his magic rising.

"That night at the inn, The Singer's Hand, I ran into something. It was like a spider's web in a narrow passage. It tried to smother me, but I fought it off. I thought... I don't know that I *did* think about it." She'd been foolishly obsessing over Bastien the next day, then had forgotten about the web-thing. "I suppose I thought it was a regular bad-magic thing that I didn't know about but everyone else did."

Bastien swore. His face took on an underlying pallor. He pulled her close in a hug. His hands rubbed up and down her back. "The things you don't know scare me. We'll keep our eyes out for this beast."

He kissed her hard, then released her and they walked faster now up to the Castle. Alexa tried *not* to think, not to visualize or extrapolate what had happened to the towns she'd visited. Not to worry whether something else was after her now.

Even though it was late when they reached the Castle, Alexa insisted on speaking to the Marshalls about Masif's news. She considered it a good omen that they were all bathing together in the main baths. She steeled herself to undress and briefly appear naked before them.

The main bath was the turquoise and white one where Alexa

had been drugged. Because of that memory and because there was usually someone from the Noble Apartments or one of the Marshalls there when she wanted to bathe privately, she usually showered. She didn't think she'd ever be comfortable bathing publicly in mixed company.

So she was brisk in her undressing, but still knew that her skin was so pale that blue veins showed under her skin—veins that were never seen in Lladranans. Her nipples were different-colored, and her pubic hair was now as silver as the hair on her head. Her coloring made people stare—even the Marshalls. And when Bastien stopped his undressing to watch her every move, it made her blush—and that was even more interesting from everyone's point of view but her own.

She jumped into the water as if it was always the way she entered a bathing pool and she didn't care where the splash flew.

Finally she was settled in, with Bastien beside her. She glanced from Bastien to his father, Reynardus, noting the scars on both their bodies, the blue aura from the jerir that seemed easier to see in the rising steam. Even though she knew Reynardus had braved the jerir twice and Bastien only once, Bastien's aura was thicker, stronger. Wild magic.

He must have caught the tenor of her thoughts because he tugged at a strand of her silver hair and said, "You glow like a blue star. Awesome. Perfect."

She snorted, not believing that for an instant. Then she sucked in a deep breath and told the Marshalls of their little trip to Town and the visit with Sevair Masif.

Faith, the Loremarshall, frowned and suddenly a book plopped gently onto the water, floating, green leather cover closed.

Alexa could read the title! Even curlicued letters in gold didn't stop her. It said *Lorebook of Monsters*. She bit her lip and slid down a little so the steam masked the stinging in her eyes. She had so missed reading!

"Not a great deal of information," Faith said, then addressed the book. "Unseen horror apparently able to manifest deep in Lladrana in the towns and cities and able to move from place to place, apparently feeding on animals then children then adults, apparently gaining strength, apparently leaving no trace except gray dust."

The book quivered, sending out tiny ripples of water. The cover opened and smacked the water, the pages riffled themselves to the end, then back, then fluttered to a halt near the end of the book. Water beaded on the pages, then ran off into the bath.

Alexa stared. Nobody seemed to think a floating book with waterproof pages was anything unusual. Wow. Again wow. Would wonders never cease? If she stayed in Lladrana the rest of her life, she figured some magic would surprise her every day.

The Marshalls drifted over to the book. "Johnsa will image for me," Faith said.

Johnsa, Faith's Sword, touched the tip of her forefinger to the drawing. Her finger and the page glowed red, then a three-dimensional image consolidated in the middle of the pool. It looked like a nasty gray cocoon.

Faith summed up the information in a cool voice. "This is a tournpench, and it meets most of the qualifications stated above. The Lorebook of Monsters is arranged by threat. As you can see, this one is near the end of the book, essentially a minor evil on the level of a snipper. It is of little threat to any being with three strands of silver at one temple, which would include most of the middle class of townsfolk and above. The tournpench is not considered a horror from over the border, but something manifesting from a miasma of magic in a certain neighborhood or town. As it grows stronger, it can move." She frowned. "This notes it should move more slowly than Alyeka reported."

"Something generated by a town. That would make it none of our affair, and Town or City business," Reynardus said.

"I agree," Johnsa said, and let the image fade.

Reynardus raised his eyebrows. "Does anyone *not* agree?"

No one spoke. Alexa struggled with an uneasy feeling. What they said didn't feel right, but she was so new to her magic that she couldn't describe *why*.

Bastien snorted, stood and walked to the pool's steps, immediately distracting Alexa. God, what an ass the man had! His back was less scarred than his front. Figured, he'd always be one to face his enemies head-on—though from the way he irritated people, she would have expected to see a knife scar in his back.... He took a dark blue robe from one of those hanging on a hook in a pillar, wrapped himself in it and stared back at the Marshalls.

"You lot are as unhelpful as ever." Then he switched his attention to Alexa, and smiled slowly.

She thought the pool heated ten degrees with that smile. He retrieved another robe and she saw that it was a lot shorter than the others. And purple.

She was torn between pride that she had a robe like the rest of the Marshalls and resignation that no one had asked her if she wanted a purple one.

Gritting her teeth and trying to appear supremely unconcerned at her nudity, she got out of the water. Bastien whipped the robe around her and tied the belt, then dropped a kiss on her wet head.

"We must hurry and leave. I'd rather not display the aroused state of my body to everyone in the room," he whispered huskily. "Good thing these robes are thick."

He rolled their discarded clothes into the parcel with his new mail tunic and hustled her from the chamber.

They walked through the Castle hand in hand. Barefoot, wet-headed and only covered in the robe, Alexa should have been cold. Instead her body was heated with the anticipation of love-making.

Bastien bent his head. "You hurried too quickly into and out of the bathing pool. I didn't get to see my fill of you. Only enough to tempt me beyond reason."

Her heart thumped harder and a low, insistent ache settled inside. She was panting by the time they entered her suite.

He dropped the parcel jingling to the floor and crowded her back against the wall. Slipping both hands inside her robe, he covered her nipples. She sensed he watched her face, but the small room was too dark for her to see him. Slowly his hands moved over her breasts, then his thumbs and forefingers lightly pinched her nipples. Magic combined with sizzling pleasure and shot straight to her core, exploding her into a quick orgasm. She cried out and gripped his shoulders.

Her release at his hands, at the smallest of love play made Bastien feel more powerful than at any other time in his life. He could drive this woman, this unique and special woman, to peak with a touch. Her heart pounding under his hand, her ragged breathing and little pleasure whimpers drove his own passion beyond delightful need to aching desperation.

Her skin was pale, her aura glowed blue, her Power jade green, in melting layers that dazzled him. The scent of her was so alluring that he doubted he would ever tire of it, knew he'd have to lick the sheen of perspiration from her body, just to pull the taste of her deep inside him.

As he would soon be deep inside her. His blood roared in his veins, drummed in his ears until he was deaf, blind, and could only touch and smell her.

Agony and ecstasy.

He lifted her, so light, so soft, so exquisitely exotic, and wrapped her legs around his waist. He wanted her lower, much lower, but had to kiss her now. With burning lips he found her cheek, glided his mouth to hers, slid his tongue along her lips. Jolted from her the taste of passion.

No control. None. He yanked the belt of his robe open, brought her onto him. Plunged into her deep.

She sang a Song of rising desire and he had to have her. Magic and body, heart and soul. Her Song plucked all his own chords, pulled at his magic to blend with hers.

He forged into her, retreated, lunged deep again, the rhythm and beat and Power nothing he'd felt before, nothing he could deny. Her hands convulsed around his shoulders, nails digging in. He had to taste her mouth as she climaxed, had to drink her Song into himself. His wild magic burst free and he shuddered, pouring all of himself into her.

That night he shared himself with her as he'd done with no other. He fulfilled unrecognized desires. Only sensation, only loving, only intimacy mattered.

20

If Alexa opened her eyes, she'd see sunlight—and she wasn't ready for the day.

"I'm sorry," Bastien whispered. The lightest of butterfly touches flowed into her mind with the lilting melody reverberating between them. Though his voice was rough with morning, waves of tenderness flowed to her from him, along with his gentle caress on her shoulder.

No use pretending she was asleep. No use pretending either, that there was no Pair link between them. The Song ran true and strong. She opened her eyes to see him on his side, leaning toward her, eyes intense. Suddenly the strangeness of him, of the bond, of *everything* hit her and she scrambled out of bed. She grabbed a throw and draped it around herself. Alexa didn't know what he was apologizing for and didn't think she wanted to know. Her face heated as she recalled everything they'd done to each other in the dark.

"Good, fine," she squeaked. She looked around. Where was Sin-afin when Alexa needed her as a distraction?

He stacked a couple of pillows and plumped them up, then sank back on them with a sigh, still staring at her. The covers rode downward and exposed his muscular torso.

"I'm sorry that I ran from you the last time we had loving, just as you're trying to distance yourself now. It's a little fearsome, isn't it, being so close to a person—physically, mentally, emotionally?"

His words were loud and distinct in her mind, in her ears. Lladranan, but better than before. The floor seemed to tilt under her feet. She let go of her tunic and grabbed the bedpost. "Llad-ranan. The language, it's even clearer now. I think I'm getting nu-ances, inflections, connotations. Whew!" And because she could, she knew how heavy her accent was. She wanted to plop down on the bed, but it was too damn high.

Bastien sat up, set his hands on her waist and lifted her back to the bed beside him with no magic, sheer muscle. Another daunt-ing thing—that he was so strong. She'd have to grab on to her self-confidence, hard, or he'd overwhelm her.

He looked smug.

His arm came around her waist and pulled her close. "I'm sorry I ran. It was rude."

He brushed a soft kiss on her mouth and her insides clutched at the taste of him. With every word, every gentle caress, she felt her options narrowing, felt more herded down a specific path.

"Shh." His large hand stroked down her back. "Don't be afraid. This will come out all right."

She fought to keep her inward trembling from showing and wondered how often the shock of being in an alien culture would overwhelm her.

"So I am sorry I ran from the situation. That was my worst fault with you, but not the only thing I must apologize for."

The warmth of his body comforted her. She could deal with this new turn of events, she knew it, she just needed a little time. Being so intimate with another could be a *good* thing, cement her status in Lladrana. The night before, he'd been so easy to talk to, so understanding. Maybe she could give him the benefit of the doubt. After all, there was no denying how far they'd explored each other. It *hadn't* been just sex.

He set her back in the curve of his arm, then tipped up her chin so her eyes met his. Since his touch was gentle, one she could break easily, she let him do it.

"I'm also sorry that I never thanked you for saving my life."

She dipped her head. "You're welcome. Last night, you said you remembered. I didn't think you could."

Bastien chuckled, stroked her cheek with his thumb. "Not remember such a face, the color of cream? Not recall such hair, so light and fine? Such striking eyes?"

She blinked. "I think you're trying to use charm on me."

His smile was simply stunning. "Is it working?"

"Maybe."

He kissed her again, a little harder, a little deeper. "Your charm works on me too. Your many charms."

The alarm claxon shrieked. Alexa was out of bed and dressed in two minutes, padding, mail and all, and heading toward the door, when Bastien snagged her arm.

"Wait."

"I can't." She struggled against his grip.

"*Wait!* You are Paired now, and so am I. We are *Paired*."

Alexa froze. "We fight together?"

"Yes," he said aloud. *Urvey, my gear, now!* he mind-called, and Alexa heard him.

This would take getting used to.

Since she was waiting, she did some stretches. Wearing chain mail hampered a person, even though it was magically "lightened." She loosened her baton and her sword in their sheaths.

Sinafin zoomed in through the window, no longer a pretty red bird with a long tail, but a hawk, ready to fight.

Jumpy at being made to stay when she itched to go, Alexa demanded, "Where have you been?" It was the first time she'd ever asked. She'd always figured Sinafin was entitled to her privacy.

The bird stared at her, at Bastien who strode to the door to open it for Urvey. *Good. You have composed a Pairing Song between you. Now we will see real results!*

"Yeah, sure." Today would be *the* day. The day she was no longer *just* Marshall Alexa. The upcoming battle would determine her status once and for all, and the longer she had to wait, the more anxious she became. It was so much easier to get into the middle of a fight and let her physical and magical training take over.

She went into her sitting room, where Urvey was garbing Bastien. Big, strong, tough. Her breath clogged in her throat. She was looking at a male in his prime, a man ready to defend his land with his life. It didn't matter that she was clothed the same way, she felt a primal wave of attraction of the female for a strong male protector. She shook her head at her reaction. She was a liberated woman, but her hormones kept tingling.

Bastien wore his new chain mail and a midnight-blue surcoat. The surcoat had his coat of arms and her purple flower embroidered on it. Alexa inhaled shakily. *Paired.* This man would work with her, fight with her, defend her. And she would do the same. Even now she felt the deep humming of the tune between them, signifying the bond that would make them a team as good as any of the Chevalier Pairs. Their energy would mix well, providing them both with strength; their communication would be flawless.

As he raised his arms for Urvey to buckle his swordbelt on, Bastien winked.

Alexa tried a smile.

He grinned, then lowered his arms and settled his sword in place. Alexa wondered which baton he would choose, if he Tested to be a Marshall. She was sure he'd pass. But would he want to Test? She frowned. He'd made no bones about not caring for the Marshalls. How would he work with his father? How would *they*?

She started her deep-breathing cycle, raising her magic, and *knew* that she and Bastien would outperform Reynardus and Ivrog. Perhaps even Thealia and Partis.

Bastien strode over, spurs jingling. His hands were still bare, as were hers. He grasped her fingers and brought both her hands to his lips, kissed her fingers, then released them and donned his flying gloves. "Ready to go, Pairling?"

Alexa made her smile brighter. "Of course." She'd rather crawl back into bed—or under it.

When they flew above the new incursion, they saw two groups of Chevaliers battling some horrors—slayers and renders, with only one soul-sucker. A few yards down the border, about fifteen monsters ran from the rocky outcroppings of their own land into Lladrana. Alexa gasped. This was the largest conglomeration of evil beasts she'd seen since coming to Lladrana.

She pointed, and Bastien nodded, his face grim. His volaran plummeted down near the new horrors.

Bastien's volaran whirled, dove, pirouetted—and lost Alexa. The flying horse's horrified neigh matched Bastien's clutching heart. He *could not* lose her, not after they'd had so very few minutes together.

Alexa found herself airborne. She drew in a huge breath of sharp, cold air and let it out in a shrilling "Eek" that was also a spell.

It slowed her descent, and seemed to slow time too, so she could think.

Being a lousy rider and flier, she'd known this would happen. Maybe often. So she and Madame had prepared for the worst. When Madame had asked what she would naturally say in the circumstances and Alexa had let out her "eek," Madame had looked appalled. Alexa always knew Madame was a tough cookie, but that had confirmed it. No doubt, Madame, if she'd been so clumsy as to fall off a horse, would have chanted "float like a feather." Alexa just figured "eek" was better than "shiiit."

She'd hit the ground and roll, had to be ready to fight.

Midair she pulled her broadsword, be-spelled to be light and magical and very, very sharp.

She cut off upraised paws, then cleaved the render's body in two furry halves as her feet hit the earth. She blocked out the sight of spurting dark blood, of mutilated monster parts. The kill had steadied her landing. She spun and her sword sliced the abdomen of the slayer open, spilling slimy green guts.

Hearing a cry, she ran toward it, panting, scanning her path for monsters. Thealia shouted again, and took the head off a soul-sucker. The monster crumpled.

It materialized from a dark thickening of the air, wings flapping with a slow, scaley thunder.

"Dreeth!" Faith screamed.

The pterodactyl-thing dove for the largest volaran on the field—Bastien's.

Then Alexa was there, before it, encompassed by it, slashing its leathery underbelly, hacking at a wickedly clawed ankle. She didn't know how to fight it. Didn't know anything save it was huge and its stench choked her and she was terrified it would kill her and if she killed it first it would fall and crush her. Her baton flew to her left hand. She stepped in, closer to the underbelly.

Alexa! Bastien shouted-sang in her ear. A whirlwind of Power snapped between them, sounding like the roar of a cannon, blinding her, deafening her, bathing her in an eerie green aura.

She jammed the flaming end of her baton into the dreeth. "Die!" she screamed, and flung all that she had, all that she was, and all she could of Bastien, into the command-spell, pouring the dark horror of Power into its convulsing body until blackness claimed her.

It's falling! Help me get her! Bastien cried, desperate to link with the Marshalls and save his lover.

Power flooded into him, more than he'd ever had even in his wildest times of uncontrolled magic. He pulled his short-sword and directed the Power. "Burn!" he commanded. The sword did, and when he thrust it into a membraned wing, the dreeth went up like torched parchment. Bastien jumped from his volaran, scooped up his fallen woman—she was so small!—and ran from the flaming monster, which was burning like a small tower.

His volaran caught him by his neck and took off, carrying Bastien and his lady, flying only a few feet from the ground and then landing in the midst of the gathered Marshalls.

Bastien sank to the ground, cradling Alexa. She was pale, but breathing, alive and strong—he knew that from their link, the Song that reverberated to the depths of his mind, his heart. Her hand still curled around the Jade Baton, which looked completely unharmed. A marvel.

"Congratulations!" Reynardus grinned and slapped Bastien on the shoulder. "You have found your fate, *Shield* Bastien."

Thealia sent Reynardus a dirty look. "It has never been a dishonor for a man to be a Shield, for a team to be female Sword and male Shield."

"Of course not," Reynardus said, his tone clearly indicating the opposite.

Settling Alexa more comfortably in his arms, Bastien used trembling fingers to smooth her silver hair back from her face. Then he narrowed his eyes and looked up at his father with an equally mean grin, baring his teeth.

"It's been a long, long time since a Marshall Pair has brought down a dreeth."

Reynardus frowned. Before he could speak, Faith said, "Three centuries, since the last one appeared. A bad sign that it has come now."

"But it is the biggest and the best of the kills." He glanced to where the flying monster still burned oily, as big as a house. "I claim the beak tip for my mate, Exotique Alexa Swordmarshall of the Jade Baton of Honor, and all the teeth that remain from the beak for necklaces for her and myself." To taunt his father. "To be used as daily ornaments."

Partis placed a hand on Alexa's forehead; he was the Marshall most skilled in medicine. "Power conduit concussion. Emotional turmoil from the battle Pairing." *Just plain shock from terror,* he added silently to Bastien. "She'll wake when she's better, but I doubt it will be before late this evening. I'd say that during one of those *three* immersions in the jerir—" now he sent a smirk at Reynardus "—Alyeka swallowed some of the stuff. It had to have helped her somehow." He stood and leaned on his staff. Like everyone else, he watched the dreeth burn.

Faith slipped her arm around her mate, Johnsa. "I *think* both the dreeth's acid sac and its heart remain after it burns." Faith gnawed at her lip. "I know all the remains have great Power, but what, I don't recall. I wish I had my books," she muttered.

Thealia laughed and squeezed Bastien's shoulder. "Whether you keep the remnants of the dreeth for their Power, or not, you do have the option of selling them to a Sorcerer or Sorceress. I'm sure they'd go for a fortune. You are a very wealthy man, now, Bastien."

"From what I know of her, my mate will only want to keep one tooth," Bastien muttered, still stroking Alexa's hair, his thumb brushing the pulse in her temple to comfort himself. "I'm a lucky man. If there's any part of the wing left, I'd like to have it mounted and hung in the Hall of the Marshalls. The best prize in the Hall."

Reynardus grunted and walked away, calling for his volaran.

"Chevaliers are arriving," Thealia said.

For the first time, Bastien realized how short the battle had been. A small group of renders, slayers and soul-suckers, outnumbered by the Marshalls, had been easily defeated. Then the dreeth…

Luthan strode up to them. Lady Hallard looked at the rest of the Chevaliers surrounding the burning dreeth wistfully, then at the group of Marshalls, set her shoulders and followed Luthan.

"Is she all right?" Luthan asked.

Bastien stood with Alexa in his arms. He wasn't going to let go of her. "She's fine, just sleeping off the shock of her first dreeth kill," he said with pride.

Luthan's eyes nearly bulged from his sockets, making Bastien laugh, easing his tension. "*She* killed the dreeth?"

"Yes, with this fair hand." Bastien indicated her fingers still holding the Jade Baton.

Luthan scrutinized the baton. "It looks no different."

"Interesting, eh?" Bastien inhaled deeply. "She's a Sword. I'm a Shield."

"Good!"

Bastien blinked.

"You have too many scars as it is, have been injured too often, too deeply." Luthan chuckled at Bastien's relieved face. "Do you really think anyone will even *think* to call you a coward, brother?" Luthan shrugged. "And if they do, you can always wear your ugly soul-sucker hat."

Feeling cheered, Bastien whistled his hat to his head. The brim shaded his eyes so he could get a better look at the flaming dreeth and the ever-increasing crowd of Chevaliers as he walked to his volaran. Reluctantly, he handed Alexa to his brother while he soothed his volaran, checked its strength and energy for the flight back to the Castle, and mounted. He scowled when Luthan continued to cuddle Alexa.

"A very nice armful, not quite as lean and tough as most Chevaliers. Very womanly," Luthan said.

"Give her back!" Atop his volaran, Bastien held out his arms for his woman.

Luthan laughed and helped Bastien arrange the limp Alexa in front of him, tying them together with spells using protection and love. "You are well and truly Paired," Luthan said.

Bastien settled his mate against himself, felt better with her body in his arms.

"When are you going to Test for Marshall?" asked Luthan.

Unlike every other time this question had been aimed at him during his life, Bastien remained silent.

"It's the only way to protect her, you know."

Bastien shuddered, remembering the curving beak of the dreeth bouncing off the shield he'd used to envelop Alexa, the punishing blow he'd taken. Better than the beak piercing her back. He recalled the awful, searing wetness of the acid the dreeth spewed, which would have covered her. Only his shield had saved her. Only their Pair bond, and the energy of the Pairing experience.

"I'll think about Testing for Marshall," he said, breaking a lifetime vow to himself.

Luthan eyed the dreeth bonfire, obviously wanting to take a good look. "A thing that big should burn all day—maybe tonight too. Nasty for the land beneath, though. Think that I learned somewhere that only those who killed it are able to handle the remains. Those trophies will be safe enough until you return."

That's what Bastien thought.

Grinning up at him, Luthan swatted the volaran on the rump. "Be interesting to see what baton you pick, little brother."

Bastien grinned at him. "Get lost."

Under the sharp eyes of Sinafin as warhawk, and of Umilla, Bastien undressed Alexa, clothed her limp body in a sleep-shift, and put her into a bed warmed by a spell and stacked with down comforters.

He sat next to her for a while, holding her hand, forcing his jumping heart and spiking emotions to calm. Seeing her in battle had been an enlightening and frightening experience, something he wasn't used to. He had good friends, and his brother, but he had never feared for them when they fought. He trusted the Song that they would come through—even after losing a childhood friend to the horrors.

But Alexa was different—very close to being a part of him now. Though he hadn't ever feared too much for himself, accepting if he died it would be at the right time, he was terrified for her.

Luthan was right. The best way to protect her was to be a full Marshall himself, but if he dwelt on that idea for very long it would make him sick. So he got up and got moving. If it had to be done, get it done *now*.

Alexa murmured in distress as he pulled his hand away, moved restlessly.

"Sleep, now. You are safe and will remain so. I promise you."

"Bastien," she sighed.

"Yes, Pairling. Sleep."

As he moved away, Umilla took his seat. Sinafin clicked her beak in approval, her eyes gleaming.

He squared his shoulders and left his lover's suite, winding down the stairs and to the Marshalls' Council Room, where they all proceeded to dissect the battle.

Alexa tossed and turned, but the dream images came, vivid and real. Bastien was marching to the Marshalls, ready to confront them about something. She tried to surface from the cocoon of sleep, but her mind and body protested and she was too weary.

Still, she tried to follow him, to help him. Or just be with him. She felt the warmth of his smile.

I thought to do this without you, by myself. For my own pride. He mocked himself. *But you're here. I should have known that the tune playing between us wouldn't allow for such an important experience to be suffered alone.*

I'm not here. I'm dreaming, she said solemnly.

Ah, is that the case? He sounded genuinely amused.

Yes. She wanted to nod, but she *was* asleep after all, so she squeezed the pillow tighter. It was so warm and comfortable here and she sensed she'd be facing a dreadful memory if she woke. She was tired, so tired she didn't want to open her eyes.

That's right, Bastien crooned. *Stay here in the back of my mind, within reach, and sleep.*

That sounded contradictory, but she didn't have the energy to ask what new magic was at work.

I cherish your presence, he said.

A very wonderful dream, she said as more than the bed gave her warmth—his words and the connection and the incredible feeling sang inside her.

Bastien felt Alexa sink into deeper sleep. He'd try to spare her his turmoil as long as he could. He'd dealt with his wild magic all his life; sometimes control had been possible, sometimes not. It occurred to him that handling Alexa would be very much like handling his wild magic—she would sometimes be completely incalculable. He grinned. Life would be constantly interesting. So *this* was the destiny the Song had had in store for him all his life.

But he'd lingered outside the door of the Marshalls' Chamber long enough. Time to face his fate. He strummed the doorharp back and forth and gave the door a rhythmic rap.

"Enter," said the cold voice of his father Reynardus.

Bastien opened the door and strolled in. Late afternoon light poured through the narrow, many-paned windows, illuminating the room and making the Marshalls look like an artist's study of privilege and power. He swept a bow, sent a glance around the table, then cocked his hip and hooked his thumbs in his belt.

"I've come to Test for Marshall."

"Blessings," murmured Thealia. "It's about time one of my godsons did that."

He grinned. "Too bad it isn't Luthan, eh, Godmama Thealia?"

She pokered up as he'd expected.

"Song seems to direct Luthan's flight path in another direction." Her brow knit. "But in the end, I think he'll be a Marshall too."

Reynardus rose. "You, a black-and-white, wish to Test for Marshall."

Bastien frowned. "No one told me you had hearing problems."

A stifled choking came from Mace.

Faith, the historian, stood. "I vote we accept the applicant for Marshall Testing and proceed with the Tests this evening and tonight, so the outcome will be determined immediately."

"I agree," said Thealia.

"And I," agreed Partis.

"Yes," said Bastien's uncle Ivrog, Shield to Reynardus, surprising Bastien.

He scrutinized his uncle and found the man's eyes clear of

drink, unclouded, even keen. With surprise, Bastien realized his uncle was no longer a drunkard. Bastien opened his mind to the familial link. His father's tune was loud, strong, angry. His uncle's melody sounded like a rushing river, with depths Bastien had never considered.

Alexa murmured in his mind, *Ivrog is a good man.*

A new surprise. Somehow Alexa and Ivrog had met, and Bastien could hear simple notes exchanged between them.

Reynardus stood alone in his opinion, and Bastien experienced another flash of understanding. His father had been on his own and against the Marshalls most of the time lately. No wonder the man was so irritable—precious control was being stripped from him.

With a *thump,* a large Lorebook landed on the table in front of Faith, along with a sheet of parchment that looked like a list, and a box that rattled.

"Any objections to the Testing of Bastien Vauxveau for Marshall?" asked Thealia.

21

All the Marshalls in the Council Room stared at Bastien. Silence for ten heartbeats increased his tension and caused Alexa to rise from dozing.

Finally, Reynardus sat.

"I will be Notator for the Tests," Faith said.

No one disagreed.

"There are several different procedures for Testing an applicant," Faith continued, looking at Bastien, "and you may choose which process you want us to follow. The first way of Testing is for you to choose three character Test tokens from the box at random—your choice of Tests is seen as indications from the Song."

She looked at him.

He figured the Song had meddled in his life enough and more roughly than he'd liked. He rocked on his heels and smiled. "No, thank you."

"We have a standard Testing combination we vary from applicant to applicant." She flipped a page in the Lorebook. "We last used combination six, so we would use combination seven."

Seven had never been a lucky number for him. He'd lost many dice games throwing seven. Still smiling, he shook his head. "Can't we make it up as we go along?"

Thealia blew out an audible breath. "The Vauxveaus are ever contrary, every one of them."

"Thank you." Bastien nodded at her.

"A possibility," Faith said, "but the last resort. So unstructured."

"And the Marshalls are ever structured," Bastien said.

Faith plowed on. "Since you are already Paired with a Sword, you can take the same Tests as she, or opposite—"

"Yes." That rang true. Struck the right chord inside him.

Faith raised her brows. "Which?"

"The same as Alexa," Bastien said.

"Any objections?" asked Faith.

Silence.

Now Reynardus smiled faintly, and something fluttered in Bastien's gut. If he thought fast, maybe he could direct this process. He recalled Alexa had bested—killed—Defau Disparu. "The late Swordmarshall Disparu Tested Alexa's fighting ability. I stand ready to be Tested that way."

More quiet. The Marshalls exchanged unhappy glances.

"I've proven myself in the field. I am every bit the warrior my Lady Swordmarshall is," Bastien said coolly. "I match Alexa—isn't that what Pairs do? Match?"

Bastien's use of her name brought her back from dozing to her dream. *Fighting. Field. Warriors.* He was talking about her? Alexa Fitzwalter? As a warrior? She took a moment in her odd dream to ponder this. Was she? She'd fought all her life to get what she wanted. She'd waged civilized war through law school and had planned on tough but bloodless fighting throughout her life—as an attorney. She'd believed in her old career. Visions of renders and soul-suckers and slayers and the dreeth curdled her guts. But she imagined them all too well invading the village on her land, setting fire to her home, and a hard, fierce burning flared in her core. She would never allow it. She would fight to the last drop of her blood to stop that. To keep her home safe. To keep Bastien safe.

In her dream, she missed a remark from Reynardus, but knew it had been snide.

Bastien laughed shortly. "Then I will balance her inexperience. I *am* a seasoned warrior." A lightness lit the tone of his mind. He began to strip, turning a sly gaze to Faith, the historian. "I believe I heard once that one Marshall Test of field experience was count- ing the number of scars. I have a goodly number of scars." He threw his shirt on the table, pointed to a small white knot at the side of the ring finger of his left hand. "We'll call this 'one.'" He frowned. "I've had it for several years—I think I got it when my childhood friend and I fought two armored snippers."

It was all before her in those scars—the recollection of the quick, nasty fight with "lesser monsters over the years," the cheer- ful, male competition with his lost friend—a loss that still echoed grief in his thoughts. Her mind whirled, trying to grasp the new information. Then her dream eyes focused on his body, his beau- tiful, muscular frame under dreadfully scarred skin, and she whim- pered. Her resolve flamed white-blue-jade-green hot and was imprinted on her soul. She would never let him be hurt again, not if she could stop it.

His laugh rippled a tune in her head. He'd never let her stand in front of him if *he* could prevent it. They'd fly into the field to- gether. They'd battle together. They'd *triumph* together.

"Oh, put your shirt back on, Bastien. I'm sure you have a hundred battle scars," Thealia said irritably. She glanced at Faith. "That was the accepted figure, was it not?"

Faith cleared her throat, turned a page of the Lorebook. "Actually, it was a mere fifty."

Bastien chuckled and pulled his shirt on. "So much for the fighting experience Test." He struck a pose. "What's next?"

"Power," breathed Partis.

Bastien's face altered subtly. He'd had Power all his life. Fragmented Power as a black-and-white.

Everyone looked at his streaked hair.

No wonder his father smirked. Bastien *had* had problems controlling his Power, especially in new situations. He didn't know what Alexa's Test of Power had been, but reasoned it must have been very difficult. Bastien swallowed. Alexa was stronger than them all in Power. He set his jaw. But he was whole now—the flaw that had fragmented and blew his inherent magic wild in all directions had been mended by Alexa. He should be able to handle anything the Marshalls could dream up.

Reynardus steepled his fingers, tapped them together, smiled a renderlike smile. "An atomball," he said softly. "Make us an atomball."

Merde! It could drain him for days. It would *take* days.

That's not right. Alexa's sleepy voice was querulous in his mind.

Shh, rest, he said, pulling his thoughts from her.

"I've never made an atomball." Hadn't known anyone who had, hadn't known the Marshalls had. He gestured to Faith. "If the Lorebook has instructions, I'd like to glance at them."

Sinafin! Alexa's call echoed in his mind.

The pages of the book riffled themselves, then stopped. Bastien stepped up to scan it. Essentially it came down to gathering all his Power, compressing it, separating it from himself and making it into a visible sphere, viable as a weapon. He had a nasty idea how the Marshalls had used it in Testing Alexa. He took the anger at the thought to make the core of the ball, white hot. No one would *ever* do such things to her again. Not while he lived.

"There is no way a single person could make an atomball of the small size and great Power that our Circle did. Let us set a size and amplitude for this Test," Thealia said.

"Agreed," said Mace. "The size to fit in my large shooting-star?"

Bastien concentrated on his task, gathering his Power. The size of a shooting-star, the round, spiked weapon at the end of a chain linked to a club, should be within his reach. Just.

"Fine," Reynardus said, and Bastien added to his ball the spurt of anger he felt at the smug tone.

Reynardus didn't think he could do it. Probably thought Bastien had already lost, since he was unnaturally quiet. The core was coming along nicely, though.

"Strength?" asked Partis. "What if it lifts Mace's shooting-star to the table?"

Bastien set his teeth against a groan, added more Power.

"To the ceiling," Reynardus said silkily.

"Midway the length of the windows," Thealia countered.

"Done!" Reynardus said with satisfaction.

Heat gathered in Bastien as he raised his energy level and poured all his Power into the forming atomball. He should have sweated, but he used that bit of energy from his pores to go inward to the construct.

The doorharp sounded a scale—with notes above and below what were set by the strings. *Ping!* A weight settled on his shoulder, but he kept steadily layering the ball. From the corner of his eye he saw a warhawk with bright pink eyes. The shapeshifter. Sinafin. For a moment he lost the slippery ball, but Sinafin snagged it with ease.

Let's put it outside you. Any more time inside you and it could do dam-age, the shapeshifter said in a sensible tone he'd never heard from her.

He shut his eyes and visualized sending the ball outside himself in a flow of energy. He shuddered as the last bit pulled away. When he opened his eyes the ball was a misty yellow nimbus the size of the huge gong in the Temple, around a white core the size of his fist. The center glowed near his gut. He gritted his teeth. This was going to be hard.

She broadcast her next words to the Marshalls. *You all had each other's help in making the atomball, as well as the ritual that brought in Power from the Song. The Song sent me to help Bastien at this time.*

Bastien sent his laughter flashing into the ball—who was going to challenge her? And what would happen if anyone did? He'd been reckless enough to dare anything and yet *he* wouldn't think of challenging the feycoocu.

No one spoke.

He panted now, compressing the sphere, sending the heat of his body to it, all the Power he could easily access.

All his strength, all his physical reactions from the trembling of his muscles to the sweat that should have beaded on his forehead went to the sphere. The task demanded a forced concentration from him that he'd never used, never could have mastered when he was a true black-and-white. Increment by increment, the sun-yellow globe shrank. How could he succeed at this Test?

How could he fail? If he failed, he'd prove to the Marshalls, to his father, that he was weak and useless, confirm the opinion many had of him... That wash of humiliation shrank the ball a good four inches. He sought to relax, to make sure any tension of his muscles went into the effort. Soon he swayed on his feet, felt his balance going.

Sinafin's claws pricked his skin as she steadied him. *I will link to your woman.*

No! She is drained enough from battling the dreeth.

The Song blessed her. Power gathers around her even as she sleeps. With every breath she inhales energy motes and they live in her skin, merge with her cells. You will help her master and wield her Power, but now you need her.

A trickle of energy, sweet energy buzzing from his lover, came to him on a threnody. The additional strength had him push the sphere tighter. From the corner of his eye, he saw several Marshalls holding their breaths. All attention was fixed on him. With slow wit, he located Mace's shooting-star. It had been moved to within an inch of his toes, but he hadn't noticed how or when.

Slowly he let the ball descend from belt-buckle level—this was more of a releasing, a deliberate relaxation of his own energy, again siphoning to the atomball. Soon the yellow was almost in the round, spiked iron, but a definite rim of white-yellow showed. Bastien tried everything, visualizing himself packing a snowball between his hands, sending more Alexa-Power to it with fierce will, incipient despair—any emotion that flitted to his mind. Yet a slight glow remained.

The strain was too much, he couldn't hold it, couldn't force it into the weapon, no matter how hard he tried. He had nothing left.

Sinafin's claws pierced his skin. He jerked, and his shout and his pain sped into the ball. The hawk lifted her bloody foot and flicked droplets of deep red with unerring aim to the last shine of white.

The atomball vanished into the spiked iron. It broke its chain, flew up, hit the ceiling, rained plaster, fell to the table, hitting the wood and embedding with a *thud.*

When the glaze of exhaustion faded from his eyes, Bastien saw no one in the room. He blinked, then noticed people huddling under the table. Humor returned. The Marshalls always had fast reflexes.

"Playing with atomballs is ever an interesting experience," Partis said, his voice echoing from under the table.

Go free it from the table, Sinafin said.

Bastien grinned weakly; he wasn't sure he could take the two steps to the table. *Let them do it themselves.*

Sinafin stretched out a wing and batted him around the head. He got a mouthful of feathers.

I'm going, I'm going! Taking one long stride, he fell against the table. The shooting-star had made a big dent and was implanted a good inch into the table. With spread fingers, he set both hands on the weapon and arched as energy sizzled back into him, setting his hair on end, top to toe. *Merde!*

The leftover energy, Sinafin said smugly.

As he pulled the shooting-star from the table, the Marshalls once again took their seats, all gazes now on the weapon. Not a bit of energy leaked from it. No glow. But it hummed very low, nearly below the hearing threshold.

Faith's pen scritched on the parchment. "Bastien Vauxveau passed his second Test. One of Power. It is the first time in the annals of the Lorebook that an applicant has made an atomball. The Marshalls will be lucky to have him with us," she muttered.

Bastien stretched, shook out his arms and legs, smiled at Mace, who was eyeing the chain and stick of the shooting-star on the floor and the round spiked ball on the table. "Want your weapon of choice back?" asked Bastien.

"I don't think so," Mace said.

Shrugging, Bastien said, "You Marshalls can decide what to do with a spiked iron shooting-star that contains an atomball. It was your idea, after all."

Sinafin cackled.

When Faith finished writing, she looked at Bastien. "The next Test is of compassion."

"Compassion," he snorted. "As if you Marshalls, who think and strategize big, are any to speak of compassion."

"How dare you criticize us!" thundered Reynardus, standing.

"Easily. You manipulated my lady. Even *after* she passed your Tests and became a Marshall, you forced her by your mistrust and your actions to leave the Castle—she a stranger, an alien with no money, and no knowledge of our land. And that is just the latest of your exploits that show true compassion," he mocked.

Thealia's face pinched white, and most of the others gave some indication of discomfort. Good. Bastien wasn't feeling charitable.

"That mistake will haunt us forever. Collectively as Marshalls and individually," Thealia sighed.

"As it should," Partis said. He met Bastien's gaze. "We regret our actions. We have no excuses."

"We are not the ones being Tested here," Reynardus said. He looked to the windows where the sunlight slanted in low. "Evening comes. Let's continue with this."

Thealia rose and sailed gracefully around the table, passed Bastien and stood by the door. "According to tradition, when the applicant appears and chooses the Tests, word is spread of his name and the Tests, and a spellsong is placed on the Castle information board. I have been informed that we have a witness who will testify to Bastien Vauxveau's compassion."

Reynardus scowled. "Fast work by someone." He scraped back his chair and sat, frowning at the atomball.

"By several someones, no doubt," Partis said. "Bastien is well-liked."

Thealia opened the door latch and looked out. "You may enter now."

Urvey marched into the room, a roll of papers in his fist. He wore Bastien's colors, midnight blue and silver. From the worn look of the clothes, they'd been altered from some of Bastien's castoffs. The teenager appeared neat, clean and nervous.

Faith gestured to a chair. "You may sit here."

Urvey thrust the rolls at Faith. "Statements by Chevaliers regarding Bastien's compassion."

From where he stood, Bastien could smell the smoke and liquor on the papers. No doubt they'd been passed around the Nom de Nom. He wondered what they said and if any of it was true.

"You're going to trust *those?* Trust *him?*" asked Reynardus.

Flipping through the pages, Faith glanced at him. "They've been sworn, witnessed and all sealed by Lady Hallard, Representative of the Chevaliers to us." Faith plucked out a sheet. "She has included testimony of her own, as has her flier, Marrec."

Bastien couldn't remember any good deeds he'd done for those two. Maybe he'd been drunk at the time. But on the whole he never consciously thought of doing good deeds.

"As for this youngster," Partis said, "have we become so superior that we won't listen to what an honest lad says?"

"Yes," said Reynardus.

Thealia sighed.

"Your name and station?" asked Faith, ready with her feather pen.

"Urvey Novins. I'm Bastien's squire."

"I remember you, and I think we have all seen you around the Castle. Tell your story, boy," said Mace.

Urvey shifted in his seat, then haltingly explained his position as stable boy at the Nom de Nom, talked about minor kindnesses Bastien didn't recall, and continued to the night Bastien had announced that the jerir at the Castle was available to anyone who cared to avail themselves of it.

"He came and he helped me in the jerir pool and he made me his squire," Urvey finished.

"But he left you here, at the Castle, when he went back to the Field, left you to fend for yourself," Faith said gently.

"He let me stay in his apartment in Horseshoe Hall, and he gave me money. Since his return, he's taught me squirely things."

"He left you," Thealia repeated.

"He gave me status. Just by allowing me to dip in the jerir with him. Just being in his rooms made me important enough for others to pay attention to me." Urvey sat straighter in his chair. "A squire shows initiative." His chin jutted. "Maybe he was just Testing me like you are Testing him!"

Mace turned a chuckle into a cough.

Urvey met Bastien's gaze. "He gave me more and believed in me more than anyone else in my life." Urvey's chest swelled with pride. "Here I am *talking* to the Marshalls of the Castle. I have clothes. I have good food— I ate sweetcheese just last night. I have a horse of my own. Soon I will have flying lessons and a volaran. Which of you would have done that for me? Which of you would have listened to me before this day?"

His hair stuck out at uneven angles. He looked no more than what he'd been, a stable boy at a rough tavern. And he looked very, very young. Bastien sighed inwardly. He didn't know why he'd taken responsibility for Urvey, but now that he had, the boy needed a decent haircut.

"I've heard enough," Reynardus said.

"And I." Partis's tone was cheerful.

Urvey stood and awkwardly bowed to the Marshalls. Bastien would need to teach him how to bow too. Lessons to Urvey and lessons to Alexa. He'd become a preceptor. Who would have thought it.

Bastien clapped a hand on Urvey's shoulder. "Good job."

The teenager reddened, then grinned. He ducked his head. "I'll be in our suite."

Alexa's suite. Bastien hadn't felt her in the back of his mind lately. "How is she?"

"She sleeps. Umilla watches over her."

"Testing is in progress," Reynardus reminded him.

As Urvey left, Luthan opened the door and walked in. "Is Urvey's testimony, along with the other witness rolls, enough, or do I need to testify?"

"You have tales of Bastien's compassion too?" Thealia asked wearily.

"Many." Luthan beamed. "And I will be glad to spend all night in the telling of them."

Mace rolled his eyes. "I don't want to hear every instance."

"But," Luthan continued, "I need only remind all of you what happens to your old volarans, too wounded or too old to fly with the wild herds, and who aren't welcome on the lands of the nobles they've served. Or those volarans who have lost a human friend and don't wish to return to the wild. They go to Bastien. And Bastien supports them. What is that if not compassion?"

"Well said." Faith made a note on her paper, set her pen aside and folded her hands. "I accept that Bastien Vauxveau has shown a history of acceptable compassion during his life. Any objections to passing the applicant on this Test?"

Reynardus grumbled under his breath. No one else said anything.

Luthan said, "As Representative of the Singer, I will stay." He slid into his chair.

Faith glanced down at the last item on her Testing chart. "Let us proceed to the greatest Test for you, Bastien—teamwork."

A bitter retort rose in his mind on how he'd cooperated with independent Chevalier Pairs, landowner units, noble corps. He stopped them on his tongue.

His emotions roused Alexa. She felt the cost of his control. *Bas-*

tien, do you need help? A wave of sleep threatened to pull her under, her body and mind demanding more rest.

Sleep, Bastien urged.

It's just a dream, Alexa said.

Sleep. You would be awake and here if I needed you greatly, but I sense your mind and body need more time to process the shock of fighting the dreeth, and creating the blood-bond.

You make no sense.

Sleep! It was more than a suggestion, it had *push* behind it. She didn't want to face the memory of being crushed, so she gave in to the tide.

Bastien faced the Marshalls with a half smile. Just the brief exchange with his sleepy, supportive, pliable woman made him feel better. He wished he was back with her in bed.

He thought of the next Test, teamwork. *Merde!* Alexa would have passed that one with flying colors, while he'd always preferred individual fighting and only Paired temporarily and when absolutely necessary for the battle.

"Do we have your attention again?" asked Reynardus in mock courtesy.

"I was sending my lady back to sleep. We are Paired. She knew of my nerves and has been with me thus far."

Mace snorted. "Nerves, ha!"

"I will do anything for my mate. It is the sole reason I am here before you now, Testing. She is a Marshall and you will not recognize me as her equal, *even if she does,* if I am not one, also. To be most effective we must be in harmony and removing the distraction that I am *not* a Marshall will do that." He'd have more status, more influence when he was a Marshall. He could protect her more.

He loved her. He hadn't known what a true, loving Pairing was before, didn't think anyone who hadn't experienced it could understand how deeply it went. He straightened his shoulders, knowing what he had to do to pass this next Test. He walked over to the table and offered his hand to his father.

"The best Test of teamwork would be to act as Shield to the Swordmarshall with whom I have the most problems. That means you."

Reynardus's eyes widened in shock as he stared at Bastien's offered hand. Bastien knew if they teamed together the blood-bond between them would kick in—a bond that would be unusual and strange since it would be the first time in many years, the first time since Alexa had removed the constriction of his Power.

Bastien smiled easily. "There are always lesser monsters creeping into Lladrana through Sly Pass. It is close enough for this Test. Shall we go, Father?"

His father stood, face stony. "No. I will not bond with you."

Why was this blow *harder* than the dreeth's? Bastien hoped his humiliation didn't show. He set his hand on his belt, curled his fingers around tough leather until the edges nipped at his hand, grateful for the small pain.

The rest of the room seemed as shocked as he.

Reynardus said, "I am not sure this whole business is true." He gestured widely. "All his life, Bastien has been a rebel, he has fought me, fought any rule that bound him, is one of those Chevaliers loudest in his condemnation of us, the Marshalls. And I do not want his black-and-white mind touching my mind."

"He does it for his lady," Partis murmured into the silence. "He is Paired. But you know nothing of that, do you? You can't comprehend that?"

Angry streaks of red showed under the skin of Reynardus's cheeks. "I don't have that weakness."

"And I think it is a weakness to believe Pairing a weakness," Thealia said.

Swordmarshall Johnsa, Paired to Faith, stood. "Bastien Vauxveau and I are distantly related through his mother's line. I don't recall that we have ever linked to work together. Since I believe we all expected Reynardus's sons to be Swords, whenever we might have trained with them as Marshalls, we would have Paired them with Shieldmarshalls. I will team with Bastien." She glanced at the windows, now red with sunset. "Since night is falling, perhaps we should use the Castle training grounds." She dipped her head in Bastien's direction. "With your consent, of course, Chevalier Vauxveau."

Bastien matched her nod. "I agree." Hurt tightened his insides, but he'd had a lifetime of plodding on through emotional hurt inflicted by his father. He wouldn't think about it. Couldn't afford to. This evening he would survive the Testing. Tonight he would curve himself, body and mind, around Alexa, and they would smooth this clash of chords into a melody that would ease the pain.

"I and my Shield will take the field against you," Reynardus said, not even glancing at Ivrog for acceptance.

Ivrog's mouth opened, then he shut it. His face went impassive, but Bastien sensed he was displeased.

Teamwork. When had his father ever truly worked as an equal partner? Never. He'd always been the controlling partner of the Pair. That was not teamwork, and surely the Marshalls knew it too, but they'd ignored it all these years. If it weren't for Alexa, Bastien would walk out of this room in disgust and leave the Marshalls to their fate.

Since he couldn't, Bastien wondered if he could exploit Reynardus's need for control in the coming Test.

"Why don't we take to the air—a volaran skirmish. With dreeths appearing again, flying skills will be vital." Bastien smiled.

Reynardus froze. Bastien's volarans were superior to anyone else's.

"A good idea," Thealia said. She was giving him an edge.

Johnsa's face lit up. "It will be a pleasure working with Bastien on volaran-back."

"Above the Landing Field, then—it's the largest area," Thealia said. "I'll broadcast word that all volaran landings this evening should divert to Horseshoe courtyard until Testing is done."

Bastien nodded at Johnsa. "I'll meet you in Horseshoe Stables."

He turned on his heel and left, fingers curling in excitement. He'd *won!* There was no way Reynardus and Ivrog could best him and Johnsa. Not when he and Johnsa were distant kin, not when his magic rolled through him, free but steady. Not when he had the best volarans in Lladrana. He laughed.

Something thunked on the door behind him.

22

"Please return, Bastien," called Mace from the other side of the Marshalls' Council Room door.

When Bastien reentered, he found Mace holding the atomball, looking irritatedly at new holes in the door. "This ball carries your blood. It is connected to you. It is yours."

Bastien took the ball. It hummed loudly in his hands, almost like a purring cat. He hoped his flush didn't show. This was a little embarrassing. On the other hand, whatever the consequences of his making the ball rested squarely on the Marshalls' shoulders.

"Do you want the chain and club attached again?" asked Mace.

In no scenario could Bastien imagine using a shooting-star. "No."

"Very well. Remember that it is your weapon now," Mace said, and opened the door wide.

As Bastien walked, the ball lifted from his hands to trail behind him. At first it felt awkward, knowing something followed him like a pony. Then, when people he met flattened themselves against a wall, a swagger entered his steps.

A few moments later, Bastien and Johnsa stood ready to mount at the southern edge of the Landing Field. She patted his shoulder.

"The Test is for a half hour only, before total night. Soon this will be over and you'll be Choosing your baton. You've been very patient, more than I expected." Her eyes sharpened. "You've matured, young Bastien."

He grunted and checked his harness again.

She sighed. "We need more Marshalls. Perhaps having you will prompt more Chevaliers to Test."

Since he wasn't done with the Test himself, he kept rash words behind his lips.

His battle mare, Inqui, stamped and lifted her wings, restless to fly. Bastien ran a hand down the arch of her neck. His main battle volaran rested in the best stall of Horseshoe Stables. The best stall for the best volaran. Inqui was for Alexa, when Bastien could get her on the mare—which might not be for years. Now the flying horse would serve him well in the duel with his father and uncle. She'd be as essential to the team as Johnsa and her volaran.

Just outside the stable doors facing the Landing Field, he and Johnsa mounted. Bastien swung up on Inqui and she stilled, flicked her ears. He hadn't been atop her since Alexa had fixed the flaw that had made his magic wild. Inqui seemed to sense the change in him. At one time part of him would merge with her, the animal inside him flow with and amplify the animal in her. It had been strange and oddly exciting, but now it wasn't necessary. They could touch the surface of their minds, him guiding her with a light thought.

Johnsa looked at him and grinned, her teeth bright in the dim evening light. "Ready?"

"Yes. I have good night vision, always have had."

"Me too." She grinned back.

"Ivrog doesn't," Bastien said.

"I know. Let us link physically to establish the connection." She held out her square, calloused hand.

Inhaling and tempering his Power, Bastien placed his hand in hers. Her grip tightened and her mind brushed his. He opened to her. A small latent tune, a distant-family tune, rose to the fore.

"Fancy that," Johnsa rasped. "A connection I didn't know we had."

"Me neither."

She dropped her fingers and laughed, drew on her gauntlets. "We are very much in accord this evening, young Bastien." Her eyes gleamed. "Let's ground Reynardus into the dust."

The hurt and humiliation he'd tried to suppress surged at the thought. "Yes."

They took off and circled the Landing Field a couple of times, stretching volaran muscles, testing their link. As they flew together, their hesitation at the new mind-touch vanished and the connection strengthened. They moved well together, Bastien first to one side, then slightly behind and to Johnsa's left.

Well done, Shield. This feels right to me, Johnsa hummed in his mind.

He didn't answer, watching Reynardus and Ivrog take the field, swing into the air.

First strike, I think, Johnsa said, lifting her knotty wooden baton and firing a stream of brown Power at Reynardus.

They caught Sword and Shield off guard, but both had fought together too long to be completely unprepared. Ivrog's Shield snapped into place, but a second too late; Reynardus took a hit. The volaran pair wobbled, Reynardus flicked his baton in riposte and ivory light speared to Johnsa, flowing around the egg-shaped Power-Shield Bastien molded.

Gasps came from the ground.

Very powerful Shield you have there, Bastien. All that fighting stood you well to become a Shieldmarshall. I am as safe as if I were behind a dreeth.

Just the thought of the dreeth made Bastien shudder. Inqui neighed and zoomed upward. Johnsa laughed.

All four volarans circled around each other, the Swords throwing magical bolts, then nipping in to engage with weapons. Each moment drew observers.

Bastien concentrated on protecting Johnsa. It was easier for him than fighting, though in a fight he could enter a mind-space that slowed time and his body reacted—he didn't think. This was different. Here he could stand ready—even nudge Johnsa, who was in the fight-react mind-set, in a direction that was strategically better for her, for them. He shifted his shoulders. This felt right, the rhythm and the energy flow, the Power. Finally, he was doing what he'd been created for—he was a natural Shield.

The thought still pinched, that his woman would be actively fighting while he stood back, but he sensed that the Power itself would soon cure him of the niggling blow to his ego. He'd be protecting her, even as he protected Johnsa; he'd send her additional energy. There were all sorts of advantages to being a Shield he'd never considered.

It was an interesting duel, since all were connected through him by family. Orchestral chords sang between them all, in the sound of pounding hearts, crafty thought note-sparks, a clashing tune. Inqui rose and fell, spoke with Johnsa's volaran, leading the mare so Bastien and Johnsa had the advantage of better light.

Johnsa was slightly ahead of Reynardus in "touches" on his body.

Then Bastien's atomball, dark and unseen in the night, punched through Reynardus's shield, one spike grazing his temple. He swayed in the saddle.

Ivrog propped him up with Power, guided both volarans to the ground. "We yield!" Ivrog cried.

"No." Reynardus's whisper was amplified with the merest Power, but all heard.

Ivrog ignored Reynardus's protest. He jumped from his volaran and went to his brother, then plucked him from the saddle and held him upright with physical strength and Power.

Reynardus struggled feebly. "No."

"You be quiet. You can't see for blood in your eyes, your mind is dizzy. I'm not so stupid as to let you get us injured further, or worse, from stupid pride," Ivrog said.

Thealia glided onto the Field. "The duel is done as one of the Pair spoke for both and yielded. The victory goes to Swordmarshall Johnsa and Shield Bastien."

Faith joined Thealia, grinned at her mate, Johnsa, winked at Bastien. "The Testing is over. To the observers, the teamwork between Johnsa and Bastien was flawless. What say you, Swordmarshall Johnsa?"

Johnsa vaulted to the ground, left her volaran to her squire. "Bastien is very smooth, as many women know." Laughter floated from the watchers. "He is strong, capable, a natural Shield. I would work with him in any fight from duel to battle." Her gaze picked out the other Marshalls. "I believe he would be an excellent Shield for any Swordmarshall."

Faith clapped once. It echoed throughout the Castle. "This Testing is over. The applicant, Bastien Vauxveau, has passed and will receive Marshall status."

Thealia gestured to Mace. "Let us adjourn to the Temple where he will Choose his baton. Mace, please retrieve the unclaimed batons." Mace faded into the night. "Partis, is Reynardus able to attend the Choosing?"

"I think it would be best if he went to his rooms." Partis's tones were as even as ever. A pair of Medicas came and helped Reynardus off the Landing Field. He stood straight, but walked slowly, as if his vision blurred.

A whirlwind of emotions swept through Bastien. He hated his father. He loved his father. He had always wanted, but had never received, acknowledgment and pride for his accomplishments from the man. Reynardus had humiliated him just an hour past, yet Bastien still wished his father were well enough to attend the Choosing. His heart still felt that if Reynardus saw him take a Marshall's baton, the man would respect him. It was futile. It was foolish. But it was true.

Urvey hurried up. "I'll care for Inqui—what a noble volaran she is." His voice fell into the lilt of a true horseman as he led the volaran away.

Bastien eyed the teenager. He could very well make a Chevalier, win some land of his own.

Barking came from near Bastien's feet. He stared down at the strange little dog—a type of dog not known in Lladrana—that was the shapeshifter Sinafin.

I will accompany you to the Temple.

"Thanks," he said. She'd reminded him that it was time to move.

Alexa will be there too.

Bastien's gut tensed. "She shouldn't—the dreeth—"

The memory of the dreeth is fragmented. This moment she is very pleased and proud of you. She is dressing in the Gold Robe the Marshalls gave her, and fussing like a woman.

He liked that image, and smiled. As he walked, his muscles stretched, the stiffened aches from the morning fight easing. Alexa would be in the Temple to see his triumph.

She was so much more important to him than Reynardus. Bastien whistled.

As he drew near the Temple, he saw her dress gleaming in the light, the pale smudge of her face and her silver hair. She stood to the right of the Temple door, calm and dignified. In her right hand, her baton glowed green, with muted flames flickering just beneath the metal ones.

On a woman of Lladrana, the golden gown would complement skin tone, but on Alexa it contrasted. She looked all silver and gold. He walked faster, and her features became clear—huge green eyes in a pale, pointed face, lips pink. She was his. His partner, his woman. His to fight alongside, his to protect. So many facets of her and him to mesh or spark each other. He wouldn't have it any other way.

He hurried to her, scooped her up and took her mouth in a hungry kiss, needing to hold her, this reason for the turmoil of Testing for the past few hours. Her body was soft and yielding against his, her arms twined around his neck, her mouth opened willingly. Their mental and emotional Song picked up pace. Her unspoken comfort soothed the hurt his father had inflicted.

I am very proud of you, she said mentally.

Bastien sensed the shadow and thought that she'd heard that very little in her own life—so she'd make sure to say it to him. When the floral scent of her teased his nostrils, he recalled he must smell of volaran and sweat. He turned the kiss tender, brushing his lips against hers, and set her on her feet. Her gown fell back into severe folds, but her complexion had turned rosy and she held herself more lightly.

"Thank you for your words," he said. "I cherish them." He lifted her fingers to his mouth for a kiss, then placed her hand on his arm.

Castle soldiers held the door open for them, as the little dog Sinafin trotted in after them. When they were inside, Thealia gestured to Alexa.

"Swordmarshall Alyeka must join the rest of us in a semicircle to observe the Choosing."

Once again the fact that she was a Sword and he a Shield tweaked his ego, and he hid his reaction from Alexa.

Alexa rolled her eyes, and to Bastien's surprise, took the end of the line in a place next to Ivrog. She reached out for Ivrog's hand. He smiled at her and took it, then offered his left hand to Thealia. Her brows raised, but she joined hands with him and took her mate's, Partis's. The Marshalls all linked.

Bastien stared, and thought they might be as surprised as he that Alexa preferred standing by Ivrog, of all people. Then he shook his head. Above all, the tradition of the Marshalls was as a single unit; every one of them would put the security of the whole above all individuals. He wondered if Alexa felt that too. Wondered if she needed that. Wondered if he could live with that thought-pattern.

Sinafin, sitting on Alexa's feet, barked once. *Make it what you will.*

Wasn't that just like wild magic personified in a feycoocu, giving advice in enigmatic words.

Sinafin grinned a doggy grin, tongue lolling. *You will hear.*

Mace strode through the doors, cradling a large bundle. Bastien's heart thumped harder in anticipation. He locked his knees against the trembling. He was about to Choose a baton—he, a scorned black-and-white, would claim the highest honor of Lladrana. He shifted his stance for maximum balance, evened his breathing, lifted his head in pride.

Swordmarshall Mace carefully laid the felt case on the pavement with the faintest of clinks. Bastien's stomach squeezed at the thought of the powerful wands inside—marble and wood and metal and glass and gemstone...which was right for him?

He felt the comforting touch of Alexa's mind, and glanced up to see her reassuring smile. She looked small and fragile. And carried the Jade Baton. Her spirit was great and her Power fantastic. But she was proud of him and had faith in him like no other, not even his brother Luthan. Bastien sucked in a breath. Of course he would Choose correctly. How could he not, with her support?

Mace opened the flap, and Bastien saw the four rows of ten batons. All were there save the ones the Marshalls carried. Near the end of one of the rows, two batons appeared dull and dim. His stomach tightened as he understood that those belonged to Defau Disparu, whom Alexa had killed in self-defense, and Disparu's wife. He choked, shook the thought from his head. Being a Marshall was a risky business. Summoning an Exotique chancy also, but Defau had attacked Alexa to kill, and she'd reacted. He looked at her again and her smile faded; he felt her Song insinuate deeper into his mind. Not wanting her to recall the event, he scanned the rods at his feet. Nothing sang to him on first glance. He opened his mind to his Power, and heard the tone of each one. Different, mingling, whispering, but none that resonated with him.

A tendril of dismay uncurled inside him. Keeping his face impassive, he squatted, resting back on his haunches. He held out a hand and passed it over the wands quickly. Once. Used both hands to test the strength of their pull, more slowly, twice.

He gritted his teeth, felt the touch of Alexa's comfort again. But he was deeply glad his father wasn't here to comment.

Bastien settled into his balance and opened all his senses. He frowned, put his hands on his knees. Something wasn't right. Reaching, stretching his Power to the limit, he called a tiny kernel of wild magic he found tucked away inside him...and probed. Two pure notes rang in response.

Narrowing his eyes, he studied the batons. They weren't for him—none of those in the pockets...but...but... He closed his eyes and instinctively reached. His fingers scrabbled at the fabric that folded over the batons, found a hard lump.

"What's that you're doing, boy?" Mace barked.

Since Bastien didn't know, he didn't answer. Opening his eyes, he examined the fabric he held, noticed a tiny gap. With steady fingers, he opened the folds of the secret pocket, slipped his hand inside, curled his fingers around a sturdy cylinder, smooth and rough. He drew out an obsidian baton, with a cord of engraved silver spiraling from silver bottom to silver top.

The Marshalls gasped as one.

"I don't think I've ever seen that baton," Mace said in a constricted voice.

Faith pulled forward, but was held back by the linked hands. "I don't know if I've read of it in the Lorebooks. A black-and-silver wand, for a black-and-white man."

"Well done!" Ivrog shouted. "Viva Shieldmarshall Bastien."

An instant's silence, then the rest cried. "Viva Shieldmarshall Bastien!"

Bastien strode over to take Alexa's hand. A wave of sheer Power rolled through him, the combined natural resting magic of the Marshalls. For an instant he was awed. Alexa looked up at him and grinned, her eyes brimming with pride. He squeezed her hand.

Bastien's touch energized her. Connected, mind, body and heart with Bastien on her right and all the rest of the Marshalls on her left, Alexa felt as if she'd finally found her place in the world.

The rainbow lamps on the altar chimed; the big gong vibrated softly, almost under her hearing range; the large crystals embedded in the beams and at the ends of the rafters brightened and dimmed, like a lightbulb about ready to die. Huh, they hadn't done that when she'd gotten her baton. Had they? Her memory wasn't clear.

But a fine tension hummed through the Marshalls. Something

was going on that she didn't know about, as usual. Bastien's fingers tightened on hers near pain. Flames danced under the surface of her baton; the silver on Bastien's blazed.

"I've heard tales…." Bastien breathed.

Bells sounded, tinkling, sparkling, like sleigh bells in Christmas commercials. Another quiver ran down the line of Marshalls, with rising excitement. The circle broke and they surged to the door.

They flowed through the door and out into the Temple courtyard.

"Look," Bastien said, angling his chin.

The bells were attached to a volaran harness. Two pure white volarans, manes ruffling in the night breeze, looking like a fantasy had flown in. Between them they carried a little, much-decorated wooden…something. A tiny carriage? Yeah, it had wheels. A little Cinderella coach, but with the horses on either side. Weird. Fabulous. Something *big* was happening.

"The Singer," Bastien whispered.

Uh-oh. The most powerful person on Lladrana, the one who listened to God—the Song. The one who did those oracle things. Alexa wanted to run away, fast and far. But Bastien stood solid, holding her hand. Everyone in and near the Castle tumbled into the ward, to see, to watch. No sneaking away. Probably didn't have anything to do with her anyway. Yeah, right. This was the seer who'd told the Marshalls to Summon her. Shi— Shoot.

All around her, breaths were held and eyes were on the coach as if Santa were coming, but no one knew if he was bringing coal and switches or presents containing heart's desires. Alexa tugged on her hand, but Bastien, the big lunk, wasn't moving. Nope, had to stay and wait to be engulfed in an avalanche.

She heard Thealia inhale, then the Swordmarshall wiped her palm on her fancy malachite robe and strode forward to press down the intricate gold handle of the coach and help out the occupant.

A tiny old woman emerged. Smaller than Alexa. Her face was a mass of lines, her bones birdlike. A shock of white hair fuzzed around her head, lifting and falling with the ripple of the night breeze. More like a fairy godmother than Santa.

She wore a gold-colored gown, made of the same fabric as Alexa's own. Alexa looked down—not the same cut, thank goodness. A minor thing, but significant, she hoped. She was not going to become this "Song." She was a Marshall. A Swordmarshall, heaven help her. A fighter. She grounded herself and shifted her balance, keeping a tight grip on Bastien.

As the lady scanned the courtyard, many shrank back, some stepped into the moonlight. Luthan strode across the ward. When he reached the woman, Thealia stepped aside, relief showing on her face. Luthan bowed, braced himself and took the tiny hand to place it on his arm. Alexa saw a tremor run through him. Bastien and Alexa took a step back, and Alexa noticed all the Marshalls did too.

"Forgive me for not giving you notice, my liegeman," the Singer said.

Alexa had never heard a voice like it. More than musical, like it carried in it the ancient answers of the stars. She'd never felt a voice like that, but it plucked chords of her inner being. She strained to hear every cadence, every syllable, every note.

"The Singer knows best," Luthan said, and took one small step to her two.

"Thealia, Partis, Johnsa, Faith…" The Singer greeted every Marshall by name. Alexa suppressed a smile. Well, if they didn't want to be famous, they shouldn't be the head honchos.

The Singer glided slowly toward Bastien and Alexa. Her head tilted back and her face lit as she saw Bastien. "Ah, my black-and-white, Bastien." She lilted "black-and-white" as if it was an honor.

Bastien bowed deep beside Alexa. She'd never seen any guy bow like that—elegant, reverent.

"And Alexa Marie Fitzwalter."

Shock stunned Alexa. No one had asked her middle and surname. No one. She'd told them to no one. Bastien glanced down at her, eyebrows raised.

Sinafin yipped, pranced around the lady's gently moving hem. A sweet chuckle poured from the Singer. Alexa sighed with wonder.

"Good evening to you, feycoocu," the Singer said.

Sinafin sat and lifted a paw.

The Singer had made Luthan, bigger than Bastien, tremble at her powerful touch. Would she blow Sinafin away?

The little lady bent down. She didn't have to stoop very far. She took Sinafin's paw in her hand. Sinafin sat rock solid. Alexa sensed the Singer hadn't modulated her Power at all; Sinafin's just met and equaled it. Sheee— Shoot. Wow.

Power—communication?—passed between the little magical being and the Singer. Then the Singer released Sinafin's paw and the greyhound came to sit proudly by Alexa, who was still gathering her wits.

The Singer stopped in front of Alexa. She was not much shorter after all, an inch or two. Her face lifted slightly so Alexa could meet her eyes. They were deep and brown with a small slant. Her features weren't Asian or Amer-Asian, they were Lladranan. For a moment Alexa had thought she would be an Exotique too.

"Hello, Alexa," the Singer said in English.

Alexa gulped. Thankfully, the woman hadn't offered her hand. "Hello, Singer."

The oracle's head tilted a fraction. "You are from Co-lo-ra-do?"

Alexa's tongue felt thick. "Yeah. Yes. From Denver."

The Singer's eyes closed briefly, opened. "As will be the next. All but one."

Alexa didn't want to hear that, didn't want to go there. "You speak English."

"Yes, I had an Exotique who taught me many years ago. He came from Mass-a-chu-setts."

That accounted for the Boston twang. So the most powerful human in the world of Amee spoke with a Bostonian accent. Too much.

The Singer slanted a look at the Marshalls. "The Marshalls of the time were perturbed that he didn't stay—we had problems even then and Exotiques are always powerful. But he didn't love Lladrana or me enough to stay when the Snap came."

Oh boy. Too much information. Way too much. Alexa thought the trembling inside her would show soon. She wasn't sure she could stop it.

Bastien's arm circled her, giving her sturdy comfort. "Alexa will stay. We need her."

The Singer raised her brows and replied in Lladranan. "You have a blood-bond from the spilling of the dreeth's ichor, and a Paired bond, but you have not completed the formal Pairing ritual." She switched to English. "Wedding."

Bastien tensed.

Oh yeah. Mention marriage to a commitment-shy man. That was good. Huh! The idea scared the crap out of Bastien, and it made Alexa a little queasy herself.

Then the woman smiled, slowly, beautifully, enveloping Alexa in an aura of bright golden warmth. "I've come for your Marshall Song Quests, Alexa and Bastien."

Oh shit.

23

"Let's go into the Temple to conduct your Song Quests." The Singer glanced over her shoulder at the range of Marshalls behind her. "I would like to use the Castle Temple privately with Bastien and Alexa, with your permission."

"Of course," Thealia croaked. She bowed deeply. "We will have refreshments for all of you in the small formal Marshalls' Dining Room."

Well, that left out a lot of people. The Marshalls were keeping the lady to themselves. Huh. The minor irritation helped Alexa beat back her fear. She'd never been a person who cared to know the future. The future was what you made it.

It was a little demoralizing to cling to Bastien, but the day had been one unbelievable event after another that sent her reeling. She supposed she shouldn't put listening to a Song Quest in the same category as killing a huge, rabid pterodactyl, but she did.

Equally unimaginable, equally new, equally something she didn't want to do.

She guessed a Marshall didn't whine. Too darn bad.

She couldn't even drag her feet. Since the Singer was as small as she was, both Luthan and Bastien kept their own steps tiny. They walked at a brisk pace—the Singer's and Alexa's pace.

She shivered.

"Are you cold?" asked Bastien.

"Very."

He gestured to Urvey, who lingered in the background. "Please fetch Swordmarshall Alexa's cloak."

The title jolted her. *Swordmarshall.* She grimaced. Sounded like she'd be swinging one often.

She wanted to know the exact procedure of a Song Quest. Another experience that everyone knew about except her, and no one had given her specifics. Would the Song Quest take place in the pentacle, near the altar? She'd skirted that part of the Temple every time she'd been in it. What else would happen?

"Will there be drugs?" she asked.

The other three stared at her. "Drugs?" Luthan asked.

Alexa sipped in shallow breaths. "Will you drug me like the Marshalls before that miserable Choosing and Bonding Ceremony?"

Bastien let go of her hand to wrap an arm around her waist. "No."

She looked up at him. He'd always been honest with her. Luthan had been a little sneaky, the Singer was an unknown, but Bastien had been brutally honest.

"Have you had a—" she took care to form the words correctly "—Song Quest?"

He grimaced. "Yes, when I was nearly a teenager." He smirked at Luthan. "It was supposed to take place before my first sexual experience, but no one told me and they were too late."

The Singer raised thin eyebrows. "I remember it well. Do you, Bastien?" Her voice was smoother and richer than honey.

Bastien gulped. "Ah, no, Singer. Not entirely. My Power was too uncontrolled. I don't remember the trance."

"Just as well," she replied serenely.

"Trance?" Alexa's voice rose. "A trance?" She didn't know if she liked the idea. Dreams were one thing, an induced trance something entirely different.

They reached the Temple's huge oak door. Luthan hurried to open it. The Singer walked on, close to Alexa, then tripped over the threshold. Alexa reached for her. The Singer linked hands with Alexa, and she was swept away into a montage of flowing visions.

Shock stilled her, with her mouth open to protest. Blackness filled with evil things descended, and the gray edge of death advanced, then was parted like a theater curtain to show scenes of Colorado! She saw the mountains outside Denver, the city itself—but changed. She blinked and saw herself, older, shedding black judge's robes, walking away from an office with a sign on the door that said, "U.S. District Court Judge, Alexa Fitzwalter." The scene shifted, zoomed in, passed a huge, beautiful house to a backyard garden, and a barbecue with many people talking and laughing, jazz in the background. Several children played, shrieking with glee, and Alexa realized with shock that two of them, a boy and a girl, were hers. The girl smiled with a cheeky, missing-toothed grin. Alexa's heart lurched with yearning and love. A man's deep voice spoke behind her and she knew it was her husband. A man she greatly cared for.

Chords of music clashed loudly in her head. She thought she cried out. Around her was Lladrana, deep green fields, misty rain, bodies of monsters and volarans littering the ground. In the distance was a tossing gray-green sea. She wiped her arm across her forehead and her sleeve came away bloody. She hurt. She grieved for fallen friends. She ached with weariness from the battle, the one the day before, the one that might come a day later. Flickering images seemed to telescope a future of endless fighting, from different angles—on foot, on horseback, on volaranback. Bastien was always there, her Shield, her strength, comforting. She loved him deeply, nearly desperately, with love that grew each day and was returned in kind. Her friendship with the Marshalls had deepened into love too. When she thought of her friendships, they were many and complex, encompassing Townmasters, Chevaliers of low and high degree, the Marshalls, Friends of the Singer.

And along the border glowed a magical boundary between live, new fenceposts.

Flickering shadows highlighted several other women—Exotiques, like her. She tried to grasp the images, but they faded too rapidly. The world spun, shrank, and she saw it—the world of Amee—the continent Lladrana was on, the seas to the far North, islands to the west. One northern island held a mountain peak shrouded with dark, evil clouds. She felt a sharp pain in her side, looked down to see herself dressed in her Colorado winter clothes, and bleeding. A great light blinded her and she glanced up to see a sunrise of shooting golden rays above a horizon, heard/felt a great shout from all of Lladrana, from the world itself, as evil died. A triumphant orchestral march rang out.

Then words echoed hollowly, words she'd heard the first night on Lladrana and many times since. "Choose, Alexa."

Alexa choked, struggled, came back to herself. Bastien cradled her in his arms. His face was pale under the golden hue, his eyes dilated and dark. Her own face was wet with tears...and something else.

"Just pure rainwater to wake you." Luthan bent down and wiped her face again with a soft, damp cloth, and Alexa figured out that Bastien sat on the stone bench against the wall of the Temple and she lay across his lap, her legs stretched out on the bench. The Singer stood beyond Luthan, her expression serene, her hands folded at her waist, out of reach. Which was good, because little old lady or not, Alexa wanted to smack her.

"Are you finished tricking and manipulating me?" Alexa asked the Singer.

"Thee was working thineself into a state," the Singer answered in English, and repeated it in Lladranan. "It was best for thee, this way."

"Huh. I'm very tired of people deciding what is best for me without consulting me." She struggled against Bastien's hold and he reluctantly let her sit up, but one of his hands smoothed her hair, pressed her head against his chest. His heart beat rapidly beneath her ear.

"The greatest decision of all will be thine alone, Alexa," said the Singer.

Alexa wanted to bury her face in Bastien's chest, inhale the comforting scent of him, but she met the Singer's cool gaze instead. "I'll do what's right."

"What is right for Lladrana or what is right for thee?"

Alexa thought of the horror of the battlefields, the comfort of the picnic in Colorado. Her beautiful estate here, and Bastien, the man she'd cared for, and children. "The decision is mine."

"That's right," said Bastien. "Leave her be." His muscles tensed under her. "I shared her Song Quest. Do I need to do one of my own?" he asked.

The Singer stared at them thoughtfully. "No. The Song Quest is done. You have seen and heard." She placed her hand on Luthan's arm. "Shall we go sup?"

"You go on now. We'll follow in a bit," Bastien said, continuing to stroke Alexa's hair, cuddle her.

After they left, his eyes met hers. "I should have had my own Song Quest, but I'm glad she spared me. I can imagine what it would show—the same as it did last time, me and Reynardus. Him looming, me rebelling."

Narrowing her eyes, Alexa said, "You're avoiding the topic of my Song Quest."

His arms tightened around her. "I can guess at the first part— that was the Exotique Terre. Lladrana did not seem to compare well." He grimaced, then his eyes gleamed, lit with sensuality. He placed his hand on her breast, and it felt fabulous. "But I can try my best to convince you to stay." He lowered his head, slowly, and his mouth brushed hers, his tongue sweeping across her lips in a sweet caress that made her heart ache, her body quicken.

She opened her mouth and let him in. Letting her tongue dance with his, treasuring his taste, reveling in the comfort of his arms around her, his strength, his warmth, his hardening body.

His fingers undid the first frog-fastening of her golden gown, the second, and slipped inside to touch her through the thin silk of her chemise. The slide of silk against her nipples made her arch, gasp and take his breath into her, surrender. Feeling was so much more delightful than thinking.

And when he entered her a few moments later and they fell into ecstasy together, it was the very best delight in two worlds.

That night it was given information and ordered back to the Castle. To kill the Exotique and drain her of magic. It would be unbeatable, then.

Slowly it coalesced from a huge spiderweb in a crumbling square tower along the city wall. It had feasted well on its travels, grow-ing strong, substantive. It could be a nearly solid man-shape.

It had liked the Tower, had been able to call victims to itself and feed. Some of those had good magic. The city was safe. It dimly recalled being hurt by the Exotique. Pain enough that it lingered in the city instead of following her to the Castle.

But more Power flowed to it from the Master and the pain was forgotten. Only the exquisite taste of the Exotique's magic stayed in its memory.

The next morning they rose a half hour before the chimes for the Marshalls' meeting, kissed, dressed, and Bastien put the atom-ball into a special box that would contain it.

Bastien was checking on the volarans and horses when Umilla handed Alexa a message. Marwey wanted to meet Alexa in the tiny, wild garden with the brithenwood, to speak with her about a matter of great importance.

Alexa smiled. She remembered being a teenager and how vital and significant her emotions had made every decision, every action. And maybe after she spoke with Marwey, Alexa could grab a minute to herself in the garden.

She *needed* time alone, and the brithenwood tree always provided solace. Homesickness wasn't too bad, but now and then the press of an alien culture, of being a stranger in a strange land, weighed on her. She had the Song Quest to think of—two futures, one on Earth, one here in Lladrana. Which should she choose? The easy or the difficult? Which would be the most rewarding? Which would fulfill her spirit?

Before she reached the outside door she met Marwey, who shrieked with glee and flung herself at Alexa, hugging her tight.

"Pascal has asked me to Pair with him! He received his volaran reins yesterday from Mace, like you wanted. Pascal asked me to Pair with him after that. We can make a future together on your land. Pascal said you gave him the volaran. He asked me to Pair with him!"

"I got that," Alexa said when she could breathe again.

"I am so glad." Marwey looked around the empty corridor, low-ered her voice. "He will make a good Chevalier. I'm not a Cheva-lier, but I think I could be a Marshall, a Shield," she whispered, stunning Alexa.

She couldn't imagine Marwey on a battlefield.

"I will take defensive magical training. I have a dowry of two volarans that I will give to Pascal. He will Test first, perhaps later this year. If he passes, I will Test. I think I could call some wild volarans to work with me, three who will say they'll stay with me for five years, and I can Test for Marshall."

"You've got it all planned," Alexa said weakly. Surely as soon as she knew all the ins and outs of the society, she would be able to strategize as well as the teenager.

Marwey lifted her chin, eyes sparkling. "My plan will succeed, I know it!"

"Ayes."

"Pascal and I will be a *great* Marshall Pair. Well, maybe not as great as you and Bastien, but very good all the same!" Marwey hugged Alexa again, waved, and whirled down the corridor.

In the direction of the guards' quarters, Alexa noted. She ex-ited through the Keep door, through the maze and continued to the garden.

Pascal and Marwey. Not unexpected, but Alexa would have a new employee soon, Marwey.

She wanted to think of that happy future today. Didn't want to think of death and destruction, of choices that would have to be made. Usually she'd analyze events, experiences, emotions. She'd planned on using time under the brithenwood to do that. But not now. Now she felt too cheerful. Right this minute, life was good.

The small walled garden welcomed her. Lush, deep green grass several inches high carpeted the area between the one door and the lovely brithenwood tree with a bench around it. That it was a single tree was uncommon, and it was found mostly near the magical borders.

The tree was in full bloom, and its fragrance drifted in the air, along with scents from other gardens, a mixture of herbs and spring flowers and blossoming trees. A heady combination. The blood sang in her veins. She chuckled at the thought. If anyone would have such a saying, the Lladranans would. Perhaps it had come from them to Earth.

She glanced up at the blue, blue sky, as blue as on a winter day in Colorado. The sight of her tower spearing into the sky made her smile. Today the sun shone and the Castle's gray stone turned a warmer color, almost golden. She narrowed her eyes. Did the bricks glow a little, like they were absorbing and storing the energy? Maybe they did. She'd had so many questions, mostly about monsters and failing magical borders and bonds and stuff, that she hadn't asked any about the Castle. She'd find out later.

But she was simply joyful. The day was beautiful. She was alive and had purpose. The raw grief at losing her friend-sister Sophie was gone, and Alexa could remember her with love and echoing tenderness. She'd made new friends. The Marshalls were becoming like a family to her; Thealia, an aunt with a stern exterior; Partis, a marshmallow surface and steel core. She grinned. Whatever else her time in Lladrana had been, it was…interesting.

A bird trilled a rippling song that reminded Alexa of the tune cycling between her and Bastien. Studying it, hearing it in her head, she found it carried a few of the same notes. A joyful, mating song. She grinned then. Their lovemaking the night before had been spectacular. So intense, so orgasmic she hadn't been able to flutter an eyelash for some time after. The man was a fabulous lover. And he was hers. Too early to think about the "L" word, but she'd let it float in her mind. He had become a Marshall, to protect her. He was her Shield.

She couldn't restrain herself, she did a little jig. Giggled. A big, pink butterfly streamed over the wall and danced in the air. Sinafin.

The bluebird sings songs good for dancing, Sinafin said.

Alexa threw out her arms and laughed, spun. The image of Sophie dancing like this from pure pleasure rose in her mind. Alexa hadn't understood then, hadn't felt the same. Now she did. What had Sophie done after that?

She'd run. Alexa eyed the garden. Not much room to run here, and dancing alone paled. But it might be fun to dart through the greenery of the hedge maze. That could be a challenge. She glanced up at Sinafin, who looked to be delicately sipping brithenwood blossoms. Probably pure magic, brithenwood blossom nectar. It smelled like it should be.

"Want to race?" asked Alexa.

Sinafin mentally slurped the last from a blossom, then waved an antenna. *Not in this body. This body does not go fast. You might kick the little dog accidentally. I will be my warhawk. Give you a real challenge,* she said slyly.

"Fine, but *in* the maze, not over it."

Alexa had no intention of losing. By the time she had passed through the door, and shut it behind her, Sinafin was settling into her feathers atop the wall.

"Ready?" asked Alexa.

Ready, said Sinafin. *Go!*

Alexa took off, entered the maze, skidded left into a passage and dodged through the first several turns—and straight into the web.

It was huge, bigger than she was. This time it wrapped her face, her arms, tangled her, took her down and started sucking the magic from her. It *hurt*—a ripping, tearing pain.

Finally she figured it out. This horror was the web at the inn, the thing that had shadowed her, draining magic and leaving heaps of dust behind.

Sharing its mind, she saw its birth from the frinks. She saw her death.

She'd burned it before. With her baton. But her mind grayed as air and magic left her. She couldn't reach her baton. Not with her hands tight at her sides. She didn't know if she had the magic to set the baton afire in its sheath, knew she had no control to keep herself from burning, but a fiery death would be cleansing after this hideous thing slipping oily fingers on her, caressing her as it suctioned her magic away, bloating, gloating.

Its mind battered hers, hissing. *So sweet your essence. So pale you look. I, black, you, white and still. I love sucking you dry, so sweet. I was sent especially for you, to suck your sweetness. You have not succeeded in restoring the posts. Soon we amass an army and invade, you will miss the battle, the invasion and I will find...*

Burn! Alexa flung all her strength into the word. A small spark lit near the bottom of the baton sheath. Not enough. She was dying. She was failing. She wouldn't allow that. No need to save any of her strength.

Burn!

The last thing she sensed was a tiny spark inching around the sheath bottom.

Bastien! The cry knocked him back from the volaran he curried. The image that followed, Alexa down, under a sticky black substance that slowly formed into a man lying atop her, shocked him.

Come now, Bastien, Shield her! It's the monster that's been stalking her! Sinafin screamed, and the warhawk's screech hit his ears at the same time. He dropped the comb, ran shouting his war cry at the top of his lungs, flung all the protective Power he had at the evil thing and had it slide off the monster. The thing raised its head, turned it, and red eyes burned. Fangs dripped sparkling drops of Power. Alexa's Power.

Bastien ran faster than he ever had. He yelled anger to the skies, at the Marshalls' refusal to act earlier, saying it was a minor monster, a town monster. No threat.

Fury ignited wild magic inside him. He zoomed to the maze, twisted, turned, bolted through it. Seeing Alexa from Sinafin's eyes. His woman lived, but was unconscious. He whirled around a corner, bumping into the hedge. There it was.

The thing ripped Alexa's clothes down the front of her body. Lifted itself like a man about to rape a woman.

Sinafin dove at it, slid away from a shield surrounding it. Her claws grew and grew, far larger and sharper than a hawk's. A roc's claws.

Bastien's baton was hot in his hand. Spell words tore from his throat, silver energy hit the thing. It shivered a little, raised a hand.

Sinafin caught the hand, snagged all the fingers with her claws, backed upward, flapping hard, stretching the monster's substance into weblike thinness.

The evil hissed, but Sinafin began to grow, changing, enlarging. A roc. The largest bird in two worlds.

He was on it now, slicing at it with hot-silver Power, cutting bits of it off—an ear, a foot, two. They fell into dirt. The monster went shapeless, filmed over Alexa's still, still body. He gathered Power in his baton, lightning power that would sizzle over her. Wild magic Power he'd only used once before, had never seen anyone else attempt.

Shouts and sounds of running came from the opening of the maze. His lip curled. The Marshalls, late as ever.

He raised his baton. The roc rose above the maze, angled to

the tower wall, still holding the thing. Sinafin's mind touched Bastien's. She was draining the energy the monster had harvested from Alexa. Sinafin wanted it all, to hold the magic, cleanse it so they could return it to Alexa. The feycoocu was desperate to keep Alexa alive.

No more desperate than he.

Bastien crouched in the maze near his Pairling. In an agony of impatience, he listened to Sinafin's instructions. More waiting...until the feycoocu had the last drop of juice from the horror. Then fry it. She'd tell Bastien the right moment.

The wild Power pulsed in him; he packed it into his wand. Holding back was the hardest thing he'd ever done. Alexa looked too quiet, too white, too fragile. The Song between them was thready. He sent energy into it, strengthening their tie, strengthening her life.

Whoosh! A lick of flame caught the thin edge of the thing. It shrieked, shriveled, contracted into a ball, tore from the roc's claws, pelleted away.

Bastien jumped to Alexa, lifted her into his arms. Her heart beat slowly, sluggishly. He hummed a healing spell, simple and powerful.

The Marshalls rushed to them. He stopped them with his gaze. "Don't come near me. *Don't...come...near...us,* you useless sacks of merde. I'll kill the one who touches her. Did you see what sort of monster had her?"

"A tournpench," Faith murmured, bowing her head. "The Lorebook said it was minor."

"That's right, a horror that drained her Power, was about to rape her. The horror you said was minor would have killed our precious Exotique! The horror you all agreed was the *Town's* problem."

"We were wrong," Thealia croaked.

He sneered. "You have often been wrong. Now you know your Lorebook can be wrong too."

They bunched near the hedges. Partis pushed through, his carved healing staff in his hand.

Bastien bared his teeth. "There is nothing you can say, nothing you can sing that will make me allow you to put a fingertip on her."

Sinafin set claws into Bastien's shoulder. He stiffened with pain, felt his blood pool under her.

Now, she said. *We will send back her Power, her magic. It will be the stronger for coming from me, flowing through you. It will contain some of my feycoocu magic, some of your wild Power. It will be good for her. Let me do this. Let me use you. You two are the future of the world.*

He braced himself, his eyes mere slits. *Do it.*

Magic gushed through him. Fast, huge, unstoppable. It swirled through every pocket of his body, every kink of his nerves, every twist of his mind, then poured into Alexa. A little sparkle of the pure magic of the feycoocu lingered in his bones, and always would.

His hair lifted; he felt the silver streaks heat as if they glowed. His skin tingled. He felt *great.* He moved away from the hedge wall. Alexa trembled in his arms. Her eyes opened, lambent green; a touch of Sinafin's sparkle was in them too. Her lips turned the color of a blushing rose.

She wriggled, and he reluctantly set her on her feet. She blinked, looked around the passageway.

"What happened?"

Sinafin sent them all quick images of events. The Marshalls shuddered backward in a lump. When Alexa "saw" the attempted rape, she flinched, swayed. Bastien caught her around the waist. Her lips whitened.

"So the fire worked," she murmured. "But even if it hadn't, my friend and my Pair mate would have saved me. Did save me by slowing the creature." Tremors ran through her. "I want a bath. Now. A bath."

Hysteria lurked under her surface.

"Of course," he said. He stared at the Marshalls. "We are going to the private bathing pool off the regular baths. We don't want company. We may never want your company again." He swept her up into his arms once more and strode away to the baths.

There he loved her, slowly and tenderly, and afterwards he held her near and tried not to think how close he'd come to losing her, and how that loss would have shattered him.

24

After they had bathed and loved, Alexa dozed in Bastien's arms. What a miserable two days! That horrible pterodactyl, Bastien's Testing, which had disturbed her dreams, the Song Quest, then the attack this morning.

Being crushed and smothered by the pterodactyl was bad enough, being smothered and drained of magic by that sticky-black-hideous monster was infinitely worse. With mordant humor, she wondered if it was her fate to be smothered. Probably better than dying fighting. Maybe. Well, if so, she'd wish it would be accidental, in bed, with a feather pillow when she was a tiny, old woman.

She breathed deeply, filling her lungs, just to know she could. It felt good.

Bastien snored softly next to her on a cushioned pallet in the private bathing room. She craned to see his face. It was peaceful, yet he looked stronger, more mature. Was it from his becoming

a Marshall and choosing a baton? Or his first use of Power as a
Marshall, saving her? She didn't think any infusion of magic from
Sinafin would make him look more adult. Alexa opened her
senses, seeking the feycoocu. Sinafin rested on a pillow on Alexa's
bed in her muff form.

Alexa smiled. It was good to have friends. She quested for the
Marshalls and found them still meeting in their Council Chamber. She should be there, and so should Bastien, but it wasn't as if
she could contribute anything. She'd enjoyed getting to know the
Marshalls, learning their quirks. Soon they would be fast friends,
like family. Irritating at times, but beloved anyway. Her family. Her
home. She'd made a place for herself here.

They were probably dissecting the attack on her instant by instant. Sinafin had seen and recorded it; they wouldn't need any
input from her. They had probably learned from the Lorebook by
now that it was sentient. Alexa shuddered, remembering the caressing fingers, the hissing voice....

She jerked up, stumbled to her feet, glanced wildly around for
her clothes. When she found them, she pounced, and dragged
them on.

Bastien groaned. Opened one eye. "What?"

"The thing. The webmonster. It *told* me something. The monsters are invading!"

"The horrors are always invading." He patted the pillows beside
him, smiled seductively. "Come back."

Alexa flung back her wet hair. "They invade in little bunches,
the small evils and creepers first, then the larger monsters. We've
been able to ward them off. In general."

Bastien sat up. "In general."

"The thing said something about amassing an army. What could
we do against an army of the things?"

He opened his mouth. Shut it. Got up. "We don't have enough

Chevaliers, enough Marshalls, enough *magic* to stop a concerted effort." He got up and dressed rapidly too.

"How many do you think we could handle?"

"No more than five hundred, and with that we could lose most of our fighters. Makes sense to field an army now, before you've reset the boundaries. Even if you find the answer to renewing the fenceposts, by then we'll have monsters throughout Lladrana."

Bastien held out a hand to her. "The Marshalls are still in session."

They ran all the way. When they reached the Council Room door, Alexa smiled as she read the script on the door: Lladrana Marshalls. Lovemaking with Bastien sure put her into a great mood. Even in her own head, she was babbling. She had to get a grip, had to present a case to the Marshalls.

Bastien flung open the door and strode through. She followed.

Reynardus looked up with irritation. Some of the other Marshalls brightened.

Thealia smiled and waved toward their seats. "Welcome, and sit."

"I have news. I recalled something the *thing* said to me as it tried to kill me." Alexa couldn't bear to sit, not with the fear rumbling through her.

Reynardus snorted. "Horrors don't think. Don't speak."

Alexa set her shoulders. "This one did." She repeated his words. The Marshalls looked stunned.

"It can't be," Faith said.

"How many?" snapped Mace.

Alexa placed a hand to her temple, trying to remember the shades and shadows of the beast's mind. "It's more than a few. More than a hundred. Maybe a thousand."

"There aren't that many," Reynardus scoffed.

"How do you *know!*" Alexa's temper heated. "You only have the

Lorebooks, and the Lorebook of Monsters was wrong about the thing that attacked me. You haven't sent any explorers North to find out where the monsters come from or why, or how many there are."

"We haven't sent spies to their deaths for a century." Mace's smile was wintry. "We lost ninety good Chevaliers, magical, noble, powerful, and twelve Marshalls that way. I know because my family line was nearly wiped out. It is against our family rules to volunteer to go North."

"Inconceivable. This idea of yours," Reynardus said. He steepled his fingers. "Do you wish to distract us from the fact that you have failed in the task for which we Summoned you?"

Anger surged through her blood. She kept her voice even. "I fully intend to fulfill my purpose and discover how to make the fenceposts. But I am telling you we must prepare for an army of monsters, for a huge battle." She looked at Thealia.

The older woman just shook her head. "They've never come more than five at a time—except the minor demons."

"And we haven't had dreeths for a century either. Or the webthing," Bastien said.

Alexa looked each one in the face. "You don't believe me." It hurt. Wrenching. She'd thought they had accepted her. Perhaps to a point, and to a point they considered her a friend. But not enough to believe her. "You don't believe me and you don't trust me, and you don't trust my judgment."

"You were near death, attacked, being drained of magic, easy prey for a lying insinuation. That is what must have happened." Thealia smiled sympathetically.

"Why would it lie as it was killing me?"

"It's evil."

Shaking her head in disbelief, Alexa stared around the table. "I know it told the truth—"

"As it knew it to be. Why should it know of this, and how, if it's been in Lladrana for weeks?"

"As if a monster can think!" Reynardus exclaimed.

Alexa set her baton down on the table very, very softly. The emotional pain was overwhelming. She'd never been more than a tool to them. Definitely not an equal to be heard or listened to.

"I can't sit here in the Castle and do nothing. I stood by when you told me not to worry about the creature in the Town. I will always regret that. There are deaths on my head for that. I can't wait to see which of us is right." Tears stung behind her eyes, tears of pain and horror, making her voice raspy. "Bastien, can we build an army of Chevaliers?" She looked up at him.

"I knew it would come to this!" Reynardus pounded both his fists on the table. "I knew she would never work with us. Never was acceptable as a Marshall. Now she will pander to those discontented, rebellious Chevaliers and split our forces!"

Bastien spoke softly. "By telling the Chevaliers there is a mass of monsters coming? And you will deny it, all of you? You have never wanted others to have information, the be-spelled weapons in your armories, the powerful battle spells of the Lorebooks. You have kept them for yourselves—and what do we have now? Fenceposts failing, the defensive border disappearing, dreeths and webthings attacking."

On the table her baton had faded to the color of light green jade. Alexa stroked it with her finger. "The Jade Baton of Honor. I can't, honorably, stand aside and watch people die when I can prevent it." She shook her head, forced her tears to dry. "Not possible."

She felt the touch of Bastien's fingers on the small of her back.

"Go gather your things. Get Sinafin. We'll leave for our estates shortly," he said.

Nodding, she opened the door and left. Left the Marshalls she'd begun to think of as family or friends. Left her baton.

Bastien closed the door behind her. Looked at the Marshalls. "How did this happen, that you can't trust her, or yourselves, or the Song?" He shook his head. "A Sorcerer from the Tower could stand here and foretell an army of evil and you wouldn't listen."

He picked up the Jade Baton. The shock of energy—Alexa's energy—was strong, pleasurable. He spun it into the air and caught it. "I'm taking this. Be assured, we won't call ourselves Marshalls. Those Marshalls who originally made the fenceposts, they were *more,* as Alexa is more. Guardians. She is a Guardian. The Guardian of Honor." His smile cracked. Whatever was in store for them, they were shaping it by themselves, for themselves. "And I am Shield Bastien. Shieldchevalier Bastien." He flipped the baton again, stuck it in his belt and swaggered off.

No sooner was he gone than Reynardus said in soft spell-voice, "We will not speak of this. Never to anyone not in this chamber now."

Thealia felt the command settle uncomfortably upon her. It did not fit. "She must be wrong," Thealia said, hoping beyond hope that it was true.

Faith blinked rapidly. "I can't think she could be right. How could she be right? The evil ones have never come in more than four or five. No noble with lands bordering the North has reported any unusual conglomeration of beasts."

"Beasts," Mace grunted. "We've always been plagued with beasts. Not thinking-talking creatures. What was that thing this morning, anyway?"

Reynardus sat. "Should we care?"

"It got away," Mace said.

They'd fallen into their old habits already, Thealia thought. When presented with the inconceivable, they couldn't accept it. How *had* they come to be so blind? So inflexible? As hidebound as a Lorebook?

She didn't know. And she didn't know what to do. These were the people she was the closest to, bonded to until death, by blood-bonds of the creatures they'd killed. She could not break that link, not even if it was right to do so.

The Marshalls were still a fighting force to be reckoned with, a team of fighters strong in magic, in training, blood-bonded as no other force. She could not afford to smash that force, especially if Alexa was right. Bile rose in Thealia's throat. She didn't like her actions, her thoughts, her conclusions. She didn't like what she was. She didn't like herself. She felt tears in her own eyes.

Under the table, Partis stroked her thigh, kept his hand on her knee. He'd said nothing during the final confrontation and she didn't know exactly how he felt, but he was by her side, touching her, offering support.

No one had spoken, as if they all were as wrapped in their own thoughts as she. She didn't want to look around the table and see doubt or anger, so she kept her gaze fixed on the closed door.

"It's time to consult the Tower, the Sorcerers and Sorceresses," Thealia said. She matched stares with Reynardus. His lips tightened, then twisted in a sneer. "Perhaps one will come when called. Perhaps not. And perhaps they will inform us why our very expensive Exotique did not perform her duty and mend the fenceposts."

Johnsa made a protesting noise, but shut up under Reynardus's withering look.

"I suppose you intend to say 'I told you so,' Reynardus," Thealia continued smoothly. "But before you do, *I* shall point out that we might have been much further along, might have convinced Alexa to stay with us, had you not made Alexa's stay here so difficult. I hold *you* responsible for this."

Before they could continue to pick at each other, Partis said, "I agree we should call in the Tower now, with all the safeguards for the one who comes. Who says nay?"

No one did. Partis nodded to Johnsa. "Johnsa, an image for Summoning, please."

Swordmarshall Johnsa inhaled deeply, steadied herself until her energy aura pulsed rhythmically. "We call the Tower." The image formed of the first Tower ever built by a Sorcerer on the islands off the coast of Lladrana. No one inhabited it now, but the Call would be heard in every Tower.

They Sang the ancient tune of Summoning for a Sorcerer or Sorceress, and looked to the lower left corner of the room, where one would appear if he or she chose to be Summoned.

A high pure note rose, deep red haze swirled, solidified into a tall, rangy man with wide streaks of silver at both temples, wearing a maroon robe. Despite the fact his features were slightly different from most of Lladranans and his eyes blue—both indications of old Exotique blood. Jaquar Dumont was a handsome man. He flung back his head to clear the long black hair that tangled before his eyes, and strolled to the seat of the Representative of the Tower, continuing to stand.

Amusement danced in his eyes, irking Thealia. She knew it irritated the other Marshalls as well.

"We wondered when you Marshalls would Call on us regarding the Exotique. I congratulate you, it has taken this group longer than all the rest. And usually we are Summoned only when something dire has occurred."

He read it in their faces. "What has happened? All was well at dawn." His eyes narrowed. "The Exotique still lives, only is not to be found at the Castle. Interesting."

Reynardus stood. "First we want your oath that you will disseminate this information freely and to all of your colleagues."

Jaquar flashed a grin but his eyes were watchful. He ostentatiously scraped back the chair and lounged into it, then waved a hand. "Done. You have my Word that I will tell all Sorcerers and Sorceresses of what transpires here, fully and impartially. My first report will go to the most powerful of us all, the ancient Bossgond."

Thealia licked her lips. That was not a name any of the Marshalls felt comfortable whispering. "We have questions."

"Naturally. Anything regarding an Exotique will raise questions, their Power and unpredictability being so much different and usually more than ours. It is reasonable that this is so. They would be powerful in their own land. Bring them through the Dimensional Corridor and they will accrue Power there, especially if they have to face a Test, as Alyeka did."

Blood drained from Thealia's face as she recalled they'd lost Alexa for a few seconds during the Summoning. Alexa had not been safe! Why hadn't she told them of the first attack? Because, with the Tests immediately following, she must have thought the first too was of the Marshalls' making.

Jaquar sat straighter in the chair, his eyes and voice cool. "You are much more ignorant than we suspected. Alyeka fought a render between our worlds."

Partis put his hand on Thealia's fisted fingers. She didn't recall having tightened them.

"So what transpired this morning?" asked Jaquar.

Faith cleared her voice and called her Lorebook of Monsters, which appeared with a harder thump than usual on the table before her. The pages flipped until they reached a picture of the creature they had thought was the pest plaguing the Town along Alexa's journey. "We thought we were dealing with a tournpench, a lesser evil."

"Watch," Johnsa said, and unrolled the events that Sinafin had shown them.

Garbled swearing came from the Sorcerer as he saw the man-thing poise above Alexa. He gave a sigh of relief when he watched the monster's defeat.

They sat in silence for a moment after the retelling.

"Fools." Jaquar's eyes snapped. With a whistle, a book three times the size and weight of Faith's banged hard before him. The pages zipped by too fast to see, then stopped. "It's a sangvile. More dangerous than a dreeth, which we've also heard has been found in Lladrana lately." His lips thinned. He placed his hand on the book, lifted it. Copies of the pages rose, floated over to Faith's book and wove themselves into it.

Jaquar continued. "In my considered opinion, the Exotique is now the only being capable of killing it. With the Power from the sangvile, cleansed by the feycoocu, added with feycoocu trace magic and the inflow of magic from her Pair mate, she is stronger than Bossgond. You have created an awesome warrior."

He inclined his head mockingly. "You also let the sangvile escape and alienated Alyeka." He swept a glance around the table, a nasty smile curving his lips. "The sangvile is too weak to follow her, which means it will linger in the Castle, trying to drain the magic from the most powerful person, turn that one into dust. That would be me. I'm leaving. All the Towers must hear of this as soon as possible and I do not want to broadcast from here."

Jaquar rose and scooped up his book.

"What do you want for that book?" asked Faith.

He looked down his nose at her Lorebook of Monsters. "I agree, an abridged version is not terribly useful." Cocking his head as if listening, he waited a moment, then said, "It is now even odds that the Towers will need our own Exotique to fight this growing evil. However, we do not cooperate well, and to form a bond strong enough for us to Summon our Exotique would take years. Something big is happening. None of us has years. On behalf of the Towers, I offer to provide eight spellbooks such as this one, of the greatest use for your Marshalls, if you Summon our Exotique for us. Bossgond will provide you with the qualities necessary for our Exotique by tomorrow night."

His nostrils flared. "We know the next moon-moment and alignment of the Dimensional Corridor is a month away, but speaking for myself, I don't want to make another visit to you idiots before that time. We will communicate by crystal ball." Plucking a maroon sphere from his robe pocket, he rolled it onto the table.

Reynardus stood. "Easy to snipe at us who have less Power——"

"You have always found it so, no?" Jaquar said.

"——but we have fought, hand to hand, these monsters to destroy them. I've not seen you fighting. As for the Exotique, she has not fulfilled her purpose. She has not revived the borders or shown how to make the fenceposts. As far as I know, even the Tower does not know how to do those things."

"The last one who had that knowledge was killed before imparting it. As for the Exotique, it is not yet time. She must bond with our world, the Amee-soul—and how quickly can one do that? The Singer was here last night. Why did you not ask her that question about Alyeka?"

Reynardus was silent.

Jaquar barked laughter. "I see. Your last Song Quest was that fearsome." He waved a hand, met the gaze of each Marshall. "Review your Song Quest where you asked for advice and heard of the Summoning. It will tell you when Alyeka will be ready, will find the knowledge you seek to defend Lladrana. It is difficult magic to gauge, magic relating to the Snap."

"The Snap!" Thealia had tried to forget about it.

"Her natural bond to her Exotique Land-soul, her bond to Amee-soul, her bonds to you all, others, Bastien... It's very hard to predict the Snap." He strode to the corner.

"Wait, Jaquar!" Thealia stood. "The pool of jerir is still in the Temple, should you wish to avail yourself."

The light was dim around him, but she thought he grimaced. With a flick of his fingers, the book was gone. "I suppose it would be wise. Since I'm here. Bastien left one of his prime volarans. I will fly it to Alyeka's estate, take a fresh one to my island. After." He strolled to the door, but a new tension showed in his muscles.

As soon as the door closed, Partis started the rendering of the Spring Song Quest where they'd been told to Summon an Exotique. His was the best memory for tune. Thealia joined hands with him and picked up a minor harmony she remembered. She Sang and held out her hand to Reynardus, wondering if he would break their circle once and for all. He stared at her open palm for a moment, then took her hand. She shuddered at the rioting energy within him, not fathoming why he should be so stirred up. Without answer, he evened his emotions, linked hands with his brother and Shield Ivrog.

So the circle connected, bonded. Partis's voice grew deeper, richer. Love for him blossomed in her and she wove it into the Song. Ivrog added fraternal love; Mace and his wife added love that had originally arisen from a Choosing and Bonding ceremony; Johnsa and Faith added their Paired woman-love. The Song encompassed them all, brought them to a level that not one of them could have achieved alone, sharpened their senses.

Partis was the first to recognize the pattern of notes. The spring mating song of the bluebird. Once, twice, thrice. "Only after the Exotique has heard the bluebird thrice will she know from Amee-soul how to raise the defenses of Lladrana. A great battle will come and if she survives, the Snap—"

The circle broke. Thrown from the stream of Song, it took Thealia a moment to gather her wits. Others blinked around her.

Reynardus had broken their connection. He sat, gray-faced.

Partis breathed heavily. She took his hands in hers, lifted them to her lips, sent all her love to him to help him ride out disorientation. Love would always support them.

Johnsa gagged, ran for the door, Faith following. Mace's wife fell into his arms.

The link-cutting had been too quick, too total.

With trembling hands, Partis stroked her hair, smiled sadly and shook his head. He'd noticed something she hadn't. It wasn't often he wouldn't share information with her, wasn't often he had knowledge she didn't.

Coldness gripped her. She hadn't heard one trill of the bluebird call. Had Alexa?

Reynardus strode from the room and Thealia hadn't the energy to stop him. "Will the sangvile go after him?" she murmured.

Partis said, "Him or Faith or Johnsa. Faith and Johnsa will likely remain together." Partis glanced at Ivrog. "Do you follow him?"

Ivrog gestured and the book with the new pages on the sangvile slid over to him. "Not until we find out how to ward off this...beast. How to lure it, perhaps kill it."

Mace gave a bark of laughter, shifted his wife onto his lap and circled her with his arms. "I suspect luring it will be no problem. Read us the monster's weaknesses, Ivrog."

An hour later they were making fire amulets to protect everyone in the Castle.

The sangvile had withdrawn to the darkest corner of the Castle, hoping the feycoocu could not sense it. It had lost much Power, and all the wonderful, shimmering magic it had drawn from the little Exotique prey. It should have been easier.

To survive, it would need a feast of magic. A while later, someone smelling rich and delicious came. Even later, the one with strong magic took a volaran back. Now compacted into a shade of its former self, a tiny speck of cobweb, the sangvile had enough energy to follow, hooking on to the wake of the volaran.

25

Alexa was blessedly numb for the flight home. She'd been placed in front of Bastien on his volaran, and the steady beat of his heart reassured her. She sensed in him a righteous anger and relief at leaving behind the Castle, and the restrictions of being a Marshall. His little farewell speech to the group echoed in her mind, so she hadn't been surprised when he'd presented her with her baton and called her "Guardian." Sort of nonsensical, when she felt like she'd been run over by war chariots...if Lladrana had war chariots, which she didn't know.

So she still had her Jade Baton, and Bastien, the black-and-silver. Sinafin flew beside them, chattering to Bastien. Alexa thought they were strategizing as to how to raise an army. She was only an attorney, she was clueless. She may or may not still be Joan of Arc, but God—or the Song—wasn't whispering in her ear.

Pascal and Marwey had met them at the door to her suite.

They'd both been stiff with pride, assuring Alexa that their loyalty was hers and they would follow shortly. Alexa had just nodded acceptance. Bastien had made another little speech. When he was done, the pair had glowed with determination.

Bastien had also had a quick word with Luthan before leaving. Alexa guessed that he'd leave it to Luthan how to tell the news, and to whom. She managed a little smile. Luthan was solid. He could be trusted. He was almost family. If she stayed, he would be family.

So much heartbreak. So much risk. So much fear. Could she stay? Right now she didn't think she could lift a finger to fight, and all she really wanted was to snuggle into an easy chair watching a video and munching popcorn. With Bastien. She rubbed her cheek on his chest and sighed. That was the big problem. She really wanted Bastien—for a long, long time.

Instead of being at home in her apartment, she was flying through the air to a mansion, *her* mansion. There she'd train to fight, and learn more spells, and practice horseback riding, and maybe learn to fly atop the volarans. Too strange....

Bastien's volaran turned its head to look back at her, eyes wide and liquid with concern. Bastien tapped it on the head.

"Watch where you're flying. She's safe with me."

Sinafin zoomed past, eyeing Alexa. *Very much shock lately.*

"That's right." Bastien sighed, squeezed Alexa a little. "But she's a very strong lady, my Pair woman, she'll bounce back."

Alexa felt like a deflated balloon, all bounce gone forever. She tilted her head and had opened her mouth to say so, when something flying behind the volaran caught her eye.

"What's that?"

Bastien and Sinafin laughed. The volaran snorted in distaste. "My atomball," Bastien replied.

Curiosity snagging her, she sat up a little. "It sure has a lot of energy."

It will be useful in the battle, Sinafin said matter-of-factly, and Alexa didn't know if Sinafin had always known of the battle, learned it from the monster, or trusted Alexa's word. Then images of a spiked iron ball zipping around a battlefield played in slow motion in her mind—blood, gore, ichor spattering, limbs ripped away, heads and bodies smashed. Alexa hid her face in Bastien's chest again, sure this would be the only "time out" she'd get. Once she reached her estate, she'd have to be Lady of the Manor—strong and decisive and responsible.

"I think the first thing we should do is have Alexa walk over my land and hers. What my dear father left out of his snide remarks was that wherever she's been, *exactly* where she's walked, no frinks fall with the rain anymore."

Walking didn't sound so bad. Walking the green fields of her land and his, the gentle hills… She could do that. It would be good to do that, to see living and sprouting and blossoming instead of wounding and death.

"When the Chevaliers come, we'll house them in my old house. It's only a couple of miles from Alexa's hall. I'll clear the old training areas, the riding and flying rings."

That sounded a little more ominous. Alexa decided to go back to sleep. She'd been sleeping a lot lately, yet didn't feel rested.

When they landed in the front courtyard of her manor, Alexa awoke and mentally girded her loins. When she'd dismounted, she lifted her chin, squared her shoulders and, with legs that wobbled only slightly, mounted the stairs.

Her butler opened the door before she reached it. He bowed deeply.

Bastien grabbed her elbow, nodded to the butler. "We have come to stay. The Jade Baton will be calling a Gathering. My squire, Urvey, follows with plans, as does Alexa's Chevalier, Pascal, and her lady-in-waiting, Marwey."

Oh boy. Obviously there was a concept for this, and proper words. Well, Bastien seemed to know them, so let him handle it.

"Yes, Shieldmarshall Vauxveau."

"Open the house, provision it, and the Jade Baton will tend to all household matters tomorrow." Bastien was moving her up the stairs. "And don't call us 'Marshalls.' We have severed our connection with them." He threw the last over his shoulder.

"Is this still my house?" asked Alexa.

"Your house, your land. They can't take it back," Bastien said with satisfaction.

"Oh. Good."

"Yes. You did very well. Have done very well since you came to Lladrana. Don't doubt that."

"All right."

Though he wanted to continue down the corridor, Alexa stopped at the landing and looked down. The butler was already organizing things. He seemed supremely unfazed by Bastien's news. She supposed he was still glad to have someone with magical power in residence. She relaxed a little, examined the house around her. It was as enchanting as she'd remembered. This was worth holding on to.

The murmur of voices and bustling came from below. The house was old, and the servants Lladranan, not of her own society. They probably all had seen power politics before.

Alexa stiffened her spine. *She* had been the one to walk away from the Marshalls. It had hurt to do so, but they were wrong. This was the right course even though it might feel like retreat, like failure. She took Bastien's hand.

"I'm glad you're here."

"I'm glad I'm here too. It's a beautiful afternoon. What do you say to a walk?"

She managed a little smile. "I say yes."

* * *

The rest of the day she walked her land. The contact steadied her, and Bastien's undemanding presence and easy company eased her bitter feeling of loss. They had dinner at Bastien's house—a charming home—then started walking to her estate. As evening fell, Urvey ran up to them, panting.

"There's a Sorcerer come to call. He flew in on one of your volarans, Bastien."

Bastien's eyes sharpened. "Which Sorcerer? Did you get his name?"

Urvey shuffled. "I didn't want to go near him. He's wearing a maroon robe and has dipped in the jerir, so he came from the Castle."

"Very old?" Bastien seemed to hold his breath.

"About your age. He has blue eyes."

"Ah, Jaquar Dumont." Bastien grabbed her hand and hustled them back to the manor house.

"Blue eyes? I haven't seen anyone with blue eyes since I've been here," Alexa said.

Bastien spared a glance for her. "Are they common in the Exotique Land?"

"Not uncommon where I come from," she said.

"Such eyes are a sign of old Exotique blood," Bastien said.

"Oh?"

She was glad evening was falling and the light was dim. She hadn't considered children and didn't want to talk about them now. When she'd first visited, her butler had said that Exotique blood was rare, that most Exotique-Lladranan couples produced no children. But now she'd run into it in two instances—with her home and with this Sorcerer. She hadn't considered birth control at all, and there was no way she'd go into battle if she was pregnant. That thought reassured her. Surely the Song, Fate, *whatever,* wanted her to be Joan of Arc, would keep her from conceiving while she had battles to win, fences to mend, dragons—pterodactyls—to slay. Alexa hadn't been a believer in destiny in her former life, but events had made her reconsider.

They reached the impressive front steps and stood under a couple of huge quartz lamps. Bastien turned her to him, ran his hands down her arms and straightened her gown, sifted his fingers through her hair. He frowned.

She shook her head at him. "How groomed must I be?"

Bastien shrugged. "You look fine. But Jaquar could help us a lot. Magical weapons, battle spells. He must know some, or have access to Lorebooks that do."

Obviously, he thought the Chevaliers would rally so they'd be ready for a battle when it happened. Since he believed they had a chance of winning, her natural optimism kicked in. She smiled back at him.

"Ah, we're going to negotiate."

"Oh yes." Bastien rubbed his hands.

"Very interesting," said a man's voice.

Alexa *knew* she hadn't heard the door open, but there the man stood, just beyond the threshold, door wide open. She couldn't see him well; he was merely a dark, lean form against the light—and the aura of blue imparted by a plunge in the jerir. He didn't look as if that event fazed him.

"You want information on magical weapons, perhaps the magical weapons the Tower has. You want battle spells. It sounds as if you have broken with the Marshalls, yet you both wear your batons," the Sorcerer said. His voice wasn't as melodious as Partis's, or even Bastien's, but there was a muscular Power in it all the same.

Inclining his head, Bastien gestured beyond the man and, to the left, to the parlor. "Shall we discuss this?"

The Sorcerer narrowed his blue eyes at Bastien and Alexa. "What can you offer me for spells to make magical weapons and great battle chants?"

Bastien used one of his charming smiles. Tugging on Alexa, they walked past Jaquar to the door of the parlor. Bastien opened it for her.

Alexa hesitated, turned to get a good look at the guy. Tall, dark, handsome. Features slightly more Caucasian and less Asian than most Lladranans. Deep blue eyes, wavy black hair. Very nice. She put out her hand.

"I'm Alexa Fitzwalter, Marsh— I carry the Jade Baton."

In a couple of strides he closed the space that separated them and lifted her hand to his lips as he bowed. "Jaquar Dumont, a great pleasure."

After the courtesy, he kept her hand, and she felt something brush against her magic. She didn't push back.

Bastien stepped close and slipped an arm around her waist. This time his smile wasn't charming.

Whoosh! The shooting-star zoomed down the stairs to hover by the Sorcerer.

He jumped back.

Bastien said, "We have vital information to trade. We killed a dreeth yesterday. Do you need any dreeth parts? My lady and I are having fighting leathers made from the dreeth, but there should be plenty of hide leftover. I also have an atomball in a mace."

"I noticed. As I said before, very interesting." Jaquar eyed the ball as he moved into the parlor and sat in a huge overstuffed chair near the fire.

With a whistle, Bastien banished the ball back to their bedroom.

"Would you like anything to eat or drink?" asked Alexa.

Jaquar glanced at Bastien, who'd moved to a sideboard with liquor, then at Alexa. She was sitting on the love seat across from the chair. "Your staff made me comfortable in the dining room with an excellent dinner when I arrived."

The image of a single man at the huge table in the formal dining room should have seemed ridiculous, but not with this man. His Power would fill the room. His elegance would match it.

"That must have made them nervous," Bastien said.

"I believe they've come to value their unique mistress and the man she Paired with—a man who once had very wild magic and was a neighbor that visited the empty estate often. They barely raised their eyebrows."

"Good." Alexa smiled.

"After-dinner drink?" Bastien asked, pouring himself brandy in a snifter.

"Thank you, yes," said Jaquar.

Alexa picked up a horn that sat upended on the side table. It was a real horn of a magical cow or something, and when you spoke into it, the person you addressed heard you.

"Kitchen," she said. "I'd like some tea and cookies, please." It hadn't taken her more than ten minutes to learn and pronounce the word for "cookies."

"Now," Jaquar said, "for your 'vital information.'"

They told him of the battle.

His face stilled. "What is your best estimate of the time?"

Alexa gave a helpless gesture. "I don't know." Her smile was weak. "I was dying at the time."

Jaquar strode over to a bookcase, placed his hand on a half-empty shelf and curved his hands as if around books, but all he held was air. He hummed a tune. A moment later three large, red-bound books sat on the shelf.

"Nice trick," Alexa said, and wondered if she could learn how to do it.

The Sorcerer's smile was crooked, but his eyes gleamed. "Not so very difficult magic, but the Marshalls don't use it much."

He glanced out the night-dark windows. "I must go, but I promise the Tower will be at the battle." He frowned. "There will be at least twelve of us, perhaps more. We will stand with the Chevaliers."

"Do you people always think in twelves? Twelve Marshalls to Summon me, twelve Sorcerers at the battle?"

Jaquar grinned. "Not exactly. I can think of six who would like to practice their magical dueling skills, five more who are dedicated to freeing Lladrana of the horrors, one that owes me a life." He shrugged. "There may be a few more."

"I hope so," Alexa said. For an embattled nation, they sure didn't have armies. She wondered what a tank could do to a dreeth. She'd like to find out. But there was no chance of that.

The small waterfall clock near a window chimed the hour.

"Time for me to go," Jaquar said. "If I might borrow a volaran with good sight in the dark...?"

Alexa frowned. "I heard you live on an island. Won't you consider spending the night instead of making a dangerous flight in the dark? We have plenty of room."

Bastien stood and smiled. "Every flight is dangerous to you, Alexa. Jaquar will be fine. My mare Inqui has excellent night vision and is curious enough to enjoy a night flight, not to mention a short stay at a Sorcerer's Tower."

Staring at Alexa, Jaquar patted his chest and smiled charmingly. "Something about you, Lady Exotique, pulls at me. So instead of vanishing into the dark on volaran-back, I'll tell you that I intend to fly only to the coastal town of Coquille where my parents reside. You may rest easy."

She returned his smile. "Thank you."

Jaquar cocked a brow at Bastien. "As for you, Chevalier, I will deliver several magical potions with your volaran, along with instructions, and perhaps a spare magical weapon or two. I'd like payment now for the books. I've heard you have a *hat,* made of soul-sucker."

Bastien relaxed back into the love seat, grinning naturally for the first time. "I do." He took the little horn and spoke into it. "Urvey, my soul-sucker hat, please."

A moment later Urvey entered the room, carrying the hat. He gave it to Bastien, then hurried from the room. Bastien whipped the hat over to Jaquar.

It had always been the ugliest hat Alexa had ever seen, but Jaquar's eyes lit up as he caught it, ran his hand around the broad rim, then placed it on his head at an angle. It looked as ridiculous on him as it had on Bastien.

Jaquar grinned. "Nice hat. The bargain is done."

The men exchanged glances.

Alexa shook her head. *Men.*

The sangvile hovered, thin as it could make its body, over the house where the Exotique prey was. It yearned for that Power. But the feycoocu was there too, and the shapechanger was strong and dangerous.

The one with bright magic that it had followed from the Castle had entered the house. The sangvile trolled the area for someone to drain of magic, but all the good ones were in the house. It would need to feast soon, and on rich magic.

It waited, and then the strongly magical one left on volaranback and the sangvile hooked itself to the *whoosh* of air in its wake.

That night, after another round of spectacular lovemaking, Alexa lay cradled in Bastien's arms, listening to his soft snoring and the birdcall outside.

The sounds should have comforted her, reminded her that she'd found a place of her own, people of her own. But she was lonely. For the Marshalls. How stupid was that?

But they'd called her and trained her and she'd thought they gave her friendship.

The birdsong was too damn cheerful. She stilled as she realized that it was the bluebird nesting for the night. Her mouth curved down and she pressed her lips hard together against a cry of pain. Just that morning she'd danced to the bluebird song, sure of her place in life at last.

Such a day, eons long, aged her second by second with trials.

And that was self-pity. A spurt of anger dried incipient tears. She'd danced joyfully in the morning, fought the sangvile and the Marshalls. It had been an eventful day, a fateful day, and she'd formed the shape of it herself with her own mind and body and magic. That was something.

She stroked Bastien's chest. She had what she'd always wanted—a home, a place, a man. All very good things, better than the loss of false friends. She thought of the thin Song-threads that still bound her to the Marshalls and considered snipping them the way she'd once threatened to cut the Song between herself and Bastien. Her pride wouldn't let her Summon metaphorical scissors. To clip the threads would be to let the Marshalls know they were important to her, and that they'd hurt her.

No, she wouldn't destroy. She'd build—a solid relationship with Bastien and the Chevaliers.

Her hand slipped down Bastien's body to caress. This is what mattered right now. Man coming into woman. Loving.

That night Thealia sat in the window seat of their suite in the Castle and looked out the bow windows. Night was falling and it was raining. Though the rain at the Castle no longer contained frinks, it still depressed her. Or perhaps it was looking at the Tower that jutted to her left. The Tower with dark windows where there'd been light when Alexa was here.

Partis came up behind her, pulled her close against his body. The cadence of their Song strengthened, deepened, and notes of desire mixed in. It lifted her spirits a little.

He rubbed her arms from elbow to shoulder. "You miss Alyeka. So do I. The Castle hadn't seen such vibrancy for a long time, not since all of the Marshalls' children were younger and still journeyed with us."

"We were so wrong in all our actions with Alyeka."

"Why do you scold yourself so? None of us had ever dealt with an Exotique before. We made mistakes——"

"Bad mistakes."

"Bad mistakes. But time will correct them."

Thealia grasped one of his hands between hers. "You think so?"

"Alyeka carries the Jade Baton, Bastien the black-and-silver. They are Marshalls to the bone. They claimed the batons and we claimed them. Alyeka is a very reasonable person——she will find her way back to us."

"I do miss her."

"And you think you should have been closer to her, had more personal contact," Partis murmured in her hair. "You are blaming yourself again. Hindsight. We did our best. If we had to do it over again, we would proceed differently, but that opportunity will not come. Stop thinking, come to bed and *feel*."

"You're sure she will return?"

"Yes."

He'd always been better at knowing people than she.

"Alyeka, Bastien, the Marshalls, the sangvile and the battle—— horrors truly invading, coming over our borders in large numbers, not twos or threes. So much to think about. So much to do. What do we do next?"

"We go to bed." With strength and magic and Song, he carried her there.

Dema and Farentha were the first Chevaliers to show up the next day, though Farentha was still healing and would not be able to fight. After that, a few more arrived every day. At first, it was the independent Chevaliers; then a minor noble Chevalier would come with two or three of his household. Soon both Bastien's and her own house were filled, and there were tented encampments around each home.

Bastien had taken on the work of a general and was good at it. Urvey and Pascal were his devoted staff and Marwey studied defensive magic with Farentha. Alexa thought she'd be hiring more Chevaliers soon to fight under her banner, as many as she could pay, though she didn't like the idea of leading others to death. The only palatable thought was that she wasn't asking them to do anything she wouldn't do herself.

So Alexa walked the land. One day she found a fallen brithenwood stick, round and tall enough to be fashioned as a staff. She hefted it, liked the weight, the slight roughness of bark under her fingers. The Song in it wasn't quite dead, and as she held it, the tune changed, deepened and resonated. For a moment a door flickered in her mind. She tried to grasp an elusive concept, but it vanished. She could only hope the idea would return.

She also trained in fighting and magic, working with Bastien to function as a team. Now and again she was sent to the nearest border to walk the line and strengthen it, keeping out the minor evils and single major ones. She studied the books and made potions, anointing the Chevaliers' weapons with magic—death magic for the horrors.

All in all, she was satisfied that she was doing her best possible effort to ensure that when the battle came, Lladrana would have a force to meet it. Though she mourned for the connection she had had with the Marshalls, she thought it had been superficial and hoped she was building better friendships with the Chevaliers.

One morning a week later, she was training with Bastien against Faucon and another Chevalier when a scream hit her brain.

Alyeka. We need you. We need you now!

The cry came in a tangle of voices inside her head. The Marshalls! All of them save Reynardus. In her time with them, she'd linked with all of them except Reynardus.

The shout deafened her, blinded her, and she fell. Breath knocked out of her, she stared up at Faucon. His sword was at her throat, and he looked determined.

"You're dead," he said.

She lifted her hands in surrender and he withdrew, but he didn't offer to help her up from the training ground. Instead, he scowled at Bastien.

"Why didn't you Shield her?"

"It was her fight," Bastien said. "And I won't Shield her from mistakes she makes on the training ground."

Alyeka! You were right. The army of monsters is massing. We Marshalls leave the Castle within the hour for the northern border. If you link with us, we can Summon you here. We go to fight now, before the army is ready. We have called in all the Chevaliers loyal to us. For the love of Lladrana, tell those with you to help! Thealia laughed bitterly. *This will be a long battle. We will need reinforcements. But with your help, right now, we might be able to prevent great loss, and strike first. We are calling on the Sorcerers and Sorceresses too.*

"What's wrong?" Faucon asked.

Her breath was back. She sat up. "The battle. It's come. The Marshalls fly to attack first. They need my help."

One side of Bastien's mouth twitched. "They finally reached you? I've been hearing them for the last quarter-hour."

She gawked. "You didn't tell me?"

"I didn't listen. I'm not a Marshall. That was a very short-lived twiddle-tune for me."

"We must go!"

"To fight with them? You have as much experience fighting with us here—" he gestured to the encampment outside her home "—as you have linking and fighting with them."

26

A sick dread twisted inside Alexa as she searched Bastien's hard expression. He would not go to the aid of the Marshalls and she could not refuse to help.

He and she were on opposite sides of a chasm. She knew it, even if he didn't, and it looked like the crack would fracture their relationship. He hadn't said he loved her, and she hadn't told him of her love, but she thought that's what they felt for each other. Could what they had survive what was coming? Or would she be left alone with the colleagues of Marshalls, but no man of her own?

Stiffly, she stood and brushed off her pants. She stared at the Chevaliers who were at the training ground, then lifted her voice. "What we have prepared for has arrived. The Marshalls leave for the North to strike at the gathering army."

Faucon glanced at her, then ran to the fence and vaulted over it, calling for his Chevaliers. Everyone rushed to the tents to prepare for flight and battle. She and Bastien were left alone. His face was tight with anger.

Alexa rolled her shoulders, sheathed her short sword. "I'm going to let the Marshalls Summon me to the Castle."

"Why? Why do you go to them, fight with them?"

"They need my help. They will be the first on the scene. With enough Power, we might forestall a huge battle." She shuddered at the thought of lost lives. Some would die. Maybe she would, but at least she would have done her best.

"You're going to *them?*" He sounded completely disbelieving. He towered over her.

She felt blood drain from her face as she tilted her head up. She tried to keep her voice steady, cool. "They *are* the best fighters of Lladrana. They have power and magic. Working with them is the best use of my skills. They need my help."

"So do we, the Chevaliers here."

Alexa walked to the training yard gate. "I can make more of a difference with the Marshalls. If we fight well, we can save lives, perhaps the lives of some of our Chevaliers here."

He grabbed her by the shoulders, his grip hard. "They've always manipulated you and used you. If you go, they will use you again. *He* will use you, Reynardus, suck your Power dry, like that damn sangvile. You, the most important part of his team, he will consider the most expendable."

"I know." Her insides trembled with fear, at the awareness of fate. "I must go."

Bastien's mind brushed hers, melded, tried to overwhelm. She was swamped by his tangled emotions—fear for her, love for her, anger at her blindness, her stubbornness.

She replied with a soft and soothing tone, comforting him, then she pulled away.

"I can't go with you. He'll use you, and through you, he'll use me. I can't..."

"I know," she said. *I'm coming,* she sent to Thealia.

The woman's—and all the Marshalls'—great relief permeated Alexa. *Your home contains a pentagram in the southwest room....*

I know where it is, Alexa said. She knew every inch of her lovely home.

"You're really going. To them. Leaving *me* for *them,*" Bastien choked out.

Alexa didn't know how to answer him. Didn't want to put it in personal terms like that. "You're really staying, coming later with the Chevaliers, unwilling to be my Shield," she said gently. She'd tried to block the sickening emotions—feelings that would weaken her. Now wasn't the time to feel, not even the time to think. Now was the time to act—and to pray that her training, *all* her training, held true.

He looked like she'd struck him, pallid under his natural tan skin. He even swayed. She couldn't take the heartbreak in his eyes, the heartbreak that clutched her insides. She ran back to him, stood on tiptoe, pulled his head down for a hard kiss of lips and tongue, savoring his taste, his scent, the strong passionate melody that still wound between them. Then she broke the kiss and stared into his stormy ebony eyes.

"I love you." She turned and bolted to the house.

She stopped in her room to gather the magical sword she and Bastien had made, and her fighting leathers and boots of dreeth hide. Her new brithenwood staff leaned against the wall and her fingers itched. She should take it into battle.

Alyeka, COME! the Marshalls cried.

She had her sword and her baton. She pelted to the room with the pentagram, stood inside it, let her tears flow. *I'm here.*

The Song that had swirled her from Colorado to Lladrana enveloped her again, plucked her from all she loved, to battle and an unknown enemy.

As she landed in the pentacle in the Castle Temple, she noticed the rhythm was slightly off. She looked up to see nine strained faces. Reynardus wasn't there.

Thealia rushed over to help her up, steadied her by putting hands on both shoulders.

Johnsa called, "Alyeka, Luthan is waiting in Temple Ward for you. The local landowner up North knows you're coming and has an appropriate horse."

"Where's Reynardus?" Alexa's breath came raggedly. Apparently the Summoning had primed her for battle already; she recognized the adrenaline buzz.

Mouth twisting, Thealia hustled Alexa into the pretty spring day. "Reynardus's volaran left in the night."

"Left? How? Where?" This made no sense.

"Volarans are more than horses. We breed many, but most of them come from a wild herd and stay with a person, sometimes are controlled by that person. If they want to leave, nothing will stop them. Reynardus's left."

It should have been funny, but dread rose in Alexa. She shuddered.

Thealia nodded. "We all have that feeling. The horrors massing—it's a fateful day and we all know it."

Alexa licked her lips. "Didn't someone offer Reynardus a volaran?"

"He rejected several. Then nobody offered any more."

Sounded like Reynardus. Alexa found herself nodding. She probably would be doing a lot of things more by instinct and training than by thinking today. She didn't want to think.

The past couple of weeks she'd worked with Bastien, and he wasn't here. The hole eating her insides would distract her if she thought about it, so she didn't dare. She could block that emotion as she rode the volaran while flying North. Yes, that could work.

Luthan strode up, face tense. He looked behind her. "Bastien's not with you?" Glancing at her face, he swore. "Never dependable."

She managed a weak smile. "He'll be there. As part of the independent Chevaliers. Just not with me." No voice catching on a sob. That was good.

"Idiot," Luthan said. He nodded to Thealia. "Mount up." Then he looked back to Alexa. "We can Pair for the battle. We work well enough together."

"Wait!" Ivrog strode up. His eyes were clear and fired with determination. "I'll Pair with the lady." He took her hand in his and a quick, easy, *strong* bond sang into place.

Luthan stepped back at the Power. "Incredible." He nodded once, pulled his riding gauntlets from his belt and slipped them on, smiled fiercely. "I'll see you at the North border, Prevoy's Pointe." Running, he jumped into the saddle and his volaran wheeled into the sky.

Ivrog tucked Alexa's hand into his arm. "I hope you don't expect that sort of acrobatics from me."

Some of her tension eased. "No."

But he was tall and walked fast, and she had to scurry to keep up.

"We will have to use distance-magic," Ivrog said. They'd reached his flying horse and he now boosted her into the saddle. "My Treasure, here—" he stroked the arch of the mare's neck "—was a gift from Bastien. I don't use distance-magic very often. She will be pleased to fly so." His smile was wry. "I only do distance-magic when going to a fight." He sucked in a breath. "And this looks to be the biggest fight of all." He swung up behind her. "Arise!"

The volaran took off, strong and steady. Alexa rested on Ivrog's chest behind her. It was like leaning on a sturdy uncle. Ivrog formed a clear bubble around them.

"I'm going to trance," Alexa said. "I need to block my emotions regarding Bastien." Again she was proud her voice didn't quiver.

Ivrog grunted. "Good idea. Try also to rest. Perhaps a little spelltune or two about how you will be at your best on the Field."

A little laugh welled in her throat. Affirmations? "I will fulfill my true potential on the Field."

She felt Ivrog nod. "Sounds good. When you de-trance, let me know, and I'll trance myself."

"I will fulfill my true potential on the Field." She tasted the words again, wondered what sort of tune to give them, then sent a last glance at the quickly disappearing Castle, her first home on Lladrana. She'd liked her suite there. Trees were in full blossom, and a rising bluebird's cheerful mating call followed them away.

Anguished, Bastien stood staring after Alexa, then looked down at himself. Funny, it didn't look like the heart and guts had been torn from him to lay spilled on the ground. Maybe the jerir had prevented it, or all the other scars on his body.

Didn't prevent the ripping pain, though. He ran his hands over his chest. No cavity. Not outside.

Cold sweat beaded on his temples, ran down his face. He doubled over, gasping with agony, and finally the torment hit his brain. *What had he done? He'd sent his Pairling off to battle without him. She could die!*

Fool! Idiot! Moron!

Fool! Idiot! Moron! The feycoocu's words echoed his own, screamed into his ears as a warhawk's cry.

"So where have you been?" he croaked.

Taking care of things.

Typical that she spoke in riddles. He jerked upright, forced his fear down and started to run to the pentagram in Alexa's home. He'd never run so fast, but as he skidded over the threshold into the entryway, he felt their Song dim. She was gone. Gone from the house.

Faucon slammed into him from behind. They both rocked before they caught their balance. Panting, Faucon said, "Just heard, the battle is at Prevoy's Pointe."

Big mountain, just over Lladrana's border. Rough country, and far. Far from the Castle and even farther from here.

Bastien jerked his head back toward outside, in the direction of the stables. All his best horses and volarans were here. He grinned at Faucon.

"Have I got a volaran for you."

Grinning back, Faucon said, "Great. Where's Alyeka?"

Bastien took off at a run. Faucon matched him.

"She went with the Marshalls."

Faucon's mouth opened, closed.

"Wise man," Bastien said. "Feycoocu!" he yelled.

The bird circled his head. *I am here.*

"Go to Alexa!" he shouted.

Not yet. I must keep an eye on you.

Bastien gritted his teeth. That sounded familiar, at least.

The volarans had left their stables, and now shifted around in the corral. As word spread amongst the Chevaliers, they congregated at the stables where the prime volarans waited.

Bastien threw open the gate. "Take your choice! I hear the fighting will be good at Prevoy's Pointe."

Alexa's stable master, Pierre, led Bastien's strongest volaran out of the stables. The stallion had flown in from a wild herd just three months before and had demanded the best. He and Bastien had trained only enough to be able to work as a team. The stallion wore no bridle, only a thin halter, reins and a saddle.

Bastien mounted.

"Wait!" Alexa's little butler puffed up to Bastien, carrying a box painted with Powerful symbols and bound with magic. "My Lord, take this."

It was the box containing his shooting-star atomball.

"You're right. It could come in handy. My thanks." Bastien stowed it in a bag behind him.

The butler wiped his perspiring face with a handkerchief and bowed as far as his large paunch would allow. "Good journeys, My Lord."

Bastien nodded. "A good journey and good fighting. A safe home to you." He settled himself again, and the volaran fidgeted a couple of steps in preparation for taking off.

The feycoocu screamed from the stable eaves. *Go to the Castle first, Bastien.*

He looked up, jaws clenching. *No!*

His volaran backed up a couple of steps, reared. Bastien kept his seat.

I have told your volaran to fly to the Castle. He will take you there with all speed. The feycoocu clicked her beak and Bastien could have sworn she smiled. *You will not arrive too long after the battle started.*

That turned his bowels to water. He wanted to be there *before* the battle started, to support his woman.

You must go to the Castle first. The Song says so. She shot into the sky.

"Urvey, Pascal!" he yelled.

They were there, volaran-back, at his elbow. "Go with Faucon, use distance-magic to reach the battlefield. Protect Alexa."

Both looked too damn young, but their faces white, they nodded, then wheeled their volarans to follow Faucon.

To the Castle, now! commanded Sinafin.

Dread made him stiffen in his saddle. He heard her faint bird cry, looked up to see a small, flapping speck. As he watched, it winked out. Gone. Some otherwhere.

For the first time since he was a child, he trembled.

Bastien tranced for most of the trip to the Castle; otherwise he'd have gone mad with the tension. When he arrived, his stallion set him down in an echoingly empty Temple Ward.

For a moment he just sat and stared. Never in all his life had he seen the Temple Ward deserted. From his earliest memory, it had bustled with life.

Then he wondered what he was supposed to do. "Sinafin?" he whispered. It was safe to use her name, and he was sure the magical being would hear.

Nothing.

He glanced at the sundial on the flat wall of the keep and decided to wait a quarter hour. Dismounting, he walked his stallion to the trough, left him there. Bastien stretched his legs by crossing to the cloister entry near the map room, then paused. He really didn't want to see what was going on. He wanted to be where the Marshalls were preparing for battle.

Testing his Song with Alexa, he found it calm but rising, building energy as she neared the Field.

His volaran's angry neigh made him pivot. He stared at his father on the ground near the flying horse.

Reynardus picked himself up and dusted off his tabard.

A sinking feeling invaded Bastien's gut. He didn't want to do what destiny had prepared for him. Slowly he walked to his father.

They stared at each other for several heartbeats.

"Is this your volaran?" demanded Reynardus.

"He is his own."

A tic appeared next to Reynardus's mouth. "It was always that strangeness that fried my temper."

"Where's your Shield, Uncle Ivrog?" Bastien feared the answer.

Reynardus's lip curled. "Gone. Shield to the Exotique, I believe."

Maybe if he hurried, fate wouldn't overtake him. Bastien jumped onto his stallion and wheeled him toward the east, where the wall was lowest.

"You aren't leaving me here!"

Bastien didn't look back. "Yes, I am."

Before the volaran could take off, the whisper of wings came to their ears, and another flying horse set down in the courtyard without a sound. Except the dull thud of Bastien's heart as it accepted destiny.

The volaran was thin and scraggly with huge, sad eyes. Bastien recognized her as the mare to the late Chevalier Perder, who'd been lost the day Alexa had saved Farentha and Dema.

Time to accept the inevitable. He and his stallion turned, observing the winged horse stepping delicately up to Reynardus, who stood frozen with fear.

"Your volaran is here, Father," Bastien said quietly. It was a time for stillness.

Reynardus opened his mouth. No words emerged. A first in Bastien's experience.

The volaran nudged Reynardus with her head. *You know,* she whispered. Reynardus looked shocked, as if he'd never heard a volaran. It hadn't happened very often to Bastien, but he'd heard an occasional word, even a phrase.

It's time. She bent her neck.

With a high two-note whistle, Bastien magically saddled her. He took a deep breath in, released it on a sigh. "I'll be your Shield."

Reynardus spun on his heel, his mail clinking. "You!"

"Me." He breathed deeply again. "Me, or no one at all." Glancing at the sundial, he saw fifteen minutes had passed. "I must fly to the Field."

The muscles in his volaran's haunches bunched.

"Wait!" Reynardus shouted and jumped onto the volaran.

The stallion whickered. *I will help in the distance-magic.*

Bastien's lips felt cold. "Let's go."

A tiny threnody unfurled from Reynardus to touch Bastien's mind. He allowed it in. The connection between them snapped into place.

And Bastien knew the burden his father had carried since his Song Quest. Alexa's and Reynardus's lives were intertwined, and one or both would die this day.

Alexa's heart started pounding as soon as they came out of the last distance-magic spell. She and Ivrog had traded off who kept touch with the volaran and who went into trance. By the time they'd reached Prevoy's Pointe, they'd found the rhythm of their Song together, and the Song they'd share during battle.

She looked down at the field and terror whipped through her—for herself, but more for Lladrana and all the people deep in the interior who had never faced the horrors. The common folk would be easy prey. Hideous visions coalesced in her mind.

All along the boundary line for as far as she could see was a snaking line of monsters, prowling. Mostly renders and slayers, but many soul-suckers, and five dreeths. Great clumps of the horrors milled near the three gaps between the fenceposts.

Ivrog landed. Alexa jumped down and staggered to the Marshalls' standard, raised by a huge, old brithenwood tree. Reynardus still hadn't arrived, but all the other Marshalls were there, along with major nobles and their Chevaliers, and some strangers. Alexa stared for a moment at richly robed men and women, then understood they were the Sorcerers and Sorceresses. She counted twenty. They stared back at her.

Thealia stood in front of another animated map, this one of the current battlefield. She nodded to Alexa, but finished with her question to the Sorcerers. "Can you of the Tower hold a force-field to narrow gaps between the fenceposts so the horrors push through at a rate we can handle them?"

Jaquar looked at his colleagues, garnered nods. "We can, if that's how you wish to use our Power, Swordmarshall Thealia. But it will take six of us at each break to hold such a forcefield. That will leave you with only two of us for offensive battlespells."

Everyone looked at the dreeths.

Thealia grimaced. "That's how it will be, then."

"What are they waiting for?" asked Alexa, pleased when her voice came coolly.

"Apparently, you," Jaquar said. "Look, they're moving, pouring through!"

"Everyone in position!" Thealia ordered, and her words reverberated across the field. She gestured to a pair of battlemares. "For you, Alexa and Ivrog."

"With your permission, Alexa, I would prefer to stay volaranback. I promise you I can Shield you best from there," Ivrog said.

Alexa mounted the horse, squared her shoulders and put on the helm that Ivrog had handed her. "Sounds good to me." She grinned, more a rictus than a real fighting grin. The adrenaline should dump into her system soon. God, she needed it. Her insides were so watery with fear, she thought they'd slop around.

She should do that old Roman salute and the "we who are about to die, salute you" thing. She shuddered and wiped her hands on a hank of saddle blanket in front of her. Her dreethskin leathers wouldn't dry her hands. She supposed this fear would always hit her.

She gulped. *We who are about to die, salute you.* She tried to remember what that was in Latin, but couldn't. She'd always been bad at languages.

"Attack!" screamed Thealia.

Alexa pulled her baton from her sheath and set her mount galloping to the nearest breach of the border, and into the fray.

Worldly power always demands a price, and I wanted power, said Reynardus, mind-to-mind with Bastien.

Bastien's link with his father seemed odd...because it was unusually easy. They were more alike than either would have wished. Their father-son Song, suppressed for so long by each, ran strong and clear.

As Reynardus spoke of Power, Bastien caught images from his mind, as if seeing a well-traced history: Reynardus young and in love with a lower-class girl. That shocked Bastien, and his father snorted. Then Reynardus's first Song Quest—where he was shown several futures.

I could wed the girl and live contentedly on our ancestral holding. Or I could wed another—a woman of great wealth, but of pitiful character— and build my own status. Then I would be a man to reckon with—the Lord Knight of the Marshalls! My name would echo through history. I wanted that, and more.

Bastien said nothing, kept his disapproval to himself. Having been the issue of that cold, passionless marriage, he wanted more. His heart wanted more—intimacy and delight. He'd found that with Alexa—passion and endless fascination.

The price of my Power was a bloodless mating with one who could never be a Marshall, never my Pairling, never my equal. His mouth curled, he slanted a stare at Bastien. *And the price was a flawed son.*

Bastien's heart lurched. He gripped his reins tight, but kept the pressure from affecting the stallion.

And to fulfill my dream of fame and fortune, the Song required a third payment—death on the battlefield at a relatively young age. This time Reynardus turned his head and his eyes glittered. *But the Song is not always right—not always inescapable. Even though it took my volaran and sent me this sad beast ready for death, the Song can be changed by the will of a man.*

Keeping his mouth shut and completely averse to talking philosophy with Reynardus, Bastien nodded. Then his father did something so touching that Bastien was stunned.

Reynardus stroked the neck of the volaran, and sang. He sang of life, of fighting for life, of determination. In doing so, he relieved his mount of the brooding sorrow and despair it had carried since its flier perished. The volaran's ears perked up, the tension of its muscles loosed. It held its head high and proudly, with eyes unclouded by grief.

Bastien could barely believe his father had done such a thing. Compassion. The man had a little compassion after all. Or was it simply self-interest? Bastien didn't know. He did know that in the coming battle, as Shield for a man marked for death, Bastien would have to be very, very careful. Though Reynardus would not allow Bastien any other than surface thoughts, he began layering defensive spells to protect them both.

Bastien and Reynardus arrived at Prevoy's Pointe to see death and destruction. Glowing Marshall batons signified the loss of a Pair—the oldest Pair, Albertus and his wife.

Blood and ichor surrounded the bodies of Chevaliers, volarans, and the horrors. Dozens of skirmishes dotted the battlefield. The aura of magic glowed in sparkling rainbows around the breaks between the fenceposts.

The thickest fighting centered on a small woman glowing green and blue and on horseback. Bastien's heart jumped to his throat.

I Shield for you, but we go there! Bastien pointed. *Where my Pair mate is.*

Reynardus grinned, screamed a war cry and dove. Caught up in his own fury, Bastien followed, accepting the rush of emotions from his father to himself, handling them, adding wild magic from himself and his mount. Linking to Ivrog, and from Ivrog to Alexa, and through Reynardus and Alexa to the Marshalls. He saw a golden net among them all. With luck, the net could close around the horrors and crush them.

Alexa knew when Bastien arrived. That he Shielded Reynardus. A bubble of wonder passed through her brain, but her hands concentrated on killing a slayer. Ducking spines. Shooting green baton magic straight to the heart.

Then Reynardus was next to her, swiping his baton around in a wide swath, killing several monsters with one blow.

"Dreeeeths!" someone screamed.

27

A dreeth materialized amidst them, its long, curved, pointed beak plunging toward Reynardus's heart.

Alexa was *there,* in front of him. How, she didn't know. Shrieking her own fear.

Bastien and Ivrog took the blow for her. The Shields held.

Her baton was in her hand, flaming green.

Reynardus's flamed white. He grabbed hers from her hand, yelled at the pain. He and his volaran shoved her aside.

She reeled.

They flung themselves in, in. Close to the thing's bulbous underbelly. Reynardus shoved both batons into its most vulnerable point. He shouted a chant and the thing exploded.

The force of it knocked Alexa to the ground. Dreeth chunks flew.

Reynardus laughed and tossed her baton to her. She caught it and gasped at his energy. Flung his magic back at him to absorb.

He laughed again and with a huge gesture and wave of his baton, Reynardus vaporized the rest of the dreeth.

He was still laughing when another dreeth appeared behind him and pierced his magical Shield, spearing his body with its beak, plunging through him and down into his volaran.

Reynardus and the flying horse gave one shudder and died.

Agony ripped through them all. All Marshalls. Bastien and Ivrog and Luthan screamed, their minds shocked at their loss, her connection to them gone.

Bastien was nearly unconscious, his Shield around his father having been brutally rent.

The new dreeth flicked its beak and Reynardus's body flew, arcing droplets of deep red blood from the back and between its legs. The volaran collapsed as it lay, blood pooling under it.

The horror made Alexa's breath catch. The Marshalls' and Luthan's and Ivrog's and Bastien's grief and anger wrenched open her own for Sophie. Suddenly the dreeth was every senseless death, every stupid mistake that claimed a life, every evil that took life and laughed. All evil.

Screaming, she ran toward the dreeth, jumped over the body of the volaran, ducked under the wicked clawed wings, and thrust her baton into the dreeth. The jade dug deep. She threw herself forward and stuck her arms up to the elbows into the dreeth.

It died.

She was crying, tears streaming down her cheeks as her heart and mind and soul wept for Sophie. And Reynardus.

The dreeth's body toppled forward.

Not again!

But the massed magic of the Marshalls plucked her away. Was too much. The Power spun her across the Field, onto the ground and under another dreeth's beak and claws. Her help gone, she stared at her own death in fascination.

Sinafin screamed and dived.

Bastien's atomball bulleted straight through the dreeth, leaving a hole. The shooting-star shattered.

That dreeth rocked forward, toppling.

Alexa rolled until she stopped against a rocky outcropping littered with debris. The dreeth thunked behind her, causing the earth to vibrate. Grabbing the edge of a boulder, she used it to stagger to her feet.

A render shrieked and swiped. His claws skimmed her back and fiery pain sizzled. She whipped around and only one claw connected, sliced her cheek. The pain cleared her brain. She would not die. She would fight and *win!*

She lunged forward, her flaming baton-point took the render in the heart. She jerked her stick back and it came with a horrid sucking noise, echoed by a soul-sucker lashing a tentacle around her. Suckers fastened on her back, along the render wounds, and blood drained from her to it, along with her energy. Another limb pulled her close, trapping her arm so she couldn't use her baton.

Desperately, she reached for a weapon, any weapon. A long branch of brithenwood stuck out from the rocks. In that instant she knew.

Brithenwood was the key to making the fenceposts. It *was* a fencepost.

Using sheer willpower, she pulled it out.

The brithenwood sang to her, music bubbling through her blood and nerves, combining with her surging magic. Yes, this brithenwood staff could become a fencepost; she only need wield it.

Staggering with the overwhelming Song, she thwacked the branch across the soul-sucker's back. The soul-sucker's ululating scream deafened her. It released her and crumpled. She stabbed the branch down, through the soul-sucker and into the ground.

The branch transformed before her eyes, glowing yellow and growing to—a fencepost! Magic ran from it to the next post down the line, a hot blue streak of Power.

Thealia skewered a slayer and it fell on the boundary, shrieked as fire engulfed it, vanished. In the monster's place was a wall of flame.

For an instant Alexa couldn't find her voice. Then she shouted, yelled with magic and triumph so all on the battlefield would hear her. "The boundaries—they are fueled by the horrors' life force!" She saw a volaran and Chevalier die under a tangle of render claws. The bodies landed on the border too. Again the boundary flared, the bodies disappeared, and the border was strong and alive at that point.

With shouts, the Marshalls and Chevaliers pressed forward, maneuvering the monsters to the line.

Soon the entire front was lit with a visible wall of magic that the monsters behind it could not punch through. The beasts on the Lladranan side of the border were trapped.

Yelling battle cries, the defenders of Lladrana encircled and killed renders, slayers, soul-suckers and another dreeth.

Alexa stumbled back into the skirmish. Her bond with Bastien returned first, then Ivrog. Their tunes were uneven, flattening and nearly disappearing at points, but she was glad of any help she could muster.

She found her wandering horse and heaved herself into the saddle. She felt better, stronger, more in control on horseback. For the first time she thought she might eventually become a volaran fighter. Alexa kicked the horse into a run and helped finish off the remaining horrors, swinging her sword, using her baton automatically until she looked around and found only Chevaliers, Marshalls, Sorcerers, horses, and volarans alive. No sign of the monsters except a very tall, very bright boundary of magical flame.

Her arms dropped and she just stared at the new border. She didn't think she'd seen anything so beautiful in her life. Safety, security, triumph. The glowing fencepost and boundary line meant all that to her.

With a press of her heels, she rode closer to the fencepost and the huddle of Chevaliers who examined it. Where the post rose from the ground was a circle of jade. Alexa shivered. She—*she* had made the fencepost and it showed that. It also seemed to tally her kill, then go on to record the other beasts that had died on the line. Almost all of the Marshalls—including the Shields— had a jeweled ring around the pole. The Chevalier kills were shown in wood.

Thealia joined her, smiling faintly and cleaning her sword. "Well done, Swordmarshall. Now we know how the posts are formed— brithenwood staffs."

"Branches," Partis said as he and his volaran landed, "and freely given. Not cut, but culled from dead fall."

Loremarshall Faith drew near too. "Did you say any spell when you thrust the brithenwood into the ground, Alyeka?"

Alexa's mind went blank. Had she? She had the vague idea that all day long she'd been praying "Oh God," or swearing, "Oh shit." She smiled weakly. "I don't think so."

Bastien's stallion trotted up. The volaran looked magnificent and pleased, as if he knew he'd participated in a fateful event. Bastien's expression was strained, but he managed to dip his head and smile at her.

All her feelings about him roiled through her. Love, despair, caution. Suddenly she wanted her feet on the ground. That might steady her.

She slid from her horse and wobbled to the fencepost as if to study it. From the corner of her eye, she saw Bastien tense. Up close the fencepost was awesome. Yellow-white, it would be a beacon at night, a warning to those evil creatures who tried to slither into Lladrana. The gemstone rings of the Marshalls sparkled in the light, bright and new, the edges of the carvings crisply incised.

Reaching out, she meant to trace the dreeth, but her fingers just brushed the column.

Mist seemed to swirl around her and it was fast and thick and white and she couldn't tell if it was behind her eyes or in front of them.

The earth under her feet vibrated.

And she heard the Song.

She'd thought the melody between herself and Bastien had been a Song, but this was more—richer, incredible.

This was the Song of a world.

And not the planet Amee or the land Lladrana.

This was the Song of her mother planet, Earth. A Song that whirled all the memories of her home planet into vivid life—the scent of snow, of spring grass, of the Colorado soil itself. Images of the law school campus, her office and battered desk, and her apartment. Of lost Sophie.

It brought tactile sensations too. The warmth of the chinook wind in February, a cashmere sweater she'd once touched in one of her foster homes, cornsilk.

Music. The real music, the crash of Beethoven's Fifth, the beat of rap, the zing of zydeco, the horns of jazz and holiday tunes and triumphal marches. The Song of Mother Earth's core-beat that called to her own blood, the beat of her own heart.

Everything, every sensory memory, overwhelmed her.

The Snap.

"Nooo!" she heard someone scream harshly.

It had sounded like Bastien, only his voice held a note she hadn't heard. She tried to turn her head but couldn't.

Rough arms grabbed her, shook. "Hold on to me! See me! Take

ME!" she thought she heard. The words made no sense. Instead, she focused on the vision of the lovely house and children and a caring man—of black judge's robes.

But they were all wrong. Her body shuddered and she sucked in deep breaths and with them another Song, fractured and frail, weeping and calling to her. Her house was redbrick, not fake half-timber. She had no children, but friends and horses and beautiful winged creatures called volarans and a funny, wonderful shape-shifter. She didn't wear black judge's robes. She wore fighting leathers of a dreeth she had killed with her own hands—and wielded a magical baton, not an authoritative gavel.

The man was all *wrong*. He was caring, not loving. Their sex was good but not desperate and consuming. He gave tenderness and support, but she could have that *and* love. She could have *more*.

She could have a man she Paired with, fought with, loved passionately. She could have a land that was strong and free because of her actions.

She could save a land and save lives. She was *needed* here. In Lladrana she had been and would continue to be the difference between life and death, for people and for the land.

The cost could be very, very high. No children. A short life. Horror and fear and pain.

The reward was immeasurable.

She grabbed on to Bastien.

Mother Earth's Song diminished, faded and left a last blessing of the taste of Assam tea.

Amee's Song sighed, and wept, and flowed through her and claimed her as one of her own.

Alexa collapsed onto Bastien. The world steadied and she found herself clutched closely to his chest, hearing the rapid pounding of his heart. She looked up and he was blurred behind her own tears. She blinked and let the tears roll down her cheeks.

"The Snap," she said.

He squeezed her until her bones creaked. "I know." His voice was thick and muffled. "I know. I love you, Alexa. Stay with me."

She hugged him back with all her strength. He felt solid, good and wild in her arms. Wow. "I love you too, Bastien. I'm here for good. Here in Lladrana."

She turned in his arms, saw the Marshalls and Chevaliers watching her, eyes wide, obviously understanding what had occurred.

Thealia looked at her colleagues. No one moved. Her mouth twitched in impatience and she hurried to Alexa. "The Snap."

When Alexa took a step from Bastien, her knees faltered. He set his hands on her hips to steady her, but didn't constrain her. She lifted her hands to run them through her hair, lift it from her scalp and dry the perspiration of her head.

She smiled at Thealia, past Thealia to Partis and the others, and called, "The Snap has come and gone and I am still here. I will remain here in Lladrana."

More Songs entwined her, the threads of connections to the Marshalls, each individual and the Pairs, notes and links to Chevaliers with whom she'd worked so closely. From each came an uplifting gladness that she'd stayed, a tune of friendship. For her, Alexa Fitzwalter.

Welcome home, said Sinafin.

* * * * *

Who will be the next person Summoned? Find out in 2006!

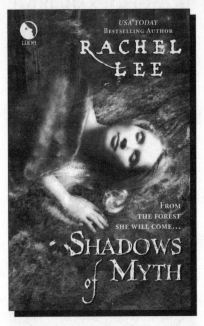